DEATH JR:

The Devil's Rebuke

JIMMIE HUPP

ISBN 979-8-89043-144-8 (paperback)
ISBN 979-8-89043-145-5 (digital)

Copyright © 2024 by Jimmie Hupp

All rights reserved. No part of this publication may be reproduced, distributed, or transmitted in any form or by any means, including photocopying, recording, or other electronic or mechanical methods without the prior written permission of the publisher. For permission requests, solicit the publisher via the address below.

Christian Faith Publishing
832 Park Avenue
Meadville, PA 16335
www.christianfaithpublishing.com

Printed in the United States of America

To my Lord and Savior Jesus Christ. It is His gift that allowed me to be able to put these words together on a page.

To my wife and children for supporting me through this endeavor, especially Heather. It was her challenge to me that started the process of this book.

Acknowledgments

Thank you to all who read this.

Chapter 1

Beep...Beep...Beep
BOOM...BOOM...BOOM
Beep...Beep...Beep
BOOM...BOOM...BOOM
Beep...Beep...Beep

Jr's eyes snapped open as his hand reached blindly for his phone to shut off the alarm. His hand grabbed the phone to silence the alarm and noticed that he had a missed call from Death.

"A call from Death." Jr chuckled. "That would freak most people out."

Being the son of the Grim Reaper, Death himself, receiving a call from Death was no big deal. He would give his dad a callback later.

BOOM...BOOM...BOOM

Jr can't tell if the booming is in his head or coming from somewhere else.

"If that is going to continue, I'm going to need some BC powder," Jr mumbled.

As he glanced at his phone again, he noticed the time. Realizing what day it was, he knew he needed to head to work. He strode into the bathroom and looked in the mirror. His bare skull was a bright white from years of being sun-bleached.

Humans have it so much better, he thought to himself. *When they go out in the sun, they get a nice dark tan going on. The more I'm out in it, the paler I get. Talk about a role reversal.*

He continued his morning routine by brushing his teeth while the booming kept happening in the background of his head. He looked in the mirror again and was thankful for the fact that people couldn't see his true self for the most part. There were a few exceptions to that rule. He went into his bedroom and grabbed his cloak. That was all he needed to wear because people would see what he wanted them to see—jeans, a trademark skull T-shirt, a leather jacket, and riding boots. That was his typical "human disguise."

Boom...Boom...Boom

Jr grabbed his phone and walked out the door of his apartment into the hall of a not-so-nice building in a not-so-nice part of town. He walked a few doors down and knocked on the door and patiently waited for an answer. Light, delicate footsteps could be heard behind the door. That gave him a little smile. He knew she was going to answer the door instead of the jerk.

"Oh, hey DJ," said a bright young woman as the door opened.

DJ was what people called Jr, except his dad, Death himself.

"Hey Claire," Jr responded. "Have you been hearing a *boom* sound?"

Before she could answer, Jr heard him—the jerk. Just the sound of his voice made his nonexistent blood boil.

"Is that the scrawny little puke from down the hall?" boomed a voice from inside. "Tell that little punk he better leave before he gets his little butt kicked."

"Sorry," Claire whispered as she looked at the ground, embarrassed. "No, I haven't heard any *boom* sounds."

"Okay, thanks," Jr said as he turned to walk away. "And don't worry about what he said. It doesn't bother me. See you later."

Jr was going to be sorry when it was her time to go. He liked Claire. The jerk, on the other hand, that one he was going to really enjoy. The official job of the Grim Reaper was to collect the souls of people, but some creative flexibility was allowed. He would ask his dad to make that one really count. That thought put a bounce in Jr's step.

As he rounded the corner at the end of the hall, the sunlight was streaming through the window of the door. The sun wasn't exceedingly high yet, just barely over the peaks of the mountains in the area. He walked out the door into the parking lot and stopped in his tracks.

"Hey," Jr hollered. "Do you mind?"

A rather large individual turned to look at Jr. It was one of the jerk's friends who lived down the street, and he was sitting on Jr's bike.

"Actually, I don't mind, you little puke," he responded. "Dan said you were overbugging Claire this morning."

He must have already been on the phone with this Neanderthal when Jr stopped by. It was becoming more and more obvious that Dan had some issues to deal with.

"I wasn't bugging anybody," Jr answered. "Now get off my bike before you regret being a jerk today."

The Neanderthal was off and lunging at Jr in an instant, frothing at the mouth like a rabid dog. Jr knew a productive conversation was out of the question. The man grabbed Jr by the neck like he wanted to strangle the life out of him. As the man's large hands curled around his throat, a smile curled on Jr's face.

"You can't kill death, you moron." Jr laughed.

"WHAT?"

Jr grabbed the man's hand and snapped two of his fingers as he pulled it from his neck. "Listen well, you—" *Ring...ring.* "Hold that thought," Jr said as he held on to the injured hand.

Jr reached into his pocket and grabbed his phone. The screen read "Death."

"Consider this your lucky day," Jr said as he released him and answered the phone. "Hey, Dad."

The Neanderthal swung at Jr as soon as his hand was free, a big swing that connected with the top of Jr's boney skull. The sound of his fingers breaking from the contact echoed through the parking lot as he howled in pain.

"What was that sound?" Death asked.

"Just a stupid Neanderthal, Dad," Jr responded. "What's up? I'm on my way to work."

"Come by after work. There is something we need to talk about."

Boom...Boom...Boom

"Sure. Hey Dad, have you been hearing a *boom* sound?"

"Just come by later."

Jr hung up the phone and looked at the Neanderthal. "Give my regards to Dan."

He walked over to his bike and undid the helmet from the latch lock that held it in place. Jr didn't need a helmet, but it was a law where he lived. He put the helmet on and got on the bike. It was a beautiful bike—a Ducati 1198, gunmetal gray, sleek, fast, beautiful. As he started it up, the engine purred like a fine-tuned machine. He pulled in the clutch and kicked it down into first gear. He looked at the door to the building and saw Dan standing there. Jr flipped up the visor on his helmet and winked as he gave Dan a wave. Dan returned the wave but didn't use all his fingers. Jr chuckled as he took off.

The feel of the bike always made Jr feel exhilarated. He twisted the throttle, only letting off to shift gears. The street flew by in a blur as he sped down the road. Ten minutes later, he pulled into the bike garage where he worked. He parked in his usual spot and dismounted as he pulled off his helmet.

"Hey DJ," said a young woman as he walked into the office.

"Hey Yvonne," Jr responded. "What's on the schedule for today?"

"The usual—fix this, repair that," she said with a coldness in her voice that Jr wasn't used to hearing.

Jr gave her a look of confusion. He thought about asking a question but decided not to. He knew things were hard for her at home right now. He walked into the back and hung up his coat and helmet. He could manifest these items to hang so it didn't look conspicuous wearing a leather jacket everywhere. He pulled his shop overalls out of his locker and started to put them on.

"Oh, hey DJ, I didn't see you come in," said a figure as he walked into the locker area.

"Hey Josh, do you know what's up with Yvonne today?"

"No," Josh replied. "She did seem cold and distant this morning. Not her usual peppy self."

"I know," Jr replied with concern for his friend Yvonne.

Nothing more was spoken of it as they started the daily tasks that went on in the garage. Yvonne hadn't lied about the schedule—fix this, repair that. He had a couple of oil changes to do and a couple of new tires to install. He was about to start a new clutch install when he heard a horrible racket echo through the concrete-and-steel walls of the shop. Jr could tell right away that somebody was bringing in a Harley. He hated working on those. They always leaked even with new seals, and the owners were always so easily offended. He was thankful when he heard Josh talking with the customer.

Jr walked out of the shop at the end of the day. Yvonne was leaving, and Josh left early for an appointment at his kids' school. Jr waved to Yvonne as she drove off. She didn't seem to notice him.

"That's odd," he said to himself.

Jr walked back into the shop, changed his clothes, and locked up. He walked over to his bike worried about his friend and wondered what his dad wanted to talk about. He stood there deep in thought.

BOOM…BOOM…BOOM

The sound snapped him out of it. He blinked, shook his head, and blinked again. He thought that he had seen a flash in the distance. He looked in that direction again, scanning for anything he could see—nothing except for a warm evening sun and a few clouds in the distance.

"Well, Rigs, you ready?" he asked the bike.

The bike seemed to shimmer. "You know I don't like that nickname." The words weren't audible but were definitely said.

"Sorry, I'm sorry, Morty," Jr chuckled.

Silence was all he got in response.

"Okay, Rigor-Mortus, I apologize," Jr said. "Ready to go to Dad's?"

"I accept your apology."

Jr got on the bike and didn't even bother with the key. His bike was, in reality, a pale horse who could shift form to suit the situation or need. Jr typically preferred the motorcycle form. He could communicate in a range of ways from telepathy to audible language. The horse and Jr phased out and headed for Purgatory, the residence of Death Incarnate, the Grim Reaper.

Chapter 2

As Jr and Rigor-Mortus approached Purgatory, the smells of a home-cooked meal filled the air. The smell of beef and spices swirled about, making Jr's mouth water. Purgatory loomed near as the horse and Jr phased back into a solid state. Since Purgatory is in between states of existence, this was the only way to get here. As they phased back in, a neigh from a horse could be heard. At the sound of this, Rigor-Mortus shifted into a horse and took off in a run, throwing Jr off in the process.

"Hey you dumb oaf, watch it!" Jr exclaimed.

Rigor-Mortus just whinnied as he trotted up to a larger and even paler horse.

"Hey Mortis," Jr said as he passed by, headed for the house.

Mortis responded with a snort and a stomping of the foot, his way of saying hi.

As Jr opened the door to the house, he was blasted by the wonderful smells of burgers, cheese, and fries that came from the kitchen. It was making him hungry.

"Dinner smells good, Mom," Jr hollered.

"Thanks," came the response from a deep voice that could only be from Death himself. "Your mother went shopping with Mother Nature. I cooked dinner."

"It still smells good," Jr stated. "When do we eat?"

"Soon, sit down, Jr. Let's talk."

Jr and Death walked into the dining room and sat at the table. There was a tea kettle sitting on a candle heater and black tea at the ready next to the cups. Death poured two cups as he looked at his son.

"Jr, you said you were hearing a *boom* sound?"

"Yeah, Dad," Jr said. "What is it?"

"The boom is basically a knock," Death bemused. "I didn't know you could hear it."

Jr looked at his dad, confused. "How could I not hear it?"

"Well, you being the son of an incarnation and a mortal, I wasn't sure you could," Death answered. "You see, the *boom,* as you call it, is a knock from a friend of mine whose life is, well, let's just say unique."

Ding!

"Dinner's ready. Let's eat," said Death.

The conversation ceased while the food was brought out to the table. Soon there was a platter full of mouthwatering cheeseburgers with all the fixings on the table. French fries piled high on a plate next to the burgers and fry sauce and mustard for dipping—truly a feast fit for a holiday weekend barbeque.

"What do you mean by *unique?*" Jr asked between mouthfuls of burgers and fries.

Death sipped at his tea as a small smile started to curl on his face. "I mean he doesn't live in the same time as us. Same dimension and space, just a separate time. He lives his time differently than us. That's why he's knocking. In order to be able to speak with him, I have to go into his reality of time."

Jr just stared blankly at his father midway through his cheeseburger.

"I'll give you a second to chew on that." Death chuckled.

"He lives in a separate time?" Jr asked.

"Precisely," Death said. "That means I am going to have to leave for a little bit to go and talk with him to see what's going on."

"Does Mom hear the *boom*? Does she know your friend? That you are taking a trip?" Jr fired off questions.

"No, she can't hear the *boom*. No mortal can, only incarnations and apparently, their kids," Death said. "She does know about it happening. I told her. To answer your other questions, yes, she knows him. He's her friend too." Death looked at his tea for a second before he continued. "Your mother does know about the trip, and she is very concerned."

Jr coughed as he blurted out, "Worried about you? What does she need to worry about? You're the Grim Reaper!"

"She's not worried about me, Jr," Death said, his eyes not wavering from Jr.

Jr sat motionless for a moment, his brain scrambling to comprehend what he was hearing. "Okay, Dad, what gives?" Jr finally managed to say.

"Follow me," was all Death said as he rose from the table.

As Jr got up to follow his dad, his heart was racing. He had never seen his dad look this way before. Jr didn't know if he should be worried or excited. They entered the office of Death. Jr always loved this room. It was large with vaulted ceilings and a large wooden desk. The desk was made from Italian cypress, also known as the Mourning Tree. It was a beautiful, polished desk—a gift from Mother Nature long ago. On the desk sat a computer, which hardly ever got used. Death hated computers! Behind the desk was a large floor-to-ceiling bookcase full of all types of books. A large book titled *The Origin of Death* was prominently displayed on a shelf by itself. Jr had never noticed this book before.

"Your mom is worried about you, not me," Death said calmly.

"Me, why me?" Jr asked, perplexed.

"Son, what do you think would happen if the collector of souls isn't around to do his job?" Death asked rhetorically. "There would be a terrible crisis if people couldn't die when it is their time. That's why you will have to fill in for me while I'm gone."

Jr's jaw dropped open. "No way, Dad, there is absolutely no way I can do that!" Jr's tone and volume were much higher than he had expected it to be.

Death reached out his hand and grabbed the book displayed by itself. His hand lifted the corner of the book, and the bookcase shimmered. Death stepped through as he motioned for Jr to follow him. Jr followed in complete shock and awe; he never knew it could do that. This was a room Jr didn't know existed until now.

"I thought all those books were real?" he asked.

"Oh, they are real," Death replied. "But being an incarnation in your home gives you special effects you can impose on your immediate reality."

Jr looked around the room. On the back wall, he saw the most renowned symbol of the Grim Reaper, the scythe—the tool that he uses to collect the souls and sometimes facilitates in the loss of their life. Jr never knew where his dad kept it when not at work. The feel of the room was unlike any other in all of Purgatory. Jr could sense the power of the role of his father in the universe. The overwhelming sense of incompetence surged over Jr.

"Da—" Death raised his hand to cut off Jr's words.

Death walked over to the back wall beside the scythe. He reached out and pushed on a brick in the wall. Like an illusion, the face of the brick disappeared. Death reached inside and pulled out a short black object. He turned toward Jr.

"It is time for you to get something, son," Death said as he handed the object to Jr.

Jr reached out his hand as his father handed him the object. The power he felt as his hand grabbed it made him reel. His mind went into a spin; a thousand thoughts, sounds, feelings, and sights flashed across the screen in his mind. They began to swirl around his mind closing in, pressing against his own thoughts and will. He opened his mouth to yell, but he couldn't even hear his own voice over everything else in his mind. He felt as though he was slipping into eternal darkness. His throat closed off, his heart pounding so hard it made his temples pulse with every beat.

"Jr, Jr, snap out of it." Jr's eyes snapped open as he felt the reassuring hand of his dad on his shoulder.

"What was that?" Jr yelped.

"Relax, Jr," Death said calmly. "What you just felt was the eternal struggle of good and evil. The sounds of every soul that they are fighting over."

Jr's eyes were wide. "They?"

"Yes, Jr, they. God and Lucifer." Death's tone was as serious as his job.

Jr's expression was blank. He couldn't make his body move as he tried to process everything that was happening. He realized he was still holding the object and stared at it quizzically. He felt the power of it pulsing through his body. It was sleek and compact. Heavy but at the same time seemed almost weightless in his hand.

His thoughts were interrupted by his dad's voice, "It's a scythe, Jr, your scythe."

Jr looked at the object. Instinctively his hand held it upright. As he squeezed it in his hand, instantly like a giant switchblade, the handle expanded, and the gleaming curved blade shot out like the fangs of a viper. The light in the room made the gleam of the blade bounce off Jr's bare skull. A wicked smile curled on his lips.

"My own scythe," he whispered. "Will that surge of…well, everything happen every time?"

"No," Death responded. "It's in tune with you now. You'll be able to tune in on it if you want to, and it will feel louder when it requires your attention. It's more than a tool for collecting souls. It's also your main source of protection, your weapon. While doing the work that both sides want to be in control of, you will from time to time need to protect yourself…and others."

"About protecting others, Dad, I have a question," Jr said.

Death chuckled as he began to speak, "Ah yes, Dan. If his time comes while I'm gone, you can make it as special as you want. If it's after I'm back, I will make it memorable as well."

"Thanks, Dad."

"You will need to practice with that scythe to become proficient with it. I have a place for that as well," Death said.

He walked back over to the wall where his own scythe hung on the wall. He reached up to grab it off the wall. He pulled it down, then pulled down on one of the hangers where it had been. The wall vanished, and beyond was the best dojo-style room Jr had ever seen.

"Whoa," was all he could say.

Death looked at his son. "Remember, with great power comes great responsibility."

They stared at each other for a second; then they burst into laughter as they enter the practice room.

Chapter 3

Jr walked out of his parents' house hours later, sore and slightly out of breath. He was amazed how quick his dad was. The old man had moves and had taught him a lot in a single lesson. His dad felt he was proficient enough to take care of things while he was away. Rigor-Mortus was in the driveway back in his motorcycle form.

"Ready to go?" Jr asked.

Morty flashed his light in response. Jr put on his helmet and put the key in this time. It wasn't really needed; it was just for show since he would be back in town. He got on the bike, and they phased out as they started out the driveway. Moments later, after phasing in behind Jr's job, they were zipping down the road toward home. It was getting late in the evening, and the sun was starting to set behind the hills. As Jr pulled into the parking lot at his apartment, he noticed a bunch of Harleys in the lot. That meant Dan had his friends over.

"This isn't going to be good," Jr muttered as he got off the bike.

He felt the telepathic response from Morty, "Maybe a good chance to practice some more?"

"Maybe." Jr chuckled. "Maybe."

Jr took off his helmet and put it in the latch lock and headed for the door. As he was walking up toward the door, he noticed the Neanderthal from earlier that day sitting with a group of angry-looking fellows. Jr just started to smile. The Neanderthal noticed Jr and stood up. One of the other fellows went inside the building. Jr just kept pace walking to the door. When he was a few feet away, three of the group stood to block the way.

"Excuse me, gentlemen," Jr said as he came to a stop a foot away.

The three didn't move or make a sound. The rest of the group started to surround Jr. Dan stepped out the door trailed by the one who had gone inside. He sneered at Jr as he stepped up to the three. They stepped off to the side for Dan.

"Jared said you gave him some trouble this morning," Dan glowered.

Jr laughed a quick chuckle. "No. No trouble. He does owe me a wax job on my bike, though. He got his grubby Neanderthal prints all over it."

Jared took a few steps toward Jr with seething anger on his face. Dan put up his hand, and Jared stopped where he was. Dan gave Jr a look up and down, then narrowed his eyes.

"You best watch your back, boy," Dan sneered.

Jr exploded with diabolical laughter. He could feel the fire starting to burn in anger. A sinister look fell over Jr's face, and a small flame started to burn in his eye sockets. He clenched his fist and was getting ready to let loose his anger. A shadow in a window caught Jr's attention. It was Claire. At the sight of her, Jr's anger fizzled down enough for him to compose himself. He didn't want her to see this.

"I would take your own advice, Dan," Jr said calmly.

Jr and Dan locked eyes as Jr walked past him to the door. As the door swung closed behind him, Jr could hear Jared complaining to Dan about letting him pass. The sound of their discussion faded as Jr walked down the hall. As he got to the door where Claire lived, the door opened. Jr stopped as Claire stepped into the hall.

"DJ, I'm so sorry about all that," Claire said timidly.

Seeing her like this made Jr's anger start to grow again. "Why do you stay with him, Claire? You have other options," Jr blurted out.

Claire was shocked at his outburst. Her mouth dropped open as Jr quickly looked away.

"I'm sorry," he quickly added. "I was out of line."

"You don't understand," Claire said defensively. "You just couldn't understand."

"I'm sorry," was all Jr said as he looked down and started to walk away.

"I'll talk to you later, DJ," she said as she closed the door.

Jr heard the door shut, and the sound made a lump pop up in his throat. He slowly walked to his door as his mind raced through what just transpired. He was kicking himself in the butt for not controlling himself better. Why had he said that? What was he thinking? Worse yet, what was *she* thinking? His hands were shaking as he got to his door, making it difficult to work his keys. He knew he shouldn't have said that. He closed the door behind him as he entered his apartment. He put his keys in his pocket and went into the living room.

"What was I doing?" He moaned as he fell back into his chair.

It was getting late, and Jr was tired. He walked to his room and plugged in his phone as he checked the alarm. He took off his cloak and flopped on the bed. He was ready to fall asleep and try to forget what he had just said to Claire. Jr could still hear Dan and his friends outside as he drifted into sleep.

Jr's eyes snapped open as he shot out of bed. "DJ, I need your assistance!" It was Morty, and he was alarmed.

Jr had his cloak on in an instant. As he reached the door, he pulled out his scythe. He flew into the parking lot and saw Jared at his bike. Jared saw Jr coming, and an evil sneer curled his lips.

"I'm gonna kill you, twerp!" Jared hollered.

"Wrong!" Jr said.

He clenched his scythe, and the blade shot out like lightning. Even in the low light of the parking lot, you could see the expression of sheer terror across Jared's face. A shriek escaped his lips as Jr swung his scythe. The blade sank into the side of Jared's neck like it was warm butter. His eyes went wide as he felt the blade in his neck. Jr looked at him as he watched the life leave his body.

"Thank you, DJ," Morty sent to Jr.

Before Jr could reply, he heard a sound coming up behind him. He turned around to the sound of hoof steps. He saw a pale horse with an ominous figure riding it. He instantly recognized his dad and the horse, Mortis.

"Well, since you're here, Jr, you might as well see how it's done," Death said as he dismounted his horse.

Jr couldn't form any words to ask the question on his mind.

"Don't worry, son," Death said, seeing his son's expression. "It was his time. We can at times go off schedule as it is, but that does mess with things a bit. Now, let me show you what to do. People often think of me as the bringer of death, which we both know is untrue. Unfortunate side effect of always being around to do the job. I simply collect the soul. The rest is automatic."

As Death finished his sentence, he reached toward Jared's body. The tip of the blade of his scythe shimmered as it passed through his body. With a quick little twist and pull, Death started to remove the soul. Jr watched in amazement. He never knew how this worked. The soul came out looking like a light cobweb but was almost charcoal in color. As Death removed it from his scythe, he spread it out and gave it a little toss in the air. The charcoal-colored web started to fall toward the ground. It hit the ground and then just disappeared.

"Not all of them are that color," Death stated. "That one was pretty obvious which way it was going to go."

"What do you mean, Dad?" Jr asked.

"Like I said earlier, I just collect the soul. The rest is automatic. Sometimes they come out extremely white, sometimes like charcoal, and sometimes they are in between. When they are as dark as that one was, it's obvious it's going down. When they are bright colored, it's obvious that they are going to float up." Death paused to make sure Jr was paying attention. "The ones that are in between are the ones that take a little patience. It can take a moment before it starts its journey either up or down. It's my job, and will be yours for a bit, to stay with the soul until it heads to its eternal home."

"How did you get the blade to do that?" Jr asked, befuddled.

"Fair question," Death replied. "Your scythe is in tune with you, like I said earlier. It knows when you want to use it as a weapon or as a collection tool." Death looked around for a moment before he spoke again, "So what happened here tonight? This was a last-minute change to the schedule. I honestly didn't expect to see you here."

"I'm not quite sure, Dad," Jr answered. "I was asleep, and then all of the sudden, I felt this urgent need to come protect Morty. When I got out here, I saw Jared standing over him, and then I just reacted. Then you showed up."

"If I may interject, sir," came the thought from Morty, "he waited until all the lights went out in the building, and then he came over to me, wringing his hands and grinning. He went over to his bike and pulled out a small flask that is filled with gasoline and a lighter. His actions looked threatening to me, so I sent an urgent help message to DJ."

"You could have defended yourself, you know," murmured Jr.

"Not without drawing attention to himself," Death interjected. "Your young stallion did the right thing.

"What are you talking about, Dad? He could have changed to his horse form and kicked him in the face!" Jr declared.

"Sure," Death said sarcastically. "Because a pale horse in a parking lot at night wouldn't draw any unwanted attention."

Jr stared blankly at his dad. He knew his dad was right but was too stubborn to admit it.

"Well, since my job here is finished, I had better head home," Death said.

"Are you going to tell Mom what happened?" Jr asked.

"Yes," said Death, sounding surprised by the question. "Do you realize what would happen if I didn't tell her and she found out from someone else? She would kill me."

Morty let out an audible chuckle, finding the irony of that statement humorous.

Death and Jr both looked at Morty. Grins curled their mouths as they started to laugh.

"Speaking of your mother, she said to tell you when the time comes, you'll know what to do," Death stated.

"What does that mean?" Jr inquired.

Death just shrugged his shoulders as he climbed up onto Mortis. "Let's go, old friend," he said as he looked at Jr. "When you figure it out, let me know."

Death and Mortis turned and started down the road. Jr watched as they slowly phased out as they went. Jr wondered what his mom could have meant. It took a moment before he realized he was still standing outside.

"Good night, Morty," he said as he headed for the door.

"Good night, DJ, and thank you."

Jr walked into his building, both physically and mentally drained. He knew it wouldn't take long to fall asleep. He walked into his apartment and locked the door. He stood there for a moment, trying to process what had just happened. He flopped down on his bed, and the world went dark.

Chapter 4

*B*ang. *Bang. Bang.*
Jr's eyes fluttered as he started to sit up.
Bang. Bang. Bang. "Open up the door. It's the police."
This was not how Jr wanted to get woken up on his day off. Jr stood up and grabbed his cloak. He headed toward the door, rubbing his eyes. Jr unlocked the deadbolt and opened the door.
"That's him, arrest that—" Dan was shouting.
"Mr. Martin," a large officer interrupted. "We have already gotten your statement. If we need you or Ms. Hagen again, we will come get you. Now please leave and allow us to do our job."
Dan just glared at Jr as another officer ushered him down the hall. The tension in the hall was high. It was evident that the police had apprehensions about the whole situation. Jr just stared down the hall. His attention had been caught by Claire. She was talking with an officer and was visibly upset.
"Mr. Deadwood," the large officer said, "my name is Officer Carson. We have a few questions for you, sir."
"Okay," Jr responded. The name hadn't caught him off guard. Dustin Deadwood was the name he used for work and his bills.
"Mr. Deadwood," Officer Carson continued. "Do you recognize this man?"
The officer held up a picture of Jared. Jr couldn't help but notice that they used a mug shot of Jared for the questioning.
"Yeah, I know that Neanderthal," Jr said.
"Mr. Deadwood, did you and Mr. Miginus have an altercation yesterday?" Officer Carson asked.

"Yeah, so?" Jr continued.

"Mr. Deadwood, Mr. Miginus was found dead this morning in the parking lot." Officer Carson started. "Right near your motorcycle. Your altercation, what was it about?'

"When I went to work yesterday, I went outside, and that jerk was sitting on my bike."

Officer Carson looked at Jr. "And then what?"

"I told him to get off my bike, which he did only to try to hit me," Jr stated, short of irritation.

"Then what happened?" Officer Carson pressed on.

"He swung at me, I dodged, and he ended up punching some truck that was out there. I heard his fingers crack," Jr said.

"Seems a little more than coincidental that following that he is found dead, don't you think, Mr. Deadwood?" Officer Carson said as he stepped toward Jr, obviously trying to use intimidation to get the answer he was looking for.

"If you're looking for someone who might have a motive to hurt that stupid Neanderthal," Jr said, staring directly at Officer Carson, "maybe you should start with the guy whose truck he dented yesterday or any family member of all the girls he's treated like garbage. Maybe start with all the people he and all his friends like Dan have cheated in town."

"Where were you at last night, sir?" Officer Carson asked coldly.

"Home all night. Dan and all his cronies saw me come in," Jr said with a tone that made it clear he was done with these questions.

"We will be sure to check that," Officer Carson glowered toward Jr. He turned and looked at another officer and said something that Jr couldn't make out. "We will be in touch."

Jr just looked at them as they walked back toward Dan's apartment. He could still see Claire talking with an officer outside the door. As Officer Carson and the other officer walked up, Claire looked up. It was obvious she had been crying. She saw Jr and gave a weak smile toward him. He was glad she had smiled; he didn't like seeing her upset.

As Jr turned to close the door, he heard his phone ringing in the other room. He closed the door and hurried to his phone. A quick glance as he answered let him know it was Josh. "Hey Josh, what's up?" Jr said.

"Dude," Josh said hastily, "the news just said that they found a body near your apartment. Did you see it?"

Jr knew he couldn't tell his friend the truth about it. "No," he said. "But the police did ask me about it."

"What? Like you're a suspect ask about it?" Josh inquired curiously.

"Yeah, in that way," Jr said wryly.

"Who was it?" Josh asked with way too much excitement.

"That Neanderthal I was telling you about."

"You mean that jerk who was on your bike yesterday?"

"That's him," Jr said.

"Whoa, man, that's crazy," Josh was saying when Jr heard a knock on his door.

"Dude, I got to go," Jr said.

"Okay, call me later, man."

"Yeah, yeah, sure," Jr responded as he hung up the phone.

Jr walked to the door, not knowing what to expect this time. He opened the door, and Claire instantly stepped in and threw her arms around his neck. Jr, shocked at what was happening, didn't know what to do. He just stood there for a second and then reached out and closed the door.

"You know you can hug me back," Claire whispered.

Jr awkwardly puts his arms around her. He could feel her pull in closer. "Umm, Claire?"

Claire let go and stepped back. "I was really worried about you when the police knocked on the door. Dan was yelling that it had to be you after they told him about Jared."

"Claire," Jr started. "Are you going to be okay? I saw you crying."

"I thought they were going to arrest you, that's why I was crying," she said as her eyes started to well up again. "Anyway," Claire continued as she started to pace back and forth in the entry. "Dan's really upset about Jared and is going on a bender. I don't want to deal with that right now, so I told him that I was going to go for a walk.

Normally he would have told me no way I was leaving, but he just looked at me and cracked open a bottle of whiskey."

Before he could even think about what he was saying, Jr blurted out, "Claire, would you like to go get some coffee?" Jr realized what he had just asked. "Oh, I'm sorry, I shouldn't ha—"

"I'd love to!" she interrupted.

"Claire, I shouldn't have asked you that," Jr stammered. "You're with Dan and everything. I'm sorry."

"DJ," Claire started. "I'm not sure what to do here. You're right, I am with Dan but not by choice anymore. I've tried to leave before. Dan won't let me, and when I did try, he beat me. I'm scared and don't know what to do."

Jr's anger flared when she said that Dan had laid his hands on her. His fists were clenched, and he was starting to shake. He felt a wave of heat pulsing up and down his body, keeping rhythm with the increasing speed of his heartbeat. He had never felt anything like this before. He closed his eyes for a second to compose himself before he spoke. He took a deep breath and exhaled slowly.

"How can we leave to get that coffee without Dan seeing you leave with me and get you in trouble?" Jr said as calmly as he could manage.

"I don't think we will need to worry about that. He's already had that bottle open for a few minutes. He won't notice anything else right now," Claire said. Then without warning, she stepped up and kissed Jr on the cheek.

Jr felt his heart skip, and he felt like he was going to fall over. "Whoa," was all he could say.

Claire blushed then smiled meekly. "Let's go get that coffee."

Chapter 5

Jr sat in his chair, replaying the events that had happened earlier that day in his head. He couldn't believe she had kissed him or had coffee with him.

Boom...Boom...Boom...Boom.

After the booming stopped in his head, he heard his phone going off. Jr answered without even looking at it.

"Hello," Jr said.

"Jr, listen," his dad said. "I have to leave now. That last knock was urgent."

"What? Now?"

"Yes, now," Death said, his tone sounding hurried. "Morty will be able to help out. Mortis has been in contact with him and filled him in on the situation."

"Morty, my horse?" Jr asked, bewildered.

"Yes, your horse, my horse. They do come from the same place, son," Death stated, "so they have the same capabilities."

"Okay, I'll do my best."

"I know you will, and, Jr, be careful."

Death hung up the phone on his end first. An overwhelming feeling surged over Jr. He wasn't ready to be the Grim Reaper."

"DJ, we have work to do," came the thought from Morty.

"It's my day off," Jr protested.

"From your day job. Death does not get a day off." Morty was sterner in tone than Jr had ever heard.

"Geez, you sound like Mortis!" The silence Jr got in response made him realize the connection. "Right, from the same place."

Jr walked out of his apartment and headed for the parking lot. As he passed by Claire's door, he could hear a drunk Dan yelling at Claire. Jr stopped and thought about kicking in the door.

"Not now, DJ," thought Morty. "She will survive. There are others who won't and need your assistance."

Jr stared at the door for a moment, his legs not willing to move toward the parking lot and a waiting Morty. The yelling was already down to a lower volume than a moment ago. His legs finally listened to what his brain was telling them. As he reached the parking lot, he saw a car parked where he had left his bike.

"Really, Morty? A car?"

"Trust me on this. It will be better in this."

Jr walked up to the car and got in. It was a nice enough car. Nothing super fancy but nice enough. He started up the engine and started down the road. He didn't have a clue where he was supposed to be headed but was sure Morty knew where to go.

"DJ, your dad worked out a plan for his absence with Fate. She agreed to not cut too many threads short in his absence. He will have to do a little catching up to do when he returns. At least this way you won't get overwhelmed your first time out. Mortis let me know how to help determine where we need to be so you can collect the soul." There was a hesitation before he continued, "DJ, your first one is Fred!"

Jr was glad that Morty had picked the form of a car. If he had been in bike form, Jr would have fallen off. Fred was Yvonne's husband and had been battling cancer for some time now. That must have been why she seemed so out of it the other day. Fred must have taken a turn for the worse.

"I won't be able to do that," Jr protested. "I can't kill Fred!"

"You won't be killing him, DJ. You'll just be collecting his soul." Morty's tone was reassuring and comforting. "You're here to make sure his soul gets where it belongs. You'll be ending his pain and suffering."

"I never imagined my dad would have to do his job to people he knows!" Jr leaned back in the seat to gather his thoughts. "I know the way, Morty. I'll drive us there."

Morty didn't respond, but Jr could feel that he was driving the car now. His thoughts turned to his friend Yvonne. How was she going to handle this? Would she be there when he got there to collect Fred's soul? He hoped that she wouldn't be there.

"I can assure you she won't be, DJ," Morty said.

The trip continued in silence. In a couple of minutes, they pulled up in front of the house of Fred and Yvonne. It was a quaint little house. Fred and Yvonne had only been married for a few years. There were both in their midtwenties and hadn't had any kids yet. For that Jr was happy. At least she wouldn't have to struggle alone to raise them. Jr sat outside for another moment before he went inside.

As he walked into the house, his physical appearance shifted into that of the Grim Reaper —cloak hanging in the skeletal frame of his body, scythe already in hand. Jr stopped in his tracks. This wasn't his normal appearance, and he hadn't wanted it to change.

"It's the office of the job," Morty thought to him. "You're on official business, so you have to be in uniform, so to speak."

"I guess that makes sense," Jr thought back.

He continued down the hall and entered the living room. His movements were completely silent. He stopped a few feet away from Fred and stood there for a moment. Fred looked pale and weak, like the life had already left his body put yet was still alive.

"I know you're there, Reaper. Show yourself." Fred was looking directly at Jr.

Jr hadn't realized that he wasn't visible. He willed himself visible. Fred's eyes went wide at the sight of him. Fred stared at him for a long moment. Jr felt compelled to say something to Fred.

"May I sit so we can talk?' Jr asked.

Fred's mouth fell open in shock. Both from the question and the fact that he could hear Jr talk. He gestured to a seat on the couch across the room from where he sat. Jr walked over to the couch and took a seat. Fred just looked on in amazement and wonder.

"Fred, I'm sorry about this. Sorry Yvonne will have to deal with this," Jr said.

"I hope I don't offend," Fred started out. "But I wasn't aware the Grim Reaper had feelings."

Jr wanted to tell Fred who he was. Fred knew him and had been at the shop with Yvonne, Josh, and himself. He knew he couldn't tell him though. So instead, he looked at Fred and said, "Know that Yvonne has friends that will look after her and the motorcycle shop. They will be there to support and comfort her."

Fred smiled a weak smile. "Thank you," he said. "That does give me some peace."

Fred's life faded as he closed his eyes. Jr stood up and walked over to Fred. He reached out his scythe. The blade shimmered just like it had with his dad. He felt the tip of the blade nudge something. Jr gave a little twist and pulled the blade back. Attached to the blade was the same cobweb-looking material. This one, however, was mostly white with a few patches of gray. Like Death had shown him, Jr spread it out and gave it a little toss in the air. It hung in the air for a second, then started to float up. It continued up and out through the ceiling. Jr looked at Fred. His body was in the chair with eyes closed and a little smile on his lips. Jr turned and walked out of the house.

"You did well, DJ," Morty said. "The rest of the night should be easier."

Jr didn't respond. He was worried how Yvonne was going to handle this. He knew she would be calling tomorrow. The rest of the night was a blur to Jr. When he finally got back to his apartment, he was spent, not knowing how he could keep this up for long. He didn't even remember walking in his apartment or going to bed. He was instantly in a deep sleep, dead to the world.

Chapter 6

Claire was looking at Jr and smiling. He loved the way her smile made her face glow. Jr loved everything about her. They sat there, talking over a cup of coffee at the local shop. Their conversation was long and enjoyable. As their coffee was almost finished, they were wrapping up the conversation. Claire reached out across the table and put her hand on his. Jr felt the explosion of butterflies in his stomach trying to escape. His face turned red. He was nervous; he never had been good with the ladies. He looked up at Claire, and she flashed another smile at him. He smiled back. They leaned toward each other. His heart was racing at lightning speed. He had been wanting to do this for so long. He felt the warmth of her breath as their lips were about to touch.

Beep, beep, beep, beep!

Jr shot upright in his bed. He was shaking with a cold sweat. It was a dream, only a dream. He shook his head as he got up and walked to the bathroom. He ran cold water and splashed it on his face. He felt the cool water cover his face, his mind racing at a thousand miles an hour. He looked at himself in the mirror.

What are you thinking? This can never happen, Jr thought.

Claire's picture was in his mind. He couldn't stop thinking about her. She was a pretty woman by any standards. Five-foot-eight inches tall, slender with shoulder-length brown hair, eyes like stars, and a smile of pearl white teeth that made her face glow when she flashed her smile. He wondered how Dan ever managed to get her. What a jerk. He didn't deserve her. She deserved better!

"Stop it, you idiot," Jr said out loud to himself.

Jr walked into the kitchen to make some coffee and breakfast. He looked in his fridge for something to make. His fridge was empty. He hadn't made it to the store yet this week.

"Coffee for breakfast it is."

There was a knock at Jr's door—a light knock. Jr glanced at the door. He wasn't expecting anybody today. He walked over to the door and opened it. Yvonne was standing there, obviously distraught and crying.

"Yvonne, come in. Are you okay?" Jr already knew why she was crying.

Yvonne walked in and burst into tears as Jr closed the door behind her. She turned to him and buried her face in his chest and continued sobbing. Jr's heart sank. He knew what she was dealing with. He put his arms around her to comfort her. He didn't speak; he knew when she was ready, she would tell him why she was there.

A few moments passed before Yvonne let go of him. "I'm sorry, DJ. I didn't know where else to go," she said between tears. "Fred passed away last night!"

She burst back into tears, and it was Jr's time to step in and hug her. "I'm sorry, Yvonne. Is there anything I can do to help?"

"Can I stay here today? I don't want to be at home today."

"Of course, you can. Do you want some tea?'

She gave and weak smile. "Yes, please. A little strong."

Jr walked into the kitchen as Yvonne went and sat on his couch. He filled the kettle with water and put it on the stove. He opened the cupboard and pulled out the black tea and his French press. As he got everything ready in the kitchen, he glanced over at Yvonne. She had been his friend since he was in school. He hated the fact that she had lost the love of her life. Jr remembered the day she got engaged to Fred. She came bursting into the office almost skipping through the air. A huge smile covered her face. She ran up to him and Josh and gave them a double hug as she was squealing with excitement.

"Fred proposed, he proposed!" she exclaimed.

Jr and Josh both gave a huge hug and congratulations. They had never seen their friend that happy. They knew that Fred would treat her well. For the few short years that they were married, they were happy, even after the cancer had been found. The tea kettle started to whistle, bringing Jr back to reality and the current issue. He poured the water over the tea in the press and let it steep. When it was ready, he poured the tea into a cup and walked over to the couch.

"Here you go, Yvonne," Jr said as he handed her the tea.

"Thanks, DJ. Have any plans for today?"

"I need to go to the store, especially since you're here, I don't have anything to cook for you."

She gave a little laugh. "DJ, you don't have to cook me anything. I'll be okay."

"Don't be silly. You need to eat. Why don't you rest while I go to the store?"

"I think that I will, thanks." Yvonne looked down at her tea for a second before she spoke again, "Thanks again, DJ. You've always been a good friend."

"I'll grab you a pillow and blanket." Jr turned and went to the closet to grab the blanket. "Do you need me to call anybody for you and let them know?" Jr asked.

"If you could let Josh know. I already called Fred's family and mine."

"Okay, I will let him know. You look tired. Get some rest."

Yvonne was already almost asleep on the couch when Jr walked out the door. He was glad she felt comfortable enough around him to relax. Jr opened the door and walked into the hall. He was thinking about what he needed to pick up from the store when his thoughts were interrupted by Morty.

"DJ, we have to go."

"What? Now?"

"Yes, now."

"Yvonne's here. I can't go now!"

"Not debatable, DJ. Sorry."

Jr started back down the hall when his mind got hit with a huge wave of emotional turmoil and agony. He reeled back and slumped on the wall. It felt like his leg had a gash. He looked and saw nothing wrong. Then his side felt like it was getting crushed. He grabbed at his ribs and again found nothing out of place. He heard wails and screams all around him, but the hallway was empty.

"What is going on?" He gasped.

"That's why we have to go, DJ. Wreck on the freeway."

The surge of emotion and pain faded away, but Jr was shaken by it. "Morty, how much info about this did you get from Mortis?"

"I have limited information on this. All I know about it is that when there is a major accident like this, you can sense the pain and terror of the people involved."

"That actually explains a lot," Jr said.

He walked outside and walked over to Morty. He had stayed in car form since last night. Jr didn't like the car as much as a bike but had to admit that the car was a lot more practical for this purpose. He got in, and Morty started off down the road.

"Where do we have to go, Morty?"

"Just outside of town."

They were at the scene of the crash in moments. There were cars crashed into other cars. Cars were flipped over on their sides and some all the way over. Smoke was billowing from a few that were on fire. Jr couldn't believe his eyes at the amount of destruction that could happen from one wreck. Jr walked over to the first person that he sensed was in critical condition. He realized that he was in his cloak already and his scythe was in his hand. He squeezed the handle, and the blade snapped out with an eerie sound. The person by the car looked up.

"I'm ready, Death. Send me home."

Jr reached in with the tip of the scythe, gave a slight twist, and removed the soul. Jr was about to smooth out the soul when he heard the sirens and the screeching of tires as the first police car and ambulance pulled up. His heart skipped a beat.

"Don't worry about them, DJ," came the comforting thought from Morty. "They can't see you. Only the ones who need you can see you."

That made Jr feel better, and he resumed smoothing out the soul. He gave it a toss and watched until it headed toward its eternal home. Turning to go to the next person who needed his services, he repeated the process of collecting and watching the souls leave for eternity. Most went toward their destination quickly; none of them lingered too long. Some saw him, some didn't. Of those who did, some thanked him; others pleaded with him to not end their pain. He felt bad for those who pleaded with him. It was beyond his power to save these people. As he walked back toward Morty, one of the people who were injured but not critical looked right at Jr.

"It's not my time yet, Reaper! Go away!"

Jr looked at him in disbelief. "You can see me?"

The man just stared at him, shaking with terror. His eyes were glassed over, and he looked at Jr. Jr could tell that the man was petrified.

"I'm not here for you."

Jr started off back to Morty, dazed in disbelief that someone who hadn't need him could see him. He got in and threw his head back for a second to take a quick rest and collect his thoughts. He noticed that he had been doing that a lot lately. He remembered then that some people, very few people, could see Death even when they weren't about to need his services.

"We better get going, Morty. I still have to go to the store."

As they started down the road, more police vehicles and ambulances were arriving. Jr was glad the injured would get medical attention. The screams he had heard in his head had started to quiet down once he started his job collecting the souls of those who needed him. Jr hadn't even noticed while it was happening. Jr leaned back in his seat and closed his eyes as Morty went toward the store.

"DJ, we're here."

Jr snapped awake as he shot up. "Sorry, Morty."

Morty gave a little chuckle. "Told you to trust me about being a car."

"Let me guess, Mortis?"

"Indeed it was. DJ, don't forget to call Josh."

"Oh crap. Thanks for reminding me.'

Jr pulled out his phone and dialed Josh's number. He picked up on the second ring.

"Hey DJ, what's up?"

"Hey Josh," Jr's tone told Josh the news couldn't be good. "Yvonne asked me to call."

Josh interrupted him. "Yvonne? Why is she okay?"

"Physically, yes, she's okay. Fred passed away last night."

There was silence on the phone for a long moment before Josh was able to speak again.

"Does she need anything?" Josh asked with concern.

"Just support right now. She's at my place sleeping at the moment."

"Give her my condolences, and let her know that if she needs anything to give me a call."

"I will, on both counts," Jr replied.

"DJ…thanks for letting me know."

They hung up as Jr got out of Morty the car. Jr walked to the door of the store and grabbed a cart. He started down the aisles, somewhat aimlessly. He never used a grocery list at the store. That's probably why his cabinets and fridge were never properly stocked. He was hoping Yvonne liked pancakes because that's what he was craving. He started to grab flour, baking powder, eggs, and oil for the pancakes when he saw chocolate chips. He grabbed a bag of them. He continued to shop until he saw frozen blueberries, so he grabbed those too. He looked at both the blueberries and the chocolate chips.

"Can't have both." He left them both in his cart. He would let Yvonne decide.

He headed for the checkout lanes when he passed by some flowers. He stopped and looked at them for a second. He saw some roses and grabbed them for Claire with a card that read, "I really enjoyed the coffee. Looking forward to doing that again." He also grabbed a little bouquet for Yvonne, hoping it would help to lift her spirits. He headed to checkout to pay for his items.

Chapter 7

Jr walked to the door of the building with his groceries in hand when he noticed Dan's bike was gone. That was good. That meant he could give Claire the flowers now instead of having to wait until later. He walked up to her door to knock. He hesitated for an instant before he knocked. He had butterflies and was nervous.

"What's wrong with me?" he said aloud.

He nerved himself and knocked on the door. He didn't her anybody coming to the door.

"Claire, are you home?"

He didn't get an answer. He felt a slight twinge of disappointment as he turned to walk away. He thought about leaving them at the door but was worried Dan would see them and cause an issue. He walked to his apartment and unlocked the door. Yvonne was just starting to stir as Jr walked in the door.

"Hey, you're awake," Jr said.

"Hey, DJ. I see you made it to the store."

"Yeah, just got back. Are you feeling any better?"

Yvonne gave a lit nod. "A little," she said quietly.

Jr walked into the kitchen and started to put away the groceries. Yvonne walked into the kitchen and sat at the table. Jr looked back at her as she rubbed her eyes, trying to get the grogginess to leave.

"Do you want some pancakes?"

"Yeah, that sounds good, but I don't see any pancake mix in your groceries, and I know your cabinets are empty."

"Pancake mix! Uh, gross," Jr playfully mocked. "I have everything we need to make them right here."

Jr pulled out the ingredients for the pancakes. Yvonne looked at him like he was crazy. He grabbed the roses he had bought for Claire and put them on top of the fridge. Then pulled the bouquet of flowers out for her and handed them to her. She looked at them before she gave them a smell.

"Thanks, DJ," she said as she gave him a little smile. "But I'm pretty sure you can't make pancakes with flowers."

They both laughed.

"Now for a serious question, Yvonne." Jr tried to sound serious. He pointed to the ingredients on the counter. "Blueberry or chocolate chip?"

"Oooh, that's a tough choice. What do you suggest?"

"Well, I prefer blueberry, but chocolate is proven to promote happiness."

"Chocolate chip it is then, DJ." Yvonne chuckled. "You always have been good in the kitchen."

"Thanks," Jr said as he pulled some mixing bowls out of the cabinets. He grabbed the griddle out of a separate cabinet and plugged it in near the stove. He went to work, measuring the ingredients for the pancakes when he heard a knock on the door. He opened the door, and Claire stepped in before she noticed Yvonne at the table.

"Hey Claire," Jr said.

"Sorry, didn't know you had company," Claire said coldly. She gave Jr a hurt look, then turned and stormed out of the door.

"What? Wait," Jr almost yelled out. He looked at Yvonne, "I hav—"

"Go you goofball," Yvonne interrupted.

Jr flew out the door after Claire. She was already at her door before he could catch her.

"Claire, wait!" he said as he caught up.

She spun around with hurt in her eyes and a hostility in her voice that caught Jr completely off guard. "You're just as bad as Dan and everyone else!" she shouted.

"No, Claire wait!" Jr pleaded.

Claire was starting to cry as she walked through her door. She didn't even bother to look back before she slammed the door behind her. The door almost smacked Jr in the face. He could feel the wind from the door blow past him. He took a step back. He stood there dumbfounded for a second before he reached out and knocked.

"Claire! Claire! Please let me talk to you."

Jr stood there for a moment with no response from inside. He slowly walked away with a sinking feeling in his heart. He slowly walked back to his apartment, hoping that Claire would come out before he got to his place. Yvonne gave him a sorrowful look as he walked back in.

"DJ, I'm so sorry," she said as she gave him a hug.

"It's not your fault. Now how about those pancakes?" he said, trying to change the subject.

Jr went in and finished making the pancakes. He put a few on a plate for Yvonne and another plate for himself. He made some coffee and put it on the table.

"Do you want syrup?' Jr asked Yvonne.

"Yes, please."

Jr grabbed some syrup and brought it to the table. The two sat down to eat some breakfast. Jr poured two cups of coffee out of the carafe and put one in front of each plate.

"DJ, I am really sorry. It feels like my fault," Yvonne said.

"No, don't worry about it."

There was a knock at the door. Yvonne gave Jr a hopeful look as he got up to answer it. Josh came through as Jr opened the door.

"I thought I smelled breakfast," Josh said as he pushed past Jr.

Josh walked over to Yvonne and gave her a hug. "I'm so sorry, Yvonne. Fred was a good man."

"Thanks, Josh," she said, hugging him back. "I take it DJ called?"

"Yeah," Josh answered over his shoulder as he went into the kitchen and grabbed a plate out of the cabinet.

"Make yourself at home, Josh," Jr said sarcastically.

"Thanks, DJ. I will."

They both chuckled as Josh brought his plate to the table. They sat quietly as they ate, glad to be able to have each other's company. They finished eating and cleared the table. Yvonne started to fill the sink with soap and water. Josh walked up behind her and nudged her out of the way.

"I don't think so, lady, go sit down," he said.

Josh started doing the dishes as Jr and Yvonne went and sat on the couch.

"DJ," Yvonne started. "I don't think I'll be able to stay at my house tonight. In fact, I don't think I could even go there right now. It's too fresh and raw. Can I stay here tonight?"

"Yeah," Jr said. "Do you want me and Josh to go get you some clothes from your place?"

"If you wouldn't mind?"

Jr didn't say anything. He just smiled, reached over, and squeezed her hand. Jr got up and walked into the kitchen. He helped finish the dishes, drying and putting them away. When they finished with the dishes, they got ready to go get some clothes from Yvonne's place for her. They didn't need to ask her where her stuff was at; they had both helped Fred and her put everything away when they moved in. They both gave her a quick hug and took off.

Chapter 8

Claire was sitting in her bed, tears streaming down her face as she looked at the bruises on her arms and chest. The visions of the night before replaying in her mind—she had just walked back in from having coffee with DJ. Dan met her as she walked in; the smell of whiskey lingered around him like a cloud.

"Where have you been?" Dan asked with anger in his voice. "I had to go get my own whiskey at the store. That's your job!"

"Nowhere," Claire sputtered. The fear of Dan's wrath was evident in her voice. "I just went for a walk."

Dan's hand smacked her across the face, splitting her lip. "Don't lie to me, you little tramp."

A small squeak escaped Claire's lips as his hand made contact with her face. Her eyes instantly filled with tears from the sting of the slap. She tasted salt in her mouth. She wasn't sure if it was blood from her lip or tears. She looked at Dan with apprehension. He was drunk; it could go either way. She was hoping that he would walk away and pass out. The other alternative was something she wished didn't exist.

"I know you were with him, you harlot." Dan's words were slurred as he stared at her with anger in his eyes.

"If I'm a harlot, it's because you made me into one!" Claire blurted out with defiance.

Dan was enraged at her words. He threw the almost empty bottle of whiskey at her. It barely missed her head. It exploded into a thousand shards of glass as it hit the wall. The shards pelted Claire in the face and neck, scratching and cutting her.

"You don't talk to me like that!" Dan yelled, causing spittle to hit Claire in the face.

Dan grabbed Claire by the arm with more aggression than normal. He spun her around, throwing her into the wall, slamming into it with a thud. Her nose exploded with blood as the wall smashed it flat. Dan grabbed her by the hair and yanked her in front of him. He spun her around to face him and punched her in the stomach. Claire doubled over from the impact. The air was knocked out of her, and she fell to her knees, gasping for air. Dan pulled her up by her hair. He was almost frothing at the mouth. He threw her against the wall again and ripped her shirt open.

"No, no, Dan, please!" Claire pleaded as she struggled to get free from his hands.

Dan pinned her to the wall by her arms. It felt like her wrists were about to snap in two. He pushed her back into the wall as she struggled even harder to get loose. Dan reached up and ripped off her bra, exposing her bare flesh.

"No!" Claire screamed as she kneed Dan in the groin.

That stunned Dan for a moment. Claire managed to get free from his grasp, and she bolted down the hall. She was almost to the door when she felt Dan jump on her from behind, causing her to fall to the floor. Dan landed on top of her and rolled her onto her back. Claire, frantic and trying to escape, spat in Dan's face. Dan let out a growl of rage and slammed Claire's head on the floor. Claire heard a sickening thud as her vision went blurry.

The rest of the night was a blur—partly from the bump on the head and partly because she disconnected from reality to survive the ordeal. For the next couple of hours, Dan raped and beat her repeatedly. When Dan was finished, he got up and walked out of the room. Claire lay on the floor, crying and bleeding. She heard Dan leave the apartment, presumably to go get high and drink some more at one of his crony's places. Claire picked herself up and went to take a shower. She felt gross and filthy and wanted to wash off.

Claire jumped, startled by the knock in the door. Her heart raced as her fear and anxiety swarmed over her.

"Claire, are you home?" she heard DJ ask.

Claire relaxed when she heard his voice. She stifled her tears and went to the bathroom to wash her face. She didn't want DJ to see her like this. She finished washing her face and looked in the mirror. She looked tired and worn out. Claire felt tears starting to form in her eyes again. She looked away and blinked rapidly to stop the tears from flowing. She dabbed her eyes with a towel and went to her room to find a nicer-looking shirt, hopefully with long sleeves to conceal the bruises. She looked at herself in the little mirror on her dresser.

"If he finds out what Dan does to me, will he think I'm gross?" she asked herself aloud.

She walked to the window to see if Dan's bike was back before she went out the door. A smile spread across her lips as she walked toward DJ's apartment. She really liked him. He made her feel safe and happy. She hadn't felt safe or happy in years. She stepped in front of his door and took a deep breath and exhaled slowly to try to steady her nerves. She had butterflies in her stomach as she remembered the conversation they had had the day before over coffee. She reached out and knocked on the door.

A smile formed on DJ's face as he saw her. "Hey Claire," he said as he opened up the door.

Claire stepped through the door, fully intent on giving DJ a hug. Something caught her attention from the corner of her eye. She looked over and saw a woman sitting at the table. She was in her mid-to-late twenties with curly jet-black hair and a figure that Claire thought far surpassed her own. Her blood ran cold when she saw the woman sitting there. It felt like a knife had been plunged into her heart. It was hard to swallow.

"Sorry, didn't know you had company," she said curtly.

She heard DJ say something as she was walking away but didn't pay attention to it. She was walking briskly so she could get to her room before she started crying. She made it to her door as DJ caught up.

"Claire, wait!" he spoke.

Claire spun around. Anger and pain welled up from deep inside her. Tears were stinging her eyes, trying desperately to spring forth and streak down her cheeks.

"You're just as bad as Dan and everyone else!" Claire shouted.

Claire turned and walked through her door as the tears broke their dam open and started to flow. She heard DJ plead with her to wait as she walked into her apartment. She slammed the door closed behind her without looking back. She ran to her bedroom and threw herself on her bed and sobbed bitterly. She heard DJ outside her door, so she covered her head with a pillow to silence him.

"How could he do this? I thought he was different. Better." The tears flowed out as she cried for the next few minutes. Claire cried herself to sleep, her heart aching like never before. She woke up to the sounds of footsteps and voices in the hall. She could tell it was DJ and his friend Josh. The sound of his voice felt like it was cutting her soul to pieces. She got up and walked to the bathroom, looking in the medicine cabinet for anything she could find. She wanted to kill herself to escape the pain and turmoil she was in. There was nothing in the cabinet except for some ibuprofen.

"Aaarrgghh!" she shouted in frustration slamming the door closed.

She stormed out of the bathroom and headed for the kitchen. She knew Dan normally hid some of his drugs in the kitchen. She tore through the cabinets, searching for anything. The frustration was getting overwhelming. She went to grab a knife from the drawer. She pulled open the drawer and saw a business card on top of the knives. Claire picked it up and looked at it. It was from the crisis hotline. One of the cashiers at the grocery store had given it to her a couple of weeks ago when they had noticed some bruises. Claire picked up the phone and dialed the number. She didn't know why, but she felt like she needed to call.

The phone only rang twice before it was answered. "Hello, crisis hotline," a friendly-sounding voice said.

"Hello," Claire said hesitantly.

"Yes, this is the crisis hotline. Do you need help?"

Claire had trouble talking. "I think so."

"Okay," the voice said. "Is it safe for you to talk? If not, just say, 'Sorry wrong number.'"

"Yes, it's safe. I'm alone," Claire said as she burst into tears.

"Good. My name is Alfie. We're going to get you through this. What's going on, dear?"

Claire couldn't explain why, but she felt like she could trust this woman. She started from when Dan had brought her to his apartment and all the vile things he and his friends had done to her—the rapes, the beatings, and other forms of physical abuse that she had endured. Alfie listened patiently as Claire recapped her life in a nutshell. She got to the part about what had happened with DJ and how she had wanted to kill herself but found the card instead.

"Claire," Alfie started, "do you know God?"

"What?" Claire asked, confused. Nobody had ever asked her that before.

"Do you know God?" Alfie asked again. "Do you know that He cares for you and wants to help you through this?"

"I don't think God cares about me. Nobody does," Claire said with both anger and loneliness in her voice.

"Oh, that's not true, dear," Alfie answered sympathetically. "Do you think you would be able to meet me somewhere tomorrow? Only if you can do it safely, though."

"Maybe, why?" Claire was hesitant about this.

"I want to give you some information about getting you out of that situation and into a safe house."

"Oh no, I couldn't do that." Claire gasped. "Dan would find out, and that would be…" Claire's words were choked off by fear.

"That's why I said only if it is safe." Alfie had genuine concern in her voice. "I don't want to put you into any dangerous situation."

Claire sat there silently for a couple of moments, her brain spinning. Her head told her that Dan would find out that this lady would tell him or betray her in some way. Her heart, on the other hand, was tugging at her, telling her to trust Alfie. She was quiet longer than she thought.

"Claire, Claire. Are you still there?" There was panic in the way Alfie had asked.

Claire snapped out of her thoughts. "Yes, I'm still here."

"Good." The relief in Alfie's voice was evident. "Could I drop something off for you?"

"I don't know. I would hate to think what might happen if Dan was home when you stopped by." Claire was curious about this lady.

"I understand, dear," Alfie said. "Call back if you need to. I want to give you my personal number so we can keep in contact."

"Okay," Claire responded. This woman seemed genuinely concerned about Claire and her well-being. She decided to trust her. "There is a planter with a fake plant outside my apartment door," Claire told Alfie. "You could drop it off in there so Dan won't know you stopped by."

"That's wonderful, dear," Alfie said. "I can drop it off later tonight. I'll make sure no one is watching."

"Thank you, Alfie."

Claire gave Alfie her address and then hung up the phone, not sure why she had even called in the first place. She looked at her door. She wanted to know who the woman at DJ's apartment was. Why was she there? Claire had to know. She heard Dan's bike pull in and shut off. She had gotten off the phone just in time. Luckily, she knew that most of the time, the day after he assaulted her, he didn't even acknowledge her existence. She hoped that would be the case today.

Chapter 9

Jr and Josh headed down the hall toward the parking lot. As they passed Claire's door, Jr couldn't help but give a sidelong glance at her door. He hoped that they would be able to talk and work things out. They exited the building as the sun was climbing high.

"DJ, where's your bike at?"

Jr just pointed over to Morty as the car. Josh gave him a weird look of confusion and disbelief.

"You're driving a car?" Josh chided Jr.

"I'm borrowing my dad's car while he's out of town."

"When's he supposed to be back?"

"Don't know yet. Hopefully soon."

They walked over to Morty and got in. Since Josh was there, Jr put the keys in the ignition and started the motor. As the car fired up, Dan rode into the parking lot. He got off and stumbled around for a second and almost fell down. He opened the bags on his bike and pulled out two full bottles of whiskey and one half-empty bottle. He took his helmet off and tucked it in his bags on the bike. Jr just watched him as he staggered into the front door of the building. Jr hoped Claire would be okay with Dan being that drunk.

"DJ, you okay, man?"

Josh's question snapped Jr out of watching Dan. He realized that he had a death grip on the steering wheel. "Yeah, fine. Just a little concerned."

"Man, you have it bad for that girl. Does she know?"

"I thought so," Jr said. "Not so sure anymore."

They pulled out on the road and headed across town to Yvonne and Fred's house. On the way there, Jr couldn't help but remember the night before when he was over to the house, how frail and weak Fred had looked. He was glad that his suffering and the battle with the cancer was over, but he felt horrible about what Yvonne was going through. He pulled the car into the driveway and shut off the ignition.

Josh's phone went off. Josh answered the phone as he got out of the car. Jr sat there for a second longer before getting out. He wasn't looking forward to going back to that house. He got out and walked to the front door as Josh was walking around the yard on the phone. Jr went to where Fred and Yvonne kept the spare key and retrieved it. He unlocked the door and returned the key to its proper spot. Josh walked up as Jr put the key back.

"Hey DJ, when we get finished up here, I need you to drop me at my house."

"Sure," Jr responded. "Everything okay?"

"Yeah, I forgot my wife has a hair appointment this afternoon. I got to go take care of the rug rat. I'll swing by tomorrow and pick up my bike."

"Sure, no problem," Jr said as they walked inside.

The smell of hospital sterilization hung in the air. They both knew how much of a toll this situation had taken on their friends—the constant treatments, medicines, and shots. The emotional toll on Yvonne was enormous. She had lost weight in the past few months and was looking extremely worn out. Working full-time and taking care of Fred after work, it was a wonder that she hadn't collapsed from exhaustion. Jr and Josh walked back to the bedroom and grabbed a bag out of the closet for some clothes. They threw together a few days' worth of clothes and grabbed some toiletries from the bathroom. Toothbrush, shampoo, and conditioner. Not sure what else to grab, they looked at each other and then turned back to the bedroom.

"You know, Josh, you being a married man, I figured that you would have some better insight on what a woman needs in an overnight bag." Jr jabbed at Josh.

Josh just laughed and said, "Remember, I'm still a guy. We don't pay attention to that type of stuff."

They walked outside and locked the door. When they got in the car, Josh looked at Jr real hard for a second.

"Alright, DJ, spill it," Josh ordered.

Jr looked at Josh. "I don't know what you are talking about."

"Spill it or I'm gonna smack you in the face." Only a true friend could threaten violence to help his buddy through a difficult situation.

"Alright," Jr said. "Claire and I went out for coffee yesterday, and I thought everything went fine. I haven't been able to get her out of my head since. I even bought her flowers today when I went to the store today after Yvonne came over. She didn't answer the door when I went to give them to her. Then she came over later and saw Yvonne sitting at the table. She looked at me and said I was just like Dan. Then she left and slammed a door in my face when I went to talk to her. She looked really hurt, man."

"Oh, wow, man, that is a crappy situation." Josh looked a Jr for a second and then continued, "I know she'll talk to you again soon. You've always been a person she could talk to about things."

"Yeah, but I don't think she will now. She doesn't trust me anymore."

"Nah, it's not you. She doesn't trust people. Look at what she has as a reference point—people like Dan and that Neanderthal. I've seen how she acts around you. She'll talk to you again. Just give her a couple days, man."

"You really think so?" Jr questioned his friend.

"I am married, remember? I do know a little about women. Trust me, dude."

Jr just smiled. "Thanks, Josh."

"No worries." His expression changed. "Now get me home before Crystal says I'm grounded from hanging out. If she misses her appointment, you may never see me again." He ended with a laugh.

Jr started up the car and headed toward Josh's house. They didn't say much to each other during the drive to Josh's. They were the type of friends who could be around each other for hours and not say a word. Jr rounded the corner to Josh's neighborhood and slowed down to almost a crawl, scanning the surrounding area for that monster that roamed the streets here. A block down the road, he spotted it. It didn't seem to pay attention to anyone else but Jr. It was large, with mangy hair, and a slobbering problem that produced about a hundred gallons of saliva a minute. Jr stopped in the middle of the street.

"Here you go, Josh."

"What are you talking about?" Josh asked. "My house is still a block away."

Jr looked at his friend and smiled a big grin. "You could use the exercise, old man. You've been putting on some holiday weight."

"It's midsummer, you nerd! And I'm only five years older than you." Josh looked down the street and saw the monster. He started to laugh. "The dog. You won't drive down the street because of a homeless, harmless dog?"

"He slobbers all over me," Jr quelled.

Josh could only laugh at Jr's hesitation. He looked over at Jr and gave him puppy dog eyes and started to whimper.

"Fine, fine," Jr said. "If he slobbers on the car, you're washing it."

Jr continued down the street to Josh's house. The dog saw him coming and started wagging his tail and trotting toward the car. Jr pulled up to Josh's, and the dog came right up to his door and sat there, wagging his tail.

"You had better say hi to your friend," Josh said. "Don't want to hurt his feelings."

Jr and Josh got out of the car. The mangy dog hopped up, tail wagging even faster as Jr walked over to him.

"Sit," Jr commanded. The dog sat. "Good boy," Jr said as he reached out to pat its head. The dog, satisfied with the attention, trotted off down the road wagging its tail.

Josh turned around as he started across his lawn. "She will talk to you again. Just be patient."

He turned back to his house just in time to catch a six-year-old son to his leg. He picked up his son, Tommy. Crystal walked out onto the porch. She saw Jr and gave him a friendly wave. Jr waved back and walked back to Morty as Josh and his family went inside. He got in and let out a sigh. He hoped Josh was right about Claire. What could he do at this point except wait?

Jr headed back toward his apartment. His mind was racing, replaying how the events of the last day had transpired. How he had gone from being on cloud nine drinking coffee with Claire, to completely crushed and depleted from losing a friend and losing Claire. He drove around, mind bouncing from thought to thought, wondering what the future would hold.

His thoughts were interrupted by Morty, "DJ, we have to go to work."

"Again, how does Dad do this? Where?"

"Australia."

"Australia!" Jr exclaimed. "How fast can you get a passport?"

The road they were on was empty except for them, so it was safe to phase out. Seconds later, they were soaring through the atmosphere at an unbelievable speed.

"I didn't know you could go this fast, Morty!" Jr shouted.

"I didn't either," came Morty's response. His thought sounded nervous.

Moments later, they descended on a long dirt road and phased back in. The road was about as smooth as an old washboard. The local terrain looked completely different from anything Jr had ever seen. They sped past a kangaroo.

"Whoa, a kangaroo. I've never seen one before!" Jr realized that he must have sounded like a little kid.

They continued down the road, speeding past local wildlife. Jr managed to keep any more excited comments to himself. They rounded a corner and slowed down as they entered a small grove of trees. They rounded another turn and found themselves approaching a small cottage nestled up next to a small lake. Morty came to a stop at the front porch. Jr donned the uniform of his duties and stepped out of the car. Jr walked through the front door and saw a middle-aged gentleman sitting in a rocking chair. He was rubbing his temples with his eyes squinted shut.

"G'day, Death," the man said as he quit rubbing his temples. "Got a cracking good headache. Is that why you're here?"

Jr wasn't sure how to respond to that question. He wasn't the bringer of death, just the collector of the soul, so he said the first thing that popped into his head. "That depends on what is causing the headache."

The man looked at Jr with a look of utter disbelief. "Not an answer I would have ever expected, mate."

"My apologies," Jr said as professionally as he could muster. "There is a misconception that I kill people. I do not. I simply collect the soul after that person passes on. I don't always know how one might die."

The man just sat there looking more confused than concerned with the fact that he was talking with the Grim Reaper. "You don't quite fit the image of Death that I had in my head, mate."

"What were you expecting?" Jr inquired rather curiously.

"Well, I suppose I was expecting evil incarnate."

Jr let out a little chuckle. "No, that job is already taken. Maybe you've heard of him, goes by the name Lucifer."

The man's expression went flat and so did his tone, "Aye, mate. I know him."

Jr could tell that the relationship between those two wasn't a pleasant one. He decided not to pursue the issue further.

"Do you know love, Reaper?"

"I know about love," Jr responded.

"Not about it," the man said. "Do you know it? Have you ever loved or been loved? I know of the greatest love ever given. That's why your presence doesn't frighten me."

Jr was perplexed by his statement. Then he saw the man go stiff and close his eyes. Jr reached out with the tip of his scythe and gently removed the soul. Jr was surprised that it was dark in color. He seemed like a decent fellow. Why was it so dark? Was that why he responded the way he did to the mention of Lucifer? Jr smoothed out the soul and gave it a little toss. His mouth fell open in complete shock. To his surprise, it was floating up!

"How can it be going up when it's that dark?" he asked aloud even though he was alone.

He continued to watch it float up until it passed through the ceiling. He stood there just looking at the ceiling. Jr couldn't believe what he had just witnessed. He walked outside, still in shock from what had just happened and got in Morty.

"DJ, everything okay?" Morty asked him.

"Yeah, Morty," Jr mumbled. "Remind me to talk to Dad later. We need to head back home."

Morty turned around and headed back out of the grove onto the long dirt road. He phased out and headed back home. Jr sat in silence on the way back, replaying the scenario in his head. Something that man said was nagging him. What kind of love would make him unafraid of the prospect of death? Both bodily and the incarnation, Jr just couldn't figure that one out. A few moments later, they phased back in near Jr's apartment. The sun was starting to get low on the horizon. Dusk was settling on the area when they pulled into the parking lot at the apartment. Jr got out of Morty and turned to get the bag out of the back. Jr squinted at a flash that happened right next to him. A man in a robe reached out and closed Morty's door and grabbed Jr by the cloak.

"We need to talk," the robed figure said. As he finished talking, there was another flash. Jr and the cloaked figure were gone.

Chapter 10

Jr blinked wildly to clear the spots from his eyes. As he slowly regained his vision, he saw two cloaked figures standing in front of him. His vision cleared, and he immediately recognized his dad.

"Dad, what are you doing here?"

"I believe, Jr"—Death chuckled—"'what are *you* doing here?' would be a more appropriate question."

Jr looked around. "Where is this place?"

"Earth," the robed figure said flatly.

Death gave him a look that feigned irritation. "Bradford, seriously."

The man in the robe just laughed. "Somebody around here has to have a sense of humor."

"Excuse me," Jr interrupted. "Can we get back to my question and then some extra ones I have?"

Death looked at Jr and said, "You're in the same place you were, just in a different time."

"Different time?" Jr questioned.

"Yes," Death replied. "You are about four seconds out of sync with the rest of the world."

"How is that possible?"

"Oh, with this," said the robed figure as he held out what looked like a pocket watch.

"And you are?" Jr asked.

"My apologies. My name is Bradford Timely. You can call me Mr. Auspicious."

"Mr. Au...what?"

"Auspicious. It means timely," the man said with a huge grin.

"Maybe you can explain to Jr what is going on, Bradford," Death suggested.

"That's Mr. Auspicious to you, Death," Bradford said. He turned his attention to Jr. "Don't mind ol' Grumpalufagus over there. Like I said, my name is Bradford or Mr. Auspicious. Even Captain Awesome if you feel like it. Most of the world refers to me as Father Time."

"You're Father Time?" Jr asked. "You don't look over fifty years old."

"Precisely," Bradford said. "I'm actually as old as time, but I prefer to appear this age. It makes me look young enough to be able to do the job yet old enough to have the wisdom to do the right thing." Bradford held up the watch and turned the knob on the top. "Look, right now we are four seconds out of sync with the rest of the world. If you look closely, you can see shadows of the people there. If I get us closer than four seconds"—he paused as he turned the knob counterclockwise—"the shadows get a little darker and more solid. If I turn it clockwise, we get farther out of sync, and the shadows start to fade."

"Wait, then why did my dad say he had to go to your reality to talk with you? Why couldn't you come to ours to talk? You obviously can. You came there to get me," Jr said.

"I live in all of time, all the time. I can appear at any moment in time, but only for a moment." Bradford could see the confusion on Jr's face. "It might make more sense if you think of it like this. Think of a drop of oil in a pan. If you spread it out across the pan, the oil is everywhere, but you can't see it. It's too thin, but it's still there. You saw the drop but only for a moment."

"Oh. Or like a puff of smoke? You can only see it for a moment, then you can't, but you know it's still there because you can smell it."

"Precisely," Bradford said.

"Then how do you know what is going on if you can't stay for more than a moment?" Jr asked, perplexed.

"Imagine the smoke again. It's there but not there at the same time. If I get to only a second out of sync, I can see and hear everything that is happening. I just can't interact with it." Bradford could see the question starting to form in Jr's mind.

"How can you go to any moment in time?" Jr's question lingered for a split second.

Bradford held up the watch again. "Like this," he said as he pushed a button next to the knob on the top of the watch.

Jr heard a click and looked around at the shadows. Everything had stopped. Not a sound could be heard except for his own breathing.

Bradford broke the silence. "You want to see a dinosaur?"

"Seriously?" Jr asked, sounding like when he saw the kangaroo. He realized how he sounded again and looked down toward the ground.

Bradford moved the hands on the watch and then clicked the button again. The shadows changed shape and size. They were huge and moved differently. Jr watched as Bradford turned the knob counterclockwise. The shadows took shape and color. The sounds started to resonate through the air. Jr could smell the foliage and smoke in the air. He saw a shadow over his head. He looked up to see a gigantic foot coming down on him. He threw his hands up, closed his eyes, and braced for the impact. He heard the sound of the foot hitting the ground. He opened his eyes to see himself engulfed by the foot before it lifted off him to move to the next spot.

"Like I said. I can see and hear everything, but not interact. Bet you're happy about that right now," Bradford said with a huge grin on his face.

"Yeah," Jr said.

Bradford could see another question forming in Jr's mind. In his best Scottish accent, he said, "Well, spit it out, laddy. We don't have much time."

Jr heard a chuckle behind him. It was his dad; he had almost forgotten that he was there.

Bradford pretended to almost fall over with shock. "Wow, the old curmudgeon laughed!"

"Just remember, we're the same age there…old buddy," Death chided his friend. "Can we get serious for now?"

"Right, serious," Bradford said as he smoothed out his robe and looked at Death with a serious expression. The corner of his mouth started to quiver a little, then he burst out laughing. "I can't do it while you're giving me that goofy face."

"I'm not giving you a goofy face," Death said evenly.

"You mean that's your normal face! I'm so sorry," he said as he burst out laughing again. Bradford was laughing so hard he was doubled over with tears streaming down his face.

Death reached into his cloak and pulled out a long, curved stick. He smacked the butt of it on the ground. The huge arcing blade of his scythe sprang out with a vicious sound. "I think your time is up," he said with a subtle chuckle.

Bradford straightened up and quit laughing. He stared at Death, and Death stared back. The standoff was intense, and Jr was starting to get nervous. Simultaneously they burst out in a hearty laugh. They fell into each other and slapped each other on the back. Jr realized that Bradford and his dad had been friends for a long time.

Bradford hit the button on the watch. Once again, time seemed to freeze.

"Doesn't it get lonely roaming around eternity by yourself, not interacting with what is going on around you?" Jr asked.

"Not at all. I'm more of an introvert anyway," Bradford stated. "Besides, your dad and I email back and forth. Well, we do if he ever turns on his computer."

"That's it?" Jr was shocked.

"No, I interact with the other incarnations all the time. In fact, I had tea with Mother Nature just last week. Now, the reason we needed you to come here"—Bradford looked around—"sorry not here." He turned the knob on the watch clockwise. The scenery changed instantly. "Here."

"Where is here?" Jr asked.

"When is here?" Death interjected.

Jr was trying to keep up with all the time changing. He knew that there was more of it coming. What is it that they could have needed him to come here for? Jr looked around to see where they were.

"This place looks like a dump. Who would want to come here?"

"Precisely," Bradford said. "It's where the person you referred to as the Neanderthal lived."

Jr looked around at the building. They were in an upstairs room with double doors that opened into a hallway. On the back wall of the room was a huge pentagram painted on the wall. Jr's mouth dropped open as he realized that the pentagram was drawn with blood. The air felt cold, the kind that sent a chill to your bones. The smell of rot and decay hung in the air. The wall next to the pentagram was missing some drywall, exposing the electrical wiring and plumbing pipes.

Jr pointed to the wall. "Is that?"

"It's only pigs' blood," Death said in a solemn tone.

"When is this?" Jr asked.

"We don't know for sure," Bradford said with obvious concern in his voice.

"How can you not know?" Jr asked. "Aren't you the incarnation of time?"

Bradford held out his watch so Jr could see the face of it. The hands were spinning back and forth, never stopping at certain time. Jr's eyes went wide. He didn't know what to think about this. As Jr was trying to comprehend the situation, the door to the room swung open. Dan and a few of his cronies walked in. Jr was about to try to hide when he felt his dad grab his shoulder.

"They can't see us, Jr." Death's tone was reassuring.

They watched as Dan and his crew walked into the room.

"I'm gonna kill that little twerp for what he did to Jared," Dan growled.

"Are you sure it was him?" one of the crew asked.

Dan threw a vicious backhand that made a loud crack as it struck the cheek of the man. "Of course it was him, you simpleton. Who else could have done it? Nobody else is stupid enough to mess with us."

The man recoiled from the backhand and grabbed his cheek. The other members of the crew looked on. The simpleton looked at Dan with shock and anger in his eyes. He knew better than to say anything else.

"Tomorrow night," Dan started. "That's when we kill her. She will be the perfect sacrifice for him."

"Are you sure you want to kill Claire?" asked one of the others.

Dan's eyes flared with anger at his crony's question and shouted, "She's a worthless piece of garbage and should feel privileged to die for this cause."

Jr heard these words and instantly flew into a visceral rage. His eyes shot out flames as he let out a primitive guttural shout. Instantly he flew at Dan. His scythe was out in an instant, blade gleaming in the low light of the room. The blade whistled as it sliced through the air. Jr braced for the impact of the swing. His blade passed harmlessly through Dan's midsection. Jr spun around from the force of the swing. His eyes wide with shock that he could have missed. He raised his scythe again, still shaking with rage. He was about to swing it again when he felt a strong hand grab his wrist. It was Death.

"We can't interact, Jr," his voice was stern yet sympathetic.

Jr was still shaking as he looked at his dad. "We have to find out when this is!" Jr shouted. "We can't let them kill Claire!"

"That's what we are trying to do," Bradford said.

Jr's shaking was starting to ease up as he looked back and forth between his dad and Bradford. Dan and his cohorts were leaving the room, still talking about what they were planning.

"How come you aren't able to pinpoint the time?" Jr was looking at Bradford when he asked the question.

"There is only one reason I wouldn't be able to. Another incarnation is blocking my ability to see when it is going to happen."

"Who?" demanded Jr.

"Look at the wall, Jr," Death said. "That's your answer."

"Then let's go confront him about it. We have to stop him!" Jr's tone was high and volatile.

"DJ, I'm afraid that's not possible." Bradford glanced at Death before he continued. "Let me explain. The Devil isn't a normal incarnation like your dad and myself. He's an angelic being, a fallen one but angelic nonetheless. We can't confront him in his own realm. We would be stuck there forever if we tried and finding him while he is out in the world would be problematic at best."

Jr sank to the floor, overcome with the reality that Claire was slated to be sacrificed. He had a thought, and he jumped up. "Dad, if either you or I, if we didn't collect her soul, then she wouldn't die right?"

"Jr, if the wound they would most likely inflict on her would be fatal, if we did not take her soul out of her body, she would suffer. The body would bleed out, but she would still be in pain until her soul was removed." Death could see the anguish in his son's eyes. "I'm sorry, Jr."

"Then we take Claire to Purgatory. She would be safe there." Jr sounded frantic.

"No," Bradford said. "If we did that, they would just use somebody else. It wouldn't stop the outcome."

"Who cares!" Jr exclaimed.

"Jr!" Death's tone made Jr jump a little. "The outcome would be the unleashing of Hell on earth. Literally! The evil that would sweep over the world would be unthinkable. Everyone you care about would suffer, and unimaginably gruesome, painful, slow death that we would be unable to expedite to save them from the pain."

Jr had never heard that tone in his dad's voice before. It made him nervous. "What do we do?" he asked.

Bradford clicked the button on the watch again, and they went back to the place and time they had started from—enough out of sync with time that the people and objects were mere shadows. "We collect information. Your dad and I will be able to get more from here in my reality than in yours. You collect as much info as you can in your reality. We'll come get you if we find out anything."

"How will I let you know if I find out anything?" Jr asked.

"Do you have a centerpiece on your table?" Bradford asked with a grin.

Jr gave Bradford a weird look. "No."

"Get one," Death said. "Get a plastic bowl of fruit. If you need to talk to us, put a pomegranate and a little hourglass on top."

"The fruit of the dead! Dad, nice touch."

"Glad you've been doing your homework," Death said with a grin of his own.

Bradford looked at Jr. "We need to get you back. Yvonne's waiting on those clothes."

"How long have I been here? It must be late."

"You'll be back just a moment after you left," Bradford said. The grin on his face said there was something up that he wasn't saying.

"Jr, you can't say anything to Claire. She can't find out." Death had a serious look on his face.

"I know," Jr said. "Dad, I have a question. The guy in Australia that I just collected, his soul was as dark as Jared's. It went up! How?"

"Fair question," Death responded. "Bradford, if you would."

"Soitenly, whoop, whoop, whoop," Bradford said with a spot-on impersonation of Curly from *The Three Stooges*.

Chapter 11

Bradford clicked the button on his watch. Time froze in place. Then he turned the face of the watch. The world took off in a whirlwind. Jr felt dizzy as the world spun. Everything was blurry and spinning like a carnival ride. As the world continued to spin, Death started to talk.

"I didn't know if you would encounter one of those souls this soon. I knew at some point that would happen." Death paused for a moment. "I probably should have had this conversation with you earlier. I honestly figured that your mom would have talked to you about it. I also wanted you to make your own conclusion and decision."

"Talk to me about what?"

"It will be easier if you see it. Sometimes the soul doesn't reflect the appearance of the person. Generally, it does, but not always."

"Here we are." Bradford turned the face of the watch back in place, and the world slowed to a stop. He clicked the button, and shadows started to move about. As Bradford turned on the knob to get them a second out of sync, Jr saw himself standing in the room with the man sitting in his chair. Jr heard himself talking.

"I know about love," he heard himself saying.

"Not about it. Do you know it? Have you ever loved or been loved? I know of the greatest love ever given. That's why your presence doesn't frighten me," Jr heard the man respond.

This comment still perplexed Jr. He still didn't understand what it meant. Then he watched the man go stiff again. He watched as he walked up to the man to remove his soul. Watching himself do that was a little eerie. The man's soul started to float up. The three of them floated up at the same rate of speed. Jr was amazed as they passed up through the atmosphere and into the open space beyond. As they went higher and higher, Jr noticed something amazing happening. The soul was starting to shed off the charcoal color. It peeled off in clumps that fell away and floated off into space, turning into tiny puffs of charcoal-colored smoke that dissipated as it floated off. With every clump that came off, the soul became whiter and whiter. It got completely white and almost glowed as it got brighter and brighter.

The soul shifted back into the man—a younger and healthier version of him. As Jr saw this, he noticed that they were slowing, and he could see an entrance to a brilliant light. A man stood outside of the entrance.

"Welcome home, Sam," the man said.

The expression on Sam's face turned to pure joy as he approached. He walked up and hugged the man.

"Lord Jesus," Sam said. "Thank you."

Jesus ushered the man to the entrance. "Our Father is waiting inside."

Sam walked inside with a look of sheer joy on his face. Jesus turned and looked at the group and gave a wave. Jr, unsure what to do, gave a wave back. Jesus smiled and walked back inside. The realization hit Jr like a bulldozer. Every soul that floats up comes here. Jr looked over at his dad.

"Do they get a similar welcome when they go the other way?"

Without getting an answer, Bradford clicked the button on the watch again and turned the face. Once again, the world around them went into a whirlwind. Jr got dizzy as the world whizzed by. He wondered if Bradford still felt like this. Bradford turned the face of the watch back into place and clicked the button. The world came into focus. They were standing on a road. On the side was a huge billboard with a charming-looking gentleman with reddish skin, wearing a rather nice suit. He was smiling, and the sign said, "Welcome to Hell."

"Is that an Armani?" Jr asked.

"Nope, it's Prada," Bradford, said trying not to laugh.

"The road to Hell. Never thought it was literal." Jr looked around, dumbfounded.

"This is all we get to see from this side," Death said.

"That's it?" Jr proclaimed.

"That's it," Bradford said. "We don't get to go further than this. Truthfully, I wouldn't want to."

"I don't get it. This is Hell?" Jr was confused.

An eerily loud silence fell over the area for a quick second, then the most awful-sounding snarls started to echo down the road. In the distance, gates appeared; and vile, twisted-looking creatures could be seen coming down the road. The pack of them, six in total, were looking about like rabid dogs on the hunt for blood. Evil shrieks and snarls escaped their mouths as they clamored down the street. Behind them walked the man from the billboard in his suit. His hair was perfect, and he had a small smile on his lips.

"What's going on?" Jr asked, concerned.

"I'm not sure," Death replied.

"Are those what I think they are?" Jr asked.

"Yes," Bradford's response was uttered without hesitation. "They can't see us. I don't know why they are coming out."

The demons and the Devil walked out just in front of the billboard and stopped. The Devil looked at his watch. He looked up and looked in the direction of where Jr, Death, and Bradford were standing. His smile melted off his lips as he squinted his eyes, straining to see something. One of the demonic creatures started to sniff the air wildly as he paced back and forth. They all looked up, and an evil little smile returned to the lips of the Devil. Coming down from above was a charcoal-colored cloud of fluff. As it descended, it coalesced into the form of a man. Jr recognized him immediately. It was Jared, the Neanderthal.

The Devil stepped forward, extending his hand as Jared landed on the ground. "Jared, so glad you're here." His voice was smooth and pleasing to the ears.

Jared smiled and stepped forward, accepting the handshake. "Glad to be here."

The Devil motioned to the demons standing around. "Show Mr. Miginus to his cell."

"Cell? What do you mean cell?" Jared was hollering. "I did your work up there!"

"I know, and it was a pleasure using you for my bidding up there." The Devil's smile turned into a sneer. "Now it will be my pleasure to watch my associates here do what they want to you. I can let you know that they typically don't kill mortals before they start to tear them apart." The devil started to laugh as he turned around.

"You can't do this to me," Jared screamed.

The Devil spun back around with sparks flying out of his eyes and smoke out of his nose. "Wrong," he roared. His voice was no longer pleasurable but bitter to the ears. "You're in my domain. This is my world, and I do as I please. You stupid humans think that if you do work for me up there that I will give you special treatment when you get here." The Devil smiled his evil little smile again and laughed as he spoke. "I do have something special planned for you though, Jared, very special."

The Devil threw his head back and let out the evilest-sounding laugh Jr had ever heard. It sent chills down his spine. The demons attacked Jared, ripping flesh off his body as they dragged him down the road. The gates of Hell opened as they went down the road. Smoke and the smell of brimstone filled the air. Jared screamed as the demons continued to pull him down into the pits of Hell. Screams echoed out from behind the gates. Once Jared was beyond the gates, the scenery returned to the barren road with the billboard.

Jr stood there in a bit of a daze. His brain was spinning, trying to make sense of what he just witnessed.

Death stepped next to Jr. "It will take some time, but in the end, it will make sense."

Jr shook his head in disbelief. With a click of the button on the watch and a turn of the face, Bradford sent the world into a whirlwind again as they slowed down at their original starting point.

Bradford stepped forward to Jr. "DJ, remember that time, for most, can't be manipulated. Make the most of it."

"Jr, find out as much as you can. We'll be in touch."

"I will, Dad."

Bradford grabbed the edge of Jr's cloak. There was a flash that made Jr blink. He found himself standing next to Morty. He looked at Bradford who gave him a sly smile before he puffed away. What did he know that he wasn't letting on about?

Chapter 12

"Welcome back, DJ," Morty said.

"Did you know that they were going to need me?"

"Not at all. After you disappeared, Mortis contacted me and filled me in."

Jr opened up Morty's door and got out Yvonne's bag. He turned and looked at the building. He didn't know what was going to happen the next time that he saw Claire. Was she still going to be mad at him? He knew that he couldn't tell her what he saw and heard Dan and his goons talking about. Whether she was mad at him or not, Jr wasn't going to let Dan do what he said. He had to find a way to stop them. Jr let out a sigh and headed for the door inside.

Jr walked into the building, and he felt every fiber of his being get stiff. A chill slowly went up his spine, causing him to shiver momentarily. He shook it off and cleared his mind. He stopped in the hall and tried as hard as possible to tune in on anything out of place. He strained his ears to hear anything. He couldn't hear anything happening. He started to walk down the hall, feeling odd.

Jr was about to pass by Claire's door, and he felt his heart jump into his throat. He heard a click and felt his body slow down as it passed by her door. When he was directly in front of the door, his entire body froze except for his eyes. He noticed that it wasn't just himself that was frozen in place but everything around him. He stared hard at the door, not sure what to expect. He felt a slow cold chill encompass his entire body. He could physically feel the evil that was in the cold. He tried to reach for his scythe but was unable to move any of his limbs. The chill passed, and Jr felt himself relaxed.

He heard another click, and his body resumed on at its normal pace. He knew that was a little bit of help from Bradford. Now he just had to figure out what he was supposed to have noticed. He continued down the hall to his door. When he reached his door, he turned and looked back down the hall. The hall had waves like you see in a mirage waving back and forth. He knew that there was something evil in that apartment. He knew that they needed to find something quick. He opened the apartment door and walked in.

"Hey, DJ," Yvonne said. She was sitting at the table with a cup of tea. She got up as Jr walked to the table. She gave him a quick hug as she was handed the bag. "Thank you."

"Did you drink all my tea?" Jr asked jokingly.

"Not all," she said, grinning. "I saved you a cup."

Jr walked into the kitchen and grabbed a cup, tea, and an infuser ball. He filled the infuser up with tea leaves and put it in his cup. He tested the side of the kettle with his hand. It was still warm. He poured the water into the cup. That's when he noticed that Yvonne was staring at him with an expression of disbelief.

"What?" he asked.

"I honestly can't believe that you're not using a press for your tea!" The shock was evident in her voice.

"I'm only making a cup," he said. "No need for the French press. The English infuser will be just fine." He couldn't help but try to imitate a sophisticated tone as he spoke.

"You need to get in the twenty-first century, DJ," Yvonne said, picking on him. "They have these new things called tea bags you know?"

Jr let out a laugh. "You know that those things never taste near as good."

"Now that I have some clean clothes to change into, I'm going to take a shower."

She turned and walked to the bathroom. Jr was letting his tea steep when there was a knock at his door. A lump appeared in his throat. *What if it is Claire?* he wondered. He wasn't sure what to say to her. Jr walked over to the door. He noticed the smell of pot roast as he got to the door. That made his mouth water. He opened the door.

"Hey, DJ," his mom said as she stepped into the apartment. She was carrying a roasting pan and a grocery bag.

"Hey, Mom, that smells delicious," Jr said with his mouth watering.

"Where's Yvonne at?" Jr's Mom asked. She set the pot with the roast in it on the stove.

The sound of the shower in the bathroom came on. "In there," Jr said, giving his mom a look of confusion.

"You do remember who I'm married to, right?" she asked sarcastically. "Here," she said as she handed him an envelope.

"What's this?" he asked.

"It's from your dad. He left it with me before he left and said to bring it over tonight." She gave Jr a hug. "Since I was already coming over tonight, I brought dinner. I knew you are busy right now, and Yvonne needs to eat. I hope she heals quickly from losing Fred."

Jr walked into the living room and sat on the couch. His mom was in the kitchen, happily pulling out pots and pans to finish up whatever feast she had brought over. His mother was a vibrant woman still. She hadn't seemed to age at all in the twenty-five years he had been alive. Technically she only aged when she wasn't in Purgatory without his dad. So she really hadn't aged that much. Jr opened the envelope and found a letter from his dad in it.

He began to read it.

> Jr, your mom should have dropped this off to you not long after we got done talking. There are some nuances about the job that I haven't let you know yet. When you are in the position of this job, you and your cloak have some extra abilities that you normally wouldn't have.
>
> The first is that your cloak can be a shroud of invisibility. This will allow you to be able to go places without being noticed. This will come in extremely useful as we try to find out the information we need to stop this evil. You can also use this when traveling for the job. It will even

have an effect on Morty. It's like an extension of your ability of people not seeing your true self. It doesn't take a lot of actual concentration on your part, but a sudden rush of emotions can cause your concentration to slip enough to render this ability momentarily void. The invisibility will remain with Morty as long as it is in effect for you, whether you are in contact with him or not. You will still be able to see yourself and Morty. You probably have already noticed that this ability is automatic when you are on the job so to speak. That's why people around others who are dying typically can't see you. This ability can be invoked when not collecting souls but need to go somewhere discretely.

The second is your cloak will allow you the ability to phase out of a solid state, much like when you travel to Purgatory, at will. This will allow you to pass through solid objects without resistance. Trust me, when you must go into a tunnel or collapsed mine while in the job, this will be extremely helpful. Unlike the invisibility, this one does require a little bit more concentration than the first. You need to be aware of where you are at when doing this. You don't want to resolidify while underground or inside of a wall or similar object. It is extremely uncomfortable, and you being half mortal, I am not sure what this would do to you.

The third one is an important one. While you have the hood of your cloak drawn about your head, you will not be able to be harmed by mortal weapons. This is only effective against mortal weapons and objects. You will still be able to be injured by incarnations and supernatural means. This prevents you from getting shot or getting stabbed when you go to collect their souls. Remember to not rely on this as protection. Don't let it become a liability for you.

Lastly, your scythe. It will respond to you however you want it to. It will remain the compact version, which is its neutral state until you grab ahold of it. Once it is in your hand, it will respond to your thoughts, both conscious and subconscious. It will expand and collapse, open and close, however and whenever you choose. We will be in touch soon.

PS, enjoy the roast.

How did his dad know that his mom would have brought roast over? It was one of his mom's best things she made. It was always so juicy and tasty. It was never dry like you always hear about when people cook a roast. "Lower heat, longer cook time," his mom would always stress about making a good roast. Jr could smell that she was also making gravy, most likely from the drippings. The smell of the potatoes, carrots, and onions mixed with the roast made Jr extremely hungry.

The sound of the shower shut off. Jr looked at the note from his dad again before he put it back in the envelope. Yvonne stepped out of the bathroom drying her hair and wearing fresh clothes. She stopped dead in her tracks and gave Jr a look.

"Do I smell your mom's pot roast?" Her eyes were wide with hope.

He just gave her a grin and nodded.

"Oh Yvonne," Jr's Mom said as she walked over to Yvonne and gave her a hug of consolation. "If there is anything I can do, dear, just let me know."

"Thanks, Mrs. Deadwood," Yvonne said, hugging her back. "That roast smells wonderful!"

Mrs. Deadwood looked at her son. "DJ, help me set the table while Yvonne finishes drying her hair."

"Yes, Mom." Jr chuckled as he got up to grab the plates.

Jr walked into the kitchen, opened the cabinet, and grabbed some plates. He turned to go to the table and almost ran into his mom. She had walked up behind him without making the slightest sound. His dad must have been giving her pointers on how to do that. He jumped back, almost dropping the plates in his hand.

"Whoa, Mom, what are you doing?"

His mom was giving him a look that he had never seen her give before. "So your dad tells me you asked him about a girl."

"Mom, really? You're going to ask me about that…now?"

"Yes, DJ, I am. As your mother, I have certain privileges. One of those is being able to ask you questions that you would rather not answer at any time I please." Her tone implied he better not deny her the answer.

"I did ask him about it," Jr started to trail off his sentence. "It doesn't matter anymore, though."

"What do you mean by that?" She wasn't going to let this issue go.

"When I came home earlier this morning after going to the store, she came over and saw Yvonne at the table." Jr paused, not wanting to relive the events from earlier. "When she saw Yvonne, she got really mad and yelled something about me being like…never mind. Anyway, when I tried to go talk to her, she just slammed the door in my face. I didn't even have a chance to explain what was going on."

His mom gave him a thoughtful look. "Does this girl know how you feel?"

"I don't know, Mom. I thought so, but then that happened, so I don't know." Jr's voice was low. "It got really complicated."

"Complicated, how?"

"Um, I can't say." Jr knew his mom wasn't going to accept that answer.

"And why not?" She was a mother scorned, and her tonality let everybody in earshot know it.

"Mom, I can't."

"Jr!" she snapped. She was really ticked. She never called him *Jr* unless he was in trouble.

"It has to do with why Dad is gone right now." Jr gave his mom a look that let her know he would take it to the grave before he would say.

His mom's expression changed from scorned to fraught with concern and understanding. She quickly changed the subject. "Let's finish setting the table."

Jr continued to the table with the plates. As he was placing them, Yvonne walked in, putting her hair up in a ponytail. Jr noticed with her hair like that, she looked like she was twelve again. He chuckled.

"What?" she asked, confused.

"You look like Pippy Longstockings," he said, laughing.

She shot him a look, then doing her best snotty valley-girl impersonation, she put a hand on her hip and her other hand in the air. "Look, okay. Pippy Longstockings had pigtails, okay? Not a ponytail." She crossed her eyes at him and made an *L* on her forehead with her hand.

"Not only looks twelve but acts like it too," he said with a grin.

"Ugh," she gasped with mock disgust.

His mom walked in carrying the roasting pan to the table. "Let's eat," she said with a smile.

"Oh my! Mrs. Deadwood, that looks and smells delicious." Yvonne looked like she hadn't eaten in years.

"Oh, thank you, Yvonne. And please, dear, I've been telling you for years, call me Susan."

"Yes, ma'am," Yvonne said, sounding a little sheepish.

Susan walked into the kitchen and grabbed a big pitcher of iced tea and three tall glasses. They sat down and poured iced tea into all the glasses as they dished up the roast with all the vegetables onto the plates. Susan looked at the table and realized the mistake that had been made.

"DJ, would you go and grab the gravy boat. I'm afraid that I forgot it by the stove."

"Sure, Mom."

"Is that gravy from scratch?" Yvonne asked.

"What do you think?" Jr asked as he went to the kitchen.

Jr returned to the table, and they enjoyed pleasant conversation as they ate. The meal was delicious and starting to wind down. As Susan and Yvonne sat, sipping on their teas, Jr got up and started to clear the table. He was putting the leftovers into plastic containers, intending to take them to lunch tomorrow. Josh was going to have a fit when he sees the roast and know that Yvonne got some and he didn't. Jr started to do the dishes. When Yvonne heard the water come on, she leaned toward Susan.

"Susan, can I get your advice on something?"

"Sure, dear. What is it?" Susan replied.

"DJ had picked up some flowers for Claire earlier today," Yvonne started.

"Is that the girl DJ was talking about?" Susan interjected.

"Yes, that's her. So he bought her some flowers today, but before he had a chance to give them to her, she saw me over here and got super ticked off. I felt so bad. It felt like my fault. When DJ and Josh went to pick up some clothes for me, she came by, and I gave them to her." Yvonne looked like she was going to explode. "She took them but didn't look like she really believed me about Fred." His name made Yvonne tear up a little.

"Calm down, dear, take your time," Susan said to comfort Yvonne.

Yvonne dried her eyes. "Should I let DJ know that I gave them to her?" she asked.

"I would say that if you feel like it would be helpful to tell him, then yes."

"That really doesn't answer my question, Mrs. Deadwood."

Susan just gave her a smile that looked exactly like Jr's. Must run in the family. "I know, dear. This is one you need to figure out for yourself."

Jr finished the dishes and walked in. He saw that Yvonne had been crying. "Is everything okay?" he asked, concerned.

"Of course, DJ," Susan said before Yvonne could respond. "Yvonne was just telling me some of the sweet things Fred used to do for her."

Yvonne gave her a nod of appreciation. Jr noticed that they had both finished their tea, so he cleared the glasses from the table and took them to the sink. Jr dried off the freshly washed roasting pan and put it in the bag that his mom had brought with her. He walked back into the dining room with his mom and Yvonne.

Mrs. Deadwood grabbed the bag from Jr and looked at Yvonne. "Now, Yvonne, if DJ forgets his manners, you call me," she said with a smile. She leaned over and gave her a hug. "Hang in there, dear."

"Thanks, Mrs. Deadwood. I mean Susan," Yvonne said, hugging her back.

Susan gave Jr a hug. "We will talk, in depth, when your dad gets back." She walked to the front door. "Good night, you two," she said as she walked out.

Jr looked at Yvonne. "I'll take care of the office stuff tomorrow. Get some sleep."

Yvonne stepped up and gave Jr a huge hug. "Thanks, DJ. I appreciate everything you are doing for me right now." She gave him a big squeeze before she let go and walked over to the couch and spread out the blanket from earlier. Jr went back to his room.

Chapter 13

Jr didn't go to sleep. The note from his dad had him thinking about the abilities he had. He had to test them out to see how well he could use them. He didn't want to be in the middle of needing those abilities and not being able to use them effectively. He tried out the invisibility first. He looked at his hand and could still see them.

"That's not good," Jr said.

He tried again, concentrating as hard as he could. He looked at his hands again—still visible.

"What is going on?" Jr asked himself aloud. "Why can't I do this?"

Jr sat on his bed, racking his brain about this dilemma. He was getting ready to try it again when he suddenly realized something he had read in his dad's note. He remembered that he would still be able to see himself to avoid bumping into things and making a bunch of noise. Invisibility doesn't work well if you are making a huge racket.

He decided to try the phasing-out ability since he would have to find a safe way to test the invisibility. He stood up and prepared himself.

"This one should be easy," he told himself. "I do this all the time when I go to my parents."

He took a breath and then walked toward his door.

THUMP!

"Ow!" Jr said with his face squished against the door.

"DJ, are you okay?" He heard Yvonne call from the living room.

"Fine," he replied, feeling slightly embarrassed.

He sat down on his bed, trying to think about what he might be doing wrong. Why wasn't he able to do this? Jr got up and walked into his bathroom to get some water. He turned on the faucet and filled a cup with water. He tipped his head back as he felt the coolness of the water trickle down his throat. He closed his eyes as he swallowed the last of the water.

"Why can't I get this?" Jr questioned. *Invisible*, he thought.

He opened his eyes as he set the cup down on the counter. He glanced up and jumped back in shock. He couldn't see himself in the mirror! What was happening? He could still see his arms, feet, legs well—everything. He looked up at the mirror. There was nothing in the reflection other than the backside of the door. He stared in amazement. He waved his hand back and forth, still nothing.

"This is amazing." His mind was racing.

He steeled his nerve and decided to try again with the phasing out. He stepped back up to the counter. He reached out toward the mirror slowly, concentrating on his hand phasing out as he reached. His hand made contact with the mirror. He could feel his hand pass through the mirror with minimal resistance. It felt like his hand was passing through a wall of water. He turned his hand over in the mirror and wiggled his fingers. He felt the mirror getting tight around his arm where it was passing through the mirror. He quickly returned to concentrating on his hand and arm being able to phase out.

He pulled his hand back out of the mirror. Jr thought to himself about being solid again. Jr reached out and touched the mirror. His hand tapped the mirror, and his fingers bent under the pressure. He realized that he could see himself again. He must have stopped concentrating on being invisible when he tried to phase out.

"That's not good." He looked at his solid hand. "This is going to take some practice."

He turned and faced the door and took a deep breath. He stepped forward as he concentrated on being able to phase out. His body made contact with the door and began to pass through it. The sensation over his body felt like breaking the surface of the water in a still pool. It felt like the door was washing over his body. He emerged on the other side of his bedroom. He turned and reached out for the door, stopping his concentration. His hand smacked into the door. Jr flinched his hand back from the door, looking at his hand in wonder. He stepped toward the door again, this time concentrating on being invisible and being able to phase out again. His body passed through the door again. He felt the door wash over his body again. He kept his head up and his eyes open as he passed through. He felt his body leaving the resistance of the door, but his reflection did not appear in the mirror.

He phased back in and made himself visible again. Instantly his reflection appeared, smiling back at him with a huge grin on his face. He felt himself begin to get excited. He had one more ability to test. How, was the question?

"DJ, we need to go." It was Morty.

Jr smiled as he turned toward the wall. He walked to the wall and simultaneously thought about the invisibility and phasing out. He walked right through the wall outside into the parking lot. He looked around to see if anybody was around as he phased back solid. He didn't see anyone so he dropped the invisibility.

"Whoa," Morty said, surprised. "When did you learn that trick?"

"Tonight," Jr said as he opened the door and got in. "Where are we headed?"

"Liquor store robbery down the road. The robber is going to be shot by the store owner."

Jr and Morty took off down the road. They turned the corner a couple of blocks away and headed for the liquor store. The store was only a few blocks away. Jr knew this store. It was a dingy, dirty little store in a poorly lit area. They heard the gunshots as they pulled into the parking lot. The robber came staggering out of the store, gun in his hand, clutching his chest. Jr could see the owner of the store ducking behind the counter on the phone, most likely with the police. The robber staggered over to the far side of the parking lot and collapsed. Jr got out of the car and started walking over to the robber. As Jr approached, he pulled out his scythe. The handle expanded in his hand. He smacked the end of the handle on the ground like he had seen Death do with his scythe. The blade sprang out with the same eerie sound as a blade scraping a scabbard as it's drawn. The sound made the robber snap his eyes open. He saw Jr and fired his gun before Jr could stop him. Jr closed his eyes and waited for the pain. He felt the impact of the bullet in his chest. It felt more like a punch from a butterfly. His mouth dropped open in shock, so did the robbers.

"I shot you. How are you still standing?" The robber gasped.

Jr remained silent as he walked up to the man. "Death can't die," he said in a voice that surprised him. It sounded exactly like his dad.

The robber's eyes went wide. He looked down at his chest as sirens could be heard in the distance coming toward them. He looked at Jr again and closed his eyes. Jr could see his chest compress as he let out his last breath. Jr reached out with the tip of his scythe and removed the soul. He smoothed it out and gave it a little toss. It sank slowly to the ground and disappeared. Jr knew where it was going and felt sorry for the man. He knew what was going to happen to him. Jr walked back over to Morty as the police cars were pulling in, screeching to a halt. The sirens shut off as the officers got out of their vehicles. The lights bounced off everything around. One officer ran into the store as the other officer ran over to the robber.

Jr got in, and they drove back to the apartment. Jr was replaying the events in his head. He hadn't even seen the robber raise his gun before he shot. That wasn't the way he had planned on testing that ability. He was glad that one didn't require practice like the other ones. It was late when they got back to the apartment, and Jr was ready for bed. He knew the morning was going to come quickly, and he had to open the shop tomorrow.

He got out and walked toward the door when he felt the same chill that he had before. He stopped and looked around. He didn't see anything, but he heard a sound that he had heard before. It was an evil sound. His eyes went wide.

"Demons," he said.

In an instant, he had his scythe drawn and was ready for a fight. He scanned the area, trying to see past the blackness of the night. He could see the monster coming toward the parking lot. It skidded to a stop as it spied Jr standing with his scythe at the ready. The twisted face of the demon tried to form a smile. Its eyes began to glisten as it slowly advanced toward Jr. When it was a few feet away, Jr swung at it with his scythe. The demon dodged and lunged at Jr. The demon grabbed Jr around the chest and slammed him to the ground. The wind was knocked out of him, and his scythe went skipping across the parking lot. The demon spun and threw Jr as hard as he could. Jr flew across the parking and slammed into a parked car. The door of the car caved in, and the windows on that side of the car shattered. Jr rolled onto his hands and knees as he tried to focus his eyes. He saw the demon limping over to him. A red flash appeared across the parking lot, and a large man carrying a broadsword lunged across the parking lot. With a huge swing, he sliced the demon in half. The demon dissipated in a poof of sulfur-smelling smoke.

"DJ, you need to learn how to not lose your weapon." He reached out his hand and helped Jr to his feet.

Jr looked at the man. He was a large man, tall and fit. His skin was an off-orange color with little speckles of brown and auburn all over. On his shoulder was a large red spot. His appearance was formidable and intimidating. He carried a broad sword in his hands and had a large battle-axe across his back. The belt around his waist had a scabbard for his sword and a couple of daggers attached to the back of the belt. He had scars on his body from many battles.

"Who are you?" asked Jr with some hesitation.

The man walked over and picked up Jr's scythe as he sheathed his sword. He answered. "Some people call me Mars. Others call me Ares. My friends call me Max."

"Isn't Ares a god?" Jr asked.

"Yes and no. In some mythologies, Ares is a god. I am not. Let's get in Morty and head to your parents' place."

Jr was floored by that statement. "You know my parents?"

"Who do you think called me?"

Max handed Jr his scythe and walked over to Morty. He turned and looked at Jr. "You coming?"

Jr walked over to Morty and got in. Max got in, and they started to drive down the road. When they got on a side street, Morty phased out and lifted off. A few minutes later, they were pulling up at his parents' place. They got out and walked up to the door. Susan met them at the front door.

"Max, thank you for helping us out," she said as she invited them in.

"Sure thing, Susan. I was a little surprised that you called instead of Torva."

"He's unavailable at the moment."

"Torva?" Jr asked.

Max chuckled. "Your dad's name. Torva Messor. You really need to brush up on your Latin."

"Latin?" Jr was confused.

"Susan, you didn't tell me it was an emergency getting to DJ."

"I didn't think it was," Susan said with concern in her voice. "What is going on?"

"DJ was in a bit of a pickle when I arrived." Max could tell Susan needed more of an explanation. "He was in a fight with one of Lucifer's creatures."

Her eyes went wide as her mouth fell open. "Torva just sent a message that he thought DJ needed some more training and that you would be able to help."

There was a three-way glance that bounced around for a few seconds before it landed on Max. "I'll go set up the training room," Max said. "Come with me, DJ."

"Thank you, Max," Susan said as they walked toward the training room.

Chapter 14

Max led the way back to Death's office and into the training room behind the bookcase. Jr looked at him in shock.

"How do you know how to get in here?" Jr asked.

Max let out a hearty chuckle. "Who do you think helped your dad build this room?"

Jr was looking at Max with confusion and curiosity. Max could see the expression on his face.

"Do you know who I am?" Max asked Jr.

"Not really," Jr answered with hesitation.

"I am known by many names from just as many cultures and societies. Like your dad and Bradford, I am an incarnation. The Incarnation of War to be specific."

"Isn't war bad?" Jr asked.

"It is unfortunate, and there is a lot of deaths because of it. Because of this, your dad and I have had to work together a lot." Max's tone was serious as he spoke. "Now, are you ready to begin?"

"Uh, begin?"

Before Jr could finish the sentence, Max swung a fast punch. The punch hit Jr square in the chest. He flew backward as he fell on his back. The punch was powerful, but somehow it didn't hurt.

"Again, are you ready?" Max asked. He sounded angry as he spoke.

Jr was still on the ground. He was confused about what had just happened. "I felt the power in that punch, why didn't I get hurt?"

"Your dad and I designed this room so that we could go full force during training and not get hurt. If you train at less than full strength, then that's how you will fight." Max looked at Jr as he extended a hand to help him up. "Listen, DJ, as we progress, you will start to feel pain from the contact so that you can also learn to not let the pain distract you during combat. Now prepare again."

"Oka—"

As Jr responded, Max threw another huge blow. Jr quickly dodged to the side. He was so happy that he had dodged that punch he didn't see the other one coming. This one made contact on his temple. His head snapped to the side from the blow, again with no pain. He was still reeling from the blow when he felt the mammoth hands of Max grab him and throw him into the air. Jr flew halfway across the training room and landed with a huge thud.

"Don't let yourself get distracted," Max said. "Now get up."

Jr started to get back on his feet. Before he knew it, Max was already at full speed, charging at him. The impact felt like it had been a grizzly bear running him down. The wind was knocked out of him as he once again hit the ground. He rolled onto his back, gasping for air.

"Hey, Max," Jr gasped. "Take it easy."

Max stood over him, towering like a giant ready to dismember him. "Do you think that those demons are going to take it easy on you? If you go easy while training, you will die!" Max reached down and helped Jr to his feet. "This is for your benefit. That creature that you were fighting when I showed up was a low-level demon. Slow and weak compared to some of the others."

"Slow? That thing was fast!" Jr exclaimed.

"No, it wasn't, and now it's obvious that they see you as a threat for some reason. Don't rely on just speed or strength. Those are both important skills but not as important as your mind. Use your senses to feel your surroundings." Max paused for a moment. "Are you beginning to understand?"

"I think so," Jr said, not sounding very sure about his answer.

"Good," Max said. "Now, again."

Max threw a straight punch. Jr ducked under it and stepped off to the side. He felt a change in the air behind his head. He ducked again as a huge fist flew over his head. If he hadn't ducked, it would have made contact with the back of his head. He was about to stop, figuring that Max was going to give him some more advice. He turned just in time to see yet another punch coming straight for his face. He threw his hands up instinctively. He felt the blow hit his hands. He looked past his hands, seeing another shot coming for his gut. He took a quick step back and threw his hands down in a sweeping motion. It was effective in stopping it from hitting his gut, but the shot made his hands smack him in the legs. As he tried to recover, he saw a flash in his peripheral vision as Max did a leg sweep, knocking Jr to the ground. Jr quickly rolled to get up knowing that it wasn't the end of the barrage of blows. A huge foot stomped on the ground a split second after Jr's head had moved from that spot. Jr sprung to his feet, ready for the next shot.

"Excellent," Max said with a grin on his face. "This time, don't just dodge the attack. Counterattack."

Jr was breathing heavily from all of this. He was tired and needed a break. A fist came out of nowhere. Jr barely had time to sidestep. He saw Max's side exposed as his arm was still extended from his punch. Jr stepped in and threw a jab as hard as he could. He felt it smack into Max's ribs. He heard a grunt from Max. Max snapped his arm down, pinning Jr's arm under it. Max spun backward, away from the pinned arm and caught Jr in the back of the head with an elbow. The force of the shot should have knocked Jr down, but his arm was still pinned under Max's massive arm. Jr struggled to get free. He felt like a wild cat in a trap, with nowhere to go. He suddenly had an idea. He stepped forward and dropped straight down as he did. He slid in between Max's legs as his arm came free. He freed his hand as he slid, grabbing Max's ankles. He grabbed ahold and gave a heave with all his strength. The outcome was not what he was hoping for. He felt Max grab him around the waist and heaved him into the air, slamming him down on his back. All the air burst out of his lungs as he hit the ground.

"Never underestimate your opponent, DJ." Max's tone was like that of a caring uncle. "It was a good plan, but you underestimated how much force it would take to get me off my feet."

Jr was still on his back, gasping for air. "I tried as hard as I could."

"Again," Max said.

Once again, Jr was up on his feet, and the fighting ensued. This time it went longer with more attacks, dodges, and counterattacks. Jr was getting faster and more adept at adapting to changing attacks. It was evident that this time the battle would end in a draw.

"Good," Max said, his breathing slightly heavy. "Your speed and strength are improving. So is your technique. Now on to the next phase." Max gave Jr a serious look. "Draw your weapon."

Jr protested, "My weapon? No way."

"Remember, DJ, this room was made to stop the weapons from inflicting harm on us." Max's voice lowered as his eyes narrowed. "Draw your weapon!"

Max flew at Jr, his sword drawn and poised for attack. He swung at Jr's head with his sword. Jr did a tuck-and-roll maneuver, dodging the attack. He drew his scythe as he rolled to his feet. The blade was out instantly. Max swung again; Jr countered with his scythe. Max swiveled his sword and used it to pull the scythe from Jr's hand. The scythe clanged as it skipped across the floor. Max spun as he swung his sword. He stopped his swing right before it would have made contact.

"You cannot lose your weapon!" Max was sharp with his words. "If you lose your weapon, you die. You have to be able to use your mind." Max's stare bore into Jr's eyes, making him look away. "Again."

Jr retrieved his weapon and prepared for the attack. It didn't come. He lowered his scythe to ask what was going on. As soon as it dropped down, Max attacked with lightning speed. His sword whistled as it sailed through the air. Jr jumped back, arching his back as far as he could. He swung his scythe to block the attack. It was barely effective. The sword glanced to the side, but the flat of the blade struck Jr in the shoulder, knocking him down. He bounced when he landed. His scythe slipped in his hand. As he scrambled to regain control of his weapon, Max attacked again. Jr tried the tuck-and-roll maneuver again. This time Max was ready for it. Max thrust his foot out, causing Jr to get knocked over. As he was going down,

Max came down with him, pinning him to the ground. The blade of Max's sword pressed into Jr's neck.

Max released Jr and got up. "You have other abilities at your disposal. Stop fighting like a human, and fight like an incarnation."

Jr gave Max a look of confusion. "What do you mean?"

"If I tell you that, you won't ever learn to think for yourself." Max was almost yelling at this point. Jr was afraid fire and smoke were going to shoot out of his eyes and nose. "Use your mind. Again!"

Jr got up as Max was sheathing his sword. He pulled the battle-axe off his back swinging it around, spinning it in circles. Jr was getting nervous. He hadn't even been able to block the sword yet. Max swung the axe at Jr's torso. Jr jumped back, dodging the swing. He counterattacked and swung at Max. Max was faster with the axe than Jr thought he would be. He blocked Jr's scythe with ease. Max knocked the scythe sideways and smacked Jr in the face with the handle of his axe.

"You're still not using your mind. Fight like an incarnation," he yelled.

Max stepped forward as Jr was stumbling backward and gave Jr a huge boot to the midsection. Jr doubled over as he was pushed backward. Max raised his axe over his head and, with a loud war cry, brought the axe straight down with a powerful swing. Jr raised his scythe over his head as he heard the war cry. A loud chink sound resonated through the room as the battle-axe sank into the floor at Jr's feet. They both stared in shock. The blade had passed through Jr before it struck the floor. Jr had phased out like he was going through a wall. He didn't think it was going to work. He swung with all his might at Max. The blade of his scythe passed harmlessly through Max.

"What? Why didn't my attack work?" Jr was shocked at its failure.

Max let out a belly-powered laugh. "Now that's using your mind. Well done, DJ."

"I don't get it," Jr uttered. "Why couldn't I hit you?"

"When you go through a wall, does your scythe pass through as well?"

"Well, yes," Jr responded.

"You will need to figure out how to phase out but have your weapon remain in its solid state." Max had a huge smile on his face.

"How do I do that?" Jr asked.

Max dislodged his axe from the floor and walked over to a closet. He opened the closet and pulled out some little triangular-shaped objects. "Practice," he said as he set the targets up on a little stand that was also in the closet. "Try to hit the targets with your scythe while you are phased out."

Jr looked at the targets, concentrating on being phased out but keeping his scythe solid. He swung at the target; his blade passed through without effect.

"Try it again," Max instructed.

Jr repositioned himself, adjusted his stance, and swung with precision. The target went sailing across the room. He turned to Max with a big grin on his face. Max was just shaking his head as he poked Jr in the chest with the handle of his axe.

"Hey," Jr exclaimed, rubbing his chest where he got poked, more out of habit than anything.

"You phased in as you swung. Concentrate," Max encouraged.

Jr turned back to the targets and started to phase out. He aimed at the target and swung again. The blade passed through without effect again. He glanced back at Max. Max just smiled and nodded toward the targets.

"I'll put the tip of my handle in your shoulder this time. Concentrate on making your scythe solid. If you feel the handle in your shoulder, you're beginning to solidify."

Jr nodded and turned his attention to the targets. He raised his scythe and concentrated on it becoming solid. He felt pain and discomfort in his shoulder. He turned his thoughts to remaining phased out. He adjusted his stance and focused his thoughts on his scythe becoming solid. He swung at the target with determination to get this right. Claire's life depended on it. The blade hit the target and sliced through it. The wind from the blade made the top part of the target to fall off the side.

"Well done, DJ, well done," Max exclaimed as he slapped Jr on the shoulder.

Jr turned to Max with a smile on his face. "I did it. What now?"

"Now, my young friend, you go home and get some sleep. You have work to do." Max didn't stop smiling.

They walked out of the training room and headed for the front of the house. Susan met them in the living area of the house.

"How did it go?" she asked Max.

"You have a fine student here, Susan. You and Torva should be proud." Max added, "He's a quick learner as well."

Susan smiled and gave her son a hug. "Before I forget, since Yvonne's staying at your place for a bit, you need to make it feel more welcoming, not so dark and gloomy." She turned to a closet and opened the door. She pulled out a colorful plastic bowl with plastic fruit in it. Susan handed it to Jr. "Here."

"How did you know?" Jr asked his mom.

"Know what?"

"Nothing, I guess. When did you get this?"

"That thing. It's been in that closet for years."

"Thanks, Mom," Jr said as he gave her a hug.

"Now go home," she said. "You have work in the morning, and it's getting late."

Jr and Max walked out to Morty. Before Jr got in, he turned to Max.

"Thanks, Max."

"Be safe, DJ, and remember to use your mind." Max gave a wink and then, with a red flash, disappeared.

Jr got in and headed for his apartment. Minutes later, they pulled into the parking lot. Jr walked into his apartment and set the plastic fruit on the table. He noticed that there was a little hourglass and a pomegranate in the bowl. He gave a little smile at that and headed to bed. He was exhausted. He walked to his room and went to bed. He was asleep within minutes.

Chapter 15

Jr heard his alarm going off. Even though he was exhausted and didn't want to get up yet, he didn't want his alarm to wake Yvonne. He shut off his alarm and walked to the bathroom. He splashed his face with water to help with the grogginess; it didn't help. He got ready for work and walked silently out of his room toward the front door. Even though he could move silently, he found himself tiptoeing through the house. As he went past the living room, he glanced at the couch. Yvonne was breathing lightly as she slept. Jr was happy that she was getting some rest. After everything that she has been through, she needed it. Jr decided to forgo his normal coffee so that he didn't make any excess noise. He quietly slipped out the front door and locked it behind him.

He started down the hall and stopped dead in his tracks. He saw Claire sitting outside her door, reading. She hadn't noticed him yet. He quickly turned invisible and started to walk down the hall. He didn't want to try to talk with her if she was still mad at him. It was killing him that he couldn't let her know what Dan was planning. He would find a way to save her! He slowly walked down the hall. He could hear her talking in a whisper as he passed by. He stopped as he passed by her and looked at her. Claire stopped talking and looked directly at where he was standing. Jr froze, breathing and all. Jr noticed that she was starting to cry.

"Cl...," he started to say, forgetting that he was invisible. He quickly stopped and stood there motionless.

Claire was startled by the sound he had made. She quickly closed the book she was reading and hid it in the fake plant outside her door. She was looking around to see if anybody was watching her. Jr realized the book that she had just hidden was a Bible. She stood up and dried her eyes, looking around once more. She reached out and grabbed her doorknob. She closed her eyes and let out a sigh.

"God, give me the strength to make it through this day."

She opened the door and went inside. Jr walked to the planter and stared at it for a second. He looked to see if anybody else was around. He reached in and pulled out the Bible. Jr never knew that she read the Bible. He flipped it over in his hands, looking it over. He opened up the front cover, and his heart leapt into his throat. Inside the front cover was the card he had put with the roses.

"How did she get this?"

Jr realized that he had spoken aloud. He put the card back in the cover of the Bible and put it back in the planter. He walked to the door of the building and turned visible again before he exited the door. He looked over at Josh's bike to make sure it was still there before he went over to Morty. He opened the door and got inside. He sat there for a second, pondering how she could have ended up with the card. He knew that he hadn't given it to her.

"DJ, you seem out of sorts."

"Yeah, Morty. I'm a bit stressed out right now."

"Do you want me to drive?"

"That would be awesome. Thanks, Morty."

"That's what friends are for."

Morty started off down the road. Jr needed to be at work early to open the shop since Yvonne was on bereavement leave for a few days. Jr was having trouble waking up this morning. He hadn't gotten much sleep last night and was in desperate need of some coffee. He saw one of those coffee huts up ahead.

"Hey Morty, pull through that coffee hut. I need some coffee."

Jr hoped that it wasn't one of those uppity places like that one coffee chain. What was its name? Jr couldn't remember; he just remembered that it had started in Seattle. They pulled into the drive-through. Jr didn't see any indication that this was that one chain. He pulled up to the window, and a very peppy girl took his order. He heard another voice in the hut sounding incredibly angry. Jr looked and saw a girl who was wearing all black—T-shirt with a bright red pentagram emblazoned on the front. She wore two exceptionally large pentagram earrings.

"I don't care what he said. You tell Dan to go to—"

Jr's ears snapped to attention as he heard Dan's name. It had to be Dan from his apartment building. Jr watched as the girl almost punched her phone to hit the off button. She tossed her phone in a black bag and then walked over to the other girl.

"Do you know what that jerk wants me to do? He told me to go to Jared's tonight and grab the planner out of his dresser."

That was the confirmation Jr needed. It was the right Dan. The other girl seemed to ignore her as she finished making Jr's coffee. She walked back to the window and handed Jr his coffee.

"She doesn't seem too happy," Jr mentioned to the girl handing him his coffee.

"Yeah, she always has something going wrong. According to her anyway."

That made Jr smile. "Do you know what's going on?"

"Not specifically, but she was on the phone with that Dan guy. Claims to be the Devil's right hand or something like that. One of their buddies just died, and he wants her to keep going to his place and keep it in order for some séance or something." The girl kind of giggled. "Seems kind of silly to me. That'll be 4.50 dollars."

Jr's curiosity was piqued. "You wouldn't happen to know when or where that is, do you?"

The girl gave Jr a weird look. "No, I know the guy who died lived down on the south end of town. In the old decrepit building next to the empty burned-out lot."

This lot wasn't too far from where Jr's apartment was. "Thanks," Jr said as he paid for his coffee and drove off.

His mind was spinning at a thousand miles an hour. This was definitely something that he needed to check into. He would head there after work. Jr continued toward the shop, sipping on his coffee. It wasn't his normal coffee, but it tasted okay. He wondered how people could drink this kind of coffee every day and pay as much as they do? Jr pulled into the parking lot of the shop and got out. He fished around in his pocket for the keys to the door. He opened the door, and his nostrils were filled with the faint smells of grease, gas, and tires. He reached out and turned on the lights. They flickered as they started up.

"We need to upgrade to LEDs or something," Jr mumbled.

He walked over to Yvonne's desk and found a piece of paper and a pen to write a note on the counter.

Please ring the bell for service.

Jr placed the note on the counter and set a bell on the counter right next to it. He didn't know if he would be able to hear the bell in the back, but it was the best that he could come up with. He walked to the back thinking about what he had seen with his dad and Bradford. He would recognize the building when he saw it now that he knew where to start. He finished drinking his coffee as he got to his locker and pulled out his coveralls. He went back to Yvonne's desk and started looking through the work orders they had for the day. Jr's jaw dropped open.

"Somebody brought in a Ducati for a race package upgrade. Definitely going to have to take that one for a test ride when it gets finished." Jr could already feel his heart starting to quicken thinking about riding that bike.

He finished looking through the work orders and split them up into different piles for Josh and himself. He walked back to the shop and looked around at the bikes. That noisy Harley that Josh had worked on was still sitting there. He got his tools ready for the day and made sure that they were all in their proper place. He grabbed a wrench and went to work.

An hour later, Josh walked in. "Hey, dork."

"Hey, dufas," Jr responded without looking up from his work.

Josh went in the back and got ready for work. When he came back out, Jr was finishing up with the oil change he had been working on.

"What's the deal with that Harley over there?"

"What isn't wrong with it? It burns and leaks oil, the cam is out of whack, and it's got three broken welds on the exhaust pipe." You could see the aggravation on Josh's face.

"Let me guess," Jr said. He looked at the Harley and surveyed the age and style of it. It was an older one with faded-out paint and ape hangers. "Older guy, can't seem to or want to get rid of the long-hair hippy days and still wants to be a three-patch outlaw?"

Josh just shook his head in disgust. "I don't get it, man. You can learn more about a person with a five-second glance at their bike than you could after spending a month with them."

Jr just gave a little shrug. "What can I say, it's a gift." He gave a grin as he turned back to the bike he was working on.

"He's not going to like the quote," Josh said flatly.

Ding. Ding. Ding.

Jr looked back at the office. There was somebody there.

Chapter 16

Jr walked into the office and saw a man wearing a suit. Not a nice suit like the Devil was wearing when he saw him but a cheap dime-store type of suit. Jr knew he was with the police.

"Hi, can I help you?" Jr asked politely.

"Yes," the man replied. "I'm looking for Dustin Deadwood."

"That's me. May I ask who is looking?"

"Oh, my apologies," the man said, flipping out a badge. "Detective St. Claire with Metro PD. Could I ask you a few questions?"

"Of course, Detective. What do you need?" Jr already knew what this was about.

"I'm just following up on the altercation that you and Mr. Miginus had," Detective St. Claire said calmly.

"I don't understand," Jr replied. "I gave all this information to Officer Carson already."

"Oh, I know. Let's just say I don't agree with his opinion on this case." St. Claire flashed the typical cop smile.

"What would you like to know?"

"Do you know how Mr. Miginus was killed?"

Jr gave a blank look at the detective. "I was told his throat had been cut."

Detective St. Claire gave a squint of the eye and a shrug of his shoulders. "More accurately, he had a gash on the side of his neck. Very gruesome. Wouldn't you agree?"

"I don't know," Jr replied. "I didn't see it."

"Mr. Deadwood, you don't seem too upset about Mr. Miginus's passing." Detective St. Claire gave Jr a long stare before he spoke again, "Obviously, Officer Carson suspects that you had a hand in his death."

"It's no secret that we had our disagreements," Jr said. "Mr. Miginus was a very vile person. I'm sure he is getting what he deserves."

Jr's smirk turned into a full-fledged smile. He knew that Jared was getting exactly what he deserved. He had got to witness how pleased the Devil and his henchmen demons had been at his arrival. Jared, on the other hand, had been unpleasantly surprised. He was morbidly curious about what exactly Jared was dealing with.

"I've personally arrested him myself multiple times," the detective said. "There is definitely no love lost between us. I don't suppose that you would be willing to let me look around your place?"

"Sure, I'll save you the trouble of getting a warrant." Jr gave a slight grin.

"Oh, I wouldn't do that. Officer Carson might, though," Detective St. Claire was saying. "He's determined to say that you are responsible. I disagree."

"Do we need to go now?" Jr asked.

"No," St. Claire said. "We can set an appointment for tomorrow afternoon if you would like."

"Aren't you afraid that I might try to hide or get rid of something?" Jr was a little shocked.

"I figure that if you were going to, you would have already done that," he said with a smile.

Josh walked into the office. "Hey DJ, do you have a…oh sorry. I didn't realize somebody was in here."

The detective gave Josh a nod and introduced himself. "Detective St. Claire, Metro PD."

"Don't you ever get tired of having to flip out your badge instead of a good old-fashioned handshake?" Josh asked as he extended his hand.

Detective St. Claire grinned and gave a slight chuckle. "Typically, people don't want to shake hands with a detective." St.

Claire extended his and accepted the handshake. "Just out of protocol, you wouldn't mind if I took a look around here as well?"

"Be my guest, Detective," Jr said, gesturing to the door leading to the back of the shop.

Detective St. Claire went into the back and started looking. Jr wasn't sure what he thought that he was going to find in a bike mechanics shop. Josh gave Jr a wry look.

"What's that all about?"

"He said that he was following up on Officer Carson's investigation. He doesn't agree with his conclusion."

Jr was watching Detective St. Claire through the window to the shop. Jr watched as Detective St. Claire walked around the shop, looking in the toolboxes and the work area around the bikes. He slowly circled around the shop, heading back toward the locker area. He poked his head around the corner and scanned the area by the lockers. He must not have seen anything that piqued his interest. He turned around and headed back to the office where Jr and Josh were waiting.

St. Claire walked back into the office. "One more question," he said. "Have you guys had any dealings with a group of bikers calling themselves the Devil's right hand?"

Josh just shook his head no while Jr said, "No."

"Well, if you have any contact with any, let me know." St. Claire handed them both a card. "Mr. Deadwood, does tomorrow around five work for you?"

"Sure, I'll be there."

Detective St. Claire gave a quick smile as he left. "Gentlemen, thank you for your time."

Detective St. Claire walked out the door as he put his hands in his pockets. Jr and Josh watched as he disappeared down the street. Jr walked over to the parts locker and pulled out the parts to give the Ducati a racing package upgrade. He gave Josh a huge grin.

"If you'll excuse me, I have a date with an 1198."

"Dude, you…suck," Josh said. "You get the Ducati, and I get stuck with the Harley! Totally unfair."

Jr just laughed as he walked back into the shop with the parts and set them on the bench. He went and pushed the Ducati to the work area and started to pull off the plastics. He loved the way that the Ducatis looked, with or without the plastics. The bare tube body made them look really mean. Josh walked over to his area and put a CD in the stereo he had set up in the shop. Josh hit play and turned up the volume. The track started with a melodic yet haunting-sounding beat. It builds quickly with drums and guitar. Before he realized it, Jr was bobbing his head to the beat as the lyrics started. The music faded down as the lyrics build.

"I thought I was in control / Thought I was invincible, I got to lock up the dark inside my soul / CUFF THE CRIMINAL!" Josh was singing along as loud as he could.

Jr listened to how incredible this song sounded. "Josh, who is this?"

Josh looked up and smiled. "It's that band Disciple I've been telling you about."

"These guys sound awesome!"

Josh smiled bigger. "It gets better."

Jr listened intently as he worked away on the Ducati. Josh wasn't lying about it getting better. Jr was really enjoying the music. A few tracks in the song started with what sounded like an old recording of an interview with a mental patient. The music dropped in heavy sounding like something that would be in *Nightmare Before Christmas*. Jr couldn't help but let the music move him. Jr was halfway through with the upgrade when a song started, and the lyrics caught Jr totally off guard.

"I only have nightmares while my eyes are open!" It started angrily.

"Whoa, this is great," Jr said to Josh.

Josh smiled back at him with pride. "I know, I told you."

They continued to listen to other albums by the same band for the rest of the morning. Shortly after lunch, Jr was putting the plastics back on the Ducati. He was ready to take it for a test ride. Jr wheeled the bike outside and put on his helmet. His heart was pounding as he put the key in the ignition. It didn't matter how many times he has ridden one of these; it always gets his blood pumping. Pretty impressive since he's a walking skeleton. He started the motor and took off like a shot. The power from the race package was amazing. He was flying down the road, the songs he had just heard replaying in his head as he headed into a set of winding corners. All his parts were working in complete unison—leaning into the corners while giving it back brake and downshifting; rolling on the throttle as he comes out of the corner; coming back to a vertical position as he shifts up a gear, not letting off the throttle. The bike felt like it was riding on a rail, holding the line through every corner. Jr couldn't wait until his dad got back so Morty could be a bike again. Satisfied that the bike was in good working order, he headed back to the shop to call the customer and then finish the day.

He passed by Morty as he was pulling back into the shop. "Traitor," Morty shot at him.

Jr just smiled. "Sorry, buddy. Part of the job."

Chapter 17

Jr walked back into the shop and saw Josh standing over by the Harley he had been working on, looking like he wanted to pull out his hair. Jr wasn't sure what to do. He had rarely seen Josh this frustrated. Josh was always the levelheaded one who didn't lose his temper unless you messed with his family.

"Problems?" Jr asked with genuine concern.

"I don't know what to do next!" Josh said, sounding exasperated.

"What's the issue with it?" Josh just shot Jr a look. "Right, it's a Harley."

"I don't understand these bikes, DJ. No matter what you do with the seals, it still leaks." Josh's aggravation and stress was showing.

"Have you tried any gasket goo on the new seals?" Jr asked as he went to his toolbox and pulled out a tube.

"It's not a gasket that is leaking. It's an O ring."

"Yeah, but if the covers are grooved or cracked, this will seal up the leaks. Just use it sparingly." Jr handed the tube to Josh.

The rest of the day seemed to drag out a bit. Jr was anxiously counting down the hours. The bell in the office rang out. Jr started to walk toward the office when the bell started ringing incessantly. *Ding, ding, ding, ding, ding, ding!* Jr walked into the office and saw a gruffy-looking man wearing ratty jeans and a faded flannel shirt with the sleeves cut off. His hair was long and stringy, pulled back into a ponytail. Jr knew instantly that this was the Harley guy.

"Can I help you?" Jr asked with irritation in his voice. The bell ringing had rubbed him the wrong way.

"Yeah," the man shouted. "I've been waiting in here forever."

"It's been less than a minute. It only takes a few seconds to get in here from in back." Jr was starting to get irritated.

"Are you idiots finished with my bike yet?" the man was still yelling.

"Oh, you must mean that beat-down crappy Harley back there!"

The man's eyes got wide, and his face turned a bright red. Jr stared straight at him, not blinking. The man stood there looking like he was going to start frothing at the mouth, nostrils flaring. Jr noticed him clenching his fists.

"Now, if you'd like to lower the volume and stop with the insults, maybe we could have a civil conversation about your motorcycle?"

Josh, hearing the commotion, came into the office. "Everything okay in here?"

"This gentleman has a question about the status of his motorcycle," Jr stated flatly, not taking his eyes off the man.

"Are you finished with my bike yet?"

"There is more than just bad O rings with your bike. It's not going to be as easy as you were hoping," Josh said, sounding very professional.

The man exploded in a rage. "What? You're trying to rip me off. I know there isn't anything wrong with that bike."

"Sir," Josh started.

"Shut up, you moron," the man shouted.

"You will either calm down, or you'll be asked to leave," Jr interjected.

"Your tailpipe has multiple broken welds among other issues. We will be finished with your bike—"

"You're finished now, you thieving idiot," the man shouted as he pulled out a gun.

Jr instantly jumped in front of Josh as the man fired the gun. The bullet bounced off Jr as he leapt across the counter toward the man. He was in a rage over the man trying to kill his friend. He could feel the fire burning in his eye sockets. He grabbed the man by the shirt. The man's eyes went wide with terror, and he was screaming. Jr looked at the man with a puzzled expression on his face. He could hear the scream, but the man was frozen with fear, and his mouth was closed. That is when Jr realized the scream was coming from Josh. Jr realized that in his rage, his true self was showing. He dropped the man who scrambled out the door as fast as he could. Jr turned toward Josh.

"Josh, it's me."

Josh wasn't screaming anymore, but his eyes were wide with fright. "Who are you?"

"It's me Josh, DJ." Jr could see that Josh was freaked out. He was calming down and able to look like his human form again. "Josh."

"What in the world is going on?" Josh was still shaking. "What are you?"

Jr knew that he had to tell him the truth. "Josh, my dad is the Grim Reaper."

Josh started to laugh hysterically. "You expect me to believe that?"

Jr let his true self show through again. "Doesn't this prove it? Josh, it's still me. I'm still DJ."

"That guy shot you. The bullets just bounced off." Josh was calming down, and he wasn't shaking anymore.

"Yeah, it's complicated," Jr answered.

"So your dad, he kills people?"

"No," Jr almost yelled. "That's a common misconception. He is around when people die, but he's not the cause. He just collects the soul and facilitates its journey to whichever place it is supposed to go."

Josh was staring in disbelief. "Can you go back to looking like the DJ I know?"

Jr forgot that he had let his true self show. He resumed his daily appearance. "I know this is a lot to take in."

"Is your mom, is she, you know?" Josh asked hesitantly.

"No, she's fully human."

"But your dad, he's a, I don't know what he would be." Josh was having trouble taking this new information.

Jr knew he could trust Josh with this information. "He's an incarnation."

"A what?" Josh's confusion was understandable.

"An incarnation. There are five that I am aware of." Jr hoped that Josh wouldn't be freaked out.

"Five, you mean that there are others?" Josh's eyes were as big as the full moon.

"Yes. Death, Time, Fate, War, and Mother Nature." Jr hadn't noticed that his tone had become stoic.

"You're serious? Mother Nature?"

"Yes. My mom goes shopping and stuff with her."

Josh's expression was starting to become less intense. "What are they like?" he asked with intense curiosity.

"They're all pretty cool actually. Except for Fate, I haven't ever met her." Jr couldn't help but smile about Josh's curiosity on the subject.

"So are there any more surprises you haven't told me yet?" Josh wasn't sure if he really wanted to know anymore.

Jr was giving him a look, trying to decide whether Josh could handle any more surprises today. He decided to tell him everything. "Go open the bay door in the shop."

"Oh man, there is more." Josh looked at Jr. "Okay," he said. "I'll go open the door."

Josh walked into the back of the shop as Jr went out front. He walked over to Morty and put his hand on the top of the car. Jr didn't have to say anything; Morty already knew. Jr got in and drove Morty around back and pulled into the bay door of the garage. He got out and walked over to Josh as he was closing the bay door.

"This isn't my dad's car, Josh," Jr started. He looked at Morty. "Show him, Morty."

Morty changed instantly into the Ducati that he was normally. Josh jumped back and looked like he was ready to scream again. Jr wanted to tell his friend not to worry but didn't think that it would help. Morty had a plan already in motion. Morty changed into a pale horse and looked at Josh.

"Hello, Josh," Morty said. "It's nice to finally be able to properly meet you."

Josh didn't scream. He couldn't even talk at all. His mouth had dropped open. His eyes looked like they were going to pop right out of his skull. Jr walked over to Josh and put his hand up on his shoulder. Josh closed his mouth and looked at Jr. He tried to talk but still couldn't speak. He looked back at Morty.

"I know it's a lot to take in. Sorry I didn't tell you before, man." Jr still had his hand on his friend's shoulder.

"Your name isn't really Dustin, is it?" Josh's voice was low and monotone.

"No, it's actually Death Jr. My dad calls me Jr." Jr felt bad for not ever telling his friend about this before.

Josh gave a small chuckle. "Death Jr, huh. Well, at least now I know where you get DJ from."

"Josh," Jr paused for a second, "are we good?"

Josh gave Jr a long, hard look. His expression was like a stone. The air was thick with tension. Josh couldn't hold his stone face any longer and busted out in a big grin. "Yeah, we're good. We've been friends a long time. Since we were kids. I just wish you had told me before."

"I'm sorry, man. I didn't think you would be okay with it." Jr's tone got low, and he dropped his head. "To be honest, man, I didn't know if we would still be friends if you knew."

Josh gave Jr a half smile and punched him in the shoulder. "You are a little scary when you lose your temper." Josh looked Jr in the eyes for a second. "If you weren't bulletproof, would you still have jumped in front of me when that guy pulled out his gun?"

"Yes. Crystal and Tommy need you."

"Jr," Morty said.

Jr looked at Morty. He was back in his car form. Jr didn't have to ask; he knew what that meant.

Josh could see it in his friend's facial expression. "What's going on, DJ?"

"You know my dad's out of town, right?"

"Yeah," Josh responded slowly.

"I have to fill in for him while he is away." Jr knew that this would freak Josh out.

Josh's face went pale. "So you're the Grim Reaper now?"

"Interim Grim Reaper," Jr responded. "Hey, you want to see something cool?"

Jr changed to the office of the Reaper. He stood there in his true form—cloaked from head to toe, covering his skeletal structure. He reached into his cloak and pulled out his scythe. He gave it a squeeze, and the handle extended. He tapped the end of it on the ground, and the blade sprang out. Josh saw his reflection on the blade. A huge grin started to curl on Josh's lips.

"That is cool," he said, sounding like any dude would when shown an awesome weapon like the scythe.

"I have to go, Josh. Sorry I can't take you to your bike."

"It's okay. I'll lock up and catch a cab."

Jr put his scythe away as he was walking to Morty. He got in as Josh opened the bay door. Jr backed out of the garage and headed down the road.

Chapter 18

As they sped down the back road near the garage, Morty started to phase out. They lifted off into the air. Jr wasn't concerned about being seen. He had gotten rather good at the invisibility thing and had invoked it as they left the garage.

"Where are we headed?" Jr asked.

"Detroit. There is a huge gang war starting there tonight."

Jr knew that this was probably going to be like that freeway accident he had to go to. He quickly pushed that thought out of his mind. He didn't want to remember that night.

It only took a couple of minutes to get to Detroit. There are some bad areas in Detroit, and the Gratiot area is one of them. When Jr and Morty arrived, they were driving down an alley. Everything was quiet, which is odd for a city like Detroit.

"Is this the right place?" Jr asked, confused.

"Yes, I'm positive."

Jr got out and started walking down the alley. His nerves were tingling. He pulled out his scythe and held it at the ready. Jr stopped in the alley; his nose was twitching. What was he smelling?

"Brimstone," he whispered to himself.

Jr clutched his scythe tightly. The smell of brimstone made him nervous. He noticed two men starting down the alley toward him. They were both about the same height and build. One was wearing a blue shirt, and the other was wearing a white shirt. It was dark, so Jr couldn't make out any other features. He was in the role of Death, but that doesn't give him super sight. Jr noticed the man in the white shirt hand the other man some money. The other stuck it in his pocket and pulled out a small package and handed that to the one in the white shirt. They parted and started walking in opposite directions. The one in the white shirt dipped his finger in the package and touched it to his tongue. He stopped dead in his tracks.

"You ripped me off," he yelled as he pulled out a gun.

The man in the blue started running down the alley. He was headed right toward Jr. The man in white fired a round. The sound of the shot broke through the quiet of the night as it rang out. The man in blue ducked and kept running. A burst of more shots rang out as the man in white fired more. The commotion had attracted the attention of others, and cars began to come speeding into the alley.

"He ripped us off," the man with the white shirt yelled as he pointed at the man running away.

The first car screeched to a sliding stop as three men jumped out—all with white shirts and fully automatic weapons. They all fired at the man running away. The night air was filled with the sounds of hundreds of rounds being fired as the bullets whizzed down the alley. The man running was struck by multiple rounds as he ran. The impact of the bullets made him stumble and fall. Jr started to walk toward the man. He knew he had work to do.

The other end of the alley exploded with a huge group of men running into the alley. They all had guns, bats, chains, or knives in their hands. The shouts of angry men echoed down the dimly lit alley. The rest of the cars had come to a stop and the doors burst open. Men in white shirts poured out in every direction. Jr heard a sound that caught his attention.

"Help me." It was the man who had been shot pleading for his friends to help.

The alley exploded in what sounded like a war zone. Bullets came from both directions in swarms. Windows in the cars were shot out as the guys in white dove behind them for cover. At the other end of the alley, the guys in blue were diving behind dumpsters and any other available cover. Jr walked over to the man who had been shot and reached in with the tip of his scythe. He pulled out the soul of the man; it was as black as coal. Jr smoothed it out and let it go.

As it slowly drifted downward, Jr felt a bullet slam into the side of his head. That made him a little agitated. Jr looked around the alley. There were a few others on both sides who had been hit with the barrage of bullets. Most of them were just flesh wounds to the arms and legs. There was one who had been hit in the chest.

Jr walked toward him as more bullets started to fly through the air. A bullet whizzed past Jr's head, hitting a door and making the window in it explode. A woman screamed from behind the door. One of the men in blue heard the scream and headed for the door. The woman screamed again as the man ripped open the door. Her scream caused the baby she was holding to start to cry.

The man started to laugh. "She's one of theirs," the man hollered to the others.

A group of five or six guys wearing blue headed for the door. They all stared at the door, starting to drool like animals. The first guy raised his gun at the woman.

"Kill the baby, then we can have some fun," he said to the others.

Jr's rage exploded in him. He wouldn't let them do this. He shot across the alley like a bolt of lightning. Everything around him seemed to slow down as he bolted across the alley. He reached them just as the second guy was starting to go through the door. Jr let out a roar of pure rage. He grabbed the one at the back of the group by his hair and threw him toward an adjacent wall. He slammed into the wall as he let out a yelp. The next one heard his fellow gang member and turned at the sound. Jr punched the man in the chest making him fly into a couple of others, knocking them down. Only the other two were left. The one who was pointing his gun at the woman spun around and tried to fire a round. Jr did a duck-spin move swinging his scythe. It passed right through the guy without resistance. The man's lifeless body fell to the ground. Jr stared in amazement; there was no blood. He looked at the blade of his scythe. The man's tattered black soul hung on the tip. Jr shook it off, disgusted at what the man wanted to do. It sank quickly down to Lucifer's lair.

"Please, no! Not my baby!" the woman screamed.

Jr grabbed the last one who had entered the room and threw him outside with the rest. The woman looked up at Jr with tears in her eyes. She was shaking and terrified. Jr looked at her baby and leaned forward. He looked her dead in the eyes.

"Today is not your time. You need to make better choices about who you let around you and your baby!" Jr's voice was harsh. He hoped she would listen.

Jr turned back to the door. The group that had been knocked down was getting up. They saw Jr standing there and opened fire on him. The woman screamed again as the bullets just bounced off Jr. He let out a diabolical laugh and advanced on the men. Seeing that the bullets did not hurt him, the men all screamed and ran away down the alley. The rest of the men continued to shoot at each other during all of this. Running out of ammo, they all started to scatter. Jr surveyed the alley. He had a few people to attend to. He didn't feel bad for them having to wait for him. That baby was more important than their suffering.

He went around the alley and began to collect the souls of the men who needed it. He couldn't comprehend why people would do this to each other. He pondered this as he went around one at a time to the souls he needed to collect. He got to the last man who was leaning up against a dumpster as he approached. Jr stepped in front of the man and did a double take. This wasn't a man; he was a kid—couldn't be more than sixteen.

Jr crouched down next to him. "Why would you be a part of this?"

Startled, the kid looked up and saw Jr. His eyes went wide. "Am I dying?"

"Yes," Jr answered. "Why do this?"

"Am I going to go to Hell?" You could hear the fear in his voice.

"I don't know," Jr said. "It depends on where your faith is."

The kid started crying. "I don't want to die!"

Jr couldn't let him suffer anymore. He reached in with the tip of his scythe and gently removed his soul. The kid's labored breathing stopped, and his tears quit flowing. Jr smoothed out his soul. He couldn't believe that somebody so young could have such a dark soul. Jr watched as it sank slowly down. Jr sat there on his knees for a moment. His mind trying to comprehend all the evil he had witnessed today.

"I don't understand this at all," he said aloud.

He stood up and put his scythe away, still looking at the ground where the kid's soul had descended. He turned and walked toward Morty with a heavy heart. He opened the door and slumped into the seat.

"Morty, we have to find Jared's place. We have to stop the spread of this kind of evil."

Morty didn't even bother to verbally respond. He revved his engine and shot down the alley like a rocket. They were phasing out and lifting off in an instant.

Chapter 19

They were coming down on the south side of town near the empty lot. Morty landed a few blocks away on a side street with no traffic.

"DJ, I feel we should stay invisible for this."

"Agreed," Jr responded.

They slowly drove around the block, searching for what could be Jared's building. They were on the west side of the lot when they spotted a building that matched the description the girl at the coffee shop had given him. They pulled up in front of the building and stopped. Jr could feel his stomach getting butterflies. His palms were starting to sweat.

"This looks like the place," Jr said.

"It does have the right feel and look," Morty replied.

"This place doesn't even look livable."

Jr got out and started toward the building. He was approaching cautiously, not wanting to get caught off guard. He reached the front door and checked the handle. It was locked.

Jr just smiled. "That's not going to work," he said with a chuckle.

Jr walked boldly toward the door and stepped right through. The stench was overpowering. Jr's eyes began to water. He scanned the room he was in. It was a fairly large foyer with linoleum flooring ripped and torn all over. The wallpaper that looked like it was from the sixties was peeling from the walls. Jr walked slowly down the foyer and into the hall of the building. There were multiple rooms on each side of the hall. At the end of the hall, there was an elevator and next to it a set of stairs.

"How could this guy own a whole building?" Jr wondered aloud.

He walked to the side of one of the rooms and checked the door. It swung open slowly, creaking on its hinges. Jr stepped inside the room; the door creaked as it swung back, almost closing again. There were empty beer cans and whiskey bottles all over the floor. Cigarette butts were scattered all about with burns all over the floor. The walls had holes in them. The room was otherwise empty. Tattered shades hung in the window.

Jr heard a thump out in the hall. He glanced at the door as he caught a whiff of something vile smelling. He stepped over to the door and peeked through the crack in the door. In the hall was a gruesome dog-shaped creature. It sniffed the air and then lunged at the door that Jr was standing behind, knocking it open. Jr spun behind the door while pulling out his scythe in an instant. The dog-like creature landed on its feet and spun around. It lunged at Jr; he jumped to the side. He spun, and with a huge swing of his scythe, he hit the creature in the side, splitting it in two. The two halves hit the floor and started to sizzle and smoke away. The smell made Jr's stomach turn. Jr poked his head out in the hall and peered around to see if there was anything else. He knew he had just encountered a hellhound. He had always thought that those things were fictional and just for scary stories.

"Nothing scarier than the truth," he muttered.

He stepped into the room directly across the hall. This room had mattresses strewn all over the place. The smell of stale urine and sweat burned Jr's eyes. As much as he wanted to leave from the smell, he knew he had to find something. He surveyed the room and saw a couple of crack pipes on the floor. In the corner, he saw used syringes on the floor. This wasn't the room that he needed.

Jr stepped back into the hall. He wasn't ready to see what he was about to. He walked to the next door and grabbed the knob. He opened the door and stepped in. In the middle of the room had a pentagram painted on the floor. In the middle of the pentagram were three hearts. He wasn't sure if they were human or not. Jr looked around the room and decided that the hearts weren't human based on the fact that there were three goat heads on platters. The melted remains of black candles sat in front of the goat heads. Behind them on a table covered with a black silk cloth sat a copy of Anton Szandor LaVey's satanic bible. Jr shuddered at the thought of what happened in this room.

The people who practiced this type of occultism could not be sane. They are fueled only by the lust for sex, power, and control. Jr could feel the evil that infused this room. He knew that there were even more vile and evil things that had and will happen in this place. Jr walked back into the hall. He had to find that room with the blood pentagram on the wall. He looked to the other side of the hall. This door was already cracked open, and he could see inside. It was a bathroom. The sink was dripping, and the mirror was broken. The room looked dingy and filthy like it hadn't been cleaned in years. He knew that wasn't where he needed to check.

Jr walked toward the steps. There was no way he was going to use an elevator in this place. He was about to take the stairs when he saw some movement at the top of the stairs. He ducked off to the side, forgetting for a moment that he was invisible. He peered around the corner, trying to see what was up there. Whatever was up there had moved away from the top of the stairs. Jr cautiously crept up the stairs. Halfway up, one of the stairs creaked. Jr froze. He scanned the top of the stairs for movement. After a moment of nothing, he was convinced and started back up the stairs. Jr reached the top without further incident.

The top of the stairs opened onto another hallway. It had a single room on either side of it and a set of double doors at the end of the hall. Jr stared down the hall toward the double doors at the end. Halfway down the hall, one of the doors on the side opened, and the girl from the coffee shop walked out. She was on the phone with somebody, and again, she sounded unhappy.

"I don't know where he would have kept it. Why don't you just ask Dan?" She snapped at who was on the other end of her call. "No, absolutely not," she continued. "I'm not going in that room! You can tell Dan that I'm done. I can't believe that he's going to kill Claire. I like her. I'm not afraid of him like you. I'm done!" She hung up the phone angrily.

The door on the other side of the hall burst open, and a demon-like Jr had seen earlier in Hell jumped across the hall, landing on the girl from the coffee shop. Another figure walked out of the room. He looked almost human but was burned looking. He walked up to the girl and the other demon.

"Iris, Iris, Iris," the humanlike demon started. "You know that we can't let you leave. You might go to the authorities. Besides, Dan will be so disappointed."

"Let me go!" she screamed.

"That's not going to happen, Iris." He chuckled. "Dan thought this might happen. That's why he asked for Ol' Gus here." He patted the other demon on the back. "Gus, have fun."

The burned demon walked back to the room and disappeared. Gus was making happy little grunting sounds as Iris struggled to get free. Gus started licking his lips. Iris screamed.

"Hey, ugly!" Jr shouted.

Gus reared up and spun around, looking for who had shouted. He started to sniff the air wildly. He stared directly at Jr. Jr dropped his invisibility as he swung his scythe with always improving accuracy and strength. The blade sailed through the air, slicing into the side of Gus's neck. Gus howled in agony as smoke issued from his wound. Jr swung again with a downward arch, landing squarely on the top of Gus's head. Gus dropped to the floor as his eyes rolled back in his head. Iris was still screaming. Jr walked up to Gus and made sure that he was done. Smoke was billowing from his wounds as his body was starting to disappear.

Jr looked at Iris. "Be quiet, and listen."

Iris surprisingly became quiet. "Who are you?" she asked timidly.

"What do you know about them killing Claire?" Jr demanded.

"Nothing," Iris screamed as she started to cry.

"Liar!" Jr roared. He drew back his scythe before he realized what he was doing.

"Nothing, nothing, I swear. I just know Dan wanted to sacrifice her." Iris was almost sobbing now. "I was supposed to find some journal or something."

"Where is it?" Jr asked, his patience was wearing thin.

"I couldn't find it," Iris said.

Jr believed her. "You need to leave town before Dan finds you."

Iris got up and ran down the stairs, still sobbing. Jr listened until he heard her go out the front door. He turned and walked to the door where the other demon had gone. He looked inside to find an empty room. That didn't make sense. He had seen him come in here. Jr stepped into the room and looked around. He didn't see anything out of the ordinary.

"Where did he go?" Jr wondered out loud.

Jr stepped into the room and looked around intently. There had to be something that he was missing. He went invisible again for some added protection from being detected. He slowly walked around the room close to the walls, scanning them as he went looking for any sign of where the other demon could have gone. On the wall directly across from the door, he noticed that the wall seemed to have a waver. He started to reach his hand out to touch. Something told him to stop. He looked at the wall again and decided to use the tip of his scythe. He reached out with the tip of his scythe, and it passed through the wall without resistance. He gave a puzzled expression. He pulled his scythe back. It seemed to be intact and unharmed.

"A portal!" He knew better than to step through.

He walked back into the hall. Gus's body had completely disappeared. He walked to the double doors and opened them. His jaw dropped open. Directly across was the pig's blood pentagram on the wall. He scanned the room for any danger before he stepped through the doors. He didn't see any immediate danger and stepped through. He was instantly hit by a wall of cold air. The feel of evil enveloped his entire body. He reeled back, trying to get ahold of his senses. He dropped down to one knee using the handle of his scythe to help support him. The coldness of the tattered wood floor was unbelievable. He took a couple of deep breaths and then stood up. He scanned the room again. He saw a book on the floor in front of the pentagram. He walked over to it and picked it up. It was Jared's planner.

Heavy, fast footsteps were coming up the stairs. Jr quickly put the planner in his cloak pocket. He saw a bar in the corner. He considered hiding behind it but thought better of it. He stood motionless near the wall with the pentagram. The door opened, and a few of Dan's cronies walked in—the same ones Jr had seen when he was with Bradford.

"We have to find that stupid book," the first one said. "Dan's pretty upset right now."

"That's 'cuz they had to get rid of Iris," the second responded. "How would you feel if your girlfriend betrayed you? She never should have said she was out."

"Just look for the book. Dan wants that list."

The two continued to look for the planner. Jr, having heard enough, phased out and stepped backward through the wall. He jumped down to the ground below as he solidified and walked around to where Morty was parked. Jr climbed inside.

"Let's get going, Morty," Jr said.

They drove off down the road toward Jr's apartment. Jr looked in the planner. It had a cryptic sentence written in it: "On the Devil's Day at the Witching Hour." Jr looked through the rest of the planner for any additional information about it. He couldn't find any location mentioned.

"What does that mean? And where is it going to happen?" Jr shouted with exasperation.

"Maybe your dad and Bradford have acquired that information."

"Maybe." Jr remained quiet for the rest of the drive.

Chapter 20

Jr and Morty pulled into the parking lot of Jr's apartment. Jr noticed that Josh's bike was still there.

"That's odd. I thought Josh was going to pick up his bike?"

Jr pulled into his normal spot and got out. He was about to walk inside when he saw Dan come out the front door. Jr's blood began to boil. He wanted Dan to suffer in the worst way. He clenched his fists.

"DJ, you can't!"

"Morty, shut up."

"DJ, I will restrain you if necessary."

Jr knew that Morty wasn't bluffing. He wasn't sure if Morty really would or even could stop him from hurting Dan, but he knew that the unwanted attention wasn't something that he couldn't have right now. He unclenched his fists and took a couple of deep breaths. Dan was staggering around in the parking lot, a half-empty bottle of whiskey in his hand. Dan saw Jr standing next to Morty. Dan glared at him and told Jr that he was number one. Jr glared back and clenched his fists.

"If he does anything as I pass, I will retaliate!" Jr's voice was quivering with rage.

"And I will intervene if needed, DJ. We can't risk him knowing we are on to him." Morty had never sounded like this before.

Jr shot Morty a dirty look. "You sound like Mortis."

Jr started to walk slowly to the door as Dan glared at him. Jr cautiously passed by Dan. Not taking his eyes off Dan, he walked by.

"I know you killed him. The cops won't do anything. I will. I'm gonna kill you." Dan slurred his words as he stood there swaying a bit from the alcohol.

Jr stopped and looked at Dan. He turned to him and stretched out his arms. "I'm right here, Dan. Do your worst."

Dan took a big pull off his bottle. "If I didn't already have plans, I would kill you." He stumbled backward a step or two.

"You know, Dan, I think you are really going to enjoy spending eternity in Hell. I mean come on, your buddy Jared is already there." Jr thought this would get to Dan.

Dan started to laugh. "You're such an imbecile. I know he is. I know that the work we have done for our lord will be repaid." The sneer on Dan's face made Jr cringe.

Jr just looked at Dan. If only he knew what was in store for him. He couldn't help but grin. He knew what Dan had in store for him. Jr walked past Dan without any further issues. He walked to the door of the building and headed down the hall and looked at Claire's door as he passed by. He felt a heavy clenched feeling in his chest. He had to talk to her. He didn't care if she was still mad. He had to explain, to tell her how he felt about her. Jr walked up to her door and took a deep breath. He reached up and knocked on the door. A lump appeared in his throat from the anticipation as he waited for a response. The was no answer. He knocked again. The lump in his throat welled up again. His chest was so tight that it hurt. Again, no answer. He turned and started down the hall again. Jr heard Dan's Harley start up as he continued down the hall. His heart sank as he walked away from the door

He could hear laughter inside his apartment as he approached the door. He opened the door and was instantly attacked by a small child. Tommy hit Jr at a dead run, throwing his arms around his leg and hugging as tight as a six-year-old can muster.

"DJ," Tommy squealed as he hugged Jr's leg.

"Hey, Tommy," Jr said, surprised that he was there.

Jr reached down and patted Tommy on the head. The laughter he had heard was coming from the living room. Jr saw Crystal sitting on the couch with Yvonne talking and laughing. It was nice to see Yvonne with a smile on her face.

Josh walked out of the kitchen, eating some of the leftover roast that Jr's Mom had made.

"Help yourself, Josh," Jr said with mock irritation in his voice.

"Thanks, I will," Josh said. "Crystal wanted to come see how Yvonne was holding up."

"Looks like that was a good choice. Yvonne's in a good mood." Jr gave Josh a stern look. "Did you save me any?"

Josh stopped in midchew and looked at Jr with a deer-in-the-headlights look. Jr was about to say something when Josh burst out laughing, almost spitting food out. Crystal and Yvonne had walked into the room while this exchange had been going on.

"Of course, he did," Yvonne said as she put her arm over Jr's shoulder from the side. "Even a human garbage disposal couldn't finish all of your mom's leftovers in one shot."

Tommy let go of Jr's leg and ran over to his mom. Crystal scooped him up and kissed the boy on the cheek. "Hey DJ, hope you don't mind I came by." The slightest hint of her Southern accent was evident when she spoke.

"Of course not, Crystal. You know you're always welcome." Jr shot Josh a look. "Your husband on the other hand."

"Hey, I'll pay you back," Josh said.

"Yeah, like you could match Susan's culinary finesse," Crystal poked at her husband.

"Hey DJ, I meant to ask you about this?" Yvonne pointed to the bowl of plastic fruit.

"My mom thought it would brighten the place up a bit. She thought it might help you." Jr walked over and put the pomegranate and the hourglass on top.

"Will you tell her I said thanks. Fred always liked the look of fake fruit. It made me smile this morning."

"Sure," Jr replied.

Crystal looked at Josh as he was finishing his last bit. "Now that you've helped yourself to DJ's food, clean up your mess so we can get this little one home and in bed."

Josh walked into the kitchen and rinsed off his plate and set it in the kitchen sink. Crystal walked into the living room and had Tommy pick up his toy car and army action figure. Crystal finished with Tommy in the living room and walked back into the dining area. "I'll pick you up around noon after my folks come get Tommy," Crystal said to Yvonne as she gave her a hug.

"Thanks," Yvonne said. Jr noticed Yvonne's eyes were getting misty. She looked at Jr. "Fred's service," she said.

"Sorry," Jr said. "I didn't realize."

"I know," she said.

Crystal walked into the kitchen and gave Josh a kiss. "I'll see you at home. Love you."

"Love you too," he said as he kissed her back.

Crystal looked at Tommy. "Come on, kiddo. Let's go. See ya, DJ."

"Bye, Crystal."

Tommy ran over and gave Yvonne a hug. "Bye-bye," he said with a smile.

"Bye, sweetie," Yvonne replied as she gave Tommy a kiss on the forehead.

Crystal and Tommy walked out and headed home. Josh was finishing up in the kitchen.

"I'm going to get in the shower," Yvonne said. She headed toward the bathroom.

"Good night, Yvonne," Josh said as he walked out of the kitchen. She waved over her shoulder. "I'll talk to you later, DJ." Josh grabbed his helmet and jacket as he headed for the door.

"Yeah, see ya. Ride safe."

"Always, brother." Josh walked out to follow his wife home.

Jr walked into his room and put the planner he had found in his dresser drawer. He heard a knock at his front door. Jr walked back to the door.

"What did you forget, goofball?" he said as he opened the door. "Claire," he said, shocked.

Claire stepped in and kissed Jr square on the lips. Jr's head began to swirl. His heart was pounding in his chest, and he felt like he was going to collapse. Claire didn't stop kissing him. He had never had this happen before and didn't know what to do. He put his hands on her hips and kissed her back. His brain was going a thousand miles an hour but not getting anywhere. Claire stepped in closer and wrapped her arms around Jr's neck and kissed him even harder and more passionately. It seemed to last for an eternity, which Jr didn't mind. He felt like he was going to float away. Claire slowly ended the kiss.

"I'm sorry, DJ," she said, sounding like she was starting to cry. "I shouldn't have jumped to conclusions."

"What do you mean?" Jr asked, still reeling from the kiss.

Claire looked at the ground as she pulled out the card that Jr had put with the flowers out of her pocket. "I came by a little later after I slammed the door on you to confront Yvonne. She handed me the roses and asked me to read the card. At first, I wasn't going to. I wanted to hate her, but I saw the tears in her eyes. She told me about Fred and why she was here. I'm sorry, DJ." Claire burst into tears.

Jr stepped forward and gave her a hug. Claire pressed her face onto his chest and cried. Jr put his arms around her and let her cry. He didn't say anything mainly because he didn't have the words to say, but also because he knew that right now, she just needed his comfort. Claire cried into his chest for a couple of minutes. She stepped out of Jr's embrace. Tears still streaked her face.

"Claire, you know we can't do this. Dan and everything."

"I know," Claire said. "You do know that I'm not with him by choice, right?"

Jr's mouth fell open. He was in shock. "I didn't know," he admitted.

"I've been talking with an abuse outreach program, and they are trying to get me into a temporary place."

The more Jr learned about Dan, the more he wanted him to suffer. "Is there anything I can do?"

"No." Claire's tears were starting to subside. "Dan's going to be gone for a while. Do you think we could have a cup of tea? I feel like I should tell you how I ended up here before you get involved in this."

Jr knew that he was already involved whether he wanted to be or not. "Yeah, I'll put the kettle on."

Jr walked into the kitchen and started a kettle of water as Claire went and sat at the table. Jr grabbed a couple of cups and brought them to the table. He put one down in front of Claire. He wanted to tell her what Dan was planning but knew that he couldn't. It was tearing him up inside. He walked back into the kitchen and grabbed the tea and a couple of tea infusers and brought them out to the table. He sat down at the table, worried about what Claire could possibly want to tell him. Jr filled the infusers with tea as he waited for the kettle to boil. When he heard the kettle start to whistle, he retrieved it from the kitchen and filled both cups with water. He set the kettle on a potholder on the table.

Claire took a couple of deep breaths as she dipped her infuser into the water. "You're the only person that I know who uses these things. Most people just buy tea bags."

Jr gave a slight smile. "These make better tea."

Claire took a small sip of her tea. "So about three years ago, I was in a real bad spot. Barely eighteen and living on the streets. My mom had died, and my dad was abusive in multiple ways. That's why I left. I ended up using drugs to cope with the pain of my life. Stupid decision." She paused for a second to take another sip of tea. "Anyway, one day when I was trying to find some, I ended up meeting Dan and some of his friends. He was a smooth talker and convinced me to come back to his place. I thought a warm place to sleep would be nice, so I accepted his offer." She stopped for a second as tears started to fill her eyes. "When we got here, he seemed nice, and we got high together, and he started giving me stuff to drink. It felt nice to be treated like a person again. The next day he said I could stay there if I wanted to. To be honest, I was skeptical, but I didn't want to be outside, and a couch was better than a bench or sidewalk, so I stayed." Tears were streaming down her cheeks.

Jr reached his hand out and put it on hers to try to comfort her. She took a sip of tea and dried her eyes before she started again.

"For the first few days, he was really nice and seemed like he cared. I can't believe that I fell for that!" Claire was upset when she said that, and her volume and tone conveyed that. "That weekend, he had some of his friends over, including Jared. We all started to drink again and get high. Jared kept on grabbing me and trying to do stuff. I kept pushing him off and telling him no. Dan got mad at me and said for everything he had done for me, I should show him and his friends some gratitude." The tears were flowing out of her eyes as the pain from the memory flooded her mind. "I told them no and slapped Dan. Dan punched me in the face, and then he and Jared drugged me to the back room. A couple other guys came back with them, and they raped me. All of them took turns holding me down and doing awful things to me. They took pictures and threatened me with them. Dan told me the police would never believe a doped-up whore like me. They finished with me, and all walked out of the room and continued to party. I just lay there and cried for hours. That was the last night that I drank or did any drugs."

Jr was infuriated and grieved at the same time. "Claire, I'm so sorry. I didn't know. I don't know what to say."

Claire continued through her tears. "When I got up and dressed, I tried to leave, but Dan grabbed me and told me if I left or went to the police, he would find me and kill me. So I had to stay. He hits me and abuses me. He does more if he doesn't have another girl to give him what he wants. Girls like Iris." Claire was sniffling, so Jr got her a tissue. "Thanks. Fast-forward until a month ago. I found a flyer for an abuse help center. One day when Dan was passed out, I snuck out to the center. They gave me a card for a crisis hotline. I called it after I stormed out the other day. The lady I talked with, she hid a Bible in the planter outside for me and started the process to help me. Resources are thin, and they don't want to put me at risk until they have a safe place to get me to."

Jr was sitting there in complete and utter shock and disbelief. Dan was even more evil and vile than he had ever imagined. "Claire, if there is anything I can do, let me know."

"Thanks, DJ. I don't know how long Dan will be gone. I had better get back."

Claire finished her tea and got up to walk to the door. Jr walked to open the door for her. Claire turned around and put her hands on Jr's shoulders and kissed him again. Jr's head was in the clouds as Claire's lips touched his. He had never felt like this before. Claire ended the kiss and wrapped her arms around Jr's waist. The hug made him feel like the kiss in a way. The warmth of her embrace caused Jr to feel lightheaded. He hugged her back.

"I have to go," she said as she stepped out into the hall.

Jr closed the door behind her as she walked down the hall. He leaned his head against the door for a minute, listening to her footsteps go down the hall. He didn't hear Yvonne come out of the bathroom.

"When are you going to tell her?" Yvonne said, startling Jr.

Jr jumped from being startled. "What do you mean?" Jr responded as he walked to the table to start clearing the cups from the tea.

"When are you going to tell her that you love her?"

Jr stopped clearing the table and stared at Yvonne. "What?"

Yvonne walked up to Jr and put her hands on his shoulders and looked him in the eyes. "DJ, you know I love you, but you have a really thick skull. It doesn't take a genius to see it."

Jr didn't respond. He turned and continued to clear the table. His mind was still spinning from the kiss and the information about Claire's situation. He hoped that his dad and Bradford had some information.

"Good night, DJ," Yvonne said as she walked to the couch and started to spread out her blankets.

"Good night, Yvonne."

Yvonne lay down on the couch as Jr finished clearing the table. He was exhausted and ready for bed himself. He walked back to his room and closed the door. He lay back on his bed and closed his eyes. He fell asleep almost instantly.

Chapter 21

Jr found himself standing in an arid desert. Juniper trees and brush scattered about. A lone oak tree struggling to grow on the top of a volcanic rock. A fig tree stands in the distance. Jr can hear a commotion in the distance just over a hill. He walked to the top of the hill and looked out. Just across a small valley, he sees a rock hill that looks like it has a face weathered into the side of the hill. At the top of the hill is a crowd of people and a procession of more people coming up the hill. The noise from the crowd sounds angry—jeering and sneering instead of cheering. Nothing in this area looked familiar to Jr.

Wanting to get a better view of what was going on, Jr set off down the hill that he was on and headed toward the other side valley. He kicked up a Cape Hare as he went down the hill. He saw a couple of desert foxes scampering across the bushes in search of food. Fast small lizards ran across the ground in front of him. As he continued down the hill, he could have sworn he saw a hedgehog run from under a bush. He definitely wasn't in an area he was familiar with.

"This is some crazy wildlife."

Jr started up the other side of the valley. At the top, he heard the sounds of a hammer pounding down a nail and cries of anguish. He crested the top of the hill to see three crosses being raised. Jr couldn't tell if time was speeding up or standing still. He couldn't see the sun to judge the time. It was dark like an eclipse was happening, but that wasn't the case. It was like somebody turned off the sun. He saw three people hanging on the crosses. He could hear them sneering at the one hanging in the middle. The cries of anguish, pain, and anger echoed through the valley. Jr could tell the man on the middle cross was the focal point of most of the tormenting. Jr walked closer and could see that he had a huge crown of thorns pushed onto His head and huge gashes oozing blood all over His face. Jr could see that His back had been lashed open. All His ribs were exposed. The man on that middle cross had a sign over His head. People were throwing garbage at Him and spitting on Him.

Jr realized that he had seen this person before. This was who Sam had called Lord Jesus when he had seen Sam's soul going to Heaven. How could people be doing this to this man? Jr looked at the bottom of the cross and froze. He saw four women and a young man standing at the foot of the cross. All of them were crying, and Jesus was talking to them. Behind them stood Jr's father, the Grim Reaper. Jr watched as Jesus on the cross was offered a sponge dipped in some kind of liquid. Jesus refused to take the sponge that they were offering him.

Jesus threw His head back and said, "It is finished."

Jesus closed His eyes and dropped His head. Jr almost jumped out of his skin from the clap of thunder that happened when Jesus closed His eyes. There was a flash of lightning that lit up the dark sky. Jr saw his father look up at Jesus. The flash of lightning made the single tear sparkle as it rolled down Death's cheek. The ground started to rumble and shake. People started to scream and run, frightened by the ground shaking.

Jr's eyes snapped open. It took him a few seconds to realize that the ground wasn't shaking, and he was in his bed. He sat up and blinked a few times, trying to clear the fog from his head. He sat on the edge of his bed. He had heard of the crucifixion before, but he had no idea that his dad had been there and witnessed it. Jr also never knew his dad to have cried before collecting a soul. He was going to have to ask him about that. Jr looked at the clock on his nightstand; it was just after midnight.

Jr got up and walked over to his dresser. He opened the drawer where he had put the planner. He picked it up and walked over to his desk. He turned it over in his hands a few times, looking it over. He opened it and thumbed through the pages slowly. It showed appointments for some of the oddest things. Things that also didn't seem to fit Jared's persona. Jr saw an entry for a pickle eating contest. He saw another one to watch a video on how to train a giraffe. Jr knew that these couldn't be real events that Jared was doing.

Jr stood up and started to pace around his room, trying to figure out what these entries could mean. He set the planner down on his desk as he continued to pace back and forth. He sat back down at his desk and continued to thumb through the pages. Jr noticed that all the dates on the pages had been crossed out.

"Why would he cross out the dates?"

Jr continued to scan the pages. The sentence "On the Devil's Day at the Witching Hour" was repeated over and over. The meaning of this sentence still puzzled him. He came to another page that was written in bold letters. It said,

> **Groceries for the party at the appropriate hour!**
> **Artichoke Hearts**
> **Kidney Beans**
> **Liverwurst**
> **Blood Oranges**
> **Inner Head Cheese**

"That's the craziest grocery list I have ever seen," Jr murmured. "Inner head cheese? What in the world is that?"

Jr continued to look through the planner when he heard a slight noise that made his ears perk up. He stopped reading and tilted his head a bit, straining to hear any sound that he could. He sat motionless, not even breathing. He heard it again. It sounded like something scratching at his front door. His nostrils flared, and his eyes went wide. It was brimstone.

Jr jumped to his feet and put the planner in his cloak pocket. He walked out into the living room without turning on any lights. He heard the sound again. He glanced at Yvonne; she was still asleep on the couch. He hoped he was hearing things and smelling things. He heard what sounded like a rake pick and a tensioner wrench being used on his lock. Jr got that tickling feeling going down his spine.

His senses went on hyperalert. He drew the scythe out of his cloak. He hoped the sound of him opening it wouldn't wake Yvonne up.

Jr heard the lock on his door disengage. The door creaked ever so slightly as it started to swing open. Jr waited quietly for the door to finish opening. The smell of brimstone filled his apartment. Jr saw two small figures enter the apartment. He lunged at them, hitting the first one on the head with the handle of his scythe. He hadn't opened it yet for fear of waking Yvonne. There was a dull thud as the first person fell to the ground. Jr spun, hitting the second person in the chest. The sound of his wind getting knocked out escaped his lungs. Jr gave him two quick hits to the head as he started to double over. The man went limp and dropped to the floor with a dull thud. Jr looked over at Yvonne; she was still asleep. He let out a sigh of relief.

Jr looked at the two guys on his floor. It was too dark to make out any details of their faces. He put his scythe back into his cloaked and bent down to move the first guy out of his apartment. He caught a glimpse of a huge gray foot coming toward his head. He didn't have time to react. The foot caught him in the cranium, and the impact made him fly up into his ceiling with a loud crash. He fell to the floor with a thud. Jr rolled over onto his back, his head still spinning. He tried to refocus his eyes. A huge hand grabbed Jr by the face and picked him up. It felt like his head was being crushed.

The creature brought Jr close to its face. "Give me the book," it said in an indescribable voice. The smell of sulfur and brimstone enveloped Jr's head.

Jr let loose with a barrage of fists to the face of the creature holding him. It let out a guttural roar as it flung Jr across his apartment. He crashed into the wall on the other side of the living room. He heard Yvonne screaming.

Yvonne ran over to Jr. "DJ, DJ, are you okay?"

Jr could hear the panic in her voice. He struggled to get to his hand and knees. He felt Yvonne trying to help him up. Jr heard the creature stomping toward them. He looked at Yvonne.

"Get to my room and hide." Jr gasped. "Go!"

Yvonne took off toward Jr's room as he staggered onto his feet. He reoriented on the creature. It was huge with blistery gray skin.

The huge foot that had kicked him in the head had three ugly toes on it. He launched himself at the creature, trying to tackle it. He hit the creature with a sickening thud. Both of them bounced as they hit the ground. Jr rolled onto his feet and charged at the creature again. He jumped up and gave the creature its own kick to the head. The kick was contacted with enough force to cause the head to snap violently to the side. The creature fell to the ground, dead.

"DJ!" Yvonne screamed.

Jr looked over and saw another creature charging through his front door. It ran straight for Jr, slamming him into the wall. Jr felt the air explode out of his lungs. The creature picked Jr up by the throat and pinned him to the wall. He heard it start to laugh the most demonic-sounding laugh he had ever heard. Yvonne was frozen by his bedroom door.

"We know you have the book," the creature snarled. "We can smell it."

Two more creatures rushed into the apartment. They headed straight for Yvonne. Jr watched as her eyes glazed over, and she let out a scream of sheer terror. Jr's rage exploded inside him. Seeing Yvonne as frightened as she was made it uncontrollable. He had already had to collect her husband, his friend's soul. He wasn't going to collect hers. He pulled out his scythe in less than an instant and cut the arm that was pinning him to the wall of its host. The creature let out a roar of anger and pain. Jr swung again, cutting the creature almost in two. Smoke billowed out of the open wound as the creature fell to the ground.

Jr launched himself across the room, putting himself in between Yvonne and the two charging creatures. There was no hiding his true form at this point. He landed in front of Yvonne, his cloak flowing around his body. His boney hands gripped the handle of his scythe. His eyes glowed as he stared at the advancing creatures. The blade of his scythe had a blue flame starting to burn around the edges. He waited until the creatures were only a few feet away. He launched his attack on the creatures. The flames on his blade left a glowing blue arch in the air as it sailed through the air. He spun around as he swung his scythe again and again. The howls of the creatures were cut short as Jr finished them both off quickly. Jr looked as the bodies hissed out smoke and dissolved on his floor.

Jr turned toward Yvonne. She was standing there, motionless and just looking at Jr. He took a step toward her.

"Yvonne, are you okay?" he asked.

"DJ?" she asked, not sure if this was her friend or not.

Jr realized that he was showing his true self. He put his scythe away and donned his human persona. "Are you okay?" he asked again, his voice and body language showing his concern for his friend.

Yvonne's eyes filled with tears as her lips started to quiver. The relief that this was her friend was evident. She fell on his shoulders, hugging him as she cried. Jr put his arms around her as he looked around his broken apartment. Jr's ears perked up. He spun around as he heard his door creaking. He put himself between the door and Yvonne. A hand reached into the door and hit the light switch. Jr blinked as his eyes quickly adjusted to the light. His mom and Mother Nature walked in.

Chapter 22

"Mom?" Jr asked with confusion.

"I got a letter from your dad today, saying to be here tonight at this time." Susan looked around the apartment. "From the looks of it, I should have been here sooner. Yvonne, are you going to be okay?"

Yvonne was standing at the door to Jr's room, looking dumbfounded. "I'm not sure," she managed to say.

Jr looked at his mom. "You got a letter from Dad?"

"Um," Yvonne started. "Could somebody fill me in on what just happened?"

Mother Nature stepped forward. "Maybe I can help."

Yvonne looked at Mother Nature. She was an attractive person. She was tall and slender and with olive-colored skin. Her hair was long and brown, but it had green highlights on it. Her clothes were modest, jeans and a shirt, both in earth tones of course. "Who are you?"

"Oh, I'm sorry. My name is Ivy Bellezza. I'm friends with Susan," Mother Nature said.

"Bellezza?" Yvonne asked. "That's beautiful. Where is that from?"

"Thank you. It's Italian," Ivy said. "It means beauty."

There was a sudden bright flash. "Evening, ladies, bonehead. Please come with me?"

Yvonne started to scream. There was another flash. They were all standing in the same room. Death was now also present. Yvonne's scream ended as quickly as it had started. She was looking around wide-eyed.

Susan walked over to Death and gave him a kiss. "Hey, honey," she said as she gave him a hug.

"Ivy," Bradford said, smiling. "We still on for tea next week?"

"Only if you can find the time, Bradford," she said, smiling back.

They both let out a chuckle at the comment. Bradford turned to Yvonne. "I bet you could use an explanation."

Yvonne stared blankly at Bradford for a moment. She slowly nodded her head. "Yes, please," she whispered.

Ivy stepped forward again. "Let me explain if I can. You know DJ and Susan I assume." Yvonne nodded in response. "I'm Ivy, this is Bradford, and that is DJ's dad, Torva." Ivy took a breath before she continued. "This part is going to take some open-mindedness on your part. Respectively our titles would be," she hesitated for a second, not knowing how Yvonne would react, "Mother Nature, Father Time, and Death."

Yvonne's body stiffened. Had she heard what she thought she just did? She looked around the room at each of them. Her eyes landed on Torva last. "Death, huh? Like the Grim Reaper?"

"In the flesh," Death said with a slight bow. A smile curled on his lips. "Well, not flesh, just bones."

Yvonne continued to stare at him. "Why did you kill Fred?" Her voice was quivering, and her eyes were filling with tears.

"No, no, my dear," Death said sympathetically. "I don't kill people. Common misconception. Unfortunate side effect of my job. I simply collect the soul and allow it to go to its eternal home. Whichever one that might be."

"Where did Fred go?" she asked Death. Her body was tense, and her fists were clenched. She was shaking from the intensity of the emotions she was dealing with.

Jr spoke up, "My dad didn't take Fred, Yvonne. I did." Jr dropped his head as he spoke.

Yvonne froze for a second. Her face was turning red, and an expression of betrayal was on her face. "How could you do this to me?" She almost screamed at Jr.

Susan, seeing that the situation was getting out of control, stepped forward quickly and grabbed Yvonne's arm. "Bradford," she said as she grabbed his arm. There was a flash, and they were gone."

"Where did they go?" Jr asked.

His dad gave him a look. "Where?"

"Really, Dad? Okay, sorry," Jr said with sarcasm. "When did they go?"

Death gave Jr a grin. "I honestly don't know. But if I know your mom, they'll be back with us in five minutes or so."

"Oh, my little nephew is all grown up," Ivy said, wrapping Jr in a hug from behind. "Torva, why didn't you tell me DJ had his first trip with Bradford?"

"Honestly haven't had the time, Ivy." Death chuckled.

"Um, Ivy, could you loosen your grip a little? You're crushing my ribs," Jr said, gasping for air.

"Oh, sorry, DJ," Ivy said as she released her grip. She was a lot stronger than she looked.

"Dad, back to my question please?" Jr said.

"I already told you, I don't know. Probably about five minutes," Death said in an even tone.

"I mean part two of my question."

Death gave a smile. "I'd be happy to answer part two of your question. You will need to ask it first though."

Jr opened his mouth to say something and stopped. He realized that he had never asked the second part. "What's Mom doing with Yvonne?"

"Showing Yvonne whatever moments in time that she needs to so Yvonne won't try to kill you."

"Kill me? Seriously, what did I do?" Jr was shocked.

"DJ," Ivy interrupted. "Right now, she thinks you are the reason that Fred isn't here. Your mom will show her that if you hadn't been there, Fred would have suffered."

"Fred was my friend. I couldn't let him suffer," Jr said softly. He was starting to get a little choked up about his friend.

"We know that," Ivy continued. "But Yvonne doesn't right now. All she knows is that Fred was here and now he's not. She heard you say that you collected his soul, and in her mind, that means that you killed him."

"I didn't, though," Jr protested.

"Jr, we know that," Death interjected. "Being an incarnation gives us an insight that unfortunately our mortal friends don't have." Death stepped forward and put his hand on Jr's shoulder. "Sometimes this job gives us sorrow and pain. It is unfortunate but necessary."

That reminded him about his dad at the cross—the tear that ran down his cheek. "Dad, I had a dream about you at the cross. You were there before you were needed, and I saw a tear roll down your cheek. Why?"

Death went a little rigid at this question. "Why to which part? That question had two parts."

"Both," Jr said quickly.

There was a flash; and Susan, Bradford, and Yvonne reappeared. Death was visibly relieved at not having to answer that question. Yvonne had tears running down her cheeks. She looked at Jr. He was concerned about what she was going to do. She walked toward Jr. He braced himself for whatever was about to happen. When she reached Jr, she gave him a little smile before she kissed him on the cheek.

"Thank you," she said as she gave Jr a hug. "You've always been a good friend. To myself and to Fred also."

A wave of relief washed over Jr as Yvonne released him from her hug.

Jr looked at his mom. "What did you show her?"

"Enough." A huge smile crossed Susan's lips as she gave Yvonne a look.

Bradford chimed in. "Look, I know I'm the fun one, but we have something serious to talk about. So take it away, Torva."

Death gave Bradford a look of derision. "Thank you, Bradford. Always the helpful one." Death glanced around the room at everybody there. "First we need to get Yvonne to Purgatory. Unfortunately, I believe that is the only place she would be safe for the time being."

Yvonne looked like somebody just kicked her. "Safe, what do you mean safe?"

"The people responsible for the attack on Jr's apartment know that you were there. Until we can stop them, you will be in danger." Death's tone as he spoke put an icy chill down her spine.

Susan, seeing Yvonne's reaction, piped up. "Don't worry, sweetie, our place is pretty nice. Plus, Ivy and I will have an opportunity to take you out shopping."

"Your place? You mean you live in Purgatory? I thought Purgatory was where souls went if it wasn't clear where they were supposed to go." Yvonne's confusion was evident when she spoke.

"No," Death said with an authoritative tone. "Souls don't get a second chance on eternity. They can't go to Purgatory to work off their sins. Their final place after death is chosen by them in life before they die. It can't be changed after."

Yvonne was looking at Death, her eyes welling up with tears again. "I need to know where Fred went."

Jr reached out and took Yvonne's hand in his. "He went to Heaven, Yvonne."

A wave of relief and emotion washed over Yvonne. She leaned into Jr's shoulder and wept. Again, Jr put his arms around her and let her cry. Yvonne wept until her eyes went dry. She hadn't fully grieved the loss of her husband yet. Jr knew that she needed this. Yvonne pulled back from the hug after a couple of minutes, drying her eyes.

"How do you know that I will be safe in Purgatory?" Yvonne questioned.

Death let out a chuckle as a grin appeared on his lips. "Nobody can enter the home region of an incarnation without permission from that incarnation."

Jr looked at Yvonne. "You had better get going." Jr paused for a moment. An expression of regret on his face. "Yvonne, I'm sorry you got mixed up in this."

"Who is it that is coming after you?"

"They're not really coming after me," Jr said, trying to sidestep the question.

Yvonne turned and looked at Susan. "Mrs. Deadwood, please help?" Yvonne was pleading with her.

Susan looked at Death. He gave her a nod of agreement. She looked back to Yvonne. "Lucifer and his minions."

Yvonne was unable to move or speak. She stood there motionless for a moment. She looked over at Jr. "You better stay safe. I can't lose anybody else."

Death stepped forward and put his hand on Yvonne's shoulder. "Hell will have to get past me first. Jr has help."

Bradford stepped forward. "Ladies, it would be my pleasure to escort you to Purgatory."

Bradford had said it to them all but was looking directly at Ivy when he said it. He extended his hand to her. You could see her olive skin get a pinkish hue to it as she accepted his hand.

"If you don't make it to tea next week, I'll never forgive you," Ivy said, blushing.

Bradford gave her a wink as he squeezed her hand. Susan grabbed Yvonne's hand and reached out to grab Bradford's shoulder. There was a flash, and they were gone. Jr just looked at the spot where they had been standing for a second.

"Dad, are we going to be able to stop this?"

"We have to, son," Death said in a low tone. "We have to."

Chapter 23

Mortis was standing at the door of the house when the four of them flashed in.

"Hey, Mortis," Susan said as she reached out to pet his neck.

Yvonne saw Mortis and got a little giddy. "Oh, I love horses," she cooed.

"Thank you," Mortis said to her.

Yvonne jumped back in shock. Her eyes glanced around at the others before she asked the question. "Did I just hear him say something?"

"Yvonne, meet Mortis. The trusted steed of the Grim Reaper," Susan stated. "Mortis, this is Yvonne, one of DJ's friends. She is going to be staying here for a while."

Mortis shimmered as he transformed into a robed figure. He did a slight bow as he addressed Yvonne. "It is a pleasure to meet you."

Yvonne was just staring at Mortis, unable to move or speak at the moment.

Mortis spoke up again, "Morty let me know that there was an incident at DJ's. I trust everything is okay?"

"Everything will be fine," Susan reassured him.

Finally, able to speak again, Yvonne spoke up. "Um, who's Morty?"

"Morty is DJ's horse," Ivy chimed in. "He's like old Mortis here, just younger."

"I've never seen DJ with a horse?" Yvonne said with obvious confusion.

"Sure you have," Bradford piped in. "I'll show you."

Bradford reached out like he was holding handlebars. He made mock kickstarting motions with his leg while making motorcycle sounds. He began to run around making engine sounds and screeching sounds as he would come to a stop before taking off again.

Yvonne just stared at Bradford for a second. "If you had told me that yesterday, I would have said you were crazy. But now, I think maybe I'm the one who is crazy."

"I know it's a lot to take in, dear," Susan said to her. "Let's go inside and get some tea."

"Okay," she responded, sounding a little shaky.

"Ladies, I have to get back," Bradford interjected. "Ivy, if I may have a word please."

Mortis shifted back to a horse and trotted out into the pasture as Bradford and Ivy walked out to the end of the driveway. Yvonne followed Susan into the house. Yvonne was looking around, trying to piece together the bits of information that her brain was actually able to retain at the moment. Yvonne was amazed at how normal this place looked. She had envisioned a dark, gloomy, and barren place for some reason.

"This is not what I was expecting at all," Yvonne said aloud.

"It does take some getting used to," Susan remarked. She looked at the front door. "I don't know why those two don't just make it official and tie the knot."

"They do seem like they really enjoy each other's company," Yvonne concurred.

Yvonne continued to follow Susan into the house, still looking around in disbelief and wonder at this place. The events so far on this night have been wild, to say the least. She was having trouble believing that she wasn't dreaming.

"DJ never has mentioned it to me," Susan said to Yvonne. "Do you take cream with your tea?"

The question caught Yvonne off guard. "Um, no, I don't think so," she stammered. "I have never tried it before. What would you suggest?"

"Typically, I go no cream, but on a crisp spring afternoon, a little cream is a nice touch."

As they entered the dining room, Ivy caught up to them. She was smiling and appeared to be blushing slightly. Yvonne watched her as she slid past her and Susan and sank into one of the dining room chairs.

"Cream with your tea, Ivy?" Susan asked.

"No thanks, Susan," Ivy answered dreamily.

"Please, Yvonne," Susan said, motioning to a chair. "Make yourself at home."

Yvonne sat down in one of the chairs at the table as Susan stepped into the kitchen to get the tea going. Yvonne rubbed her hands across the smooth polished finish. She could see the distorted reflection of her hands as they slid across the top. Yvonne leaned back in the chair and closed her eyes. She could feel her mind starting to drift off to sleep. She hadn't realized how tired she was during the events that had happened.

Yvonne's eyes fluttered as she heard Susan setting the tea kettle and cups on the table. Susan looked up at her and smiled. They both glanced over at Ivy who was just coming out of her delirium.

"What?" Ivy asked, not knowing why the two were staring at her.

Yvonne let out a giggle. "You remind me of how I used to be around Fred." Her giggle quickly faded at the thought of her husband.

"About that, Yvonne. Do you need help making the arrangements?" Susan asked her.

"Crystal was going to help me with that tomorrow." Yvonne looked around as she paused. "But I don't think that is going to happen now. I mean she can't come here. Right?"

"Not without letting her know about, well, us," Susan said. "I don't know if she knows about DJ?"

Yvonne tipped her head back slightly as she struggled to find some information in her memory. "I don't think so. I didn't." Yvonne looked at Susan with a sorrowful look. "Why didn't he ever tell me?"

"Honestly, what would you have done if he had just come up to you and said, hey I'm a walking skeleton?" Susan gave Yvonne a little smile. "Or said, hey I'm the son of the Grim Reaper?"

"You're right," Yvonne admitted. "I would have thought that he was crazy."

Ivy picked up a cup of tea and took a small sip. "Susan, how serious is this situation they are dealing with?" Ivy's lip was quivering as she spoke.

"I honestly don't know, Ivy. Torva hasn't let me know, and DJ won't say." Susan had a tender tone as she spoke to her friend. "I'm worried too. We don't need to worry about that now. Let's focus on helping Yvonne with the arrangements for Fred's service."

Yvonne gave Susan a look of gratitude. "Thank you, Susan."

Ivy piped up as she sat up quickly. "Totally off-topic for a second. Susan, could you help me make some crumpets for tea with Bradford next week?"

"Wouldn't it be easier to just pick up some English muffins?"

"Easier, yes. The same or as tasty as your crumpets, absolutely not."

This caught Yvonne's interest. "English muffins? I thought a crumpet was like a cookie."

Susan let out a small chuckle. "You aren't the only one. Most people do. They are fairly simple to make. I prefer mine with honey."

"Honey makes them so good," Ivy added. "So will you help, Susan?"

"Of course, Ivy. I will help you make crumpets," Susan told her. Turning to Yvonne she said, "Now, what still needs to be done for Fred's service?"

The next hour or so was a bit of a blur for Yvonne. They all discussed what needed to be done and what Yvonne already had accomplished. They also talked about who needed to be invited and what they could say to Crystal about why Yvonne wasn't around for her to help. They sipped tea as they discussed what needed to be done. They tried not to think about what Bradford, Death, and DJ were doing.

Yvonne let out a big yawn as she fluttered her eyes, straining to keep them open. Ivy looked like she was ready to go to sleep as well.

"Good night, you two. I'll see you in the morning." Ivy poofed out with a green flash.

Yvonne's eyes went wide. "I will never get used to seeing that."

Susan just laughed. "I'll show you to your room."

Yvonne followed Susan down the hall to a beautifully furnished room. The only thing Yvonne cared about was the huge plush bed in the middle of the room. Yvonne walked in and turned a circle to view the whole room.

"Thank you, Mrs. Deadwood. I appreciate everything that you guys are doing for me."

Susan smiled a big smile. "It's my pleasure, dear. Now get some sleep."

Yvonne rushed in and gave Susan a hug. She started to cry a little. Susan wrapped her arms around her to give her some comfort. Yvonne let go and dried her eyes and walked over to the bed.

"Thank you. Good night, Susan." Yvonne managed a smile.

"Good night, Yvonne. Sleep well."

Susan closed the door behind her as Yvonne flopped on the bed. She was completely drained both physically and emotionally. She closed her eyes. She was grateful for everything that they were all doing for her. She drifted off to sleep as she was replaying the day's events.

Chapter 24

A second later, there was another flash, and Bradford reappeared. "If I miss having tea with her next week because you get me killed, I will not be happy with you!" Bradford said, pointing a finger at Jr.

"How would this be my fault?" Jr asked Bradford.

Bradford looked at Jr, crossing his eyes. He made his voice sound like Vincent Price's. "That book you have will bring destruction to all!"

Death looked at Jr. "Let's see that book you found?"

Jr pulled out the planner from his cloak pocket. "It's Jared's planner, but it's written in code."

Bradford perked up at the mention of a code. "Code, what kind of code?"

Jr tossed the planner to Bradford. "Have a look. Pickle eating contest, some giraffe video, and a really weird grocery list. What in the world is inner head cheese?"

Bradford was looking through the planner. "Torva, have you ever seen something like this?"

Death walked over to Bradford and looked at the book he was holding. "It smells," Death said.

"What?" Bradford asked, sniffing the book. "I don't smell anything."

"You wouldn't be able to," Death sounded serious. "It smells like souls!"

Jr's eyes went wide. "What?"

Bradford looked at Death. "I agree with DJ. What? Can you elaborate?"

"Souls have a smell. It's hard to describe what they smell like." Death took the book from Bradford and peered closely at it. "The smell is faint. It was years before I could smell them. I guess it's an acquired smell."

"That's how they knew where the book was. One of those creatures told me they could smell it," Jr said.

"Um, I'm not in the soul business like you guys, so I'm a little out of my league," Bradford said. "Could you explain why or how it smells like souls?"

Death gave Bradford a look that Jr had never seen before on his dad's face. "Trust me, old friend, you don't want to know."

Bradford swallowed hard when Death said that. "If they can smell it, then we're going to have to keep it here," Bradford said. "Or take it to Purgatory."

"Having it there will do us no good," Death said. "Bradford, you're good at codes. Can you make anything out of this?"

"Why wouldn't it be good for the book to be in Purgatory?" Jr asked, a bit confused.

"Bradford can only pop in for a couple of moments at the longest, so having the book where he can't stay for an extended period makes no sense."

Bradford took the book back from Death and started to flip through the pages. His face was twisted with concentration as he tried to decipher the code. He looked at each page again and again. Flipping through the book, back and forth. He finally looked up from the book.

"This doesn't make sense. The Devil's Day is October thirtieth, but that is months away. We know whatever they have planned isn't that far in the future." Bradford looked in the book again. "This grocery list I should be able to figure out. The pickle thing and the giraffe thing though, those are going to be tricky."

"Then the book needs to stay here with you then so you can figure it out," Jr said.

Death started to pace back and forth, his hand rubbing his chin as he talked through the problem to himself. "The Devil's Day, but too far away to be the right day. What else could be the Devil's Day," Death bemused as he continued to pace back and forth.

"Dad, in the building where I found that, in one of the rooms, there is a portal. I saw a demon go into it."

Bradford slammed the book closed. "A direct path to Hell. Torva, that's not a good sign."

Death stopped pacing. "Well, I guess know we know where it's going to take place. That's not necessarily a good thing."

Jr looked at his dad. "How is that not good?"

"Direct path to Hell means bad mojo, DJ. Lots of demonic creatures come through," Bradford said. "An endless flow of adversaries. Unless we can close it."

"If we know where it's going to happen, can't we just like stake it out?" Jr asked.

Death shook his head. "No, for a couple of reasons. First and most importantly, if Lucifer is involved in this, which we have to assume considering the portal, he would detect our extended presence there, and Bradford already explained about the endless path of adversaries." Death started to pace as he continued to explain, "Also, you wouldn't be able to stay all the time. You have a job that can't be neglected. It's just not feasible, Jr."

Bradford looked at Death. "We have to break this code. Can I use your library?"

"Of course, Bradford. It's at your disposal."

Jr looked around at both of them. "What do I need to do?"

"You will have to go back home and continue your day-to-day routine," Death said. "And continue in your other duties."

"Won't those creatures come back, though?" Jr asked, sounding concerned.

Death looked at Jr. "Yes, they most likely will return to your place. But I'm fairly sure that you can handle it."

Bradford let out a laugh. "Your flip technique could use some improvement, though. You wouldn't get good scores at the Olympics with that form."

Jr shot Bradford a look. "I didn't see you joining in to help."

"The time has not yet arrived," Bradford said in a tone with mock seriousness. His face was quivering, trying to hold back a laugh. Bradford couldn't hold it back any longer. He burst out laughing.

"Both of you need to focus," Death snapped. "We have serious issues to figure out. Let's get back to the issue at hand."

Bradford was looking in the book again. "This list, the grocery list. I think if we work on it while DJ works on the pickle and giraffe thing, we could solve this quickly."

Death stood there rubbing his chin in thought. "Yes, I think that would be best."

"How am I supposed to figure out what a pickle eating contest and giraffe video are?" Jr asked bluntly.

"Isn't there a library where you live?" Bradford asked with a grin.

"Sure, I can just look up pickle contest is code for what? I'm no master of the Dewey decimal system, but I'm fairly positive that it won't be in there." The sarcasm was oozing out of Jr's comment.

Death jumped like a thought just slammed into him. He snapped his fingers. "Fate," he exclaimed.

"What about her?" Jr asked.

Bradford caught on to Death's thought. "Torva, you're a genius."

Death chuckled. "I know, but thanks for noticing."

"How is she going to be able to help?" Jr asked, not making the connection.

Death looked over at Jr. "She cuts the threads. She should know."

"Well, let's go then," Jr said.

"You won't be going, Jr," Death said. "You will need to go back home, plus she's not a big fan of visitors."

Jr wasn't looking forward to going back home, especially since he had to clean and repair his apartment. "The sooner we finish this, the sooner I can get back to normal."

"Normal, unfortunately, Jr, no longer exists." Death gave Jr a quizzical look. "You have friends that know your true identity now. It can never be back to normal."

Bradford walked up to Jr pulling out his watch. "Look at the time." Bradford chuckled. "Time to go."

He reached out and grabbed Jr's shoulder. There was a brilliant flash, then Bradford and Jr were standing back in Jr's apartment. Bradford walked over and took the pomegranate and hourglass off the top of the plastic fruit.

"I can't believe that your mom still had this." Bradford turned to look at Jr. "I know how you're feeling right now. I can't guarantee anything, but I know your dad. He knows how you feel about Claire. He won't stop until this is finished."

"Thanks, Bradford."

Bradford gave Jr a serious look. "Don't tell anybody I said that. I'm supposed to be the funny one."

There was a flash, and Jr was standing in his apartment alone. He glanced around his apartment. It was in complete disarray. Jr let out a sigh and went and grabbed his broom to start cleaning up.

Chapter 25

Jr grabbed the broom out of the closet and a garbage can. He started down the hall toward his room when he noticed the big caved-in section of the wall from where he had been thrown.

"Well, that sucks," Jr said, a bit irritated. "Maybe Josh knows how to do drywall repair."

Luckily that was the only major damage. Jr was in the middle of sweeping the hall when there was a knock on his door. He glanced at his phone.

"Two thirty a.m. Who would be here this late?"

Jr walked to the door. Not knowing what to expect, he prepared for anything. Jr opened the door and was shocked to see Detective St. Claire.

"Oh, Detective. What brings you here at this hour?"

He flashed the typical cop smile. "I was on this side of town working on a case, so I figured I would stop by. May I come in?"

"Sure," Jr said, stepping aside and gesturing for Detective St. Claire to enter. "I wasn't expecting you until this afternoon."

"I know," the detective said as he glanced around the apartment. "I apologize for the hour. Honestly I'm surprised that you were up. Since I'm already here, do you mind if I look around now?"

"Couldn't sleep, so I was doing some reading."

"Anything interesting?" Detective St. Claire asked.

"Not really. I'm sure it wouldn't interest you," Jr responded.

Detective St. Claire was wandering around the apartment when he stopped in front of the couch. He pointed at the blankets spread out on the couch. "Do you have company?"

"Had company," Jr said. "A friend, who just lost her husband, was staying. She's not here at the moment."

"Does that big dent in your wall have anything to do with her leaving?" Detective St. Claire's voice sounded serious.

"No," Jr stated coldly. "Please, Detective, have a look around."

"You know, Mr. Deadwood, this building is known for having a lot of trouble. Parties, fights, and that sort of thing. You ever involved in those?"

"I don't drink but have had some problems with Dan and his jerkwad friends." Jr wasn't pleased with this line of questions.

"I thought you told me earlier at your shop that you had never met any of the group, the Devil's right hand?"

"That's right," Jr was curious where he was going with this.

Detective St. Claire again flashed the cop smile. "So you're telling me that you didn't know your friend down the hall and Mr. Miginus are part of that club."

Jr's eyes went wide. "No, I didn't know that."

Jr started running through everything he had learned in the past few days. It was all starting to make sense. What wasn't making sense was why the detective was pushing the issue so much. Jr thought he might be able to get some information from the detective.

"Detective, have you ever been to a pickle eating contest?"

St. Claire gave Jr an odd look. "No. Planning on entering one?"

Jr laughed at the question. "No. I wasn't even sure they existed."

"If I hear of one, I'll let you know," the detective said. "Mind if I look in this room back here?" he asked as he headed for Jr's bedroom.

"Be my guest, Detective."

Detective St. Claire gave a nod as he headed down the hall. He entered Jr's room and walked around the perimeter slowly. He opened the closet, looked under the bed, and opened a couple of drawers in Jr's dresser. Finished with his look around, he came back out in the hall.

"Mr. Deadwood, the Devil's right hand is a bad bunch of people. They won't hesitate to kill somebody. I would advise that you stay away from them." The detective's face showed obvious concern for Jr's safety.

"Thank you, Detective, I'll keep that in mind," Jr said with a smile.

"Good night, Mr. Deadwood," the detective said. "Thank you for your time."

Detective St. Claire walked out of the apartment and headed out. Jr went back to cleaning up from the demon attack that had happened earlier. He finished sweeping and bagged up the trash. Jr took the bag of trash and walked out of his apartment. He made sure he had his key before he locked the door. He picked up the bag and headed down the hall. As he was passing Claire's apartment, he once again felt the chill of evil air coming from inside. He shivered as he walked by. He walked outside and headed across the parking lot toward the dumpsters.

He flipped open the lid, startling a raccoon. It took off in a hurry, hissing at him as it went passed. Jr shook his head and tossed in the bag of garbage. He turned and was headed back toward the door when he heard a woman screaming down the street. He tilted his head to figure out the direction that it was coming from. He heard the scream again, but this time it got muffled as it echoed down the street. Jr started down the street in the direction the scream came from. As he got closer to the alley, he could hear a struggle.

"No, no, get off me!" a woman was screaming.

"Shut up you…" The resounding smack of a slap drowned out any other words that had been spoken.

Jr rounded the corner and saw a man straddling a woman on the ground. She was screaming and struggling to get from underneath him. He was yelling at her and hitting her. She had blood on her face, and her clothes were ripped. Jr's blood instantly started to boil.

"HEY!" Jr screamed at the man.

The man snapped his head around. Jr started toward the man. His fists and teeth clenched. The man slapped the lady again. He quickly drew out a gun and fired three shots. All three shots hit Jr dead center of the chest. The man didn't even watch to see if Jr went down. He returned his attention back to the woman. He grabbed the woman's blouse and ripped it open. The woman was screaming as Jr walked up. She saw Jr. Her eyes went wide, and her throat closed off.

"Excuse me, I think you dropped these," Jr said, extending his hand.

The man turned his head. He was looking at a skeleton hand holding three bullets that looked like they had hit a steel plate. The man's face went rigid, and his complexion went pale. Jr reached down and grabbed the man and picked him up by his head. The woman scrambled out from underneath the man. Jr looked at her.

"Go and get looked at. There's a hospital ten minutes from here."

The woman managed a weak thank you before she took off down the street.

Jr brought the man's face close to his. The man saw his bare skull, and his body began to tremble. The man's breathing became shallow and rapid.

"You're not on the schedule for tonight," Jr growled at the man. "Know that when that day comes, I will know what you've done since tonight. If you continue in this lifestyle, next time we meet will not be pleasant for you."

Jr let the man go. He fell to the ground, scrambling away. He staggered to his feet and dropped his gun, shaking profusely. Jr took a step toward the gun. The man let out a gasp as some of his motor skills were returning. The man had turned as white as Jr's sun-bleached skull.

"You need to leave," Jr said to the man.

The man was frozen in fear again. Jr wasn't in the mood to deal with this. He reached into his cloak and pulled out his scythe. He smacked the butt on the ground. The blade snapped out instantly. The pale light in the alley gave the blade an eerie glow. A small, weak sound escaped the man's mouth as he turned to run away. Jr walked up to the gun and reached down to pick it up. He put his scythe away as he retrieved the gun.

"Can't leave this out here."

Jr stuck the gun in his pocket and turned to walk back to his apartment. Morty pulled up to the end of the alley as Jr approached.

Jr walked around to the driver's side and got in. Morty started down the street.

"Where are we headed?" Jr asked.

"Beijing."

"What? China?"

"Yes, an unfortunate string of events is unfolding," Morty said.

Morty lifted off and phased out.

Chapter 26

The sun was already getting low on the horizon when they got to Beijing.

"Did we skip a whole day?" Jr asked, sounding befuddled.

"No, Beijing is fifteen hours ahead of us," Morty responded as he was coming down in an alley away from the busyness of downtown.

As they drove down the street to where they needed to be, Jr marveled at the architecture of the buildings. He saw the little houses on the outskirts of the city. He remembered from school that these were called Minka. He always wondered why they had curved roofs. He would have to ask somebody about that. The woodwork was amazing. He looked up ahead and saw a pagoda. It was a tall one, four stories. He looked out farther and saw the Forbidden City. The ancient palace of Emperor Chengzu.

"That thing is huge," Jr marveled.

"Nine thousand nine hundred ninety-nine rooms," Morty said. He paused for a second. "And a half room also."

"That's a lot of rooms. I would hate to have to clean all those."

They turned and headed away from the Forbidden City. They headed into a busy part of town and slowed to a stop. Jr looked around and didn't see anything out of the ordinary—or so he assumed; he had never been to China. Jr got out and looked around.

"Are you sure this is the right place, Morty?"

"Yes, DJ, I'm positive."

Jr looked around, feeling a bit confused. Jr's attention was caught by the sounds of screeching tires and scraping metal sounds coming down the street. He heard people scream as they scattered off the streets. Others were honking their horns. Jr looked down the street at the commotion. It looked like complete chaos. The car was swerving back and forth, smashing into cars on both sides of the street, smashing on doors and bumpers, windows shattering from the impact, and glass flying everywhere.

He heard a woman screaming frantically. He looked and saw a woman scouring the sidewalks for something and not finding anything. She was running back and forth, spinning around, looking in every direction. She was hollering something that Jr couldn't make out. He heard her scream it over and over.

"*Wo de baobei, wo de baobei?*" she screamed.

"What is she saying?" Jr asked nobody in particular.

He concentrated as hard as he could on the words. He heard them in his head.

My baby, my baby?

The words sent a chill down his spine. He scoured the road and saw a toddler trying to cross the street to its mother. She couldn't get across from all the people running to and fro. Jr saw the car careening down the street and headed straight for the toddler. Jr was at least fifty yards from the child.

"Oh no," he uttered.

Jr shot down the street at the speed of a bullet. He had to get there in time. He didn't care if it was her soul he was supposed to collect. He couldn't let her get hit by that car. He made it to the child in less than a second. The car was only a couple of feet away when Jr got to the child. He slid to the child, wrapping her up in his arms as he turned his back to the out-of-control car.

The impact was enormous. It made Jr stumble forward a few steps. The sound of crushing metal and broken glass was deafening. He saw the broken glass and twisted metal shoot past his body. Smoke and dirt were flying all around. He glanced up and saw the car flipping over his body. Sailing through the air, upside down, smashed and mangled looking. It landed with a loud crash and the sound of the remaining glass exploding out of place as it slid to a stop on its roof.

The street went eerily quiet. Jr looked down at his arms. The little girl was looking up at him with tear-stained cheeks but otherwise unharmed. Her little eyes were wide as she looked at Jr. He could hear people starting to whisper on the streets.

"*Sishen! Sishen!*" They were all saying.

Jr looked for the mom of the child, the woman who had been screaming for her. Jr saw her, and their eyes met. She was holding her hands to her face. Her entire body was trembling. He scooped the child up and started walking toward the mom.

"*Sishen!*" she spoke.

The word sank into Jr's mind.

Grim Reaper!

He could see the fear in the faces of the people on the street, especially the mother of the child in his arms. He stopped directly in front of the mother. He handed the child to her. As she reached out for her daughter, a wave of relief and tears overwhelmed her. She broke down sobbing as she held her child tight in her arms. He turned and started toward the car. Murmurs were echoing down the street as people watched in shock and suspense at the events unfolding in front of them.

Jr reached the car. His nose wrinkled at an overpowering smell. He saw at least eight bottles scattered about the car. They all read, *Baijiu*. Jr could tell by the smell that they were alcohol. He looked at the man in the car. He was unconscious and bleeding profusely from the head. Jr pulled out his scythe as he looked at the man.

"When are people going to learn that alcohol and vehicles don't mix?" he said as he shook his head.

He tapped the butt of his scythe handle on the ground. The blade sprang out. He reached in with the tip of the blade and gently pulled out his soul. It looked splotchy in color. He stood up and smoothed it out. It didn't hesitate long after he gave it a toss. It sank quickly to the ground. Jr grimaced as he watched it sink. He knew what awaited the man down there. It wasn't a pleasant thought.

The people were still gathered in the street—all staring at him. He wasn't sure if they were able to see the soul as he collected it or not. He turned and headed for Morty, slowly turning invisible as he walked over. He must have lost his invisibility when he saw the child in danger. That had made his heart skip a beat. Jr was glad that she was going to be okay. Jr opened the door and sat down. He leaned his head back as he closed the door. The rush of adrenaline and emotions wearing off.

His phone alerted him of a text. He pulled it out of his pocket and looked at it. It was from his dad.

"You did well tonight. It wasn't her time. It won't be for a long time."

That made Jr smile slightly. At least he hadn't screwed up the schedule or anything like that.

"Let's go home, Morty," Jr said, leaning his head back again.

Morty started down the road slowly. The woman and her child where still standing on the sidewalk as Morty got close. He pulled to a stop and rolled down the window and used a bit of his talent to make Jr visible to only her. She saw Jr, and her mouth dropped open.

"*Xiexie, xiexie!*" she exclaimed to Jr.

Jr gave her a smile and nodded his head. "You're welcome."

Morty started down the road again, rolling up the window as he went. The ambulance and first responders where now arriving at the scene. Jr was sure that they would have an unbelievable story told to them. Morty increased his speed as they phased out and lifted off. Jr was glad to be heading home. Hopefully he could get a few hours of sleep before he had to get up for work.

A few moments later, they were coming back down near the apartment. As they landed, Jr resumed his day-to-day attire of flesh and clothes. Morty completed phasing back in as they rounded a corner a block away from the parking lot. As they pulled into the parking lot, Jr let out a sigh.

"Thanks, Morty," he said. "I couldn't do this without you."

"You're welcome, my friend. It will always be my pleasure."

Jr got out and walked toward the door. He could almost hear his bed calling his name. He walked in the door and saw Claire sitting outside her door, reading. He assumed it was her Bible. He could see her lips moving as she read and could her the melodic sound of her voice but couldn't make out the words. She looked up and saw Jr and gave him a smile. Her smile seemed to light up the surrounding area. It had a radiant glow that made Jr feel warm inside. He smiled back at her. She closed her book and put it back in the planter. She stood up and met Jr as he walked up.

"Can I walk you to your door?" she asked with a shy-looking smile.

"What about Dan?" Jr inquired, not wanting to cause her any extra grief considering what she was going to have to suffer through.

"Oh, he had a whole bottle to himself tonight. He's not going to wake up for a while."

"In that case, I'd love it if you would walk with me."

The started down the hall toward Jr's door. As they were walking, Claire reached over and grabbed Jr's hand. His heart swelled as she did this, and he felt a little dizzy. He looked down at their hands linked together and then up at her. She smiled and gave him a wink. They got to Jr's door and stood there for a moment. Jr didn't want to go inside yet. Claire leaned forward and kissed him on the cheek.

"Dan's leaving town tomorrow for a few days," she started. "Do you think that we could go get something to eat tomorrow evening?"

Jr's face exploded into a huge grin. "I'd love to."

"Great," she said, smiling her radiant smile at him again. "Call me when you get home tomorrow."

She handed Jr a piece of paper. He looked at it for a second. "Do you know where he's going?" Jr asked a little hesitantly.

"Not completely," she said with a quizzical look in here face. "He said something about a giraffe. He did mention something about the house in Amityville. Why do you ask?"

"Just call it morbid curiosity. I'm sorry, I shouldn't have asked." Jr needed to know where he was headed and why.

"I can't wait to get away from him. He's been getting more violent lately." As she was talking, her eyes were getting moist with tears. "I'm getting scared, DJ."

Jr stepped in and gave her a hug. It was killing him that they couldn't take her to Purgatory to keep her safe. He was going to get her out of this, somehow.

"Try to stay strong, Claire."

She looked up at him and gave a weak smile. It wasn't the same radiant smile she had just had. She perked up on her tippy toes and gave him another kiss on the cheek. "Good night, DJ."

She turned her head a bit and gave him a quick kiss on the lips. That sent Jr's world spinning once again.

"Good night, Claire."

Claire turned and headed back to her apartment. Jr leaned back against his door, trying to get his head to level out and stop spinning so he could unlock his door. He watched Claire walk down the hall. He had to find a way to stop Dan. He unlocked his door and stepped inside halfway, expecting to see Yvonne on the couch. Jr walked over to the bowl of plastic fruit and put the pomegranate and hourglass on top. He glanced at the clock; it was 3:30 a.m. Time for some shut-eye. He went into his room and pulled out his phone. He texted Josh: "Late start tomorrow, start at nine, I'll explain later."

He set an alarm on his phone for eight. Hopefully, he will hear and wake up on time. He stripped off his cloak and flopped on his bed. He was out as soon as his head hit his pillow.

Chapter 27

Jr blinked wildly trying to get his eyes to adjust to the light. A few seconds later, his vision began to come into focus. He heard a sound rushing toward him from behind. He whipped around ready to fight whatever was coming at him. Jr stopped as he realized what it was. He saw a ram running past him down the hill. Jr recognized where he was. He was on the hill from his dream from before. Jr could hear the commotion on the other hill again. There were the same flora and fauna he had previously seen here. Jr started down the hill toward the other hill, again. As Jr neared the top of the other hill, he was overwhelmed by a sense of fear and uncertainty. He knew what he was about to see but still had trouble believing that his dad would shed a tear. Jr crested the hill and saw the crowd across the way. Again, they were jeering the three people hanging on the cross, especially the man on the middle cross. Jr knew this was Jesus—the same Jesus he had seen in Heaven.

Jr looked across and again saw his dad standing behind the four women and the man at the base of the cross. The sky was rapidly getting dark, and the scene appeared to be playing at an incredible speed. Suddenly it slowed in speed as Jesus threw His head back.

"It is finished," Jesus said.

There was a brilliant flash of lighting followed by a huge clap of thunder that once again made Jr jump. Jr looked across at his dad and saw a single tear roll down his cheek. Death stepped forward from behind the women and the man who were all crying tears of grief and agony. Jr watched as his dad slowly walked toward Jesus's limp body on the cross. Death stood there motionless for a moment, then slowly, he reached forward with his scythe. The blade of the scythe paused for a moment before passing through the flesh of Jesus. The blade shimmered as it entered his body. Jr watched as Death slowly twisted and pulled the soul of Jesus from his body. The blade of the scythe didn't come out with the cobweb-like substance that Jr knew should have been there. Instead, it pulled out a thick black tarlike substance. It oozed off the tip of the blade and plopped to the ground. It seeped into the ground. Jr jumped as his dad threw his head back and let out the most grief-stricken cry Jr had ever heard.

Jr shot out of bed like a rocket, shaking like a leaf and sweating bullets. His breathing was heavy and rapid. The sound that his dad had cried out at the sight of Jesus's soul descending instead of floating up toward Heaven had sent Jr into a panicked state. Jr glanced over at the clock. It was five in the morning.

"I've got to get some sleep," Jr uttered to himself.

He walked over to his cloak and pulled out the piece of paper that Claire had given him. He pulled it out and unfolded it. It was Claire's phone number written with little hearts floating around it. That made Jr smile. Little hearts floating around was the way his head felt every time he was around her. At the bottom of the page was a little note: "And the blood of Jesus, His son, cleanses us from all sin" (1 John 1:7).

Jr sat there, staring at the note for a minute or two. His mind was bouncing back and forth from the words on the note and what he had seen in his dream. How could Jesus's soul be that black? If He was supposed to cleanse us of our sins, then how could he have so many? Jr couldn't seem to wrap his head around the whole situation.

"What am I missing?" Jr asked himself.

Jr got up and started to pace back and forth in his room, mad with himself for not knowing what was going in in his head. What did these dreams mean? What was he missing?

Jr.

Jr spun around, instantly pulling out his scythe. He was shaking. He hadn't heard anything other than his name. No footsteps, no door swinging in or out, nothing at all but his name. Jr closed his eyes for a second, trying to calm his nerves and clear his head, as well as try to sense, well, anything. There was nothing there.

Read the book.

Jr spun around again, completely around, full circle. He saw nothing. He stood there motionless except for his eyes. They were darting back and forth, scanning every inch of his room, looking for anything that was out of place. His breathing was quick and shallow. A small drop of sweat was starting to form on his forehead.

"What is going on?" Jr grunted.

He continued to scan his room for anything that seemed out of place. He concentrated on calming his breathing. Slowly in, slowly out. He knew he had heard his name. Was it audible or in his head? A few minutes later, Jr was still motionless, but his breathing had settled. Convinced that he was alone, he slowly relaxed. Jr put his scythe away and looked around his room again. He saw Claire's phone number on the floor by the door. He walked over to it and picked it up.

"The book?" he questioned himself as he read the quote at the bottom.

Jr walked toward his front door as he invoked his invisibility, and he phased halfway out. He walked through his door and down the hall. He got to Claire's door and was standing at the planter. He reached down and picked up her Bible. He looked at it while he held it in his hands. Something about reading this without her permission just felt wrong. He put it back in the planter. Jr was about to return to his apartment when he glanced over at her door.

Jr's vision went blurry as he stepped through the door. Everything seemed to have a dark hue to it, like a shadow was trying to take over the surrounding area. He noticed that the shadow hue wasn't entering the living room area. It stopped at the threshold of the door. It looked like it was trying to grab and claw its way into the living room. The sight sent a chill down Jr's spine. How could an inanimate object such as a shadow act like this?

Jr walked to the living room and looked in. His breath sucked in. He was standing on the threshold and could see what the shadow was trying to grab. Claire was sleeping on the couch. She was wearing a pair of shorts and a T-shirt. Jr noticed bruises on her arms and legs.

A lot of bruises. They were fresh and deep, turning purple and dark brown. Jr's anger started to grow. He could feel his eyes starting to glow, and his fists were clenched. He could hear the shadow whispering but wasn't able to make out the words.

Jr walked to the couch and looked at Claire for a minute. He reached down and brushed her hair behind her ear. Jr leaned forward and kissed Claire on the forehead.

"I love you, Claire," Jr whispered.

Claire gave a small sigh and smiled. Jr heard muffled voices coming from the back of the apartment. He looked at Claire again before he headed toward the voices. He walked down the hall and stopped at the door farthest from the living room. Jr could tell that the person talking was Dan. Jr was having trouble making out the words. He slowly passed through the wall a few feet away from the door. Jr froze. Dan was talking with the demon Jr had seen at Jared's place.

"Dan," the demon started. "You can't be so violent with Claire. If she is injured or killed before the day is here," he paused for a second and then let out a small chuckle, "well, let's just say that our lord will not be pleased."

A wave of fear washed over Dan's face. "You don't understand," Dan pleaded. "She wouldn't stop struggling."

"I don't care!" roared the demon. "And neither does our lord Lucifer. He has chosen her for this purpose. Therefore, you must find something or someone else to satisfy your urges." The demon glared at Dan. "She must not be completely broken in spirit. She must be far enough along in her misery to want to die but not willing to do it herself. She must want death to come so that the offer to be released from her pain by becoming our lord's bride will be accepted. She must believe that it is her escape from the pain." He gave Dan an even crueler stare. "She must never suspect that in doing so, she will be willing to allow our master to ravish her soul for all eternity." He chuckled an evil chuckle.

Dan started to protest only to be silenced with a backhand from the demon. It took everything Jr had to not chuckle. The demon looked around, scanning the room for a second. Satisfied that no one was there, he turned his attention back to Dan.

"Silence," the demon shouted at Dan. "Why do you think that he has let you have her for as long as you have? To get her to that point, not beyond it." The demon paused for a moment, making sure Dan was going to follow orders. "Get the items you require in New York. Do not fail!"

The demon turned and started to walk toward the wall. He snapped his fingers as he walked, and a pentagram that Jr hadn't noticed before started to glow. He vanished as did the pentagram when he passed through it. Dan started to rub his face, trying to ease the sting of the backhand. Dan started to pace around the room, grumbling to himself.

"I don't care what he says. If she doesn't do what I want, I'll beat her if I want to." Dan smiled as those words came out of his mouth. "And if she doesn't give me what I want, well, let's just say I'll have a lot of fun getting it from her." Dan laughed maniacally saying those words.

Jr's anger flared when he heard Dan say that. He instantly pulled out his scythe. He froze, unable to move, unable to speak. What was going on? Why couldn't he move? Jr's eyes darted around. He noticed Dan wasn't moving either. Bradford! Jr struggled as hard as he could to move. He wanted to scream in anger but couldn't utter a sound. There was a flash to his side.

"DJ, you really need to calm down." Bradford was looking at Jr with an intensity that Jr wasn't ready for. "I will unfreeze you in a second. Do not try to kill Dan!"

Bradford pulled out his watch and clicked the button. Jr felt his muscles ease from being frozen in place. He slowly lowered his scythe. Jr shot him a look of anger and confusion at Bradford. His anger intensified from the feeling of betrayal from someone he had come to consider a friend. Jr turned to look at Dan. He could feel his eyes glowing again. The only thing he could think about was taking all his anger and rage out on Dan.

"What makes you think you can stop me?" Jr growled at Bradford.

"I won't need to," Bradford said. There was a dark flash next to Dan. "He will."

Jr looked over and saw his dad standing next to Dan. His eyes were glowing as well.

"Jr, I know how you feel. Hearing him talk about doing those evil and vile things to her makes my blood boil too." Death was looking at Jr with empathy. "We both have to control our tempers, though. We're too close to finishing this to let it get away from us now. We can't let evil win."

Jr looked at his dad for a second. He dropped his gaze to the floor as he put his scythe away. "What do we do then?"

"We stop them when they try to set evil loose on earth!" Death's tone was serious.

Chapter 28

Bradford stepped forward. "Gentlemen, if you're ready."

He looked at Death and Jr. They both gave a nod. Bradford pulled out his watch and clicked the button. Jr felt his head spinning and started to get woozy. A second later, they were still in the same room, but Dan was no longer there. Jr looked around the room. He could still smell Claire's perfume in the air.

Death stepped toward his son. "We saw the sign. What have you learned?"

Jr looked at his dad. "Claire told me Dan is leaving town tomorrow and going to someplace called Amityville."

Death and Bradford looked at each other.

"Well, that's not good," Bradford said without his normal jovial sound.

"What's the deal with Amityville?" Jr asked, not knowing the backstory.

"Let's just say bad things happen there," Bradford responded.

"Did Claire mention why he was going there?" Death questioned.

"No, but when I came over here, I overheard Dan talking with a demon I have seen before at Jared's place. He looks almost human but really burned looking."

"Sinder," Death and Bradford said together.

"Who's Sinder?"

Death looked at Jr. "Pretty much the VP of Hell. He does whatever Lucifer tells him to do without question and relishes in dealing out tortures."

"A real pleasant fellow," Bradford added. "Where did he go?"

"He snapped his fingers, and a pentagram started to glow on the wall. He stepped through it and disappeared," Jr answered.

"A temporary portal?" Jr couldn't tell if Bradford had made a statement or asked a question.

Death looked at his son. "What were they talking about?"

"At first Sinder was basically scolding Dan for leaving marks on Claire and for hurting her. He said that Dan would be in serious trouble if he hurt Claire. That Claire had been chosen by Lucifer for whatever they are planning." Jr stopped for a second to catch his breath and see if his dad and Bradford were still following along. "Then Dan started to complain, and Sinder slapped him right across the cheek." A huge smile spread on Jr's lip as he replayed the moment in his head. "That was awesome. Then he told Dan to get what he was going for, and he emphasized not to fail. By the way, how did you get here so fast? It's only been a couple of hours."

"What are you talking about, DJ? It's been days." Bradford had a huge grin on his face as he spoke.

"No, it's only been…" Jr stopped midsentence as he realized who he was talking to.

"Did either of them mention what he was going for?" Death asked Jr.

"No," Jr replied. "Sinder just said the items he was going to get."

Bradford jumped up like somebody lit a fire under his feet. "The list," he shouted. Death and Jr just looked at him confused. "The weird grocery list in Jared's planner." Bradford dug around in his pocket for a second. "Look," he said as he pulled out the planner. "Listen to the list. Artichoke hearts, kidney beans, liverwurst."

Jr's eyes snapped wide just like a bomb went off in his head. "Oh man. Hearts, kidneys, livers. How did I not see that before?"

"None of us did, Jr," Death said.

"Torva, there's only one place he would be able to get these items. Unless he was going to kill somebody." Bradford wasn't smiling at all when he spoke.

Death's tone was low. "I know."

"What are you two talking about?" Jr didn't have a clue where you could get these items.

"Did they say anything else?" Bradford sounded urgent when he spoke.

"No, but Claire said that Dan mentioned something about a giraffe in Amityville."

Bradford's mouth fell open. "I know what the giraffe video is a reference to."

Death and Jr both looked at Bradford. Their expressions were obvious. "Please explain!"

Bradford caught the hint. "Oh, right. Look." Bradford pulled out a pad and a pencil and started to draw a rough sketch of a giraffe. "If you look at this," he said as he continued to draw. "The head of a giraffe roughly resembles the head of a goat, and the neck could be the blade."

He finished his sketch as he showed it to them. Off to the side of the giraffe sketch, Bradford also had sketched a knife. It was a long curve blade that arched back and forth. The handle was adorned with a goat's head atop a humanlike torso. It looked like the handle was carved from bone, and the goat head was gold.

"What is that?" Jr asked.

"It goes by many names. It's best known as Cupio Me Daemonia or the Devil's Desire." Bradford gave Death a look. "Torva, this is serious stuff."

"I know, Bradford." Death was staring at the sketch.

"What did Fate say? Does she know when this is happening?" Jr asked, hoping to get some positive news for a change.

"No, Jr." Death's tone sounded fraught with concern at the event's ambiguity. "She couldn't tell. Claire's thread is blurry and unable to see when it is slated to end."

Jr looked at his dad with disbelief. "How is that possible?"

"We know that Lucifer has his hands in this. That's the only explanation." Death was looking directly at Jr when he spoke.

"So what do we do then?" Jr asked.

"You'll have to tail Dan to Amityville," Bradford said. "That's the only thing we can do."

Jr looked at Bradford. He knew that they had to find out when this was going to happen. Jr's thoughts turned to Claire. The way she looked. The way she smiled at him. The way he felt when she kissed him. How her hugs seemed to warm his entire body. Her perfume scent still hung in the air, barely detectable. Its scent tugged at Jr's nasal passages. He closed his eyes for a second to help his brain stop swimming.

He opened his eyes and looked at both Bradford and his dad. "Let's get a plan together."

"Do you know when he is leaving?" Death asked his son.

"No, Claire didn't tell me. I would assume earlier in the day," Jr paused as he tried to hold back a smile spreading across his face. "She wants to go get something to eat tomorrow after work." He couldn't control it any longer. The thought of being on a date, so to speak, with Claire made a smile explode across his mouth.

Bradford had a huge grin on his face. "Torva, do you see that? Your boy is smitten."

Death looked at Jr with an unchanging expression. "You can't let your emotions get in the way. Keep your head about you, Jr."

"I will, Dad," Jr added.

"Bradford, do you think you could pop around and find out when Dan leaves and when he gets to Amityville?" Death asked.

Bradford just grinned and with a flash; he disappeared.

Death walked over to his son. "I have a feeling that the pickle contest mentioned in that planner is of importance."

"What could that even mean, though?" Jr had a look of confusion trying to figure out what a pickle eating contest could even have to do with human sacrifice.

"I don't know, Jr. I don't know," Death demurred.

Bradford popped back in with the typical flash of light. "He has a really crappy flight," Bradford said with pleasure. "He'll leave here this morning at 7:00 a.m. Then he has a really long layover in Houston. When I say long, I mean six hours long. And in Houston, talk about a bad place for a layover. Anyway, he leaves there and arrives in Amityville at eight fifteen tomorrow night."

"Jr, you will need to get on Dan's tail at the airport." Death's eyes were unwavering.

Jr had never seen his dad this way. It was a little unnerving. "I will."

A yawn caught Jr off guard. He wasn't expecting to yawn. He couldn't even remember if he had ever yawned before.

"You need to get some rest, Jr." Death walked to his son and put his hand on his shoulder. "You will need to be fully alert while you are following Dan. He will have protection with him."

"I can't, Dad," Jr protested. "I have to open the garage in a few hours."

"No, Jr," Death snapped.

Jr actually jumped. His dad had never snapped at him before.

Bradford looked at Jr and interjected, "DJ, if you get seen or tip them off that you are there, it won't end well for you or the rest of us."

"Don't worry about the shop," Death stated. "We have that under control."

Jr snorted with shock. "What, you're going to open the shop?"

Death laughed. "Not on your life. I wouldn't know how to fix those things. Why do you think Mortis stays like a horse? Besides, I can use this opportunity to do a little catching up on the schedule."

"Then who?" Jr asked, perplexed.

Bradford let out a chuckle. "We made a call. Don't worry."

"The fact that neither of you will say causes me some concern."

"Get some sleep, Jr." Death paused momentarily. "You're going to need it."

Jr was yawning again as Bradford put his hand on Jr's shoulder. Jr was so worn out that the flash as they popped to Jr's place didn't even make him squint his eyes.

"Good night, DJ. Well, it's actually morning," Bradford said, grinning. "You know what I mean, though." Bradford left with a flash.

Chapter 29

Josh was sitting at his table, sipping on a cup of coffee when Crystal walked into the kitchen.

"Late start this morning?" she asked with a slight hint of her Southern roots filtering into her accent.

Josh looked up at his wife. He smiled when he saw her pouring a cup of coffee. She was still in her pajamas, and her hair was a mess. "Yeah, DJ texted really early this morning and said we would start at nine. Don't know why yet."

Crystal walked over to the table and sat down next to her husband. She leaned over and gave him a kiss as she smiled at him. Josh smiled back at her. Crystal was originally from Georgia and had met Josh at Lake Tahoe when they were both there on vacation eight years ago. Her hair was strawberry blonde, a trait their son, Tommy, had inherited from her. In less than two years, they were married and getting ready to have Tommy.

"Maybe Yvonne was having a bad night? She was holding back yesterday. I don't think she has started the grieving process for Fred yet." Crystal reached out and squeezed Josh's hand. "I don't know how I would be if I suddenly was without you."

"I know," Josh replied. "I can't believe that Fred is gone." Josh stared at his coffee in his cup for a second before he took a sip. "They weren't married for that long either. That relationship was definitely cut short."

They looked at each other and said in unison, "Cancer sucks!"

Tommy came stumbling out of his room, rubbing sleep out of his eye with one hand, while dragging a sock monkey by the tail. He walked up to the table and crawled up in a chair. He looked up and saw his dad sitting there, and he grinned.

Tommy looked at Crystal with a smile. "Daddy's home."

Crystal reached over and ruffled his strawberry locks. "Only for a little bit, sweetie. Just has a late start today."

"Oh," Tommy said as his smile disappeared.

Crystal put her finger under his chin and raised his head to look into his eyes. "Do you want some banana pancakes for you and monkey?"

His smile returned. "Yes, please."

Crystal got up and walked into the kitchen. "Honey, do you want some as well?" she asked Josh.

"No thanks, baby. I wouldn't have time to eat. I have to leave in a couple of minutes."

Josh got up from the table and held his hand up in front of Tommy. Tommy giggled and gave Josh a high five. Josh picked up his coffee cup and took the last swallow as he walked into the kitchen. He put his cup in the sink and rinsed it out. He walked up behind Crystal as she was reaching into the cabinets to get the ingredients for pancakes. He wrapped his arms around her waist, making her give a little squeal as he hugged her and kissed the side of her neck. Josh put his head on her shoulder. Crystal rubbed the side of his head as he continued to hug her.

"You okay, hon?" she asked with the drawl that Josh loved to hear.

"Yeah," he said. "Just thinking about what Yvonne must be feeling. I can't help but be concerned about her."

Crystal turned around in Josh's arms to face him. She put her arms around his neck as she looked him in the eyes. "You're a good friend to her. I know she appreciates your empathy. But she is a strong woman, and she will be able to get through this. Especially with the help of you and DJ." She gave him another kiss. "Now go fix some bikes."

Josh let go of his wife and walked back to the table and gave Tommy a kiss on the head. "I have to leave for work, buddy. I'll see you tonight."

"Okay, Daddy," came his reply. "I love you, Daddy."

Josh smiled at those words. "I love you, too, Tommy."

Josh walked over to the closet by the front door and grabbed his helmet and jacket. He set his helmet on the table as he put on his jacket. He walked into the kitchen to grab the lunch he had made earlier and put it in his backpack. Crystal was at the stove, pouring some pancake batter onto the flat top. The smell of pancakes with fresh bananas filled the air in the kitchen. Josh smelled it and started to get hungry. He pushed the thought of food out of his mind as he finished putting his lunch in his pack. He flipped his pack around and slung it over one shoulder as he walked over to Crystal.

"Bye, babe," he said as he leaned in and gave her a kiss. "See you tonight. I love you."

Crystal smiled as she said, "I love you too. Have a good day."

Josh walked past the table and grabbed his helmet on the way to the front door. He opened the front door and walked over to the garage of his house to start his bike and head to work. He opened the garage door and heard a whimper behind him. He turned and saw the stray neighborhood dog sitting there. When Josh looked at him, it started to wag its tail.

"Hey doggy," Josh said as he started to smile. "Hold on a second."

Josh sat his backpack on the floor of the garage and put the key in his bike. It was a nice bike by most standards, not a Ducati but still nice. He has a Suzuki GSXR 1100, blue base color with white-and-red graphics on the plastic. He turned the key on, pulled in the clutch, and hit the start button. The engine fires to life. The dog stood up and walked a few feet farther away from the bike. Josh walked into the back of his garage and grabbed a dog biscuit from the box on his shelf. He turned toward the stray dog. Its tail started to wag even faster as Josh walked over.

Josh held up the biscuit. "Sit."

The dog sat down, tail still going a million miles an hour, kicking up the dust from the driveway.

"Good boy."

Josh held out the biscuit. The dog walked up and took the biscuit gently with its teeth and trotted off to eat his prize. Josh chuckled as it trotted off. He couldn't understand why DJ had a problem with that dog. He put on his helmet and backpack and backed the bike out of the garage. He closed up his garage and hopped on his bike. The weather was nice this time of year, late spring. The air was warm, and the sun was usually out. Josh headed out of his neighborhood and got on the highway and headed to the shop. Traffic wasn't bad for the time of day it was—fairly light and running smooth. He was pulling into the shop fifteen minutes later. He pulled into his parking spot and shut off his bike. He didn't see DJ's bike. He pulled off his helmet and noticed that the open sign was on.

That's odd, he thought to himself.

Josh walked into the shop area and saw somebody working on one of the motorcycles in the shop.

"Hello?" Josh said with questioning in his voice.

A mammoth of a man stood up and turned around. He was tall and fit. His skin was an off-orange color with speckles that resembled freckles all over his body. He was wearing a pair of overalls. Josh could hardly believe that he fit into them. The man stepped forward extending his hand.

"Good morning," his voice boomed. "You must be Josh. I'm Mars. Some people call me Ares, but most people just call me Max."

Josh reached out with a perplexed look on his face and shook Max's hand. Max could see the expression on Josh's face.

"Don't worry. I may be the Incarnation of War, but I'm still a nice guy." The grin on his face told Josh that he wasn't in any danger.

Still in shock, Josh managed to ask, "But isn't war bad?"

"Absolutely," Max answered. "Imagine how bad it would get if someone wasn't there to govern its progression. You humans sure have it out for each other. Never could figure out why. I mean you are all human."

Josh's expression changed when he heard that. "I guess you're right about that. We sure do fight a lot, but there is a lot of evil in the world."

"Evil's not my department. Somebody else deals with that." Max's tone and expression were stern when he said that. His expression softened. "Hope you don't mind I started early this morning?"

"Not at all," Josh said, his shock wearing off. "I thought DJ was going to be here?"

"He had some things that he needed to take care of today." Max's tone said that was all he was willing to reveal.

"You know bikes well?" Josh asked.

A smile spread across Max's face. "Oh yeah," he said. Max pointed to the helmet in Josh's hand. "What do you ride?"

Josh was a little shocked by the question. "GSXR 1100."

"Oohh, nice bike," Max said, grinning.

"What about you?" Josh asked. His interest was piqued.

Max let out a booming laugh. "Look at me. Do you really think that there is a production bike out there that would fit me? I built a custom bike to fit my, well, my rather large stature. I modeled it after the Ducati Monster 999. The motor is larger than normal like the frame. Around 6,000 cc. She's a real beauty."

Josh's jaw fell open. "Alright then," he said. Josh could hardly believe the size of that bike. "I guess if DJ trusts you with bikes, I will too." Josh was still a little dumbfounded that he was talking with the Incarnation of War. "I'm going to get changed."

Josh turned toward the locker area and took off his backpack and coat. He hung them in his locker and set his helmet on top. He was going to have to have a talk with DJ. A little warning would have been nice. He pulled on his coveralls and got ready to go to work. Josh walked back out to the work area and noticed how fast Max was moving already finishing another bike's work order. Josh's eyes almost popped out of his head as he watched Max pick up the bike he had just finished and carried it over to the staging area, pick up the next, and carry it to his work area. Josh shook his head; it was going to be an interesting day.

Chapter 30

Jr was sleeping when a knock on his door woke him up. He tried hard to blink his eyes and see his surroundings, but his eyelids felt like lead. The knock was at his door again. Jr managed to get one eye to open, barely. His other eye was refusing to open and let the surrounding light to enter. He managed to get out of bed, standing up on his feet but feeling a little wobbly. He slowly walked toward the front door, pulling on his cloak before he got there. He opened the door to find Claire standing there. Her smile made her face glow. She was wearing jeans with a T-shirt that matched her hair and jacket. Most likely to hide the bruises on her arms and legs.

"Hey, DJ," Claire started. She saw how Jr looked, and her smile faded. "Are you okay? I saw your car outside." She paused before adding, "You look exhausted!"

Jr mustered up a weak smile. "I'm fine. Just really tired." He blinked his eyes, still trying to get the grogginess out of his eyes and brain. "Would you like to come in? I could make some coffee."

Claire's smile reappeared as she stepped in. Claire turned and closed the door, then turned back toward Jr. Seeing her smile like that made Jr feel warm inside. He couldn't help but smile back.

"No coffee, thanks," Claire said as she stepped in and gave Jr a quick kiss on the lips. "I just wanted to see you this morning before I left."

His head started swimming from the kiss, but hearing those words made a wave of fear and apprehension sweep over him. "Leave? Where are you going?" Jr asked a little more quickly than he intended.

Claire giggled seeing how nervous Jr was. "I am just going to meet up with a friend of mine. Her name is Alfie. I'd really like you to meet her sometime."

Jr wasn't sure how to respond to that. "Um, okay," he managed to mumble. "Why do you want me to meet your friend?"

Claire gave Jr a coy smile that made his heart swell. "Well, if we are going to be around each other, I think you should know the people who have helped me out. Alfie is one of those people."

Jr was looking at Claire, not knowing what to say. She seemed to have that effect on him. It was like his brain would just shut down. Claire's phone went off, snapping Jr back to the moment at hand. She gave it a quick glance before she put it back in her jacket pocket.

Claire stepped close to Jr and looked directly into his eyes. "I have to go," she almost whispered. She popped up on her tippy toes to give Jr a soft kiss on his forehead. "I'll see you tonight?"

"Of course," Jr answered.

Claire reached out and grabbed both of his hands in hers. "I need to tell you something, DJ," her words were interrupted by her phone going off again. She let go of his hands as she turned to leave. "I'll talk to you tonight. I really need to go." Claire turned around, pulled out her phone as she opened the door, and walked away, typing frantically as she hurried down the hall.

Jr stood there at his door and watched her walk away. He felt his heart sinking as she walked away. He hated being away from her. His mind quickly went running, wondering what she could possibly want to talk to him about. Jr's brain was going in a thousand different directions with what Claire could possibly want to tell him. Jr's thoughts were interrupted by his phone going off in his bedroom. Jr closed the door and headed back to his room. His phone went off again.

"Must be popular today," Jr bemused.

He picked up his phone and saw two text messages. He opened up his messages. The first message was from Josh.

"A little heads up that War would be here today would have been nice!" It read.

Jr didn't have any idea that Max would be at the shop. He looked at the other text. It was from his mom.

"Go back to bed!" was all it said.

Jr figured that he better not question that order or text back. His eyelids were still filled with lead, and he was having trouble keeping them open. He walked back over to his bed and took off his cloak. He slipped back into the bed, his eyes already closing as he grabbed at the covers. He was asleep again within a nanosecond.

Jr felt like he had only been asleep for less than a minute when he felt a hand shake his shoulder. He fluttered his eyes, trying to get them to open. He perked his head a little higher as the smell of freshly brewed coffee entered his nostrils. He managed to get his eyes open and was looking into a bare skull holding out a cup of coffee.

"Wake up, Jr. You need to get ready to go to Amityville." Death set the cup of coffee on the dresser. Death turned and walked out into the living room.

Jr crawled out of bed and pulled his cloak over his head. He grabbed the coffee and took a swig as he headed out of the bedroom. He walked into the living room where his dad sat on the couch, sipping his own cup of coffee. Jr took another drink of coffee as he sat down in his chair. He was still groggy and felt tired. The coffee would help, he hoped. Jr had never felt this tired before.

Death took a drink of coffee before he spoke, "It was horrible, you know."

Jr gave his dad a quizzical look. "What was horrible?" he asked, confused.

"Watching His soul ooze of my scythe like black sludge." Death's words almost seemed to be choked off. His eyes began to faintly glow red. "We have to stop this, or else the entire world will have to feel the agony, doom, and sorrow of that day." Death's tone was solemn and unwavering.

"Dad, why were you there during that whole ordeal? Shouldn't you have only shown up when you were needed?"

Death looked Jr in the eyes. "There was extenuating circumstances during that moment."

Jr looked at his dad. "What do you mean?"

"I'll explain it to you later. Right now, we have other things to be concerned with." Death stood up and started to pace as he spoke, "You will have to be on high alert while in Amityville. There is certain to be lots of Satan's minions afoot."

"Afoot?" Jr asked with befuddlement in his voice.

"Yes, Jr, afoot." Death was giving his son an eerie look. "Around, about, circulating. Seriously, Jr, read that thesaurus I gave you."

"Sorry, Dad," Jr said as he took another drink of coffee.

Death continued, "As I was saying. There is sure to be a lot of Lucifer's henchmen around with Dan. I'm sure that he has a few just there to watch Dan and make sure he does what he is supposed to do. I'm sure that you have figured out by now that he doesn't trust anybody, nor can he be trusted."

Jr almost sprayed coffee out his nose when his dad said that. "People actually trust him? Evil incarnate."

"Not only trust. Some people pledge their lives to him and spend their entire lives trying to give him control of the entire world. This is not just some thugs trying to control a neighborhood or a street corner." Death paused from pacing and took a drink of his coffee. "We are, at this moment, the last line of defense before Armageddon."

"Armageddon? You mean the end of the world?" Jr was finally grasping the severity of the situation.

"Yes," Death answered. "That will not be a day that we want unleashed on this world."

Jr felt a cold chill wash over his body. His bones literally started to shiver. His mind was now becoming fully alert. Jr closed his eyes for a second. He saw the words flash in his mind.

"Read the book."

Jr snapped his eyes open. His dad was staring at him. A smile curled his lips as Death took a sip of his coffee.

"What?" Jr asked.

Death just smiled back at him for a second. "Don't ignore those messages you see and hear."

Jr looked at his dad with shock. How did he even know about those? Jr sat there for a second longer, pondering what the messages could pertain to. He took a small sip from his coffee before standing up.

"Let's do this," Jr said.

Death chuckled as he looked at Jr. "Slow down, son. Don't you have a date first?"

"Oh no!" Jr exclaimed. "What time is it?"

"It's ten till six," Death said. "I woke you up with a little time." Death looked at Jr for a brief moment. "I would wear something nicer than jeans and that T-shirt."

Jr looked down at himself. He shifted his clothes. He was wearing a pair of pressed dark-blue jeans and a button-down gray shirt cleaned and pressed. He looked over at his dad.

Death smiled. "You can't go out without these."

With a small poof, a bouquet of flowers appeared in his hands. He reached out and handed them to Jr. Jr accepted the flowers. It was a nice bouquet. It had roses, carnations, and some lilies—all of varying color.

"Thanks, Dad," Jr said as he accepted the flowers.

"Keep an eye on the time," Death said evenly. "You do have an appointment at eight."

Death popped out with a dark flash. Jr's expression went blank. It dawned on him like the dark flash that had just occurred. His dad had never popped in and out like he had been doing recently. He was going to ask how he was able to do that now. Jr took a deep breath to calm his nerves before he stepped out into the hall, locking his door behind him. He headed down the hall with his heart pounding in his chest. A lump was in his throat, making it hard to swallow.

Chapter 31

Jr stopped in front of Claire's door. He took another deep breath, exhaling slowly before reaching up to knock on the door. Taking a deep breath didn't help. Jr's heart was still pounding in his chest, and he felt like he was about to start sweating. He heard the sound of light footsteps behind the door. The footsteps stopped behind the door. It was a good couple of seconds before the door started to open. Jr felt like his heart was going to come flying out of his chest. The door swung open, and Jr's mouth almost dropped open when he saw Claire. Claire was standing in her doorway, looking a bit nervous and bashful. She wore a yellow sundress. The light fabric of the dress rippled as the wind from the door opening swept the cloth around her legs. Her shoulder-length hair draped around the back of her neck, sweeping over her shoulders. Jr couldn't believe his eyes.

"You look amazing!" Jr said, slightly awestruck. He remembered the flowers and handed them to Claire.

Claire's eyes went wide, and so did the smile that spread across her lips. "Thank you, DJ," she said as she took the flowers. "These are beautiful."

Jr was thinking the same thing about her. The flowers complimented her dress, causing her eyes to sparkle. Her smile was radiant as she put the flowers to her nose and took a long smell of the flower's fragrance.

"Let me put these in water before we go," Claire said as she gestured Jr to follow her into the house.

Jr stepped in, and Claire closed the door behind him. She turned around and headed toward the kitchen to get a vase and some water. Jr could feel the evil inside the apartment trying to pry into his mind. That brought him back to the reality of the literal Hell that Claire had to live in. Jr's spine started to stiffen. Jr could feel that he was starting to clench his fists. The marrow in his bones was starting to tingle with anticipation of what was to come. He heard Claire opening up a cabinet in the kitchen and turned on the faucet. Jr's eyes were darting around the apartment. The shadow that he had seen in here before seemed to be absent at the moment. Jr heard the water in the kitchen shut off.

"Are you ready to go?" Claire asked as she rounded the corner back into the foyer.

Jr quickly released his fists and forced a smile. "Yeah, let's go."

Jr opened the door and stepped out into the hallway of the building. Claire stepped out and turned to close and lock the door. As the door was closing, Jr heard a low demonic laugh come from behind the door. The sound sent a chill up and down his spine. He shuddered at the thought of what could have made that laugh.

Claire turned to face Jr. "I've been waiting for this all day," she said as she grabbed his hands. "So where are we going?" she asked.

Jr was caught off guard. He hadn't thought about where to take Claire at all. He had been so caught up with the fact that he was actually going to go out with her that he forgot about a major detail of the evening. His heart started pounding in his chest again.

DJ. It was Morty. *There is a Fifties Café not too far from here.*

Thanks, Jr thought back to Morty. "There is a Fifties Café down the road a bit. Do you want to go there?" he asked Claire.

"Sure," Claire answered. "I could go for a good burger."

That shocked Jr a little. He wasn't expecting her to be a burger fan. He stood there looking down at his hands in Claire's hands. He looked back up at her face. She had one of her cute smiles on her lips. Jr had butterflies in his stomach. He was captivated by her beauty and couldn't take his eyes off her. Before he knew what he was doing, he leaned down and kissed her on the lips. Claire let go of his hands and put her arms around his neck and kissed him back. Jr's head and heart exploded with emotions that he had never felt before. He felt dizzy and lightheaded as he wrapped his arms around her waist. The moment seemed to last for an eternity.

After a minute or two, Jr ended the kiss. "Sorry," he almost whispered.

"Don't be," Claire whispered back. Her arms were still around his neck. "We better get going, though."

Jr could feel the warmth of her breath. Their faces were only inches apart. He didn't want to let go of her. He had a wave of fear and anxiety wash over him as the thought of failing in what he had to do. He had wanted to be in her embrace for so long. The thought of her dying sent his heart down to his toes, and sorrow and anguish tugged at his heart. He forced those thoughts out of his mind. He knew he had to defeat Dan and the Devil at their scheme.

"Yeah," he said as he unwrapped his arms from around Claire. "Let's go."

He took one of her hands in his as he turned to walk down the hall. She squeezed his hand and gave Jr a wink as they headed toward the door. The sun was starting to get low on the horizon as they exited the building. It was a warm evening, and there was a gentle breeze in the air. The smells of late spring filled the air. Jr took in a deep breath as they exited into the warm evening air.

Claire glanced over at Jr. "You look really nice tonight, DJ."

Hearing that made him smile. "Thank you," he replied. "You look even more amazing than normal tonight." He gave Claire another long look as he said that.

Claire started to blush from the compliment. They got to Morty, and Jr walked around to the passenger side and opened the door for Claire. She stopped in her tracks.

"What are you doing?" she asked, seeming confused by the action.

Jr looked befuddled at the question. "Opening your door for you. Is that okay?"

"Nobody has ever done that for me," Claire said.

Jr just smiled slightly. "Chivalry is a dying characteristic."

"Thank you," she said, still a little shocked by his action. "That's really sweet of you."

Claire got in Morty, and Jr closed the door for her. He walked around to the driver's side. His heart was racing and his head still in the clouds from the kiss. He opened up his door and got in. He put the keys in the ignition and started Morty.

Okay, Morty, Jr thought. *You know the way.*

Jr put the car in gear and pulled out of the parking lot. He started down the road in the direction that Morty had indicated to him. He glanced over at Claire, still enthralled with every aspect of her. He couldn't help but let a smile cross his face.

"Penny for your thoughts?" Claire asked.

"What?" Jr responded.

"You just had a smile cross your face. Any particular reason?" She gave a smile as she asked him the question.

It was Jr's turn to blush a bit. "It's because of you," he answered a little sheepishly.

Claire reached over and put her hand on his. "DJ, there is something different about you. Something that I'm not used to."

Jr had a nervous laugh escape his throat. "I don't know what. I'm only doing what my parents taught me to do. How to treat people."

"I hope I get to meet them someday," Claire said. "It would be nice to meet the people responsible for making you as sweet as you are."

Jr blushed again at the compliment she had given. He turned the next corner and headed down the road. As they rounded a bend in the road, the audible sound of a Harley could be heard. Claire visually stiffened at the sound. Her hand pulled off his, and she slumped down in the seat. The look of fear crept across her face as she scanned the distance to find the source of the sound. Jr saw the change in her demeanor and could tell that she was frightened. His eyes darted around the area trying to pinpoint the origin of the sound. About a half a mile ahead, he saw the Harley. It was a newer Road King, nothing that Dan or his cronies would have.

"It's a newer Road King up ahead," Jr said to Claire. "Looks like an older gentleman riding it."

Claire looked around and saw the motorcycle in question. A wave of relief washed over her. Jr could visibly see the tension leaving her body. She relaxed a bit and leaned back in her seat, waiting for her anxiety to subside.

"Sorry, DJ," Claire said, sounding a little embarrassed.

"It's okay," Jr replied. "I understand." He paused for a moment, not sure if he should ask a question. He decided against asking an awkward question.

A minute later, they were pulling into the parking lot of the diner. It was a nice-looking place. It had a large neon tubing sign above the door in the classic neon pink color. The doors were in the design of an old jukebox. Just outside the door, they parked an old Woody station wagon with white wall tires. Randomly parked around the parking lot were old Chevy Bel-Aires and Studebakers with the big fins above the taillights. There was a huge yellow curved arrow with flashing bulbs and a flashing neon word that read Eat. Jr found a place to park and got out and opened Claire's door for her to get out of Morty.

"Thank you," Claire said, still amazed at the chivalry Jr displayed toward her. She had never had a person treat her with this type of respect.

"You're welcome," Jr said as he extended his hand to help her out of the car.

They walked slowly from the car toward the door of the diner, holding each other's hand as they went. Jr couldn't help but let himself get caught up in the excitement of being with Claire tonight. They entered the diner and found a booth to sit in. The booth had the old-style vinyl seat cover with a white speckled Formica table with polished aluminum wrapping around the rim of the table. They sat down at the table and grabbed the menus out of the jukebox-shaped bin on the table.

A young woman wearing a pink-and-white striped skirt with a matching shirt and hat walked up to the table. She also had on a white apron with pockets for her ticket book for orders and pens. There were others wearing the same attire as this server, while other servers were wearing poodle skirts and saddle shoes.

"Hello. My name is Julia, and I'll be your server today," she said in a peppy tone. "Could I start you of with something to drink?" she asked as she pulled out her ticket book and pen.

"Could I get a strawberry shake please?" Claire asked her.

"Of course," Julia replied. "And for you, sir?" she said to Jr.

"Iced tea please?" Jr said with a smile.

"Sure thing," Julia answered. "Are you two ready to order, or do you still need a few moments?"

Claire and Jr looked at each other before Jr answered, "Could we get a few moments please?"

"Of course," Julia said with her peppy tone. "I'll get those drinks started and check back in in a few minutes."

Jr started to look over the menu with Claire. It had your typical burgers but with intriguing names. They had the Honolulu Luau burger, the Backyard Barbeque burger, the Longhorn Ranch burger, etc. The other food items were similarly named—Long Board fries, Totem Pole tater tots, Hula Hoop onion rings, and things of that nature. Jr's ears perked up as he heard a song he remembered from his childhood start to play on the overhead speakers.

"I loved this song as a kid," Jr said.

Claire's eyes went a little wide. "You know, it's an itsy bitsy tinny weeny yellow polka dot bikini?"

"Yeah. You too?"

They both started laughing at the situation. As their laughter was dying down, they both started to sing along with the chorus, which caused them to start laughing again. Julia was walking up to the table with their drinks as Jr started to dab his eyes to catch the tears that were coming out.

"Looks like you two are enjoying the evening so far," Julia said as she set the drinks on the table. "Have you two had a chance to look at the menu, or do you still need a few moments?"

Jr looked over at Claire. "I'm ready to order if you are."

Claire looked up at Julia. "Could I get the double Longhorn Ranch burger, please?"

"Of course," Julia responded. "Would you like fries or tots with that?"

"Longboard fries please," Claire answered meekly.

"And for you, sir?" Julia asked Jr.

"Could I get the same thing except with the Totem Pole tater tots, please?"

"Of course," Julia said as she finished scribbling the order down on the ticket. "I'll get this to the kitchen, and it will be out shortly." Julia turned and walked off toward the kitchen.

As Julia was walking off, Jr looked over at Claire. "What?" she asked.

Jr grinned as he looked at her. "You just ordered a half-pound burger. How does a girl as small as you manage to eat a half-pound burger?"

Claire just giggled as she answered, "It's a ranch burger."

"Yeah, but it's a half-pound burger."

Claire gave Jr the same look he was giving her. "Yeah, but my taste buds still work."

"Touché." Jr chuckled.

"You know, DJ, I noticed that you ordered iced tea. Do you ever drink anything else?" Claire inquired with a radiant smile on her face.

"Absolutely," Jr responded with his own smile. "Sometimes I drink hot tea or coffee. Even water on some occasions."

"That's not what I meant. I meant do you ever drink soda or juice or energy drinks?"

Jr wrinkled his nose at the last suggestion. "On rare occasions, I might drink a soda. I do enjoy orange juice, but energy drinks, no, thank you. Too much sugar and that sticky film it leaves in your mouth." Jr could see Claire's expression of disbelief. "What?" he asked as she looked at him.

"I thought everybody drank those!" Claire said in astonishment. "I don't think I could survive without them."

"You should try. I've discovered that the consumption of energy drinks only makes your body dependent on the caffeine and sugar that is in them, and your body doesn't rely on its natural functions of melatonin and sleep to give you the energy you need to get through the day-to-day activities that we all have to do."

Claire was looking at Jr like he had just stepped off a spaceship. "You just said a lot of words that made me cringe. No energy drinks, that's just wrong!" As she finished talking, a smile spread across her face.

Jr smiled back at her. He loved her smile. It seemed to make the whole room illuminated. He knew that it was getting close to the time that he would have to leave for Amityville. That made him want to enjoy the time left in the evening even more. He remembered that Claire had wanted to tell him something that seemed important, to Claire at least. He wasn't sure if he should broach the subject or not. The concern on his face must have been evident.

Claire's smile faded a little bit. "What's on your mind, DJ?"

Jr wasn't sure if he wanted to answer that question. He reached out to his glass of tea and twisted it, making the ice and tea swirl inside the glass. He looked at her before he slowly started to answer. "To be perfectly honest," Jr started. "You said earlier today that you wanted to tell me something and I'm a little worried that I won't like what it is that you need to tell me."

Claire's expression showed mixed emotions about his statement. Claire steeled herself and began to speak. "You know how I have a friend named Alfie? Well, she works at the crisis hotline. That's how we met actually, but since then, she has become a great friend and someone I can depend on to help me out. She has been working hard to find me a place to go to, to get away from Dan." Claire had to pause for a second to hold back the tears that were starting to sting her eyes.

Jr reached out and put his hand on hers. "Claire, I'm sorry. I didn't mean to upset you."

Claire looked up at Jr. "No, it's not you. This is just really hard to say." Claire grabbed her napkin and dried her eyes before she continued, "Alfie found a place for me to go. Unfortunately, because of the funding for their housing, there isn't anything around here that is available."

Jr's mouth dropped open, and his throat went dry. He couldn't believe what he had just heard. He quickly took a drink of his tea so he could speak. "Where is it?" he asked, knowing that anywhere would be too far in his mind. He couldn't imagine her being farther than down the hall. He didn't want to imagine that.

"You're going to think that I'm making this up," she started hesitantly. "Alfie's sister just moved to North Pole, Alaska, and has an extra room in her house that she said I could stay in until I can get a job and get on my feet."

Jr almost laughed at that. He did start to think that she was making it up. "North Pole?"

"Alaska," Claire added for clarification.

Jr could tell by her expression that she wasn't kidding. "Well, that would get you away from Dan." Jr also knew that it would take her away from him, but if she was leaving soon, that would stop Dan from trying to sacrifice her. "When are you leaving?"

"In two weeks. Alfie and I are trying to get the money for a plane ticket or a train. Whatever we can afford by then."

Jr knew that that wasn't soon enough to stop Dan's plans for the sacrifice. Their conversation was interrupted by Julia walking up, carrying two plates of food.

"Okay," she said as she walked up to the table. "I have two Longhorn Ranch burgers. Longboard fries for the lady," she said, setting the plate in front of Claire.

"Thank you," Claire said with a smile.

"And Totem Pole tater tots for the gentleman," Julia said as she set the plate in front of Jr. "Is there anything else that you guys need?"

Jr looked around the table. "Could I get some mustard please?"

"Sure," Julia politely responded. "I'll be right back with that."

Julia turned and walked away to fetch the mustard. Jr noticed that Claire was giving him an odd look.

"What?" he asked Claire.

"Are you going to put mustard on your burger?"

"Yes, and the tater tots."

"On the tots! You are an odd one, DJ. Why don't you just use ketchup?"

"Ketchup," Jr said, wrinkling his nose again. "I'm not a big fan of vinegar and sugar on my fries or tater tots," Jr responded. "If you use ketchup, I would consider you the odd one."

Jr couldn't help but laugh after he said that. Claire was squinting her eyes in mock irritation as she picked up a French fry from her plate and shook it at Jr like she was shaking a finger. It was only a short moment before Julia returned with the mustard.

"There you go," she said with a smile. "Do you two need anything else?"

Claire and Jr gave each other a quick smile. "I think we're good," Jr said with a smile of his own. "Thanks."

"I'll check on you guys in a bit," Julia said as she excused herself from the table.

Claire and Jr continued their conversation and laughter as they enjoyed their meal. It only felt like a few minutes before he got a thought from Morty.

Time to go, DJ. We can't be late.

I know, Jr thought back. *Give me a minute.*

Jr was finishing the last little bit of his burger as Claire sipped on her shake. She had already finished her burger. Jr couldn't believe that she had even been able to finish it. She flashed him one of her radiant smiles as he took a drink of his tea. That made him smile back, feeling like he was dreaming this whole evening.

Julia walked up to the table. "Do you guys want any desserts or more shake?"

"No, thank you," Jr said. "Could we get our check please?"

"Sure," she said as she pulled the ticket for their meal off her booklet. "Just come to the register when you're ready."

"Okay, thank you," Jr said. He looked over at Claire. "Are you ready?"

"Yeah," she said as she slid out of the booth.

Jr got up and picked up the bill. As they were walking toward the front, Claire reached over and grabbed Jr's hand, intertwining her fingers with his as she leaned her head over on his shoulder and let out a comforting sigh.

"Thank you, DJ," she said as they continued to walk. "I haven't felt this happy in a long time."

"You're welcome, Claire," he responded. It gave him a twinge of grief knowing that she wasn't happy normally.

As they approached the counter, Julia gave them a smile from behind the register. "How was everything?"

"It was wonderful," Claire piped up. "And the food was good too."

Jr's head snapped to the side when she said that. She shot him a huge smile as Julia let slip a slight giggle from behind the counter. Jr could feel his face turning red. After a brief second, Jr remembered why they were standing at the counter. He handed the bill to Julia and pulled out his wallet. He handed her enough to cover the bill plus a decent tip.

"Keep the change," he said as he and Claire turned to walk out.

"Thank you," Julia said with a smile. "Please come again."

Jr held Claire's hand as they slowly walked out to where Morty was parked. Jr knew that he had to get to Amityville, but he didn't want this moment to end. He loved Claire, and he loved being around her. He looked over at her as they got to the car. He opened the door for Claire so she could get in.

"Always the gentleman," she said as she put her hands on his chest and gave him a quick kiss on his cheek.

Jr couldn't help but smile from that. He could get used to being kissed by her, he thought to himself as he closed the door after she sat down. He walked around to the other side of the car feeling like he was floating. He got in and put the keys in the ignition. He started Morty and pulled out of the parking lot and headed for their building. Neither of them said much as they drove back. Claire was sitting in the passenger seat with a slight smile on her face. She seemed to be truly happy at the moment. The drive only took them a few minutes.

Don't take too long, DJ, Morty thought to him as they pulled into the parking lot.

I know, Jr thought back.

Jr got out and walked around to open the door for Claire. He helped her get out and they walked toward the door. They walked slowly as they walked toward Claire's door. They looked at each other as they came to a stop in front of Claire's apartment.

"Do you want to come in for a few minutes?" Claire asked as she put her arms around his neck.

She looked him in the eyes for a second before she leaned out and kissed Jr. He felt his knees go weak as he closed his eyes.

Jr! Focus!

Jr heard his dad's voice loud and clear in his mind. He snapped his eyes open and stepped back from the kiss. *"I wish I could,"* Jr responded.

He heard his dad again. *Say you have to go help your mother.*

"I promised my mom that I would stop by tonight," he continued. "I have to get over there."

"Okay," Claire said. "Can I see you tomorrow?"

"I really hope so," Jr said. "Good night, Claire."

"Good night, DJ," she said as she gave him another quick kiss. She opened her door and stepped inside.

Jr stood there and looked at the door for a second. He wasn't sure how he was feeling at the moment. His mind and heart were going at a million miles an hour. He loved how she made him feel, but at the same time, he was anxious and nervous about what was about to happen.

"I love you, Claire," Jr whispered as he turned to walk away. *"I will stop this!"*

As Jr turned to walk down the hall, he heard his dad again. *Come to your apartment.*

Chapter 32

Jr headed toward his apartment, wondering how he was hearing his dad. Jr walked into his apartment to the smell of fresh-pressed tea. Jr's head tilted up as he smelled the air. He heard the sound of conversation coming from his living room. He peeked around the corner to see his dad, his mom, and Yvonne sitting in the living room.

"Please, let yourselves in and help yourself to my tea," Jr said with semiseriousness.

"Hey, DJ," Yvonne said as Jr walked into the living room.

"You're getting a little low on tea, Jr," Death said as he handed Jr a cup of tea.

"Thanks, Dad," Jr said as he took the cup of tea. "What are you guys doing here?"

"We had to come into town so we could tell Josh and Crystal the time for Fred's service tomorrow," Susan said with a small grin. "And your tea is delicious."

Jr shot his mom a glance. He knew that she was teasing him about drinking his tea. Yvonne got up and started to walk over to Jr.

"I also wanted to give you this," Yvonne said as she handed Jr a book. "It was Fred's. I want you to have it."

Jr looked at the book in his hand. It was a Bible. The cover was worn thin, and the binding was starting to show signs of wear. Jr turned it over in his hands, wondering why Yvonne would have given him this. He opened the front cover and saw his friend's handwriting on the inside. It was a prayer that Fred had written. It was simple and to the point, asking God to guide his path and to allow him to lead his wife and friends to Jesus. It named Jr and Josh specifically. Jr's mouth fell open when he read those words. He looked up at Yvonne; she had tears starting to form in her eyes.

"Why would you give this to me?" Jr asked Yvonne.

"Because you were the one who had to collect Fred's soul. I know that you blame yourself for that." Yvonne had to stop to hold back her tears. "Fred wouldn't want you to beat yourself up about it. Neither do I." Yvonne gave Jr a small smile. "Read this and help free yourself from the guilt that you are holding on to."

Jr couldn't ever remember a time in his life when he had cried. He felt his eyes starting to sting as the tears started to form. As Jr blinked his eyes, trying desperately to stop the tears from flowing, the words he had heard the other night popped into his head. *Read the book.* He looked up at Yvonne and gave her a weak grin. Yvonne did her best to smile back as she stepped in and gave Jr a hug. As Jr returned the embrace, Yvonne burst into tears. The room fell silent except for the light sobs from Yvonne.

Susan stepped forward and gently put a hand up on Yvonne's shoulder. "We need to head back to Purgatory, dear."

Yvonne nodded as she pulled back from the hug. "Okay," she said as best as she could between sniffles. She looked at Jr. "Fred's service is tomorrow at three."

Jr gave his friend a solemn nod. "I will be there."

Susan put her arm around Yvonne's shoulders. "Let's get you back so you can rest." Susan looked over at Death. "Torva, if you would be so kind, dear."

"Of course, my love," Death said with a smile. He looked over at Jr. "I'll be back in just a minute to help clean up the tea and so we can go over some last-minute details."

Death stepped over to Susan and Yvonne. He reached out and held his wife's hand as she still had her arms around Yvonne. There was a dark flash as the three disappeared from the room.

"Dang it," Jr exclaimed. "I forgot to ask about that."

He felt the weight of the Bible in his hands. He examined the cover of it as he moved it closer to his face. It had a nice leather cover—the thick, soft leather. The cover had deep wear marks from where Fred's hands had been as he read. The corners were curled from lots of use. Jr noticed that there was a ribbon bookmark attached to the bindings. Jr opened the Bible to where the bookmark was. In the middle of the page was a couple of lines that had been highlighted. Jr read the highlighted part.

"Fear not, for I am with you; Be not dismayed, for I am your God. I will strengthen you, yes, I will help you. I will uphold you with My righteous right hand." Jr looked at where the highlighting stopped. "Those who war against you shall be as nothing, as a non-existent thing." Jr read it again. His brain was swirling around, trying to grasp his emotions. He had just read the very thing he needed at that moment. He was scared about what was about to happen. He needed to be told not to be afraid. He closed the Bible, leaving the ribbon where it had been.

Death flashed back into the room. Jr looked up at his dad. "I've been wanting to ask you something."

"Okay, what?" Death said, looking a little caught off guard.

"How are you able to do that flash thing that Bradford does now? I mean, I've never seen you do that before," Jr said as he put Fred's Bible in his cloak pocket.

Death's lips curled into a huge grin. "I couldn't before," Death said as he pulled back the sleeve of his cloak. "Check it out."

Jr looked at his dad's wrist. He was wearing a watch. The face of the watch had an outline of the Grim Reaper. One of his hands had a scythe in it. This hand pointed at the hour mark. His other hand pointed a finger at the minutes. It had three small buttons on the side of the face. Jr chuckled at the design on the face.

"Bradford thought it would help facilitate with the task at hand," Death said. "It obviously doesn't do everything his watch can do, but it does allow me to pop over to wherever in time Bradford is at the moment and get back to our correct time. Plus, it looks really cool." Death sounded more like Jr than the Incarnation of Death as he talked about the watch.

Jr was looking at Death, grinning from ear to ear, desperately trying not to laugh. He failed in his endeavor. He burst out laughing at the way his dad had been acting as he showed Jr the watch.

The grin disappeared from Death's face as he pulled his cloak sleeve back down as a glimmer of red started to glow in his eye sockets. "Now, back to the situation at hand," he said, sounding more ominous than necessary. "When you get to Amityville, you will need to be very attentive about your surroundings. Even to the supernatural realm. Dan will have demons following and protecting him."

"I know, Dad," Jr responded. "I've been reminding myself to be cautious and attentive."

Death gave Jr a serious look. "Bradford and I have been seeing a lot of increased activity at Jared's place. That is a definite confirmation that his place is where the event is taking place. We just need to figure out the day. Hopefully, you can find that information out when you are in Amityville."

"I know," Jr agreed. "I'm hopeful that we can find out all the information we need to finish this."

Death gave Jr a quizzical look. "You seem less worried about this than I assumed you would be right now."

Jr gave a half laugh. "No, I'm still worried. Extremely worried. I'm just not afraid right now."

"That's good," Death demurred. "Fear can cause you to hesitate or make snap judgments that can lead to disastrous outcomes." Death walked over to Jr and put his hand upon his shoulder. Looking Jr directly in the eyes, he spoke, "Be careful out there, son."

"I will, Dad," Jr said as he gave Death a loving tap on the upper arm.

"It's time to get going, Jr," Death said. "Get as much information as you can without putting yourself in danger. I have to get work caught back up tonight, then get back to helping Bradford."

Death reached over to his watch and pushed one of the buttons. There was a dark flash as he disappeared. Jr blinked since he was looking at his dad when he hit the button. For being a dark flash, it was still kind of bright. Jr looked around his living room and realized that they had forgotten to clean up the cups from the tea. Jr let out a sigh of exasperation as he started to grab some cups. Before Jr could grab the first cup, his front door opened, and Ivy walked in.

"Hey DJ, you need to get going. I'll take care of the cleanup," she said as she stepped through the door.

"Oh, hey, Ivy. I wasn't expecting you," Jr said slightly startled.

Ivy let out one of her giggles, causing the green highlights in her hair to shimmer in the light. "You wouldn't have been. Your mom texted me and let me know that your dad and you probably would forget to clean up." She paused for a moment as she gave Jr a look. Her deep-green eyes filled with concern. "You two do have a lot to deal with right now."

"Thanks, Ivy," Jr said, filled with a little relief about the mess.

Jr headed for his front door. As he passed where Ivy was standing, she threw her arms around Jr, squeezing so tight Jr again thought his ribs were going to crack. Jr could tell that she was pressing the side of her face into his back. Her olive-colored arms were quivering as she held her grip around his chest.

"You better be safe out there, DJ," Ivy said in almost a whisper. She gave one last big squeeze before she let go of him.

She turned around and started picking up the cups before Jr had a chance to turn around to respond. Jr assumed that she wasn't wanting him to see the emotions that were evident on her face.

"Ivy?" Jr inquired with concern for her in his voice.

"You better get going, DJ," she said without turning around. Jr could hear the tears starting to form in her voice. "Be careful."

Jr turned to walk out the door, his heart feeling a little heavy for the worry he was causing her. She was his aunt in a sense. He had known her since he was born, and she had always been a part of his family. The gravity of the situation was becoming more evident with every passing moment. He could see that it was more than just Claire's life and soul at stake. This event was going to have a massive impact on a lot of people if Dan isn't stopped.

Jr walked down the hall with more resolve to end this evil plan of Dan's. Jr was a little cautious as he was getting ready to pass Claire's door. He didn't want her to know that he hadn't left yet. As he started past her door, he could feel time slow down. He could hear his slow breath as he exhaled with every step. The click of his boots as they hit the ground was slow and methodic, echoing down the hall. This wasn't Bradford's doing. This felt different. Jr felt a shiver run up and down his spine as he passed through a pocket of ice-cold air. His eyes darted back and forth. He heard the same demonic-sounding laugh that he had heard when he picked up Claire. It was louder and somehow sounded even more evil and vile as before.

"You will fail!" it said as he passed Claire's doorway.

Jr's heart started to race as time resumed its normal passing as he got beyond the edge of the doorway. He reached down and felt the Bible in his pocket. He remembered the words that had been highlighted on the page. "Fear not, for I am with you; Be not dismayed, for I am your God. I will strengthen you, yes, I will help you. I will uphold you with My righteous right hand." Jr felt his wave of fear starting to dissipate as he continued down the hall.

He stepped out the door of his building into the cool night air. The sky was dark and must have had a cloud cover. Jr couldn't see the stars. He walked over to Morty.

"Are you ready for this, buddy?" Jr asked.

The door opened up. "Let's go," Morty responded.

Jr got in the car and closed the door. Morty started out of the parking lot. He turned down the side street to get ready to phase out and take flight. Morty came to a sudden stop.

DJ! Morty shot to him in a thought.

Jr looked up as he saw two hellhounds coming down the road. Jr got out and pulled out his scythe. The sound of the blade springing out caught the attention of the hellhounds. They stopped in their tracks as their ears perked up, and they scanned the road for the source of the sound. They spotted Jr and snarled viciously as they leapt forward, bounding toward him—teeth glimmering in the low light of the street as they bared them in an act of aggression, saliva dripping off as they lunged forward. They darted in opposite directions, trying to get on both sides of Jr.

The situation seemed to freeze in his mind as everything he had learned from Max came rushing into his forethought. Jr felt the edge of his lips curling into a smile. He darted two steps forward, spinning his scythe like a samurai sword. He stopped just in front of the first hellhound, scythe still twirling around as he sidestepped the hellhound. The blade of his scythe went easily through the midsection of the hound. It split in two as smoke issued out of the corpse of the hound. The hair on the back of Jr's neck sprang to attention. He spun around instantaneously, scythe still spinning like a samurai sword. He caught the second hellhound with a powerful down stroke. The force of the swing sent the two halves flying off in opposite directions, leaving a trail of smoke as they sailed through the air.

The two halves hit the ground with a squishy-sounding thud. Jr surveyed the situation as the four halves of the hellhounds dissolved into wispy smoke trails. He didn't see or feel anything else in the area. Jr's attention was drawn to a red flashover by Morty. He saw Max leaning against Morty with a huge grin spread across his face.

"You remembered well," Max's mammoth voice boomed. "What's the saying? 'You've done well my little,' whatever that word is."

"Padawan?" Jr looked at Max, a little dumbfounded. "Like in *Star Wars*?"

"Let me tell you the war that's playing out in the stars right now is nothing like in the movies." Max's tone was serious, and his body language matched the tone. "Be careful out there tonight, DJ."

"I will, Max," Jr assured him. "And thanks for the training."

Max gave Jr a slight grin and a nod as his red flash made the Incarnation of War, disappear.

"We better get going, DJ," Morty reminded Jr.

"Yeah," Jr agreed as he trotted back over to where they had stopped.

Jr got back in and Morty headed down the street, phasing out and lifting off as he sped up. As they sailed through the air toward Amityville, Jr reached into his pocket and pulled out Fred's Bible. Jr flipped it open and started to thumb through the pages. He wished that he had time to sit down and actually read it. Those words, *Read the book*, kept coming to mind. As he continued to thumb through the pages, he saw some more lines that Fred had highlighted. "In God I trust; I will not be afraid. What can mere mortals do to me?" Jr was looking at those words when Morty's thought came through.

"It's not mere mortals we are dealing with, DJ," Morty said.

"I know that," Jr replied. "But I can't help but notice almost everything that I have seen, what Fred found important is to not be afraid." Jr rubbed his thumb across the cover as he pondered his words. "It's funny how it seems to be what I have been needing to hear right now."

Jr continued to thumb through the pages. As he continued scanning the pages and not really reading, something caught his eye. "For He will give His angels orders concerning you, to protect you in all your ways."

"Hey, Morty," Jr started. "Do you believe in angels?"

"Since I have firsthand knowledge of demons, it would be foolish to believe that the other end of that spectrum wasn't in actual existence," Morty answered, sounding more intellectual than Jr cared for.

"A simple yes would have sufficed," Jr said with a touch of sarcasm.

Jr could tell that Morty was chuckling in his thoughts. Jr closed Fred's Bible and put it back in his pocket. He could see the lights on a runway up ahead. Morty came down near the end of the runway and drove toward the terminals. Morty phased back in, but they remained invisible. Morty veered toward the edge of the runway as a plane came down on the runway next to them. Jr looked out the window as the plane passed them as it was slowing down. He saw Dan sitting in a window seat. His face was pale, and he appeared to be sweating. Jr could tell by the stiffness of his body that he was white-knuckle gripping his armrests.

Jr let out a laugh. "Check that out, Morty. Big bad Dan is afraid of flying."

"I bet the rest of his gang doesn't know that little bit of information," Morty replied with a chuckle of his own.

They drove next to the plane until it completed its taxi into the terminal. As the plane was waiting for the Jetway to extend out to its door, Jr got out of Morty and looked for the door leading into the gate area of the airport. Jr spotted the door and headed toward it.

"I'll be out front," Morty told Jr and drove off.

Chapter 33

Jr was standing at the gate, waiting for Dan to emerge. A stream of passengers started to funnel out of the Jetway. Dan emerged from the tunnel, walking beside him, Jr saw two demons. They looked similar to large fauns like one would see in fantasy books. They had goat heads instead of human heads. Their horns were long and spiraled out of their heads. Long boar-like tusks protrude from their lower jaws. Nobody seemed to notice the trio as they walked out to the terminal. The one on Dan's left walked directly into another passenger and passed right through her. Dan and his companions started down the terminal toward the baggage claim area. Jr heard Dan complaining to the one on his right.

"I don't know why Sinder had to send you two along." Dan was irritated with the situation.

"Sinder doesn't trust you," the demon responded with noticeable irritation.

"The least he could have done was sent Delilah," Dan groveled.

The other demon burst out laughing. "You think he would have sent Delilah? Sinder despises you. He's not going to do something that you would enjoy." He continued to howl in laughter.

Dan's face turned red with anger as he struggled to keep his composure. Jr felt a slight desire to join the demon in laughter. Dan and his demon companions continued toward the baggage claim area. Dan was clenching his fists as he walked down the corridor. The two demons continued to laugh at Dan.

"Why does Birsha want to meet at that stupid contest?" Dan asked.

"How should we know? That's where Sinder said to meet him," the demon on the left snarled.

"Come on, Tyre, you know if you could, you would join that contest," the other said.

Trye snapped his head around to look at the other demon. "Shut up, Sai, you imbecile."

Sai laughed at Tyre as they continued down the corridor. A light bulb went off in Jr's head about their names. Satyr, like in Greek mythology. They continued down the corridor and turned the corner following the signs for baggage claim. Jr rounded the corner a few seconds later and spotted Dan over by the belt waiting for his bag. Sai and Tyre were not there. Jr's senses went on high alert. He scanned the area looking for any sign of the two demons. He saw one of them on the other side of the room, going from person to person, sniffing them. Jr spotted the other one on the other side of the room, also going up to people and smelling them. The expression on their faces was unpleasant.

Dan glanced over at the one on the right side of the room. "I haven't found him," the demon growled.

Dan glanced over at the other demon. "I haven't found him either," the other demon glowered. "I did find somebody who could use a shower, though." The demon wrinkled his nose as he spoke.

Dan looked at the conveyor belt like he was waiting for his luggage. The two demons continued to go from person to person, sniffing each one as they went. Jr didn't know if they were searching for him or for somebody else. He decided to step back around the corner and watch from a farther distance. A moment later, an odd-looking piece of luggage came out of the opening for the conveyor belt and started to make its way around the conveyor. Dan walked over to the luggage and grabbed it off the conveyor. He glanced over to the two demons and gave a little nod as he headed toward the exit. The two demons slowly started to follow, looking around and sniffing the air as they went. Jr followed them out at a distance.

Jr stepped out of the airport and saw Dan and his two escorts getting into a taxi. Jr looked around and saw Morty parked off to the side. Jr walked over and got in.

"Follow that car!" Jr said as he pointed toward the taxi. Then he let out a laugh. "I've always wanted to do that."

"You watch too much television, DJ," Morty replied as he started off down the road, following the taxi.

Jr and Morty followed the taxi out of the airport and merged onto the freeway that would take them into Amityville. They continued down the freeway and took the exit and crossed over the Queensboro Bridge. Once they crossed the East River onto Long Island, the taxi ventured off into the residential area toward the village of Amityville. Jr wasn't sure where they were headed. Ten or fifteen minutes later, they turned onto Ocean Avenue. Jr remembered from a book that he had read once that the Amityville murders happened in a house on Ocean Avenue. The address used to be 112 Ocean Avenue before the city changed the address to 108 Ocean Avenue to deter tourists and others from coming to the house due to the bloody murders of six of his family members by Ronald DeFeo Jr. The Lutz family bought the house later but didn't live there long because of paranormal activity.

The taxi stopped in front of 108 Ocean Avenue. Dan and his two companions exited the taxi. The two demons started scurrying around as Dan paid the taxi driver. Morty parked a ways down the street to observe the situation. Dan walked up to the lawn of the house as the taxi driver drove off. The house was a large house, Dutch Colonial in architectural style. Dan reached the center of the yard and opened up his odd luggage. He pulled out a folded-up cloth that looked like a sheet or tablecloth. He unfolded it and spread it out on the grass. Jr noticed a huge pentagram on the cloth. Dan placed black candles on each point of the star of the pentagram. Sai and Tyre started to dance around the outer edge of the cloth on the ground. A few neighbors peeked through their curtains but retreated quickly when they noticed the pentagram. They had seen this type of activity before and wanted nothing to do with it. Ignoring it was their best defense. Dan lit the candles and stood in the center of the pentagram as Sai and Tyre continued to dance around. Dan lifted his hands to his sides and started to chant in a language that Jr couldn't recognize.

The pentagram began to glow. A red flame formed and ran around the circumference of the pentagram.

"This doesn't look good," Jr said to Morty.

"Indeed, DJ. Not good at all."

Jr watched as Dan began to chant louder and louder, raising his hands as he chanted. The red flames grew larger the higher Dan raised his hands. The flames grew to five feet in height as Dan raised his hands above his head. The eerie light from the flames illuminated the entire yard. Puffs of smoke popped behind each of the candles. Demons, much like Sai and Trye appeared behind four of the five candles. The fifth candle at the top of the pentagram, directly in front of Dan, had a huge swirl of thick black smoke and began to coalesce in front of the candle. The smoke slowly started to dissipate to reveal a large ugly demon. It stood over seven feet tall. It had shackles around its wrists with broken chains dangling from each shackle. There was another shackle around its neck also with chains hanging about. Its belly drooped over the edge of its tattered shorts. Its arms were large and muscular, a complete contrast from the rest of its overweight body. It had a blank expression on its face as it stood there staring at Dan. There was another smaller swirl of thick black smoke appearing next to Dan in the center of the pentagram. It quickly dissipated to reveal Sinder standing next to Dan.

An expression of disgust spread across Sinder's face as he faced Dan. "As much as it displeases me to do this, our lord said he wants you to have some protection." Sinder pointed to the overweight demon. "Shackle here will serve that purpose."

"What about Tweedledee and Tweedledum over here?" Dan asked with seething irritation in his voice.

Sinder's eyes narrowed to slits. The despise he had for Dan was evident. "These two will continue to accompany you to make sure that you don't screw this up." Sinder paused to make sure Dan was paying attention. "Shackle will not be with you at all times but will be nearby if needed. Try not to screw this up like you seem to do at every opportunity."

Dan opened his mouth to protest what Sinder had said but was silenced by a searing pain from a demonic backhand. The force of the hit made a resounding smack echo through the neighborhood and caused the red flames to flicker and bend from the wind.

"Don't complain to me, you sniveling putrid troglodyte! If it were up to me, I would kill you now and relish in torturing your soul for the rest of eternity," Sinder flared with rage. "You will do as you are instructed. Lucifer's patience with you is beginning to wear thin," Sinder sneered as he glared at Dan.

Dan stood there rubbing his cheek to try to ease the pain in his face. "I will do as my lord asked me. Not because you want it done."

Sinder turned to walk away. "Shackle, be on guard for this...," he paused as he glared at Dan, searching for the right word. A small evil smile cracked his lips. "This ignorant slug trail." Sinder vanished as he stepped out of the pentagram.

Shackle looked at Dan and then vanished, leaving a whisp of smoke to dissipate into the night air. One by one, the rest of the demons disappeared around the pentagram until only Dan, Sai, and Tyre were left. Dan blew out the candles and gathered up his things as he grumbled under his breath about Sinder. He folded up the cloth that had the pentagram and placed it back into his luggage.

"Let's go, you two," Dan commanded the pair of demons.

Tyre stood up with a low guttural growl. "You don't order us, you maggot. You heard Sinder."

"Fine," Dan questioned him. "What do we do?"

Tyre looked at Dan for a moment, then over to Sai. "What do you think, Sai?"

Sai just looked blankly back at Tyre and Dan.

"That's what I thought," Dan said as he walked past them. "Let's go. I have a hotel room just down the road."

The two demons started to follow Dan as he walked down the street. Jr watched as the trio left the house. He had an uneasy feeling about what he had just seen.

"Let's be extra cautious as we follow them," Jr said to Morty.

"I agree, DJ. I don't know where that big one went, but I'm sure he is around."

It only took a few minutes for Dan and his demon companions to walk to the hotel. It was a ratty run-down place that looked like it was meant for doing quick drug deals and prostitutes. Just looking at it made Jr's skin crawl. You could almost feel the evil oozing out of its walls, permeating the surrounding area with crime and rampant drug addiction. There were used needles strewn across the parking lot. Sai and Tyre seemed to be in love with the place, running up to the doors and sniffing in the aroma of disease and poverty and smiling as the scent entered their nostrils. Dan walked into the office of the hotel as Sai and Tyre continued to run around the building going from door to door. Dan walked out of the office and to a room a few doors down from it. He didn't even acknowledge the two demons running around; he just entered the room.

Jr glanced at his phone. It was almost midnight. "I wonder what time Dan will be going to gather the items?"

"I don't have a clue, DJ," Morty told him. "You had better get some rest. I'll keep watch for now."

"Thanks, buddy," Jr responded as he leaned back in his seat.

Jr couldn't get his mind to shut off to relax. He tried for a while to just keep his eyes closed but was unable to fall asleep. He sat up and pulled out the Bible Yvonne had given him. He opened it up and started to flip through the pages again. It was so thick; Jr didn't have a clue where to start. As he flipped through the pages, he noticed Fred had marked a lot of the words in a book called Psalms. Jr started to read all the pages in that book that Fred had marked up. Almost all of them told of God's protection and were words of encouragement. As he read all the verses that Fred had marked, he began to feel a sense of calm come over him. Jr wanted to know more. He did a quick Google search on his phone about where to start in the Bible. Most of the inquiries came back with the Gospel of John. Jr found it and began to read.

"DJ," Morty's thought interrupted.

Jr looked up from the Bible and saw Dan coming out of his room. Jr looked at his phone again. It was a little past 1:30 a.m. He had been deep in thought as he read and hadn't realized how much time had passed. Jr put the Bible in his pocket and watched as Dan walked over to the side of the parking lot where the light had been busted to keep it dark. There were a couple of women standing near the lamppost that Jr hadn't seen earlier. Jr could see the glow from their cigarettes as they took a drag from them. He could only make out the outlines of their bodies in the shadows. Dan walked up to them and began talking to them. Their body language indicated that they were trying to make some kind of agreement. A moment later, the two women dropped their cigarettes and crushed them out with their high heels. The three of them started to walk back in the direction of Dan's room. As they crossed the parking lot into a more lit portion, Jr could make out their clothes. They were both dressed in extremely short miniskirts with ripped stockings and blouses that barely covered anything. The material was so thin that it didn't matter what it covered; you could see right through it.

"I hope that he catches something from them," Jr said angrily.

Morty let out a chuckle. "I don't think that we are going to get that lucky."

Jr watched in disgust as Dan and the two prostitutes disappeared into his room. Sai and Tyre were outside still. They weren't running around anymore. They seemed to have gotten their fill of the scent of the disease and poverty that was abundant in the hotel. Jr watched them as they wondered around the parking lot, looking into broken-down cars with missing windows. A man who was visibly twitching emerged from a doorway a few doors down from Dan. He continuously was scratching at his neck as he looked around nervously. He was thin and pale. He looked like he hadn't slept or eaten in months. His clothes were soiled and stained. His hair was thinning and looked oily, and it appeared that he hadn't bathed in weeks. He continued to scratch his neck as he clumsily walked to the edge of the road. He was frantically checking his watch and then looking up and down the street. A car came around the corner and slowly rolled down the street. The guy started pulling wadded-up bills from his pocket and straightening them out to count. The car stopped in front of the man. He scurried up to the car and shoved the money at the guy in the car. The person in the car handed the man a tiny little package that he smelled, then clung onto like his life depended on it. He scurried back to his room to take part in his prize.

"I've always wondered how people can get that down and out and not see what's happening before it's too late?" Jr spoke aloud.

"It is sad to watch," Morty responded. "The Devil definitely has a way of getting his hooks into these people."

A few moments later, the door to Dan's room burst open. The two prostitutes came flying out of the room. Their faces were bloody. They only had on panties; the remains of their tattered see-through blouses hung loosely off their bodies, exposing their bare flesh for the whole world to see. Dan followed close behind. He came out the door wearing only his pants, screaming a slew of profanities at the women. Jr reached into his cloak and grabbed his scythe, infuriated at how Dan treated women. Prostitutes or not, they were still human.

"DJ, you can't!" Morty barked.

Jr put his scythe away. "You're right," he begrudgingly agreed.

Dan ventured no further than a couple steps out of his door. He continued to yell profanities as the women ran in fear for their lives. Sai and Tyre—filled with glee at the sight of the frightened, half-naked, beaten women—began to pursue the prostitutes. Luckily for them, they couldn't see or hear the two demons as they chased after the smell of fear. Dan went back into his room, obviously upset that he hadn't been able to finish his plans with the two prostitutes. Jr was shocked at the fact that the loud commotion hadn't attracted the attention of any of the hotel guests or the management. Unfortunately, this type of incident was all too common around here so nobody would raise an eyebrow to it.

Sai and Tyre came walking back through the parking lot, having had their fill of the smell of fear and insult from the prostitutes. They walked past a large shadow that Jr hadn't noticed earlier. He strained his eyes to see past the veil of darkness. He was able to get his eyes to focus on the dark shadow and saw Shackle sitting there motionless, patiently waiting for any adversary that might come looking to harm Mr. Martin. Jr continued to focus on the shadowy figure of Shackle. His breathing froze as he stared. It looked like Shackle was looking straight at him. Jr shook his head to get his eyes to refocus.

"Can he see us?" Jr asked Morty.

"He shouldn't be able to," Morty said, not sounding as confident of his answer that Jr had hoped for.

Jr checked the clock on his phone again—2:45 a.m. Jr saw the light in Dan's room go out. He knew he was going to sleep. That made Jr happy. He was starting to get really tired and sleepy. A yawn escaped from his mouth, catching him off guard. Jr shook his head, trying to get the grogginess out of his mind.

"Get some rest, DJ," Morty told him. "I'll wake you if you're needed."

"Good idea," Jr agreed.

Jr leaned back in the seat again. This time he had no trouble getting his mind to quiet down. He fell asleep quickly. The rest of the night was uneventful, and Jr was able to sleep well until the morning sun started to creep up over the horizon.

Chapter 34

Jr awoke to the sunlight started to creep over the horizon. He glanced around the parking lot to where he had seen Shackle the night before. He wasn't there. The rest of the parking lot was empty as well. No signs of life. It looked completely deserted. The hotel was even more dingy and run-down looking in the daylight than it had last night.

"Good morning, Morty," Jr said as he fluttered his eyes to adjust to the light.

"Good morning, DJ," Morty replied, sounding as though he had been sleeping as well.

"What time is it?" Jr asked.

"It's morning," Morty replied sourly. "I don't have the exact time."

"You know, Morty," Jr began with mock smugness in his voice. "Most cars today can tell you the exact time."

"I agree," Morty fired back with the same mock smugness. "But most cars can't go invisible, phase out, or fly at the speed of sound."

"Touché," Jr said as he chuckled. "Do you think we can find some coffee?"

"Um...," Morty started. "I can't drink coffee."

"Noted," Jr said. "I'm sorry about that. I wish you could. Do you know of any around that I can get?"

"Sorry, DJ. There is none around that I know of," Morty said, not sounding sorry at all.

Jr was in the middle of a yawn when the curtains in Dan's room slid to the side of the window. Jr could see Dan was on the phone, and his facial expressions told Jr that he wasn't pleased. Dan was pacing back and forth in front of the window. He wasn't wearing a shirt; he turned a complete circle as he paced. Jr saw all his tattoos—pentagrams, demonic little figures, and the typical naked women tattoos. As Dan made another circle, Jr saw the tattoo on his back. Jr's eyes went wide, and his blood ran cold. His eyes instantly blazed red with anger. It was a portrait-style tattoo depicting a rape scene. Jr could see every revolting detail even from the distance he was at. It had a maniacal-looking Dan laughing as he stood over a beaten, bloody Claire with tears streaming down her face, screaming in agony as she was being raped by two demons.

In a rage, Jr grabbed the door handle and tried to fly out of the car. Morty had seen the tattoo as well and knew what Jr was going to do. He locked the doors and wouldn't let Jr out. Jr let out a guttural roar as he beat his fists against the door and window, trying his best to break out.

"DJ!" Morty shouted. "You must stop!"

"Let me out, Morty!" Jr screamed.

"No!" Morty said in a more commanding tone than Jr had ever heard him use. "You must calm down!"

Jr stopped trying to get out caught off guard by the tone Morty had used. Jr closed his eyes, his body shaking with rage. He slowly opened his eyes and spoke, "Morty. Thank you. I know we have to finish this."

"DJ, I was able to read his lips for part of that conversation," Morty started. "His anger is in part for being woke up this early and because his meeting got moved up."

"Meeting with who?" Jr asked.

"Somebody named, Birsha."

"Birsha, that's an odd name," Jr said. "Do we know when he's going?"

Morty didn't have a chance to answer before a cab pulled up in front of the hotel. It honked its horn with two quick beeps. Dan came out of his room carrying his jacket as he finished a beer. He threw the can down in the parking lot as he opened the cab door and got in.

"Wow, he starts drinking early," Jr said with some shock.

Morty followed as the cab pulled out. Sai and Tyre were nowhere to be seen. Morty and Jr both knew that they and Shackle weren't very far away. Dan's cab headed out toward the freeway. After a brief travel on the freeway, the cab pulled off into a suburban neighborhood. It wound its way back to a large park. The cab came to a stop at the park entrance. Jr's eyes popped out as he read the huge banner. "Amityville First Annual Pickle Eating Contest." Jr stared in utter surprise for a moment before he could speak.

"The pickle eating contest wasn't a code?" Jr's voice sounded pitchy from the surprise.

Morty also sounded befuddled as he responded, "It would appear not."

Dan got out of the cab and put on his jacket. He handed the cab driver money for the fare. He turned and started toward the park, looking less than pleased as he went. Dan continued looking around as he ventured farther into the park.

"Looks like I'm on foot," Jr said as he exited the car.

"DJ," Morty said, sounding concerned. "Keep your, cool and be careful."

"I will," Jr replied with a small grin.

Jr followed Dan as he went to the center of the pickle eating contest. Dan approached the middle of the contest area and began to scan the surroundings. A very large sinister-looking man approached Dan. Jr was too far away to hear as the two exchanged some words. The sinister-looking individual pointed off in a direction, indicating where he wanted Dan to go. The two of them set off in the direction where he had pointed. Jr sped up to keep sight of them as they rounded a corner. Jr turned in time to see Dan and the other person step into a door off to the side. Jr approached the doorway cautiously. He could hear the two talking as he approached.

"I don't know why Sinder insisted that the organs be in these jars?" Dan asked the sinister-looking individual.

"Sinder is not the one who insisted," boomed a large voice. It sounded as sinister as he looked. "He was just telling you what he was instructed to say. It is lord Lucifer who requires these jars."

Dan became agitated as he said that. "Yeah, whatever. You got them?"

"That depends," the sinister voice replied. "Do you have my money?"

Dan let out a laugh. "Get real, buddy. The jars first."

Jr peeked around the door to see the demeanor of the sinister-looking one change drastically.

"Goodbye, Mr. Martin," he said as he turned toward the door. "Give my regards to Sinder when you see him."

"Fine, Birsha. Here." Dan shouted as he pulled a thick envelope out of his pocket.

Birsha stopped and grinned as he turned back toward Dan. "That's more like it, Dan."

Birsha grabbed the envelope from Dan and looked inside, fanning through the bills with his thumb. After he was satisfied that the whole amount was there, he walked over to a brick wall. He placed his hands on the wall and began to chant. His chants grew louder as two small pentagrams appeared on the wall under his hands. Birsha pushed on the two pentagrams, and the wall rumbled as it slid apart, revealing a hidden cavity. Birsha reached in and pulled out a wooden box containing five ivory jars with gold lids. Each lid had a carved image of a pagan deity. Birsha handed the box to Dan so he could examine the contents. As Dan inspected each jar, Birsha reached into the cavity again and pulled out an ornamental knife.

"The Cupio Me Daemonia," Dan said in awe of the knife.

Birsha extended the handle to Dan. An evil, twisted smile spread across Dan's face as he set the box down off to the side. He took the knife from Birsha and retracted it from its scabbard. The sound of steel scraping on steel echoed in the room as Dan slid the knife's curved blade out into the light. The light bounced off the blade, throwing a light spot on Dan's face. He reached up and put his thumb on the edge of the blade.

"I wouldn't do that if I were you," Birsha cautioned as Dan was about to slide his thumb down the blade.

Dan hesitated for a second, then thought it better to heed Birsha's advice. He pulled his thumb away from the blade. Dan's attention was drawn to his hand as he noticed a drop of blood forming on his thumb. Dan blinked as he looked at the drop of blood. He brought his thumb to his mouth and licked off the blood. He chuckled as he slid the knife back into its scabbard. He slid the scabbard down the back of his pants, then covered it with his jacket. He picked up the box of jars before looking at Birsha.

"These will do just fine," Dan sneered at Birsha.

"Do not fail our master, Dan, or you may find the Cupio Me Daemonia used upon you." Birsha threw his head back in laughter. He glared at Dan for a hard moment. "Now, if you'll excuse me, I have a pickle eating contest to win."

Birsha turned and headed out the door, forcing Jr to duck out of the way. Birsha slowed as he passed Jr, looking around for whatever had made his hair stand on end. Jr was astounded that Birsha didn't see him. He had momentarily forgotten that he was invisible. A sigh of relief washed over Jr as Birsha continued to walk down the path back to the pickle-eating contest. A few seconds later, Dan emerged from the room. He glanced around before he proceeded toward the front of the park.

"I can't wait to see the look on that wench's face when I plunge this blade through her pathetic little heart." Dan chuckled to himself as he walked down the path.

Hearing that made Jr's rage flair instantly. Jr instinctively started to reach for his scythe. His mind flashed a picture of the tattoo on Dan's back. He quickly reigned in his motor skills and emotions, stopping his hand from grabbing his scythe. Jr knew that he had to stop Dan at the right time and place. He was not going to let the tattoo become a daily occurrence for Claire. Jr slowly followed Dan as he wandered aimlessly through the park. He entered the area that was holding the pickle eating contest. The event was about to begin. Dan stopped at the viewing area and looked up onto the stage. It was lined with a set up like you would see at the county pie eating contests. Instead of pies though, in front of the contestants was a large bowl filled with pickles.

A man wearing a top hat that looked like a pickle walked onto the stage. "Ladies and gentlemen, welcome to the Amityville first annual pickle eating contest. The contestants will have sixty seconds to eat as many pickles as they can," he said as he waved his hand back to sweep over the row of contestants.

Dan found a seat and sat down, holding the box in his lap. Jr stood off at a distance. Why would Dan want to see this? The only conclusion Jr could fathom was because of morbid curiosity. The man on stage wearing the pickle hat was reading off the names of the contestants. He had a huge grin when he brought out the trophy for first place. It was green and large and resembled the Lombardi Trophy, except where the football should have been was a large pickle. Jr shook his head in disbelief. Jr had to give it to the pickle hat guy; he sure had enthusiasm.

"Contestants, to the ready," shouted the pickle hat guy.

He raised a starter's pistol and pulled the trigger. A loud shot rang out as smoke shot from the side of the cylinder. The contestants on stage attacked the bowl of pickles in front of them, as an official pickle judge watched each contestant keeping a tally of how many were eaten and properly done. As soon as somebody would take the last pickle out of the bowl, the pickle judge would place a new bowl in front of the contestant. It was an extreme feeding frenzy. Jr saw Birsha starting his fourth bowl of pickles. Everybody else was only on their first or second bowl. It looked like Birsha was literally inhaling them.

The pickle-hat guy raised the pistol again and fired another shot. "Time's up, contestants," he shouted. He turned to the audience of spectators. "Ladies and gentlemen, the judges will give the official count and announce the winner in just a few minutes."

Dan, satisfied with the event, stood up out of his chair and began to head out of the park. Jr noticed and began to follow Dan. Dan meandered slowly through the paths of the park. He took a turn down what barely looked like a game trail, let alone a path for park goers. He pushed his way through the brush and sat down on an old stump. He set his box of jars down in front of him and pulled a joint from his jacket pocket. He put the joint in his mouth and lit the end, taking a deep long drag off it. The end glowed a fiery amber as he took the drag. He held the drag in his lungs for a moment before exhaling. He pulled the Cupio Me Daemonia out of the back of his pants and admired it as he pulled it from the scabbard. The joint bobbled around as he held it loosely with his lips. An evil, sadistic smile spread across his lips as the sunlight reflected off the blade.

"You better not let Sinder find out you're playing with that!" Sai said as he and Tyre stepped out from the bushes on the other side of Dan.

"Yeah," Tyre interjected. "He will kill you if that knife gets tainted."

Dan took another pull off his joint as he gave to two demons a vile glare. "I don't care what that little weasel has to say. I have the Cupio Me Daemonia, not him."

Both of the demons fell over, laughing. "We'll be sure to tell him that you said that," Tyre said, laughing hysterically.

Dan threw his joint down and stomped on it as he grabbed up his box of jars. Jr stood back and watched as the interaction unfolded. Sai and Tyre couldn't stop laughing at what Dan had said. Dan gave another glare at the two demons before he stomped off down the path. Jr was about to follow Dan when he spotted Shackle coming through the bushes in the same direction Sai and Tyre had emerged. He walked up to Tyre who was rolling around on the ground, laughing. He reached down and picked him up by the head. Tyre let out a howl of pain. Shackle chuckled as he set Tyre down on his feet and patted him on the head.

"You big oaf!" Tyre yelled at Shackle. "That hurt, and quit patting me on the head. I'm not your pet."

Shackle continued to chuckle as he lumbered down the path after Dan. Jr decided to keep a safe distance away as he followed. It took a few minutes of winding through the paths of the park before Dan was once again near the entrance to the park. He sat down on a bench and pulled out his phone. Shackle walked up behind where Dan was seated and stopped. He stood there stoically as he scanned the area in front of the bench. Jr stopped at the edge of the trees and waited as Dan sat on the bench with Shackle standing behind him.

"I don't need you babysitting me," Dan gruffed at Shackle.

Shackle just responded with a grunting sound but remained behind Dan. Jr remained where he was as well. He couldn't help but wonder what Shackle was looking for. Dan and Shackle waited for what seemed like an hour. Neither of them moved a muscle until a cab pulled up to the entrance to the park. Dan grabbed his box of jars and stood up. He looked back at Shackle and said something that Jr couldn't make out. It couldn't have been pleasant since Shackle's body started to quiver as Dan gave a sneer as he walked to the cab. Dan opened the back door to the cab and slid the box of jars into the back seat. Dan got in and closed the door as he turned to flip Shackle the bird. Shackle clenched his fists, and a blast of smoke shot out of his nostrils. Shackle faded back into the trees as the cab drove away. Jr knew he had to get to Morty and follow Dan.

Chapter 35

Jr got back to where Morty was waiting and climbed inside. "Did you see where he went?" Jr asked, hopeful that Morty would know.

Morty didn't answer with words. He shot off like a rocket, driving at breakneck speed, cutting in and out of the little amount of traffic on the road as he quickly caught up to the cab that Dan was in. Morty and Jr followed Dan around as the cab drove lazily through the town toward the direction of the sleazy hotel.

"He sure doesn't take the most direct path to his destinations," Jr noted.

"Agreed," replied Morty. "It sure doesn't seem like he is worried about paying for a cab fare."

The cab's brake lights came on as it slowed to a stop at a red light. As they waited at the red light, Sai and Tyre ran up and jumped in the cab with Dan. They weren't going to let him be unchaperoned with the jars of internal organs and the Cupio Me Daemonia. Jr noticed Dan turn his head as the two little demons jumped in the car. His expression changed from contentment to frustration. Dan was trying his hardest to ignore the two little demons. They obviously annoyed him to the most extreme sense of the word. The cab continued its lackadaisical route through the city. Jr and Morty slowed down and pulled to the curb as they watched the cab stop in front of a liquor store. Dan exited the cab carrying his box of human parts and entered the store. As Dan entered the store, the person attending the counter scurried over and locked the door, flipping the open sign over to Closed.

"What is that all about?" Jr wondered.

"Whatever it is, it can't be good," Morty responded with a hint of disdain in his voice.

"I'm going to get a better look," Jr said as he exited the car.

Jr carefully made his way his way over to the liquor store, keeping his eye on Sai and Tyre. They were still in the cab. Jr wondered why they hadn't followed Dan into the liquor store. Jr approached the window to the store cautiously. He peered through the glass and saw Dan putting a couple bottles of whiskey on the counter. Dan and the person who had locked the door were laughing as they held a conversation. The door to the back area of the store opened, and a frightened-looking woman hurried out, carrying a dress. Dan smiled as she hurried up with the garment. Dan grabbed the dress from the woman and held it up to look at it. It was long like an evening gown, shimmery gold-colored cloth with thin black lines on either side. It had a split on both sides that went up to just below the waistline. The front of the dress had a swirl shape missing in the midsection that would expose the midriff. The top was a very low-cut V shape.

"DJ!"

Jr heard the sound of Morty's voice as a sharp blow connected with his temple. Pain shot through his head as he went flying sideways. Two demonic laughs echoed through his brain as he bounced off the sidewalk. He rolled as he landed and scrambled to his feet. Sai caught Jr with a club to the head just as he got to his feet. Jr reeled backward from the blow and tried to steady himself. He kept his attention on Sai as he regained his balance. That was a mistake. Trye kicked Jr in the back of the knee, causing him to drop to his knees. Trye hit Jr in the back of the head with the butt of a huge knife. Jr's head was spinning, and his vision was going dark.

"AGAIN!" he heard Max's voice rocket through his mind.

Jr's eyes snapped open as he heard the sound of hooves striking the asphalt. Everything started going in slow motion. Jr felt the air pressure change behind him. He dropped down to his belly as the huge blade of Tyre's knife sailed across where Jr's neck had been. He rolled to his back and shot his heel toward Tyre. It struck Tyre in the chest, sending him flying backward. Jr continued to roll as he kicked

Tyre. He rolled up on his knees to see an angry, pale large horse slam into Sai, ramming him to the ground. Jr pulled out his scythe as he sprang to his feet realizing the horse was Morty. Morty began stomping on Sai harder and harder with every hoof drop. Little wisps of smoke began to issue out of Sai's body with every blow. Jr felt a tingle run up his spine. He dropped to his knees as he spun around. Sending the blade of his scythe in a quick circle. It caught Tyre in the knees. Removing both his lower legs from the rest of his body. Smoke began to billow from the stumps of his legs. Jr completed another circle as he launched to his feet. A high arcing swing removed Tyre's head and right shoulder, silencing his howl of pain as soon as it started. Jr spun around to see Morty stomp on Sai one more time, hoof connecting with head. Sai's body went limp as smoke boiled out from his skull.

"Morty?" Jr asked, confused.

"I'm sorry, DJ. I didn't see them in time," Morty said with regret in his voice.

"It's okay, Morty. I didn't see them leave the cab either. I don't understand it. How did they see me?" Jr said, perplexed.

"I don't believe that they did see you. I think that they smelled you," Morty explained.

"Are you saying that I stink?" Jr asked, shocked.

"Not in the typical sense," Morty answered. "But you do need to remember that you are the son of an incarnation, which means that you do have that type of scent."

Jr looked around at the two dead demons as he put away his scythe. Smoked issued out of all the stomp wounds of Sai as his body began to dissipate. Jr looked over at Tyre. Most of his body had already dissipated into smoke and was wafting away in the gentle breeze in the street. Jr glanced over at the liquor store and saw Dan putting the dress and the bottles of whiskey into his box with the jars and started toward the door. The woman who had brought out the dress was nowhere to be seen. She must have returned to the back of the store. The person behind the counter walked with Dan toward the door.

"We need to go," Jr said as he ran and jumped up onto Morty's back.

Morty launched into the air and galloped through the air. They made it to the top of the liquor store just as Dan and his friend exited the front door. Jr dropped off Morty's back onto the roof of the liquor store to try and listen to what the two were talking about.

"We had that robe anointed by one of the dark priests in the area," Jr heard the man tell Dan as he peered over the edge of the roof.

"Seems like a waste for such a worthless little tramp like Claire," Dan responded. "Sinder won't even let me touch her anymore. What a total jerk. I can't wait until Lucifer puts him in the chambers. On the bright side though, once her soul is in the clutches of Lucifer, I can find a new woman. You know, one who is a little less used," he said with a chuckle.

The other man gave Dan a slap on the shoulder and smiled. "She is a tasty little piece, isn't she?" He gave a good laugh before continuing, "Make sure the next one likes to fight and squirm like she does. It makes it more enjoyable."

Jr's blood boiled as he listened to these two talk about Claire like that. He could feel the heat beginning to grow in his eyes. His anger was at its boiling point, and he was clenching his fists as the rage began to course through his entire body. He felt a strong, comforting hand come down on his shoulder. Somehow he could feel its comfort, and a sense of peace came over him. He glanced over to see who it was but saw nothing. There wasn't anyone there. Morty, still in horse form, was just standing there, looking at him in bewilderment.

"Did you see anybody just now?" Jr asked.

"No," was all Morty replied.

Jr turned his attention back to Dan and his friend. They were still laughing and talking.

"Thanks for the bottle, Ed," Dan said. "It will be nice to tie one on and not have to listen to that sniveling wench."

"No problem, man. When are you flying back?"

"Tomorrow afternoon," Dan answered. "You still coming for my birthday?"

"I wouldn't miss it for the world," Ed replied.

"Can't wait to plunge the Cupio into her heart and take my place beside our lord, Lucifer," Dan began to laugh a sinister, diabolical-sounding laugh.

"See you in a couple of days," Ed said.

Dan looked around as he walked toward the cab. "Where did those two little snitches run off to?" he asked nobody in particular. "Oh well, good riddance."

Dan got in the cab with his box as Ed went back into the store. He flipped the sign back to Open as he entered the store. Jr and Morty watched as the cab pulled out and headed down the road.

Jr looked at Morty with his mouth hanging open. "We know when it's going to happen."

Morty looked back at Jr. "We need to tell your dad and Bradford."

"Agreed," Jr said as he pulled his phone out of his pocket, checking the time. It was past one o'clock. "We need to get back for Fred's funeral."

Jr climbed back onto Morty's back. Morty turned and started to gallop across the rooftop. They reached the edge, and Morty leapt into the air. His hooves continued the rhythmic beating of horses at a run. He climbed higher and higher in the air, running on literally the air that we breath. Jr grabbed onto his main and squeezed his knee tight against Morty's side. Jr hadn't ridden a horse since Mortis as a kid in Purgatory and never in the air.

"Hey, Morty," Jr shouted over the air rushing passed him.

"Yes, DJ,' Morty responded.

"We have to do this more often," Jr shouted with a smile on his face. "This is almost more fun than motorcycles."

Morty sent Jr the image of a smile. It didn't take long to make it back home due to the rate of speed that Morty was traveling. As Morty was coming down to the street around the corner from Jr's apartment, he morphed into his typical Ducati form. As he touched the road, he released the controls, and Jr felt the release. Jr leaned forward and grabbed the handlebars. A huge smile spread across his face. He hadn't ridden in what seemed like an eternity. He gave the front brake lever a quick pump as he down shifted a gear. As the front shocks rebounded from the braking, Jr twisted the throttle. Morty's front tire came off the ground as Jr gave him more gas.

"Hey!" Morty yelped. "If I had known you were going to do that, I would have changed back to a car."

Jr let out a chuckle as he brought Morty's front tire back to the street. Jr turned the corner and pulled into the parking lot. Josh's car was parked near Jr's normal spot. Hopefully Yvonne was here too. Jr pulled Morty into his usual spot and turned off the engine. He got off and started toward the door. He stopped a few feet away and turned around.

"Thanks, Morty," he said solemnly. "You saved my life today."

"A friend is always willing to lay down his life for his friend," Morty answered.

Jr smiled as he turned back toward the building. Morty truly was a good friend. Jr was glad to have him as a companion. He approached the door, trying to mentally prepare himself for the funeral of his friend—a funeral that he still felt responsible for. That was kind of ironic; he had never held his dad responsible for any of the people he had known who died in the past. Jr opened the door and walked into the gloomy hall of his building.

Chapter 36

Jr walked down the hall heading for his apartment. He stopped as he got to Claire's door and knocked. He didn't know why or what he was going to say. He just had the impulse to knock. He stood there with nervous anticipation. It grew more intense as he stood there. The seconds barely seemed to be ticking by. He gave another knock on the door. There wasn't an answer at her door. He knew that he would see her soon enough. He turned and continued toward his apartment, not sure if he was relieved or concerned that she hadn't answered.

Jr turned to walk away and stopped dead in his tracks. As clear as day, he heard a low demonic laugh and the same voice he had heard before.

"You will lose." It hissed and laughed again.

A chill ran up and down Jr's spine. His whole body shivered. He felt a comforting hand on his shoulder again. He looked over but saw no one there. The chill stopped, and a warmth of calmness washed over his body. He smiled and continued down the hall toward his apartment. He reached his door and didn't even bother trying to fish out his keys. He knew Josh was in there. Josh had had a key to Jr's apartment ever since Jr had the apartment. He barely got the door open before he had the wind knocked out of him by the head of a six-year-old.

"DJ," Tommy squealed with delight.

"Oooff," Jr gasped. "Hey, Tommy," he said, trying to catch his breath.

"Tommy, get over here," Crystal said, chasing after him. "Sorry, DJ."

"It's okay," Jr replied. He noticed Josh walking out of the kitchen with a sandwich. "Why is it every time you come over you eat something?" Jr asked.

Josh shrugged his shoulders. "I don't know." He paused to swallow the food in his mouth. "Why is it every time I come over you have extra food in your fridge?" he asked as he took another bite with a grin on his face.

Crystal walked over and gave Jr a hug before trying to pry Tommy away from him. "Yvonne and your mom said that they would meet us there," Crystal said. She paused and gave Jr a weird look. "Yvonne wanted me to ask you if Claire was going to be there. She really took a liking to that girl."

"I don't know," Jr started. "I knocked on her door just a minute ago, but she didn't answer." He paused for a second. "What was that look for?"

Crystal gave a big Southern grin. "When are you going to tell that girl?"

Jr squinted his eyes as he spoke, "Tell her what?" he asked flatly.

Crystal gave a laugh as she looked over at Josh. "You're right, babe," she said. "He does have it bad for her."

Josh grinned back at his wife. "I told you."

"What are you two talking about?" Jr snapped.

"DJ, sweetie, listen," Crystal started as she pried Tommy from his waist. "We need to talk about this," she continued, her Southern drawl really starting to show through.

"We don't have time," Jr stated. "Fred's funeral."

"We have all the time in the world," Jr heard as a bright flash appeared.

"Captain Awesome!" Tommy squealed with delight as he ran across the room to Bradford.

"Hey, Tommy," Bradford said as he kneeled down to Tommy's level. "What's up?"

Tommy started clapping his hands with delight. "Can you show me dinosaurs again?"

Bradford looked over at Crystal to get her approval. She gave him a nod. "Sure, Tommy. But remember you have to hold on tight."

Tommy jumped forward and grabbed onto Bradford's leg with all his might.

"Thanks, Bradford," Crystal said.

Bradford simply gave a tip of the hat and flashed out. Jr's eyes were wide in disbelief. His jaw dropped open as he witnessed what had unfolded in front of him. His eyes went back and forth between Josh, Crystal, and where Bradford and Tommy had been.

"What?" Crystal questioned, her Southern accent thick as ever. "You really think my husband and I don't talk? Now sit down so we can talk."

"I'll make some tea," Josh said.

Jr walked over to the table and sat down as Crystal followed. Josh headed into the kitchen and filled up the tea kettle. Jr's mind was racing, wondering what to say or how he could get out of this uncomfortable situation. He could hear Josh getting cups out of the cupboard as the tea kettle sat on the burner of the stove. The light tick sounds could be heard as the kettle heated and the metal began to expand.

"I can't find your Earl Grey tea," Josh said from the kitchen.

Jr grabbed a piece of paper off the table and wadded it up, sending it sailing into the kitchen.

Josh stared laughing. "You missed."

Crystal reached out and put her hand on Jr's. "DJ, we've been friends ever since Josh introduced us, and you have always treated me like a sister. It pains me to see you tormented like this. You need to tell her how you feel. In case things don't go well." Jr's eyes went wide. "Josh told me about what Dan is planning."

"I can stop him," Jr said flatly.

"I believe that you can. I have been praying that you will," Crystal said with a slight tremor in her voice. "I also know that the Devil is evil like no other and will stop at nothing to get what he wants."

"I know," Jr responded. "But what does that have to do with me telling Claire how I feel?"

"Just telling somebody that they are loved can change their whole outlook on things," Josh said as he came in carrying three cups and a French press filled with steeping tea. Jr looked at Josh and glanced at the press. "Hey, you always told me if you're making multiple cups to use the press, not the infuser," he responded.

Jr grinned as his friend defended his actions.

"Seems messed up to me though to use a French invention for an English drink," Josh added with mock disgust. The two of them let out a chuckle.

"Do you guys really think that is the best thing, to tell her?" Jr asked.

"Yes!" Josh and Crystal said together. Crystal added, "If nothing else, it might get her away from that slimy jerk."

"She is already working on that. She has a friend, Alfie, from the crisis hotline helping her. I don't want to tell her and have her end up staying," Jr said with genuine concern that he might screw up her chance to leave.

Josh pushed down the plunger in the press and poured three cups of tea. His expression showed that he was deep in thought. He set the press down when he was finished pouring the tea before he spoke. His normal peppy tone was gone. He sounded solemn and serious. "I see your point, DJ. I wouldn't want that on my conscience either." He paused as he formulated his next thought. "What do we do?"

Jr looked at Josh for a second. "You. Nothing, you do nothing." Jr took a sip of tea and gave a grin. "This is nice tea. Me, on the other hand"—his demeanor snapped back to a more serious type—"I fight, and I have no choice but to win!"

"Then I will fight with you!" Josh almost yelled.

There was a huge dark flash behind Jr. The Grim Reaper stood there—arms crossed with his scythe leaning against his shoulder, blade arching eerily over his head, cloak flowing with an unfelt breeze. Crystal's mouth fell open at the sight, and her face turned pale. Josh fell silent. They both now knew that Death was Jr's dad but had never seen him in his true form.

"You will do nothing of the sort, Josh," Death said in a tone that commanded obedience. "You have a wife and small child. I will not allow you to risk your life for this fight."

Josh nodded slightly in agreeance at Death's decision.

"Would you like some fresh tea, sir?" Crystal asked with a trembling voice as she pointed to the press.

Death's tone shifted. "That would be delightful. Thank you, young lady," he said cheerfully.

"I'll get you a cup, Dad," Jr said as he got up from the table.

"Thank you, Jr," Death said as he put his scythe away and sat opposite from Josh and Crystal. They sat there staring at him. "I'm sorry, where are my manners. I realized we haven't been properly introduced," he said as he extended his skeletal hand across the table. "I'm Torva."

"Nice to finally meet you, sir," Josh said, excepting the hand with a firm handshake.

"Likewise," Death said as Jr sat a cup in front of his dad.

Death reached over and picked up the press and poured a cup of tea. He watched as the steam rose as the liquid filled the cup. He picked it up, allowing the steam to fill his nostrils before he took a sip. Josh and Crystal sat in amazement at the sight of a skeleton drinking tea. The tea entered his mouth and disappeared. They both had assumed that it would have just poured out of the skeleton form sitting in front of them. A smile curled across his fleshless teeth.

"I agree with Jr, Josh. This tea is excellent," Death said. "It's not Stash brand, is it?"

"I'm not sure, sir. You would have to ask DJ. It was in a red tin," Josh said.

"Harney & Sons, Dad," Jr said. "Mom and Ivy brought it over."

"Excuse me, sir," Crystal started. "Is DJ's mom, I mean Susan. Is she...?" Crystal trailed off.

"Oh no," Death stated. "She is a mortal like you guys. And please call me Torva."

"Um, okay," Crystal responded.

"Jr," Death said as he looked over to his son. "After Fred's service, come by the house. We need to discuss what happened in Amityville."

"Sure, Dad," Jr said as Bradford flashed back in, Tommy still clinging to his leg.

"There you go, Tommy," Bradford said. "Now if you'll excuse us, Torva and I must attend to some things."

Tommy let go and ran over to his mom. "Mommy, I saw the coolest…"

Tommy stopped dead in his tracks as he noticed Death sitting at the table. Tommy looked over at him. Death's fleshless skull managed to give a wink of an eye at Tommy. Tommy smiled and continued his thought to his mom.

"I saw a T. rex and a stega, um…stego something," he said with excitement that only a toddler could have.

"That's great," Crystal said as she scooped Tommy in her arms.

Death took another drink of his tea before he stood from the table. "Don't forget to swing by later, Jr."

"I won't, Dad," Jr replied.

Death walked over by Bradford. "You have company," he said as a dark and bright flash appeared simultaneously, causing the four left in the room to blink. There was a light knock on Jr's door.

Chapter 37

Jr opened the door to find Claire standing there. She was wearing a black dress that made her look astonishing. Jr's eyes widened a bit at the sight.

"You look gorgeous," he said before he realized what he was saying. He dropped his gaze to the ground. "Sorry," he apologized.

Josh walked over and gave Jr a slap on the back. "We'll see you at the funeral, DJ."

Crystal walked over as Josh stepped outside the door. "And you, too, Claire," she added. "Yvonne asked if you were going to make it."

Josh and his family exited Jr's apartment and headed down the hall. As they were walking down the hall, Crystal turned around and mouthed the words, "Tell her," before Tommy grabbed her hand to get her attention to tell his mom more about the dinosaurs.

Jr closed the door behind them as they walked down the hall. He turned around to an unexpected kiss from Claire. Jr froze in place, his head feeling like it was going to blast into orbit. He couldn't figure out why he felt this way every time she kissed him. He felt the warmth in her breath as her lips touched his. His heart was racing again. Claire reached out and grabbed both of his hands and laced her fingers through his. Jr forced his thoughts to coalesce back into tangible form. Claire ended the kiss and stepped back but kept ahold of Jr's hands.

"Thank you for the compliment," she said sweetly. "Is it not appropriate for the funeral?" Claire asked.

"What do you mean?" Jr asked, still having trouble forming coherent thoughts.

Claire blushed a bit as she tried not to smile. "You said I was gorgeous. I don't think that is the look you should go for to attend a funeral."

"No," Jr stammered. "It looks great is all I was trying to say. It would be fine for a funeral."

"That's good," Claire said as she leaned in for another kiss.

Jr prepared for the kiss. It still took his breath away. Claire's lips were so soft and wonderful. He knew that they had to leave for the funeral but wished he could freeze time to stay in this moment for a long time. Claire placed Jr's hands on her waist and wrapped her arms around his neck. Claire's kiss was making Jr's knees weak. She pulled his head in tighter with her arms as she kissed him deeply. Jr was in absolute heaven, feeling the warmth of her embrace. The scent of her perfume filled his nostrils, causing his heart to skip a beat. Jr managed to have enough willpower to break the kiss.

"We need to get to the funeral," he said quietly. He kept his hands on her waist.

"I know," Claire said regretfully as she put her forehead against Jr's. "I hope you can give me a ride," she said with a half smile.

Jr froze for a second remembering that Morty was back in his Ducati form. Before Jr could answer, he heard Morty's thought come through. *Your chariot awaits,* Morty said with a British accent.

Jr let out a little chuckle as a smile formed on his lips.

"What's so funny?" Claire asked, a little taken aback.

"Nothing," Jr demurred. "Just a little surprised that you thought that you needed to ask," he said.

Jr opened the door and gestured for Claire to start walking out. Claire paused before she looked at the door. She reached out and closed the door. She turned to Jr, her eyes filling with tears. Jr was shocked to see her crying. She flung herself into Jr's chest and began sobbing.

"Claire, what's wrong?" Jr asked shocked.

Claire didn't answer. She just kept her face pressed into Jr's chest. He could feel the moisture from her tears soaking through his cloak. He didn't know what had happened to make her begin to cry. Jr wrapped his arms around her shoulders and held her as she sobbed lightly. Jr could feel her pulling his cloak pressing her face harder and harder into his chest. A few moments later, her sobbing eased up.

"I'm sorry, DJ," she whispered with her face still buried in Jr's chest.

"What's wrong, Claire?" Jr asked again.

She sniffled as she pulled back from Jr's chest. "Nothing," she said, feigning a smile. "Let's get going. We don't want to be late."

Jr knew from watching his parents not to challenge the issue when a woman says that nothing is wrong. Jr opened the door again, and he and Claire stepped into the hall. As the two walked down the hall, Claire reached over and grabbed Jr's hand. He looked over at her as they approached the door and could see the anxiety creep across her face. Claire stepped to the other side of Jr, putting him in between the door and herself. Jr didn't say anything, not knowing who of the Devil's minions might be eavesdropping. As they reached the end of the hall, Morty shot Jr a thought.

Heads up, we have company.

Great, Jr thought back. *Who?*

A couple of the Devil's right hand, Morty answered.

Jr opened the door and stepped out in front of Claire. He walked right into the first one of the bikers. The stench of whiskey and beer filled the surrounding air.

"Hey! Watch it, you little puke," he slurred.

He stood there staring at Jr, trying his best to intimidate him. Unfortunately for him, Jr wasn't the type who was easily intimidated. Claire stepped out of the door as the man was slurring at Jr. The other biker who was there saw Claire and spoke out.

"Where do you think that you are going, you little tramp?" he slurred angrily.

Claire froze at the unexpected arrival of two of Dan's little gang. She opened her mouth to speak, but no words came out. She was frozen with the fear of what Dan was going to do when he returned.

"We have a funeral to attend," Jr interjected. "Now if you two will kindly let us through."

The first one started to laugh. "If you don't walk away, there will be an additional funeral to attend."

Jr looked at the drunk man and smiled an eerie-looking smile. "I don't know you or like you," he stated flatly. "I won't be attending your funeral."

The other biker stepped forward and reached for Claire. "Dan said we could come over and have some fun. It's gonna be real fun now. And even more when Dan hears about this."

"Screw you, Floyd!" Claire screamed at him as she stepped back to avoid his grasp.

Floyd lunged forward, trying to reach Claire. Jr grabbed his arm and spun him around, placed a foot in the small of his back, and shoved Floyd away. Floyd stumbled a few feet before he regained his balance. The other biker lunged at Jr, pulling out a knife as he came. Jr grabbed his hand with the knife and began to squeeze. The biker's face twisted in agony as the light cracking of bones could be heard.

"I don't think the lady wants your idea of fun," Jr glowered, his eyes began to glow with anger. "I suggest that you leave."

Floyd had regained his footing and turned around to face Jr again. "You're that little twerp that Dan is always talking about." He began to laugh. "Oh, Dan is going to love to hear about this." He continued to laugh. "He might even give us a whole week with that little wench when he finds out what we are going to do to you." He pointed at Jr as he finished his sentence.

Jr stepped right up to Floyd, their faces almost touching. He stared at Floyd, anger flickering in his eyes. As Floyd received Jr's glare, his face began to turn pale, and his laughter subsided. The other biker was holding his broken hand.

"I suggest you leave now," Jr spoke softly.

Floyd didn't argue. He stumbled backward, away from Jr. "Come on, Hank," he stammered. "Let's get out of here."

The two bikers scurried away like a couple of cockroaches when the lights came on. Claire was standing there in complete silence. She had never seen any of Dan's group turn away from a fight before. Jr turned and looked at Claire. He could see the fear on her face.

"Claire," Jr started. "Don't worry about them."

Claire's eyes filled with tears as she spoke, "They're going to tell Dan." She broke into tears of fright. "He's going to beat me bad. And worse, he's going to, to…" She couldn't finish her sentence. She was overwhelmed by huge gasps in between sobs.

Jr stepped to her and wrapped his arms around her. "Look at me, Claire," he said in a tone that Claire had never heard him use before. She looked up at him. "I promise, they won't be saying a word about this to Dan."

"How can you say that, DJ?" She wailed.

Jr just smiled at her. His smile made her stop crying for a second. "Think about it," he said with a grin. "If they did, they would have to admit to Dan that they failed in killing me and hurting you. Do you really think they would do that and have to deal with the consequences?"

Claire couldn't help but laugh at the thought of that. "No," she said.

"Come on," he said, offering his arm to her to escort her to the car.

Jr walked Claire over to Morty. She put her head on his shoulder as they walked. That made Jr's heart skip a beat. He really did love her. Jr opened the door for Claire and held her hand as she got in. He closed the door and walked around to the other side and got in. Jr pulled out of the parking lot and headed toward the funeral home where Fred's service was at. Claire looked in the mirror and fished out a compact to touch up her makeup to erase the evidence that she had been crying.

A few minutes later, they pulled into the parking lot of the funeral home. Yvonne, Josh, Crystal, and Susan were standing outside. Yvonne saw Claire and walked over to the car. When Claire got out, Yvonne gave her a hug.

"Thanks for coming," Yvonne said. "I was hoping that you would make it."

Claire gave an uncomfortable smile. "I'm not sure why you wanted me here? I didn't even know Fred."

Yvonne reached out and put her hand on Claire's shoulder. "Ever since that day at DJ's apartment when we had that chance to talk, I know Fred would have wanted you here."

"Thank you," Claire said to Yvonne.

Jr walked off to the side as Yvonne and Claire continued their discussion. Jr looked around the parking lot and was shocked at how many cars were there. Fred had a lot of friends and business acquaintances. His kind nature and temperament touched a lot of people's lives. Jr turned back around and almost jumped out of his skin. Crystal had snuck up behind him, and he almost walked into her.

"Wow, Crystal," he almost yelped. "You can't sneak up on people like that."

She eyed Jr for a second. "You didn't tell her!"

"What are you talking about?" Jr knew; he just wasn't going to admit to anything.

"DJ, sweetie, look," Crystal started. "You're an idiot." Crystal gave Jr a hard look before she continued. "You're going to lose that girl. She's going to leave, and you'll only have yourself to blame if you don't tell her."

Jr looked up and noticed Yvonne and Claire walking over to where Jr and Crystal were standing. "It's time to go in," Yvonne said.

The group walked toward the funeral home. Jr felt a hand on his shoulder. He looked back and saw his dad. The Grim Reaper looked his son in the eyes and gave a slight nod and then flashed away. Jr knew what he meant. Jr couldn't blame himself for this. He paused for a second and looked up at the sky. He continued into the funeral to say his final goodbyes to his friend.

Chapter 38

Jr and his friends gathered in the viewing room of the funeral home. Yvonne was putting on a bold face. Her eyes were red-rimmed and a little puffy. The group was shown to a row of seats near the front. Jr looked around at the amount of people who had shown up for Fred's service. A minister walked up to the front of the room and did the typical start of the service. Jr didn't hear much of what he had said. He couldn't shake the feeling of immense guilt of Fred's passing. A moment later, the minister finished up and walked over to the side of the room. Josh got out of his seat and walked to the front of the room.

Josh looked out at the roomful of people and cleared his throat. "Yvonne asked if I could give a eulogy for Fred. I've never given a eulogy before, so please be patient with me." Josh shifted his weight on his feet as he continued to look around the room. "Fred Masterson was a good friend, apparently to a lot of people based on the amount of people here today."

Josh's comment caused a few people in the room to chuckle. Yvonne's bold face left, and she began to cry. Crystal reached over and gave her a hug and held her hand for support. Jr felt an unfamiliar sting coming to his eyes. Jr heard Josh sniffle.

"I met Fred a few years after high school when he and Yvonne started dating. He was a smart businessman even back then." Josh's eyes welled with tears, and he gave a half laugh as he continued. "I remember he had this crazy idea about making a pair of wings that would attach to a motorcycle. Our buddy DJ offered to be the test pilot. After a few months of designing and building, Fred finally had a pair. He attached them to the bike that DJ had at the time." Josh laughed a little harder at this point. "DJ didn't even make it half a block before those things fell off. One bounced off the back tire, the other ended up getting caught in the chain. It completely ripped off the back sprocket and messed up the chain." Josh paused to compose himself. "I was shocked that Fred wasn't upset that his wings had failed. I looked over at him, and he had a huge grin on his face. He gave me a wild look and said, 'I have great idea.' So it wasn't a big surprise when a month later, Fred told DJ and I that he was opening a motorcycle repair shop."

Josh stopped at that point to catch his breath. He was having a hard time holding back his tears. Jr reached over and gave Yvonne's hand a squeeze, hoping she didn't blame him for Fred's passing. Yvonne squeezed Jr's hand back. He glanced over at her, tears were running down her cheek as she cried quietly. The sight of Yvonne crying like that made Jr's gut tie into a knot. He could feel his face getting hot.

Josh cleared his throat and resumed where he had left off. "What was a surprise though was when he asked DJ and I to work there as his mechanics." Josh closed his eyes, and Jr saw a tear run down his cheek and pause at his chin. "Fred was a great guy to work for. He always had a smile and big ideas."

Jr looked at the tear that was stuck on Josh's chin. His eyes began to sting as his vision became blurry. Jr lost control of his body and emotions. He erupted out of his chair. The hood of his cloak flew back as red flames jumped off his bare skull, tickling the ceiling. A loud primitive yell filled with raw emotion and anguish leapt from his throat. The windows in the room rattled as his voice echoed around the room. His hand was clenched around his scythe as the echoes faded. Jr slowly realized what he had just done. He looked around the room, horrified that everyone just witness Jr in full-on Reaper mode. His eyes darted from face to face. The faces were unresponsive, frozen in time. He heard footsteps on the hard floor behind him. Jr's head snapped around. His mouth fell open, and his eyes went as wide as the full moon.

"Fred?"

Jr couldn't believe what he was seeing. Fred was walking into the room, looking directly at him. Fred's face had a warm smile as he approached Jr. His walk wasn't hurried or forced. It looked as if he was just out for a stroll.

"DJ," Fred said. "You can't blame yourself for this. It wasn't your call. You, unfortunately, were in a position where you had to do a job."

Jr's eyes welled with tears as he tried to speak, "Fred," he choked out. "I'm so sorry."

Jr saw movement to his side. His head snapped to the side, fearful that one of the funeral goers was watching. He saw his dad standing at the back of the room. The Grim Reaper looked at his son and once again gave the assuring nod before he turned and walked out. Jr looked back at Fred, unsure what the next few moments were going to hold.

"It wasn't your fault," Fred assured him. "It was the cancer and my time." Fred smiled at his friend.

Jr couldn't find any words. His throat was closed off, not allowing any sounds to escape. His eyes quivered as he stared at Fred. His heart was pounding in his chest. He could feel his thoughts swirling with anguish. Fred reached out and put his hand on Jr's shoulder. Jr's head snapped back as he saw a vision of Dan laughing manically as he looked at the Cupio Me Daemonia. Jr's eyes opened as his head slowly returned to its original position. Fred was looking at him dead in the eyes.

"You know what has to be done, DJ," Fred said sternly. "Now go do it."

Jr looked at his friend and nodded. "I will."

Fred glanced over at Yvonne. "Watch out for her for me."

Fred took his hand off Jr's shoulder as he gave him a smile. He walked over to Yvonne and gave her a kiss on the forehead. Fred turned around and started to walk back out the way he had come in. His walk was slow and unhurried like before. Jr watched as his friend slowly exited the room. Jr felt a tear roll down his cheek. His friend had given him his forgiveness about collecting his soul. Jr felt a wave of relief envelope him as he turned around. He put his scythe away and sat back down. His boney hand reached up to wipe the tear off his cheek. As he was wiping the tear away, he felt Claire's hand reach over and give his hand a squeeze. Jr realized that everyone was moving again, and he could hear Josh finishing up his eulogy. Jr glanced back toward where Fred had come from and smiled.

"Everything okay?" Claire asked Jr.

Jr looked at her with his smile. "Yeah, I'm good."

Claire leaned over and put her head on his shoulder as Josh returned to his seat. The minister returned to the front of the room and announced that there would now be an open viewing for anybody who would like to say their final goodbyes to Fred with a reception to follow in the main hall of the funeral home per Yvonne's request.

The rest of the funeral was filled with people telling stories about Fred and how he would always make you laugh. Yvonne was always talking to or getting a hug from somebody giving their condolences for her loss. She was keeping in good spirits considering the situation, which was good. Crystal was keeping close to her for the emotional support that she needed.

Jr was standing off to the side like usual. He had never liked being around a lot of people. Claire was with Yvonne and Crystal, talking and truly enjoying being part of a group. She looked over and saw Jr standing off to the side and flashed him a smile. Jr felt his face get warm as he saw her smile. Her smile had an odd effect on him; it always made him smile back, feeling like a kid with a schoolyard crush. He saw Clair reach over and touch Yvonne's shoulder and say something to her. Yvonne smiled and answered back. Claire started her way over to where Jr was standing.

"Hey," she said as she walked up.

"Hey," Jr answered back, feeling a little awkward.

"Can I ask you a favor, DJ?" Claire asked softly.

"Of course," Jr answered a little more hastily than he had wanted.

Claire looked down at her feet as she began to speak. "I'm a little worried about going home, especially since Floyd and Hank had stopped by." She continued to look at her feet as she slid one across the floor in front of the other. "Um, do you think it would be okay if I stayed at your place tonight?" she asked, not lifting her eyes from the ground.

Jr reached out and lightly lifted her chin up with the side of his hand, looking her in the eyes. "You can stay at my place as long as you want to," Jr told her. He leaned over and gave her a light kiss.

Jr noticed her blush as the kiss ended. He felt his cheeks also getting warm. "Thank you," Claire said a bit timidly.

Josh and Crystal walked up as Claire had finished talking. "Aww, look at you two," Crystal said. "Getting all cozy and kissing and stuff," she chided Jr. Claire blushed again.

"Hey buddy," Josh said, carrying a limp Tommy in his arms. "We're taking off. Tommy is a little tired as you can see."

"Alright, guys," Jr said as he gave Crystal a hug. "I'll catch up with you guys later."

Crystal leaned over and gave Claire a hug. "You," she said as she released Claire from her embrace, "need to come with Yvonne and I next week for coffee."

Claire gave Jr a quick glance. She hadn't let anybody else know that she was leaving. "I'm not sure if I'll be able to make it."

Crystal gave Claire a look before she spoke, "Well, we'll just have to try to make sure that you can." She gave Claire a smile. "I don't want to have to tell Yvonne you can't come."

Crystal and Josh turned to head out with Little Tommy asleep in his dad's arms. "See you later, guys," Jr said as they walked away.

Little by little the remaining guests finished up their stories about Fred and made their way toward the exit. Claire was holding Jr's hand and had been since Josh and Crystal had left earlier. As the final remaining guests were heading toward the exit, Jr and Claire walked over to Yvonne. She looked tired and worn out. Her eyes were red around the edges from the multiple times of crying throughout the day. Yvonne walked over to a chair and slumped into the seat.

"I am so mentally drained right now." She sighed as she leaned back in the chair.

Susan walked over to Yvonne and sat next to her. "I'm pretty sure that Ivy has a crème brûlée waiting for you."

Yvonne looked over at Susan and gave a weak smile. "That sounds delicious," she said. "And a bed directly after. That sounds amazing."

"DJ," Susan started. "I know you need to go see your dad. Why don't you give Yvonne a ride to the house, and I'll give Claire a ride back to her place?"

"Actually, Mrs. Deadwood," Claire said. "I'm going to be staying at DJ's tonight." Claire realized how that sounded and quickly added, "For safety reasons."

Susan smiled at Claire with that motherly smile that makes everyone feel safe. "No need to try to justify your reasons, sweetie. Besides, I raised my son to be a gentleman. Isn't that right, DJ?"

Jr just gave his mother a look as Yvonne dragged herself out of the chair and put her arm over Jr's shoulder to hold herself up. "I'm tired, DJ. Let's go," she said.

The four of them walked out together to the parking lot. Jr and Yvonne walked over to Morty as Susan and Claire walked toward Susan's car. As Yvonne and Jr drove off, Susan looked over at Claire.

"Let's get you to DJ's, shall we?" she said cheerfully. Claire had a look of sadness on her face. "Is something bothering you, dear?" Susan asked with a less cheerful tone.

"Mrs. Deadwood," Claire said in a whisper. "Can we talk?"

Chapter 39

Jr and Yvonne drove down the street a ways before they found a side road to turn down so that they could head toward Purgatory. They lifted off as Morty phased out. His speed increased, and within seconds, they were in a place that didn't even closely resemble earth. As they sailed through time and space, Yvonne turned in her seat to face Jr.

"DJ, what happened at Fred's service today?" she asked, looking at Jr with steely eyes.

Jr froze for a second before he tried to answer, "Um, could you be a little more specific?"

"With you is what I mean," she said. "While Josh was giving the eulogy, one second you were all tense and looked ready to cry. Then you were wiping a tear away and smiling. When I saw you smile, it gave me a sense of peace. It felt like Fred gave me a hug." A tear ran down Yvonne's cheek as she was speaking.

Jr gave a slight sigh. "Fred was there," he said hesitantly. "I don't know what came over me, but I just lost it. From the guilt I felt about Fred and having to be the one who, well, you know." Jr looked at Yvonne, and the expression on her face told him to continue. "I shot out of my seat, hood flew off, and my scythe was in my hand. I let out a scream that scared myself. I froze, thinking that everybody in that room just saw what I truly am, but everyone was frozen in place." Tears were streaming down Yvonne's face as Jr continued. "I heard somebody walking into the room, and I turned around, and it was Fred. I was shocked, frightened, and wasn't sure what was going on. Fred spoke to me and let me know that he didn't blame me for any of it. He told me to finish what has to be done with Dan. Then he turned around, gave you a kiss on the forehead, and left."

Jr watched as Yvonne let everything he had said sink in. Her eyes were filled to the brim with tears, ready to overflow and wash over her cheeks. She had a smile on her face. "I really love that man," she said as tears began to stream from her eyes. "Fred was right, DJ. You have to finish this."

Yvonne looked at Jr with the tears easing up from her eyes. She gave him a weak smile and turned to face forward in her seat. The rest of the drive to Purgatory was in complete silence. They came down in the driveway of Death's abode and slowed to a stop. Yvonne dabbed at her eyes before she opened the door. Death was walking out of the house as Jr and Yvonne exited the car. As soon as the doors were closed, Morty morphed into his horse phase and trotted off to see Mortis.

"Thanks for the ride, Morty," Jr said aloud.

Morty just whinnied as he trotted toward the field.

"Yvonne, I put a fresh kettle at the table if you would like some tea," Death said as she walked toward the house.

"Thank you, Torva, that would be nice," she replied. Yvonne turned toward Jr before entering the house. "DJ, remember what Fred told you, and finish this."

Jr gave his friend a nod in response. Yvonne turned and walked into the house. Jr looked over at his dad. "Thanks for showing up today."

Death looked at Jr for a second with a look of fatherly approval. "You're my son, and you needed to know that you have people to support you during your trials. Let's get some tea and talk."

Death turned and headed for the door as Jr followed. They entered the dining room as Yvonne was mindlessly bobbing a tea infuser up and down in her mug of tea. Death sat in a chair near the tea kettle and grabbed two cups. He slid one over to Jr.

"Actually, Dad," Jr said a little hesitantly. "Do you have any iced tea instead?"

Death looked over at Jr with a stone-cold blank expression, unchanging and unwavering. Jr began to get a little uncomfortable from the look his dad was giving him. Suddenly a huge toothy grin spread across the Grim Reaper's face.

"It's in the fridge," Death said, grin still plastered on his face.

A wave of relief swept over Jr. "Thanks, Dad," Jr said. He looked quizzically at his dad for a moment. "What was that look for?"

"Honestly, I thought you were going to say that you didn't want tea. At which point I would have had to taken you to go get checked out. You know, mentally," he said, almost laughing.

Jr got up and walked into the kitchen and grabbed a glass from the cupboard. He walked to the fridge, grabbed the pitcher of tea, and poured a glass. He stood at the fridge with the door open, a huge no no in this house, as he drank the entire glass. He refilled the glass and returned the pitcher of tea to the shelf and closed the door. He returned to the table to find Yvonne and her dad laughing and talking as Yvonne told stories about Fred. He was glad that she was feeling okay after Fred's service.

"Hey DJ," she said as she got up from the table. "I think I'm going to hit the hay. Thanks for the talk, Torva."

"Anytime, Yvonne," he said with a slight nod.

Yvonne walked over to Jr and gave him a hug. "Thanks, DJ. I really needed you guys today."

"You're welcome, Yvonne," he responded as he hugged her back.

Yvonne headed into the kitchen to put her cup and infuser in the sink. She stopped at the doorway and turned around. "And if you don't tell that girl how you feel about her, I will." With that comment, she turned and exited the room to retire for the evening.

Jr walked to the table with his glass of tea and sat down. "What's your opinion on this issue, Dad?"

"My opinion on anything that has to deal with emotions and relationships is ask your mother," Death said flatly. "Now, what did you learn in Amityville?"

"It's going to happen on Dan's birthday," Jr started. "Which, based on the conversation that we overheard at a liquor store, is in a couple of days." Jr stopped to recall everything that had happened. "He picked up these jars with the organs inside and the Cupio Me Daemonia from a guy at a pickle eating contest."

"As Bradford and I had expected," Death responded. "Wait, an actual pickle eating contest?"

"Yeah," Jr answered. "Who was he?"

"His name is Birsha. It's Israeli for 'An Evil.' He fits the name quite well. He has been doing Lucifer's bidding for years. Doesn't look like he is planning on stopping anytime soon." Death thought about that information for a second then asked, "What else?"

"After that Dan went to a liquor store and meet this guy named Ed. He gave Dan a ceremonial robe that he said had been anointed by some dark priests or something." Jr hesitated for a second.

Death, seeing the hesitation in his son's face, pressed the issue. "What is it, Jr?"

Jr knew he had to answer. "Those two little demons that Dan had tagging along with him. Well, they ended up catching my scent and attacked Morty and I. We had to defend ourselves," Jr answered. "Sorry, Dad."

"Well, that is unfortunate," Death responded. "Did anybody see it happen?"

"I don't think so, and Dan didn't care that they were gone."

"Let's hope that these two were prone to this type of behavior," Death said. "Nevertheless though, we need to be extra cautious from now on."

"Okay, Dad, I will," Jr said, starting to worry that he may have messed it all up.

"I will let Bradford know," Death said. "Now, you better get home. You don't want your mom to talk too much with Claire," Death said with a grin.

Jr had a look of fright and anxiety flash across his face. He got up and hastily finished his tea. He took the glass to the kitchen and put it in the sink. He walked out the door, and Morty was standing there, ready to go. As Jr walked out, Morty morphed into a car and opened the door. Jr got in and closed the door. His heart was racing. Morty took off like a rocket as Jr sat wondering what exactly his mom and Claire could be talking about. Even though the trip was only a few minutes, it seemed like an eternity.

Chapter 40

Jr hastily exited the car as Morty pulled into the parking spot and walked toward the door to his building. His heart was racing as he briskly walked down the hall. He could hear the sound of conversation and laughing as Jr reached his door. He cautiously opened the door hoping to hear what was being said before they noticed him. He slowly twisted the knob and very gently pushed on the door, hoping that the hinges wouldn't squeak.

"Come in, DJ," came his mother's voice from the living room.

Jr knew he had been busted. No sense in continuing to try to open the door slowly. He stepped through the door and walked into the living room. Claire was sitting on the couch with his mom. She looked up at Jr and flashed a coy smile. That made Jr's heart skip a beat.

Claire's phone rang. She looked at the screen, and her smile faded. "Um, excuse me for a minute. I have to answer or...," she trailed off as she got up and walked to the door. She answered the phone as she stepped into the hallway.

"You know, son," Susan started. "It's not a wise decision to try to eavesdrop on your mom. Unless your thought that I might be telling a certain young lady how you feel about her." Susan had a grin on her face as she teased her son.

"Mom, no!" Jr gasped.

"Don't worry, DJ. I didn't tell her," Susan said as she gave Jr a look. "She already knows. She's just waiting for you to tell her."

Jr looked at his mom with utter confusion. "How can I tell her? She has to leave to get away from Dan."

"I'm sure that you can figure that one out on your own." Susan got up from the couch and gathered her purse and keys. She gave Jr a thoughtful look. "DJ, whether she stays or goes, you need to tell her, or you will question whether or not you made the right choice for the rest of your life."

Jr looked at his mom without saying a word. His throat had a lump in it, and his heart felt like it was sinking down to his toes. He opened his mouth and realized that he had the ability to speak but didn't have the words to say. What could he say? He had no idea what the right decision with Claire would be. He slumped onto the couch, his head spinning like a whirlwind. "Mom, what do I do?" he asked in agony.

"You have to figure that out on your own, DJ," Susan replied. "I have to get going." She paused for a moment. "DJ, be careful. I love you, son." Susan turned and headed for the door.

"I love you too, Mom," he said as Susan walked out the door.

Jr stayed on the couch for a minute, trying to focus and get his head to stop spinning out of control. A moment later, Claire walked back through the door. She had a confused look on her face. Jr saw her expression and jumped off the couch.

"Claire, are you okay?" Jr asked, sounding more alarmed than he had anticipated.

Claire looked at Jr with her eyes starting to well up with tears. "I don't know, DJ. That was Dan on the phone. He said that he wanted to apologize for everything and wants to take me out for his birthday on Saturday." Her voice was trembling as she spoke. "He said that he got a special dress for me to wear."

Jr's heart leapt into his throat when he heard her mention the dress. He fought with himself on whether or not he should tell her that it wasn't a dress but instead a sacrificial robe. Jr couldn't bring himself to tell her what Dan was planning. "Um," was all Jr could manage to get out. Jr quickly turned his head. He wanted to scream out. He wanted to scream that he loved her, to tell her that Dan was evil and wanted to kill her to get power from Satan himself. His fear, anger, and agony was welling up inside him. He clenched his fists and took a long, deep breath.

"DJ?" Claire said quizzically.

Jr didn't respond. He couldn't. He knew if he did, he would blurt out everything that was running through his mind. He felt Claire grab his hand. She turned to him so he would look at her. Jr lifted his head to look at Claire. Looking into her eyes made him lose all control over his better judgment.

"Claire," he blurted out. "I think I'm falling for you."

Jr froze as he realized what he just said. He knew he couldn't take it back. It was out there now. Claire's eyes swelled with tears instantly. Claire walked forward, pushing Jr back toward the wall. She kissed him, firmly pressing him back. She started to pull at his cloak as she pushed him back. Jr was caught totally off guard. This wasn't what he had expected. Claire was being aggressive with the way she was pressing against him. Her hands started to grab at his body. Jr didn't know what to do. He put his hands on her shoulders and pushed her off him.

"Claire, what are you doing?" Jr asked, shocked at her behavior.

Claire recoiled from Jr's push and instantly slapped him as she screamed. "I thought you liked me?" She wailed. "Isn't this what you want?"

Jr rubbed his face, trying to ease the searing hot pain that was in his cheek. "Not like this," he said flatly. He was confused about what had just happened. "I really do like you, Claire, but this isn't what I want."

Claire was standing there, shaking as tears were streaming out of her eyes. Her body was tense as she stood with her fists clenched. "You liar!" she screamed. "That's all men want. You're just like him, you jerk!" she screamed again, slamming the door behind her as she ran out of the apartment.

Jr sat there in shock as he continued to rub his cheek. He didn't know what to do. He had never been in this type of situation. Should he go try to talk to her? Should he leave her alone? He didn't know what to do. So he just sat there rubbing his cheek for a few moments. Jr couldn't just forget about what happened. He got up and walked over to the door. He drew in a deep breath to calm his nerves and opened the door. Jr opened his door and stepped out into the hall and collided with Claire.

"Oof," escaped his mouth from the impact. "Oh my gosh, Claire, are you okay?"

Claire was sobbing uncontrollably in front of his door. "DJ, I'm so sorry," she wailed.

Claire fell into Jr's chest and sobbed uncontrollably for what seemed like hours. Jr, not really knowing what to do, wrapped his arms around her shoulders and let her cry into his chest, soaking his cloak. Jr's heart was pounding in his chest, and his mind was spinning. He was completely confused. Just a minute ago, she was yelling at him and saying he was a jerk, and now she was crying.

"Claire?" Jr asked tentatively. "Are you okay?"

Claire dried her tears as best as she could. She pulled her head off his chest and looked up into his eyes. "I'm sorry, DJ. I never should have said that. You aren't anything like Dan. Or anybody else I know for that matter." Claire sniffled as she still had a few tears trickling out of her eyes. "I guess I don't know how to properly accept affection. Most men have only wanted my body."

Without realizing what he was doing, Jr reached out and wiped a tear from Claire's eye. He looked into her eyes as he brushed her hair away from her tear-streaked face. Jr smiled at her for a second. "Claire, you are beautiful, but that's not the reason I love you."

Claire took a step back. Her mouth fell open as her eyes went wide. Her bottom lip began to quiver slightly as her eyes again filled with tears. Jr's smile faded. He thought what he had said made her upset somehow. He began to stammer to try to say something that could make her feel better. Before he could get anything out, Claire stepped into him and kissed him, not like she had earlier. This time it wasn't aggressive; it was soft, sweet, and filled with emotion. She wrapped her arms around his neck as she kissed him. Jr felt his knees getting weak and his head swooning. He didn't push her away this time. He leaned in closer as he wrapped his arms around her waist. He was confused by the turn of events, but he didn't care at the moment. He was lost in a flood of emotions.

Claire slowly ended the kiss as she leaned back slightly. Jr could feel her soft, warm breath on his face. "I love you too, DJ," Claire whispered.

Claire put her head on Jr's shoulder. She pulled her body in closer to Jr. He could feel the soft beat of her heart as she squeezed herself as close as she could. Jr loved the way her heartbeat felt against his body. As they stood there holding each other, Jr felt Claire gently kiss his neck. That made Jr smile, and he gave a slight sigh of relief.

"Claire?" Jr asked. "Do you want to go get something to eat?"

Claire lifted her head from his shoulder and gave him a befuddled look. "That's an odd subject change," she said.

"Is that a yes?" Jr asked with a slight smile.

"How about tacos?"

"Let's go," Jr said as he reached behind him to close his door.

Claire and Jr started down the hall toward the exit. The confusion from the events that had just transpired still bounced around Jr's brain. This was uncharted territory for him. He had never opened himself up to anyone before. Claire reached over and grabbed his hand. He looked at his hand with hers, and he smiled. He was happy that she finally knew how he felt. They exited the building and got into Morty. They drove off toward the taco stand.

Chapter 41

They returned a little later after having tacos and a lot of conversation. They walked into the building and started down the hall. As they approached Claire's door, she clutched onto Jr's arm. He gave her a look of concern as her grip increased with every step toward the door.

"Are you okay, Claire?" he asked with genuine concern.

Claire looked back at Jr with obvious fear in her eyes. "I don't want to stay here, especially alone. There is something in there that scares me. I don't know what." Her voice echoed the fear in her eyes. "Can I still stay at your place, DJ?"

"Of course," Jr replied.

He gestured toward his apartment's direction. As they turned to head down the hall, a dark chill shot up Jr's spine.

The time is near, Jr heard the demonic voice say.

He glanced at Claire. She obviously didn't hear it. They continued down the hall as Jr tried to get rid of the chill in his spine. They got to his door and went inside. Jr wasn't sure how to approach the sleeping situation. He decided to not worry about it for the moment.

"Want some tea?" he asked Claire.

"Sure," she said. "Thanks for letting me stay here tonight, and don't worry, I'll take the couch."

A wave of relief came over Jr as Claire said that. "You're welcome," he said.

Jr walked into the kitchen and filled the kettle with water, placed it on the stove, and turned it on. He walked over to the cabinet and pulled out two cups and a couple of tea infusers. He set them on the table and brought out the tin of tea. Claire was sitting on the couch as he gathered the items for the tea. He finished putting the things on the table and went and sat on the couch with Claire. She grabbed his hand as she pulled her feet up on the couch and leaned her head against his shoulder.

"Penny for your thoughts?" Jr said.

Claire gave a slight sigh before she responded, "I'm not sure how to respond to this situation. I've never been shown affection from any man before who wasn't trying to get sex from me." Claire got a little emotional as she spoke.

Jr gave her hand a squeeze. "I'm truly sorry that you have had to go through that type of stuff."

Claire continued to lay her head on his shoulder. "Did you mean what you said earlier? Do you really love me, DJ?" She was starting to cry a little as she asked the question.

"With every ounce of my heart and soul," Jr said without hesitation.

Claire lifted her head off his shoulder and looked at him for a second. They leaned in together and kissed. Jr reached his hand up and began to softly caress her cheek. Their kiss was cut short by the high-pitched whistle of the tea kettle letting them know that it was ready. Jr got up to retrieve the kettle as Claire moved from the couch to the table in the dining room. Jr returned to the table with the kettle and a hot plate. He poured the water into the two cups and sat the kettle on the hot plate. Claire had filled the infusers with tea as Jr was getting the kettle, and she dropped them in the cups after he poured in the water.

Claire stared into her cup for a minute. Tears began to fill her eyes before she said anything. "DJ, I'm sorry about this."

"About what?" Jr asked, a bit confused.

"Dan is going to be back tomorrow afternoon." Tears were beginning to stream faster while she continued, "I can't be here when he gets back. I don't trust him, and I don't want him to take me out or apologize. I'm going to go to Alfie's tomorrow morning and get on the bus to her cousins on Sunday." Tears were flowing heavily out of her eyes now.

Jr's heart sank, and he felt a pain like he was being stabbed when she said that. He didn't know that it could hurt like this. He couldn't seem to get any words to come out. He had no idea what to say or do. He felt a sting in his eyes. He closed his eyes to collect his thoughts. He felt a hot tear streak down his cheek. He knew it was for the best that she leave, but he didn't know that it would hurt like this. Jr blinked rapidly to keep the tears back that were threatening to streak out of his tear ducts.

"You could come with me," Claire said.

Jr finally found his voice. "I couldn't leave Josh and Yvonne to run the shop by themselves. It's always been us together." Jr's heart was breaking into a million pieces as he spoke.

Claire got up from her seat and sat in Jr's lap. She pressed her face onto his shoulder as she wept quietly. "You had better at least come see me," she said between her tears.

Jr put his arms around her and closed his eyes. He cried silently with tears only. "I will," he told her quietly.

The two of them sat there and held each other for a long while as the reality of their situation sank in. Finally, after a long while, they were cried out. Claire returned to her seat at the table and took a sip of her tea. Jr sat there blankly, swirling the tea around in his cup. He took a sip of his tea, still fighting the urge to cry. He got up from the table and began to clear the tea kettle and the tin of tea. He knew that they wouldn't be needing another cup of tea.

Claire walked into the kitchen with the two cups and set them in the sink. "Will you drive me to Alfie's tomorrow so we can spend a little more time together?"

"Of course," Jr replied. "It's getting late. I'll get you a pillow and some blankets."

Jr got some blankets and a pillow out of the closet and brought them to the couch. He began to spread out the first blanket to make a decent place for Claire to sleep. She walked up behind him and put her arms around his waist and hugged him tightly from behind. She released Jr from her grip. Jr finished making the couch into a place to sleep.

"Thank you," she said as Jr turned around.

"You're welcome," Jr responded weakly. His heart was heavy as he turned to walk to his room.

Claire reached out and grabbed his arm as he turned. She turned him toward her and gave him a kiss before he could leave. "Good night, DJ. I love you," she whispered after the kiss.

"Good night, Claire," he said. "Sleep well."

Claire pulled out her Bible as Jr turned toward his room. She sat down and began to read before she went to sleep. Jr got to his room and pulled out Fred's Bible. He was hoping that it would have some comforting words for him. He read quietly for a while before he began to get sleepy. He put the Bible up and looked out to see if Claire was still awake. The lights in the living room were off, and it was silent. Jr closed his door and turned out his light. He was still heavy hearted as he lay down.

"I love you, Claire," he said aloud as he drifted off to sleep.

Chapter 42

Jr felt a hand gently rubbing his cheek and a soft pair of lips kiss where his ear should be. His eyes began to flutter open.

"Claire, what are you doing?" he asked sleepily.

"It's not Claire," responded a sultry voice.

Jr sat up quickly to see a dark-haired female standing next to his bed. She was wearing a see-through night robe that allowed all of her fleshly features to be easily seen. Jr felt a sense of concern about the fact that she was in his room, but at the same time, seeing her naked body under the see-through nighty made something arouse in his body that he had never felt before.

"Who are you?" Jr asked.

"My name is Delilah," she said in that sultry voice as she sensually walked toward him. She put her hands on his chest and pushed him back onto the bed. "Now relax and we can have some fun."

She pinned him to the bed and began to kiss his neck and work her way down to his chest. Her hands began to probe around his body. Jr felt something that he had never felt before. It felt good, but something on his mind told him this was wrong. As her moist mouth pressed against his, she used her tongue to part his lips. A vision of Claire flashed in his mind.

"No," Jr said as he leapt out of his bed. His cloak was on in an instant. "What do you want?" he demanded.

She gave a seductive laugh as she allowed her hands to run around the curves of her body. "Why, you of course," she said as she licked her lips.

Jr was having trouble concentrating. He didn't know who this was or how she had gotten into his room. Watching her hands explore her body made Jr want to let her do what she wanted with him. Again, a vision of Claire flashed in his mind, snapping him out of this weird trance he seemed to be falling into.

"Oh, I see," she said with a seductive tone as her hands continued to explore all the curves and soft parts of her body. "I believe this is what you would prefer."

Her body shifted into a perfect replica of Claire. Jr was staring at a naked Claire in front of him, and his mind went into a tailspin. His heart began to pound in his chest, and his palms began to sweat. The Claire-looking Delilah licked her lips as she walked toward Jr. She opened her robe as she approached him, removing the thin veil of fabric between her skin and his eyes. She let the robe fall to the ground as she walked slowly toward him. He heard the slight rustle of the fabric as it slid down her now naked body.

"Come on, handsome," she said as she reached Jr. She pressed her naked body against Jr. "Come on, explore my body. Use your hands or your mouth or anything else you would like to use." She grabbed Jr's hand and tried to place it on her bare breast. Jr recoiled as she touched him. The words from what he had read earlier jumped to the front of his mind. He stepped back.

"For the commandment is a lamp and the law of light. Reproofs of instruction are the way of life. To keep you from the evil woman, from the flattering tongue of a seductress. Do not lust after her beauty in your heart," Jr said allowing the words of Proverbs to resonate aloud.

Delilah gave a wicked laugh. "Come on, honey. You'll enjoy it more than you think." She once again approached Jr while her hands explored the intimate parts of her anatomy.

Jr steeled himself against her attempts at seduction. "For the lips of an immoral woman drip honey and her mouth is smoother than oil. But in the end, she is bitter as wormwood. Sharp as a two-edged sword. Her feet go down to death, her steps lay hold of hell."

The words hung in the air like a thick smoke. Delilah glared at Jr with rage and anger in her eyes. A glowing pentagram appeared on the wall of Jr's room. Lucifer stepped into the room. His pressed suit and tie sparkled as he entered the room. He walked up to where Delilah was standing and smacked her bare buttock. Her glare turned into a seductive smile as she felt the slap on her rear end.

"Remember this look," he said to her as he grabbed her by the waist. Lucifer looked at Jr. "Are you really going to follow the words of a man who had literally hundreds of wives and concubines? Do you really think he is the best person to take advice from about sexual relations?"

Delilah rubbed her hands up and down on Lucifer's chest as she looked back and forth between him and Jr. "I could show you a good time if you'd let me," she said to Jr.

"Not interested," Jr said flatly.

"I'm willing to make you a deal," the Devil said as he took his arm from around Delilah's waist. "If Claire is what you want, then Claire is what you can have. Either her or a very sexy likeness of her, who I'm sure will be more pleasurable than that washed-up little tramp."

Jr's anger flared as he heard the Devil refer to her in that way. "But a succubus would be better? Hard to believe that a succubus would be more pleasurable. If that was the case, you wouldn't be so hellbent on getting your evil, lying hands on Claire."

Lucifer gave a pouty-looking face. "Consider it for a moment. Let me have the little tramp, and I will let you have access to any succubi that you desire, in any likeness that you desire." Lucifer gave him a devious smile. "Trust me, Cleopatra can be very entertaining."

"I'll pass," Jr replied. His nerves were shaky, but he was standing his ground. He wasn't going to give up Claire.

Lucifer snapped his fingers, and the pentagram on the wall began to glow again. It began to pulse on the wall. With every pulse, another succubus appeared in the room. The room was filling with dozens of succubi, all in varying degrees of nakedness. They were all voluptuous and well-formed, appealing to the eye. Jr tried to concentrate on what was important. He knew he had to fight to keep his composure. As the room filled with sexual, naked succubi, they began to look at Jr. They all started to run their hands over their bodies, trying to seduce Jr.

"Take your pick," Lucifer spouted out. "Any of them will make your toes curl with pleasure in any fashion that you want. With as many as you want, at any time you want." The Devil looked around the room. "Ladies, show him a good time."

Lucifer grabbed the Claire-looking Delilah and kissed her as his hands went groping all over her naked body. The rest of the succubi began to approach Jr. He reached in his cloak and grabbed his scythe. He slammed the butt of it on the ground, causing the blade to explode out of the handle.

"No!" Jr shouted as rage pulsed through his body.

Lucifer stopped his sexual playing with Delilah and shot Jr an evil glare of loathing. "Big mistake, son of Death," he yelled. "All you had to do was go along with my deal." The Devil's face turned bright red as his anger increased. Flames shot out of the pentagram, heating the room instantly. "You delusional little twerp. I could have my luscious, delicious succubi tear you to shreds, and we could have sex in your blood." His face twisted into an evil, sadistic smile. "But I have a much better plan for you. Grab him!" he shouted. "And take the girl."

Multiple succubi lunged at Jr with lightning speed, grabbing his arms before he could react. One of the succubi wrenched Jr's scythe from his hand and threw it across the room. Jr heard Claire shriek in horror as other succubi grabbed her and drug her toward the glowing pentagram. Lucifer walked toward the pentagram behind the kicking, screaming Claire, with Delilah back in her dark-haired form, not far behind. Lucifer stopped right before passing through the pentagram.

"Shackle, have fun with your new toy." He laughed as he passed through the pentagram.

Jr struggled to get free from the grip of the succubi that held him down. Shackle stepped through the pentagram and looked at Jr. An evil smile curled on his fat lips as he wrung his hands together.

"I've been waiting for this since Amityville," his loud voice boomed. He marched toward Jr as the seductive demons held him tightly.

Chapter 43

"I knew you saw me," Shackle said as he lumbered toward Jr. "I knew and I wanted to let you know that I saw you also. Your stupid horse can't fool me." Shackle stopped at Jr's feet and looked him directly in the eyes. "You will lose."

Jr's eyes snapped wide. That was the voice he had heard coming from Claire's apartment. Shackle looked down at Jr as he struggled to get free. Shackle's shoulders began to bounce as an eerie, evil laugh escaped his lips. Jr struggled to get free from the grip of the succubi. They were no longer trying to seduce him to do their desires. They were now clawing and scratching him. Shackle's shoulders stopped moving, and his face turned grim. He raised a giant foot and brought it down with a crushing force on Jr's chest. Jr felt the air blast from his lung. A huge hand reached down and grabbed him by the throat. His body was ripped from the clawing grip of the succubi as Shackle hurled him into the air. Jr flung around violently, trying to right himself as he descended back toward the floor. The huge punch from Shackle sent him flying into the nearby wall. Jr's eyes began to roll back in his head.

"Leave us be," Shackle boomed. The succubi hissed at Jr as they all scurried toward the pentagram on the wall.

Shackle lumbered toward Jr. He began to lick his lips as he came, anticipating the meal on Jr's corpse. Fear swept over Jr as he watched Shackle lumber toward him. Jr scrambled to get to his feet. He rolled over on to his knees, ready to spring up, when a giant foot kicked him in the stomach. Jr lost his breath again. He yelped as the force of the kick brought him off the ground. He tried to crawl away as he hit the ground. The giant hand grabbed him by the head and yanked him off the ground. He dangled from the grip of the hand, trying to catch his breath. Shackle turned him around so he could look him in the eyes.

"I am going to make this enjoyable," a huge grin curled on his fat lips. "Well, enjoyable for me anyway. You, on the other hand, I am going to make suffer."

Shackled began to laugh as he threw Jr across the room. Jr knew the pain that was coming as his body tumbled uncontrollably through the air. It felt like his bones were about to break as he slammed into the wall. His whole body ached as he tried to roll over. His body wasn't cooperating with the commands from his brain. He could hear the heavy footfalls of Shackle coming up behind him. Jr rolled to his knees and lunged at Shackle's legs. He felt the sharp pain in his face as Shackle threw his knee at Jr. Jr's body fell limp to the ground.

"That's right. Keep fighting," Shackle grunted as he picked Jr up. "It makes it more fun."

Shackle slammed Jr back down to the ground. Shackle threw multiple large punches at the back of Jr's head. His head bounced with a sickening thud with every blow. Jr knew he couldn't take much more of this. His body struggled to lift itself from the floor.

DJ, Jr heard echoes through the room. He tried to clear his head. It was Claire's voice. *DJ!*

Jr tried to find the origin of the scream. He got his eyes to focus for a second. The pulsating glow of the pentagram caught his attention. He looked over as rage swept through his body. Just beyond the wall in the pentagram, he saw Claire, her arms stretched out with a succubus holding each of them by the wrists. Her clothes were torn. Her shirt hung loosely from her body, exposing her skin beneath. Her bra was the only thing covering her breasts from all of the minions of Hell to see. The Devil stood behind her with a look of pure lustful desire in his eyes. He ran his hands over Claire's chest as he licked her neck. Tears streaked down her face as she felt the Devil caressing her body.

Jr's rage kicked into overdrive. His adrenaline coursed through his veins. He shot up at a dead run, heading for the pentagram. The Devil began to laugh as Jr charged toward him. The second Jr reached the pentagram, the pulsing glow stopped. Jr slammed into a solid wall. He could see Claire and the Devil on the other side. He could see the Devil laughing manically as Claire cried in fright and disgust. He could see but not hear them. He pounded his fists on the wall as he screamed at the Devil. The pentagram disappeared from the wall. Jr stopped midswing of his pounding in shock as it vanished before his eyes.

Jr's attention was broken as he felt his body being hurled backward. He opened his eyes to see Shackle running at the same speed he was flying backward. Jr hit the wall with a huge amount of force. It felt like his back snapped in two. With even more force, he felt Shackle run into his body with the force of a runaway train. Shackle began to deliver a series of huge blows to Jr's rib cage. They were fast and powerful; Jr could feel his ribs starting to crack with each additional blow, each blow knocking more and more wind from his lungs. His breath ran out as the barrage of punches continued. His body went limp and fell to the floor. Shackle wrapped a huge hand around his neck and squeezed as he lifted Jr from the ground. Shackle pinned him against the wall by his throat. Jr could hear Shackle begin to laugh as his vision faded.

Jr saw a dark flash pop behind Shackle. His laugh suddenly silenced, and his grip eased up. Jr gasped for air as his throat was opened. Shackle's face had a twisted expression of confusion and pain. A huge point of a scythe popped through Shackle's chest. Immense blue flames flickered from the blade as smoke began to hiss out from his chest. As Jr's vision began to become clearer, he saw two huge pitch-black wings spring up from behind Shackle. Jr's face looked at this with enough confusion to stifle the armies of Babylon. Shackle's face lost all expression as a loud guttural roar filled the air from behind him. Shackle's hands released Jr. He fell to the floor, gasping for air. Shackle's limp body violently flew backward across the room. Death stood there, shoulders heaving with anger as he held his scythe, blue flames still leaping about the curved blade.

Jr saw a vision of Claire jump to the front of his mind. It was when she was reading her Bible in the hall. He heard what he couldn't before. "So I looked, and behold I saw a pale horse. And the name of him who sat upon him was Death, and all the power of Hades followed behind him." Jr's jaw dropped as the words Claire had read echoed through his brain.

The Grim Reaper spun around. With thunderous sounds of pure anger, he shouted, "Lucifer, you vile deceiver. Come out from your place of hiding, you cowardly little worm. I swear by the Almighty One that the Angel of Death will chase you to the very bowels of Hell itself to find you. I will be the one to bring you before the White Throne of Judgment. You will pay for your sins, oh Fallen One!"

The thunderous sounds of Death's words echoed around the room, bouncing from wall to wall with all the force it started with. Shackle's body was fizzling into wisps of smoke as Jr slumped against the wall in shock at what he had just seen and heard. Death turned and walked over to Jr's scythe and picked it up. He turned to his son and hand it back to Jr. Jr stared at his dad with confusion.

The flames on Death's scythe were beginning to get smaller as he spoke, "I'm sure you have a lot of questions right now."

Jr couldn't get the words out, so he just nodded at his dad. Jr looked down at his scythe in his hands. It looked small compared to his dad's. His mind was swirling from the last few minutes. Was his dad the Angel of Death? An actual angel? Jr's eyes went wide. "Morty!" Jr exclaimed.

Jr took off running. He reached the wall and phased through it. He was still running as his feet hit the ground. He saw Morty lying on the ground, motionless. Mortis and Max were there fighting off the last few demons. Jr pushed himself to run faster, he snapped the blade of his scythe out as he ran. Blue flames ignited around the sharp curved blade as it sprang out. Jr swung as he reached the area where Morty lay. His blade sliced clear through the demon in front of him. A vile squeal escaped the mouth of the demon as he disappeared in a wisp of smoke. Jr looked up to see Mortis, with smoke shooting out of his nostrils and fiery red eyes, put his hoof completely through the head of another demon. Max had a demon in each hand and was using them to clobber another one in front of him. Each blow caused wisps of smoke to come off each of the three in the mix. Jr dropped to his knees next to Morty, his eyes stinging with tears as he placed his hands on the side of his friend on the ground. He felt a weak heartbeat beneath his hands.

"Morty," he whispered. "Why didn't you call me for help?"

The Grim Reaper walked up behind Jr and put his hand on his shoulder. "He couldn't. Lucifer knew he would try and put up a block so that you couldn't hear anything from outside."

Max and Mortis were finished with their demons. Mortis walked over to Morty and nudged him with his nose. Jr thought that he saw a tear roll down the long nose of the horse as he nudged Morty.

Max walked over to join the others. "They jumped him. Even if he had wanted to call to you, he wouldn't have been able to." Max still had his fists clenched as he spoke. "Sorry, DJ, we didn't get here soon enough."

"Dad, is he going to be okay?" Jr asked, tears still welling up in his eyes.

"Ivy should be able to help," Death responded. He turned to Max and to Mortis. "Take Morty to Ivy, and meet us back at Purgatory."

Max nodded, his mammoth figure strode forward and picked up Morty. Mortis put his nose against Morty's side. They all vanished with a bright-red flash. Jr slowly stood up. His head was hung low as he looked down at the spot where Morty had been. He squeezed the handle of his scythe tighter as his anger swept over him. Huge blue flames arched off the blade of his scythe. He turned toward his dad, his eyes burning a bright red.

"Dad," Jr said quietly. "We have to end this!"

"We will, Jr," Death replied. "We will."

Bradford appeared with a bright flash. "Torva, we need you to in Purgatory." With that, he flashed away.

Death looked at his son. He reached out and touched Jr's shoulder. Jr saw the dark flash from the inside this time. When his eyes readjusted, he was in his dad's office.

Chapter 44

Bradford was already there looking at a large clock. Jr walked around behind Bradford. The face of the clock had images that were blurry moving around it. Bradford reached up and turned the dial on top counterclockwise. The images blurred even more moving backward.

"Anything yet?" Death asked him.

Bradford looked up with an expression of frustration. "No," he almost snapped. "It's still being obscured somehow."

"What's obscured?" Jr asked perplexed.

"Tomorrow," Death replied solemnly.

"If we can't figure out what is going on tomorrow, we won't be properly prepared," Bradford stated.

"What?" Jr asked, confused.

"We need to know how many of Hell's minions are going to be at the ceremony," Death said flatly. "If we underestimate how many are going to be there, it won't end well for us. We need to make sure that we have an effective plan of attack."

A big red flash off to the side of the room caught Jr's attention. Max walked toward Jr and stopped right in front of him. "Morty is with Ivy. She says that she will be able to help. He's going to be okay."

A wave of relief swept over Jr as he heard that. He closed his eyes in an attempt to stop from tearing up. A mammoth hand landed on his shoulder. Jr looked up at Max. "Thanks," was all he could manage.

Max nodded in response, then turned to Death, "Torva, Mortis is going to stay with him until he gets better."

Death nodded in acknowledgment. Bradford was turning the dial back and forth on his clock, his face getting redder and more distorted with every turn of the dial. In a moment of pure irritation and frustration, Bradford jumped out of his seat and threw the clock against the far wall in Death's office. He stood there breathing heavily as everyone stared at him.

"What?" he questioned. "Haven't any of you wanted to see time fly?" A huge grin spread across his face.

Max's red face grew even more red as he tried to stifle a laugh at the overplayed joke. Death shook his head at the pun his friend had made, and Jr just stood there in disbelief. He had never seen Bradford lose his temper in the short time that he had known him.

"Torva, I can't get through to see what is really there. It's blocked well." Bradford's frustration was evident in his tonality. "I'm sorry."

"We will figure it out," Death replied. "We have to," he mumbled.

Jr didn't know what to do or to say. He felt small in the room with these three—out of his league so to speak. His eyes went back and forth between the three of them as he tried to figure out what to do to help. His mind was still running in circles, trying to process everything that had just transpired. He could still see those huge black wings and hear the rage in his father's voice. Jr's thoughts were interrupted by his dad's voice.

"Max, we need you to formulate the best strategy for this attack," Death said. "The rest of us, we need to make sure we are prepared for this battle." Death's tone was serious when he spoke. "Jr, how are your injuries doing?"

Jr realized that he didn't hurt as bad as he had earlier. "Better," he said, surprised.

"Good," Death replied. "You're healing quickly."

"Dad, can I ask you something?" Jr inquired.

"Of course, Jr. What's on your mind?"

"If I couldn't beat Shackle, how am I supposed to beat Dan and the Devil?"

Death looked at Jr for a long moment before he answered, "Well, for starters, you will have help this time. Having and knowing that somebody has your back makes all the difference in the world." Death slowly drew out his scythe as he continued, "Also, we are going to use these. You didn't have yours in your hand when you fought Shackle. You let your guard down a little when the succubi were around. Whether you are willing to admit it or not, your fleshly desires where interfering with your concentration."

"I felt something that I had never experienced before when they were there," Jr admitted.

Bradford jumped in at this point, "Oh, you mean lustful desires?"

"What?" Jr yelped in shock. "No!"

"DJ, trust me on this one. I've been around since, well, the beginning of time, and I still get those on occasion." Bradford's tone wasn't its usual jovial state. "Every male deals with it."

"He's not lying," Max's voice boomed. "Every male and a lot of females too."

"Then how do I stop it?" Jr implored the trio.

Death stepped in front of Jr and put his hand on his shoulder. "That is something you will have to figure out on your own. What works for us might not work for you." Death looked at his son and then around the room. "Now, Max, if you can work on a plan, Bradford, keep trying to break through that blockade. And, Jr, it's going to be difficult, but you need to get some rest. Tomorrow is going to be tough. I have work to attend to. I'll be back soon." With a dark flash, he was gone.

Bradford looked at the other two. "Well, I guess it's back to work for some of us." With that, he pulled another huge clock out of his cloak and sat back down, scanning the face for anything.

Max pulled out what looked like a map and a list of weapons and somehow managed to squeeze into a normal-sized chair, his mammoth frame bulging from every place possible. He towered over the small desk that he sat at. He began to scan the papers that he had and a look of concentration spread across his brow.

Jr walked out of his dad's office. He slowly walked up to his old room in the house. He didn't see or hear his mom or Yvonne in the house. They must be with Ivy helping with Morty. He didn't know how he was going to get any rest. The pain left in his body let him know that somehow though, he needed rest. He opened the door to his room. His mom hadn't changed it any. It was still just a bed and a dresser in the room. He walked over to his bed and sat down. He felt Fred's Bible in his pocket. He pulled it out of his pocket and flipped it over in his hands. He put it back in his pocket before he stretched out on his bed. He put his head on his pillow and closed his eyes.

Jr's eyes snapped open as he heard his name. He looked up at what should have been the ceiling in his room. It wasn't. He could feel the heat in the area. This wasn't a very pleasant place. It had rough walls and ceiling. The floor was dirty and covered with tiny pebbles.

DJ, he heard a voice call. *DJ, please?*

The voice sounded distressed and in pain. Jr shot up as the voice finally registered in his brain.

"Claire," he shouted as he leapt out of his bed. That was curious; how was his bed in this strange and dingy place? He started walking in the direction he thought he had heard Claire's voice come from. As he continued down the corridor that he was in, the smell of sulfur started to creep into his nostrils. Jr knew where he was; he was literally in Hell. He rounded a corner and saw Claire tied to a set of cross beams. Her arms and legs spread apart, and her clothes were still torn.

"Claire," Jr said as he ran forward.

Claire looked up at the sound of his voice and looked around. She spotted Jr, and a scream of sheer terror shot from her mouth. She started thrashing about, trying to free herself from the binds that held her to the beams. She looked up again and shouted, "Get away from me, Death. I'm not going to die yet!"

Jr stopped dead in his tracks. He realized that he must look like his father coming to collect a soul. "Claire, it's me, DJ," he said as reassuringly as he could.

Claire stopped struggling to get free and looked up at Jr. The confusion washed over her. She dropped her head. "My mind must be delusional. I know you're the Grim Reaper. I can feel it. Why do you sound like my friend? Do you always taunt your victims?"

"Claire, no. It's really me, DJ." Jr was worried that he wouldn't be able to convince her that he wasn't Death. "You have to believe me."

Claire slowly raised her head. "I don't believe you."

Jr's heart sank as Claire dropped her head again. He felt the pain of that rejection. It was like a knife to the heart. He knew that he didn't have much time left to convince her. "Claire, I love you," he almost whispered.

Claire's head popped up when she heard that. "DJ," she said as she began to weep. "It really is you!"

Jr rushed to the beams she was strapped to. As he reached out to grab the ropes, it felt like he was hit with a bolt of lightning. He was thrown back as a bright flash was followed by a clap of thunder. Jr hit the ground with a thud as the wind was knocked out of his lungs.

"DJ," Claire screamed as he hit the ground.

Jr rolled to his knees and got up. He turned back to Claire. He walked toward the beams again. Jr paused as the sound of footsteps started to echo down the corridor. He looked down in the distance and saw a well-dressed figure walk around the corner out of the shadows.

The Devil started to chuckle as he walked up to Claire. Tears started to stream down her face as he put his hand on her shoulder. "Not very smart, son of Death," Lucifer started. "Did you really think that you would have any power in my domain?" His chuckle grew a bit louder. "You have no power here. I just wanted this tasty little tart to see your true form. I knew if she saw you as who you truly are, she would be more willing to come to my reality for the rest of eternity." He ran his fingers down her cheek, caressing the contours of her chin as he spoke. "After all, how could she ever love you, the son of an incarnation, or the son of on incarnation truly love an overused little wench like her."

Jr charged toward the Devil with visceral rage coursing through his veins. He pulled out his scythe as he charged forward. The Devil just grinned as Jr ran toward him. Jr reached Lucifer and was once again hit by what felt like a bolt of lightning and thrown backward. Jr hit the ground again with the wind knocked out of him.

"I tire of this," Lucifer said dismissively. "Be gone."

Jr blinked as he rolled to his knees. As his eyes refocused, he saw the floor of his room, his scythe still in his hand. As he got back to his feet, the door to his room opened. Death walked in. "It is time!" Death said flatly.

Chapter 45

Death turned and walked out of the room without another word. Jr was shocked it had only felt like he had been there for a few minutes. As Jr followed his dad out of his room, he kept visualizing the wings he saw spread from his dad's back. As they entered the dining room, Jr couldn't restrain his query any longer.

"Dad," Jr said, "can I ask you a question?"

Death stopped, his cloak flowing around him like a wall of water. He turned around, causing it to flare out around the base. "You may," he responded.

"Dad," Jr started as he cleared his throat a bit. "Are you an angel?"

Before Death could answer, the sound of a whistling tea kettle pierced through the air. Bradford appeared carrying a tray with four cups and the steaming kettle of water. "If Torva is going to tell this story, we're going to need some tea. Plus, Max made some food thing that is supposed to help us retain our strength during battle." Bradford set the tray on the table and took a seat.

Max walked into the dining room, carrying a plate with what looked like sandwiches. "We need to eat these before we go. They look and taste like tuna fish but have an added protein to help with strength and stamina." He looked over at Death. "I also would like to hear this story again. It's been a while." Max took a seat as he set the plate on the table.

Death walked over to the table and poured water over the tea infuser that was already in the cup. He handed it to Jr and motioned for him to take a seat. Jr took the cup and sat as he looked at his dad. Death seemed nervous; Jr had never seen him like this before. "Yes, Jr. I am an angel. The Angel of Death that is mentioned in the Bible. I'm sure you have read that in Fred's Bible that you carry in your pocket."

Jr's mouth fell open. He had read a couple of portions that had mentioned the Angel of Death. He never made the connection. "I thought angels lived in Heaven?"

"They do," Death responded.

"Then why aren't you?" Jr asked, more confused now than when he first saw the wings on his dad. "And how did you end up in Purgatory?"

"Maybe it would be better if you saw it rather than an explanation," Death said. He turned to face Bradford. "Bradford, if you would please."

"Sure," Bradford said as he swallowed a bit of the sandwich that he had. He poured three more cups of tea and handed one to Death and Max, putting the final one in front of himself. Bradford stood up and twisted the dial on his watch. The whole room lurch as it started to speed backward through time. As it slowed, the wall in the dining room turned to match the arid terrain of the desert. It came to a stop, looking at the cross as Jesus hung on it. Time began to move forward again at its normal rate.

"It is finished," Jesus said as he threw His head back.

The brilliant flash of lightning lit up the entire sky and dining room. The thunderous clap of thunder hurt Jr's ears as he once again saw a tear roll down the cheek of the Grim Reaper. He slowly stepped from behind the small group of women that stood in front of the cross. Death stood in front of Jesus, motionless for a moment. His head hung low as he stood there. He looked up a Jesus and reached out with the tip of his scythe. The blade paused slightly before passing through His skin. Death gave the scythe a quick twist and pull. As the tip emerged from Jesus's body, a big blob of black tar oozed off the blade. The substance hit the ground and seeped in. Death threw his head back, and a loud grief-stricken yell escaped his throat. Death dropped to the ground and pawed at it, trying to retrieve the soul of Jesus.

He dug at the ground with his boney fingers, trying to dig down to the bowels of Hell to retrieve Jesus's soul. The dirt flew past his kneeling body in a fury as he struggled to reach it. After a fruitless attempt to retrieve the soul, Death pounded his fists on the ground. Death leapt to his feet. His huge black wings sprung out as he gave another guttural roar. He shot into the sky at lightning speed. He sped through the sky, heading upward. He passed through the atmosphere and into the stars. He kept going until a brilliant light shone from some clouds in the distance. Death landed at what appeared to be a large gate that shone white. Death walked through the gate into Heaven. There was a large black cloud hanging over the center of the area. Angels stood around, mourning and crying. There was a deep sorrow that filled the atmosphere. Death walked toward the center of Heaven. An angel ran up to Death.

"Torva," the angel said. "You mustn't go in. Father is grieving."

Death looked at the angel. "As we all are, Gabriel. I have to tell him. I can't do this anymore. I'm sorry, brother."

Death walked into the center sanctuary and disappeared. The scene stayed outside of the sanctuary. Gabriel stood there with a look of confusion and grief on his face.

"Hey, what gives?" Jr questioned. "How come the scene stayed outside?"

Death turned to his son. "No mortal can view the face of the living God and live. They are sin, and He is righteousness. You are part mortal, so the timeline knew that and stopped it from going inside."

The wall turned back to its solid state as the room blurred back to the present time with the four of them sitting in the dining room.

"So what happened?" Jr asked.

Death took a deep breath before he spoke, "I let the Father know that I couldn't handle watching the person who created me die and not be able to deliver His soul to Heaven. God understood my torment and proposed an alternative to the situation. He told me he would give me this place and have me continue in my duties if I was willing." Death paused for a moment to control his emotions. "I knew Jesus was supposed to return but not until He defeated his sentence in Hell. His soul was black and tarlike because at that moment, every sin ever committed—past, present, and future—were on Him. It was over forty days later that He returned to Heaven. I could have went back, but I was ashamed of my decision, so I have remained here ever since."

Jr looked at his dad. He didn't know what to say or do. He never knew that this had happened or that his dad was ashamed of anything. "Dad, I'm sorry. I don't know what to say."

"There is nothing to say, Jr. It was my decision."

Bradford and Max had remained silent until now. It was Max who broke the silence. "We need to eat these protein sandwiches and prepare for the day ahead. It will not be an easy task. The minions of Hell will be many." His tone was stony and flat.

"Yeah," chimed Bradford. "But there is four of us. Seems like decent odds." Jr, Death, and Max all turned their gaze to Bradford. "What, you guys don't think so? C'mon, we've got the Angel of Death, the Incarnation of War, Jr who will be fighting from the heart, and I can cheer you guys on from another time."

Death gave Bradford a steely glare as he took a bit of the sandwich that Max had given him. "You know, Bradford, you're lucky that you are time itself. That way your time is never up."

"Torva, it's hard to tell if you're serious or not. I can't tell with those hollow eyes," Bradford said without trying to maintain a straight face.

Jr took a bit of the protein sandwich that Max had given him. It actually tasted pretty good. He took a sip of tea as he swallowed the protein mix. His mind was spinning a little, and he was having trouble focusing on the present moment. He took a breath and closed his eyes to regain his focus. As he closed his eyes, he remembered how Morty had looked lying on the ground after Lucifer's minions attacked him at the apartment. Jr felt his blood beginning to boil. He felt a hand gently land on his shoulder. Jr opened his eyes.

Death looked him directly in his eyes. "Channel that anger you have boiling inside you. You have to control it. Don't allow it to control you."

"Dad," Jr started to say before Death stopped him.

"He will recover, Jr. He has your mother and Ivy taking care of him."

"Thanks, Dad." Jr said feeling a slight bit of relief.

Jr heard a sound coming from where Max was sitting. He turned his head to focus on the source. He noticed that Max's shoulders were beginning to heave up and down. Max had a grin starting to spread across his face. He threw his head back as he began to laugh a loud deep laugh. His shoulders were heaving heavily.

Bradford gave him a wry look. "What's up with this guy?" he said as he pointed at Max with his thumb.

Max's laughter began to subside. He took the last bite of his protein sandwich and took a swig of his tea. He slammed his cup down as he almost leapt from his seat. "Let's go win a battle and save that girl you love, DJ." He grabbed his battle-axe, which had been leaning against the wall, and slung it across his back as he started toward the door.

Bradford took the final drink of his tea. "Well, I guess it's time," he said with a grin. He stood up and followed Max toward the door.

Death took out his scythe and tapped the butt on the ground. The blade sprang out with its trademark sounds as the glimmer of the lights made it cast an eerie light spot on the wall. He ran his cloak sleeve across both sides of the blade. "It's time, old friend," he said as he closed the blade and put it back in his cloak. He turned to walk toward the door. He stopped and turned around to look at Jr. "Son, do you truly love this girl?"

"Yes, I do."

"Then let's go save her," Death said flatly. He turned and walked out of the room, heading for the door.

Jr closed his eyes and he saw Claire, battered, bruised, and crying. "God, help us." He opened his eyes and walked toward the door.

Chapter 46

Jr stepped out the door into Purgatory proper. The other three were standing there.

"When we get there, Bradford won't be able to be there the entire time," Death stated. "He will pop in and out to help as much as he can."

Jr looked around the group standing near. His heart was pounding, and he was nervous. They all three turned to look at him. He swallowed hard, "I want to say thank you, guys, for doing this."

Max took a step forward and slapped a huge hand on Jr's shoulder. "DJ, this is war. Do you really think that I wouldn't be here?" Max gave a huge grin. "It's what I was made for."

"Yeah, DJ," Bradford chimed in. "He's made for it. Me, on the other hand, I'm not. But if you feel for Claire like I do for Ivy, then I'm going to fight with everything I have in me." His tone wasn't its normal jovial sound. He was serious, and his tone showed it.

Death gave a long look at his son. "Jr, you know how I feel about you and your mother," Death said stoically. "I will battle all the minions of Hell to protect you and the people you love. Death is not my pleasure. It's my job."

The group looked around at each other with different feelings coursing through each one of them. The mood was serious and grim. Max took the initiative. "DJ, you've been in this place. Give us the lay of the land."

Jr began to give them a detailed floor plan to the best of his recollection. He explained what he had seen in the lower rooms and warned them all of the stench. Jr continued his detailed description of the stairs and warned them about the step that creaks. He continued to walk them through the layout of the upstairs hallway. He took special care to tell them about the wall upstairs that had the portal. He began to tell them about the double doors that led to the room with the giant pentagram on the wall. As Jr recapped the room, his blood ran cold, and his anger began to grow. He finished his detailed account of the layout and stood there in silence for a moment. His mind was focused on Claire and how she had looked when they had taken her. He knew that he had to win this to save her. He reached into his cloak and pulled out his scythe. He tapped the end on the ground, causing an arch of huge blue flames as the blade sprang out.

"Now that's more like it," Max hollered. "When this is over, we feast!" his voice trailed off into a laugh that shook his whole body.

Max reached out and put his hand on Bradford's shoulder. This started the chain reaction of the others reaching out to the next and doing the same. It was Death who ended the rounds as he placed his hand on Jr's shoulder. Jr looked at his dad as a red, dark, and bright flash all mix in his vision. As his eyes cleared, they were all standing in front of Jared's old decrepit building. It looked like it was breathing, and the smell of sulfur and brimstone filled the surrounding area.

"It look almost alive," Jr said aloud.

Death stood there with a slight glare on his face. "And the smell of evil oozes out of there."

"I'll see you guys in there," Bradford said as he popped out with a flash.

Max was ready to run in at full speed and just start swinging. He was itching for a battle; he hadn't been in a major one in a long time. "DJ, when we get in there, your main objective has to be Claire. That is the main objective. It won't be easy getting to her, but that is what has to happen."

"I know, Max. It's all I can think about." Jr paused for a quick second to gather his thoughts. "Every time I close my eyes, all I can see is how she looked when Lucifer had her. She was terrified, and she saw me for who I truly am. Not the human facade that I wear around and she still called out for me to help her. She wasn't afraid of how I looked."

Death spoke suddenly, almost making Jr jump, "Jr, you have to remain focused right now. Lucifer knows how to get into your head and make you doubt yourself or not be aware of your surroundings." Death reached out and grabbed his son's shoulder. "Keep your wits about, and don't let that deceiver get into your head."

Jr looked at his dad and gave a weak smile. "I will, Dad. Thanks."

Max gave a hearty laugh. "Let's go save the world!"

The trio began to walk up the walkway to the entrance of the building. The sulfur in the air made Jr's lungs burn with every breath that he inhaled. His eyes stung as the tears threatened to wash out the sulfur that was irritating them. The demonic sounds of chaos grew louder as they approached the building. Max reached behind him and pulled out his huge battle-axe as they approached the door. Jr, scythe still in his hand, gripped it tighter with every step. Death's boney hand reached into his cloak and brought out his scythe. A slight tap on the ground made the huge gleaming blade that had served him for centuries spring out.

"Wait here," Death said as he held out a hand.

He walked forward and passed through the doorway. A few seconds later, a boney hand reappeared through the door, waving them through. Jr stepped forward and passed through the door. He was standing there with his dad looking around the building. It looked the same as before but had a new aura about it. His mind was focused on the events at hand. His thought was broken as a red flash entered his vision. Max was there, taking in the surroundings.

"You lead DJ. You know this place," Max said in a whisper.

Jr began to move forward and instantly froze as he heard a familiar sound coming from behind the door to their right. It was a hellhound that had caught their scent. The trio heard it scratching at the door. Max raised his axe, ready to swing. A muffled whimper came from the other side of the door, and the scratching stopped. The door slowly began to open, Max at the ready. Jr and Death raised their scythes, ready to battle whatever came out of the door.

Bradford popped his head around the corner, instantly ducking as he saw three blades coming for his head. "Whoa," he whispered sharply as the three pulled their swings. "Geez, you guys are jumpy.

By the way," he continued, "I hate these dogs." He popped back out with a flash.

"I think we might all be a little edgy," Max stated. "Let's try to not kill our allies."

Jr and Death nodded in agreement before they began to slowly move forward again. Another door in the hall flew open as two hellhounds came bounding out. Max threw his axe, hitting the first one and pinning it on the wall. It quickly began to disappear as it turned into smoke. The other hound had leapt into the air, flying toward Jr. He gave his scythe a high arching swing, catching the hound in the midsection. The two halves plopped to the floor with a squishy sound as smoke bellowed from the two halves. The three gave a quick glance around to make sure nothing else had heard the scuffle before they once again began to move toward the stairs. Max pulled his axe from the wall as they passed by. They stopped at the bottom of the stairs.

Jr pointed up the staircase. "It's the sixth or seventh stair up," Jr said. "I can't quite remember exactly."

As the three were looking at the stairs, an eerie red glow began to appear at the top of the stairs. The sound of dozens of running feet began to grow louder and louder. Shadows began to bounce off the walls at the top growing larger as the foot falls grew louder.

"What's that?" Jr asked in an anxious whisper.

"The minions of Hell have appeared," Death said, not bothering to whisper anymore. He gripped his scythe and began to move forward.

A large number of demons in all assorted sizes and shapes began to flood over the top of the stairs and charge forward toward the trio at the bottom. Sinder appeared at the top, looking down at them as the demons continued to flow down the steps. Death saw Sinder, and his eyes turned red with fury. Sinder stood at the top with a smug look on his charred face as he looked down at Death.

Max was looking around as a broad smile flashed across his face. "Oh yeah," he hollered, almost laughing. "Let's do this," he said as he charged up the stairs.

Death followed as Max was ascending the stairs. Jr knew that the battle he had feared was finally at hand. He steeled his nerves and charged up the stairs with his father and friend. Sinder turned and walked away as the wave of demons rushed to meet the trio. Jr saw a flash appear in the middle of the wave of demons. It was Bradford. He wasn't in his robe, though. He was wearing what looked like a Samurai outfit. He had twin katana blades in his hands. He caught two demons with his blades and flashed back out as the smoke issued from the two he had cut. Another flash and two more demons cut down in battle.

The wave of demons collided with the trio as Jr's foot landed on the squeaky stair. The force of the impact of the demons almost knocked Jr over as he swung his scythe. As Jr was battling a couple of demons, Bradford flashed in right next to him. He swung his katanas with precision, hitting two demons, one on either side of Jr. The two dropped to the ground as smoke flowed out of the wounds inflicted by Bradford's blades. He gave Jr a wink and flashed back out. The flow of demons over the top of the stairs began to slow.

Jr turned as he saw a glint in his peripheral vision. The huge blade of Death's scythe whistled as it sailed through the air. Two demons, who had launched into the air with their claws glistening in the eerie red glow, were instantly sliced in two. Death's blade trailed with smoke as the two demons screeched in agony as their bodies were halved. Death spun on his heels toward Jr. His eyes were glowing with fiery red anger. He stopped as he stared at Jr. He instantly threw a vicious right punch.

"Whoa," Jr said as he tried to dodge. His reflexes where slower than his father's punch.

Death's punch landed on the face of a demon that resembled Shackle, standing directly behind Jr. The large overweight demon flew backward from the impact of the punch. Death spun around as he delivered a pinwheel kick catching two smaller demons, coming from the other direction, that resembled Sai and Tyre.

As the two went flying into the large fat demon, Death grabbed Jr by the cloak. "Focus, Jr," Death almost shouted.

Death shoved Jr in the direction of a cluster of Hell's minions. Jr continued to swing his scythe with all the skill and precision that he had learned from his dad and Max, cutting down multiple with each swing. Demon remains were strewn all over the stairs, and the smoke from the dead demons filled the air. Visibility was slowly diminishing as the body count grew higher. The flow of demons stopped, and the sound of the rushing feet disappeared while the sounds of the swinging blades subsided.

Jr looked around; his breathing was labored. Death and Max were standing a few feet away. A bright flash appeared next to Jr, and Bradford stood there.

"That was only the first wave," Max said. "They know we are here, and they will come again."

Death looked at Bradford. "Did you get Sinder?"

"No," he responded. "He went back through the portal."

Jr was looking at Bradford in confusion about his outfit. "Where did you get that?"

Bradford grinned as he twirled his twin katanas before sheathing them. "You like it? It was a gift from Max a long time ago. During the Ming dynasty," Bradford responded. "Haven't had a chance to use them until know. Glad I made time to practice," he said as he let out a laugh.

"Let's move," Death said in a low growl.

Chapter 47

Bradford gave a wink to Jr as he flashed back out. The trio returned to climbing the stairs. Jr was looking at his dad. He had never seen him like this before. It wasn't like him to lose his temper and show this kind of rage. The trio crested the top of the stairs and stopped. Across the hall was a huge glowing pentagram that hadn't been there the last time Jr had been there. Jr snapped his eyes shut and reopened them, trying to get them to refocus. He couldn't believe what he saw.

Standing in front of the pentagram was a cloaked figure with its head bowed down. It was a long black cloak that looked the same as the ones his father and he wore. The figure was holding a scythe that looked identical to the one that Death held in his hand. The cloaked figure slowly raised its hooded head. As it raised its head, the pentagram behind it began to pulse like a heartbeat, and a low red glow began to brighten on the face of the star. Jr recognized the figure in the cloak as it removed its hood. Under the hood was the face of Sinder. An evil sinister smile was curled across his burnt face. He raised his scythe and twirled it around before letting the butt of the handle hit the ground. A flash of red flame began to dance along the curved blade of his scythe, seeming to taunt the trio to a battle.

"Max, you and Jr continue in ahead and save that girl from Lucifer's clutches," Death said in a tone of complete and utter seething rage. His words almost hissed as he spoke. "I will deal with this one."

Max grabbed Jr by the shoulder and gave him a push toward the double doors before Jr could object or ask a question. Jr knew not to interfere with this and felt an even more pressing urgency to get to Claire. Jr and Max continued past Death as he turned toward Sinder. Death held out his hand as if to stop someone from passing. A bright flash appeared, and Death's hand was already stopping Bradford from advancing on Sinder. Bradford looked at his friend who was staring him right in the eyes. He gave a slight nod and flashed back out.

"We could have worked well together, Torva," Sinder stated. "You should have come with us."

"As I recall, Sinder, you and your master did not leave willingly," Death responded with zero emotion in his voice.

A chuckle escaped from Sinder's mouth. "Do you honestly think that that buffoon you call Father could have actually made lord Lucifer leave if he didn't want to?" Sinder sneered as he glared at Death. "Lucifer can do whatever to whomever he pleases!"

"What happened to you, Sinder?" Death asked. "You used to be an angel of light doing the work of our Father. Instead, you chose to be a pawn for Lucifer and his evil plans. He doesn't care if you survive or not, as long as you serve your purpose."

"Well, isn't that the pot calling the kettle black," Sinder sneered viciously. "As I recall, you no longer reside there either, Torva." Sinder was becoming increasingly enraged as he began to foam at the teeth like a rabid dog.

"I wasn't forced out as you were, you vile creature," Death snapped. "I stepped down from that place but still abide in the Father and do His will!"

"Enough," Sinder shouted. "There is a difference between us. Unlike you, Torva, death is my pleasure and can't wait for you to taste it, Angel of Death.

Two large batlike wings sprang out from behind Sinder as he launched into the air, heading toward Death. His scythe was covered in ominous red flames engulfing the entire curved edge of the jagged blade. Death spread his large black wings and launched into the air to engage with Sinder. Death's own scythe blade cast light around the hall from the blue flames that were fanned by the wind rushing past as Death flew toward Sinder. The two collided in midair as their blades slammed into each other. The impact caused a sound like a cannon to reverberate around the hallway. Blue and red flames intertwined with the others casting purple light about the area. The blades were locked in a battle for dominance as the two foes glared at each other.

Sinder pulled his knees up and kicked Death in the torso. He used the force of the kick to propel himself backward. He flipped in the air and with a snap of his black, batlike wings shot toward Death to deliver another attack. Death quickly recovered from the kick to the midsection and was ready as Sinder flew toward him. With a quick flap of his wings, Death dodged out of the way and caught Sinder by the back as he flew past. Using Sinder's own momentum against him, Death spun him around and launched him into the wall above the pentagram. Sinder smashed into the wall causing large chunks of the dilapidated drywall to fall toward the floor.

As quickly as Sinder had flown into the wall, he shot out of it. A loud snap from his batlike appendages, and he shot out of the crater in the wall. The blast of wind as he launched himself back into the air caused a cloud of drywall dust to plume out of the crater. He slammed into Death with a vengeance, propelling them straight toward the wall directly across the hall. Sinder forced the fiery red blade of his scythe toward Death's skull. Death could feel the fury of Hell's flames against his face. They crashed into the wall and sent particles of drywall and wood splinters flying apart as they crashed through the wall. Sinder again planted his legs in Death's midsection and, with a forceful kick, slammed Death into the floor.

"Face it, Torva," Sinder shouted. "I've always been better than you. Just release your soul to Lucifer and become an ally."

Death hit the ground and rolled to his feet. "My soul always has and always will belong to our Father."

Death launched back into the air. Sinder snapped his wings and shot toward Death. Sinder drew back his scythe, waiting until they were in close proximity to swing. Death flapped his wings to increase his speed. He knew if his timing was off, Sinder would land a devastating blow. Sinder's eyes widened slightly as Death approached. Death saw it and knew it was time. He folded his wings and dropped like a stone. Sinder, not anticipating this, swung with fury, wanting to finish his longtime rival. His scythe sailed through the air, aiming for Death's skull. The red flames on his scythe danced as it sailed through the air, almost as if dancing with joy that they would finally get to make the marrow of his bones seep out.

"No!" Sinder exclaimed as his eyes widened at the sight of his blade missing its target.

Death saw his opportunity. He flipped in midair and snapped his wings back out. With one powerful flap, he rocketed toward Sinder. He hit Sinder with incredible speed, jarring him from behind. Death gave another powerful flap of his wings, increasing his speed toward the ceiling. They hit the ceiling with a massive impact, causing chunks of painted plaster to break off and fall to the floor. Death spun Sinder around as they bounced off the ceiling and headed for the floor. Using the handle of his scythe, he pulled Sinder's head up and delivered a massive punch to the face. They slammed into the ground with enormous force.

Death didn't notice that the pentagram had a flash of red flame and smoke. A demon standing ten feet tall lumbered through the portal straight toward Death. Death drew back his fist to deliver another blow to Sinder's face. A giant ham fist from the demon caught Death in the back of the head. The punch had enough force to cause Death's body to dent the floor as it bounced next to Sinder, knocking his scythe free from his hand. The giant paw grabbed Death by the head and picked up his limp body and dangled it in front of Sinder. Sinder got up off the ground, rubbing the side of his face.

"Hold him," Sinder told the demon.

The other giant hand grabbed both of Death's arms, closing them together behind his body. Sinder slowly walked over to Death's scythe as it lay on the ground.

"Oh, the great scythe of the mighty Torva," Sinder said with great sarcasm.

Sinder reached down and grabbed the handle to pick it up. The blade snapped shut as his finger wrapped round the handle. Sinder gave a slight jump as it snapped shut. Sinder gave it a sidelong glance. Death was starting to recover from his blow and was struggling to get free from the grip of the large demon. Sinder held up the scythe and gave it a tap on the ground. His eyes narrowed as nothing happened. He smacked the end on the ground with greater force. Again, nothing happened. His eyes became slits as he glared at the scythe handle. He threw it down to the ground in disgust.

"Uh, worthless piece of garbage," Sinder sneered in disgust. He glared at Death through the slits of his eyes. "I have a very special surprise for you, Torva," Sinder said in a sinister tone.

Sinder moved the tip of his scythe toward Death's face. The flames danced around the tip of the blade and lapped at Death's skull. Death's eyes focused on the tip of the scythe. Sunder inched it closer to Death's skull. He struggled to get free from the grip of the large demon.

"Hold him tight!" Sinder snapped.

The demon tightened his grip on Death's arms. Sinder shoved the tip of his scythe against Death's skull. Death let out an agonizing scream as the flames charred a crescent shape into his cheekbone. He struggled to get free as the pain shot through his body. The large demon tightened his grip even further.

"Now for that surprise I was telling you about." Sinder laughed as he remove the tip of his scythe from Death's face. "While my rather large associate has his way with you," Sinder paused momentarily as he began to pace back and forth in front of them, "I will be having my way with your sweet little Susan." A diabolical laugh escaped his lips. "I can't wait to use her entire body to make me feel good!"

"Not today, jerkwad," Bradford said as he popped in above the large demon.

He dropped down with his katana pointed downward. He matched the speed of the blade with the velocity of his fall. He plunged the blade down into the demon's head. A guttural roar escaped its lips as smoke billowed out of its mouth. It released its grip on Death as he reached for his head. Death hit the ground and rolled to grab his scythe. A huge arch of blue flames exploded as the blade sprang into position. Death lunged as he swung a downward slash with all the anger left in his soul. He let out a roar of rage as his scythe pierced the top of Sinder's head, pinning it to the ground.

Sinder's body exploded into a ball of smoke. Death stood there with his breathing labored.

"Sorry it took so long," Bradford said as he popped in next to Death.

The pentagram on the wall exploded with a blast of red flames that shot out in all directions. Death and Bradford quickly dodged to not get burned by the fires of Hell that leapt into the hall. A huge plume of sulfuric gas ensued after the flames billowing into the hall, filling it with putrid, acidic air. The sound of a rushing waterfall began to echo off the walls as the entire floor began to rumble. A huge wave of demonic creatures of all shapes and sizes rushed out of the pentagram into the hallway. The wave advanced toward Death and Bradford at an amazing amount of speed.

Death turned around quickly. "Jr, look out!" Death shouted. The wave of demons swarmed over the top of Bradford and Death.

Chapter 48

Jr stopped in his tracks as they crested the top of the stairs. *Who is that?* Jr thought to himself. He was confused. It looked like a shorter version of his dad. A horrible thought shot through his brain. *Could that be an evil reflection of my soul?* Jr was almost relieved when he saw the hood pull back. "Sinder!"

"Max, you and Jr continue on ahead and save that girl from Lucifer's clutches. I will deal with this one." Jr heard his dad say.

Jr felt Max grab him by the shoulders and shove him toward the double doors. They ran past Death as he turned toward Sinder. He felt Max pushing him toward the double doors down the hall.

"What's the deal with Sinder having a cloak and scythe?" Jr asked Max as they ran down the hall.

"Long story let's just say there is a lot of bad blood there," Max responded as they ran along.

Jr felt a sudden sense of urgency to get to Claire. He willed his legs to carry them faster. He could feel the tension in the very marrow of his bones. Max and Jr were matching strides as they raced toward the door. Jr could feel his heartbeat with every step closer they got to the door. A few feet from the door Jr heard a cannonic boom, the concussion from the boom knocked Jr and Max through the door. The doors slammed open as the two went sailing through the door.

Jr sprang to his feet as he was still sliding through the doorway. He reoriented himself. The heat and red glow of the room was making it hard for his eyes to focus. Max stood up right next to Jr. The two looked around the room. The amount of demons in the room was too high to count. Jr spotted Dan in the center of the room.

Claire was strapped to a table in front of him. She was wearing the ceremonial robe that he had seen Dan pick up in Amityville. The slits in the sides of the lower portion caused the fabric to fall between her legs, exposing her flesh and the curves of her legs all the way to her upper thighs. Dan held the blade above her midsection where the cloth didn't cover her belly. She had tears streaming down her face.

Dan seemed like he was in a trance as he stood there, chanting. He had dozens of succubi dancing around him. They were running their hands up and down Claire's exposed legs. She struggled to get free from the restraints. Lucifer stood behind Dan with his hands spread wide, like he was absorbing the words Dan was chanting. The sight of this made Jr's blood run cold. His eyes narrowed to slits as he tightened his grip on his scythe. The commotion of Jr and Max being blown through the door had caught the attention of a group of demons standing off to the side.

"Looks like we are going to have some company," Max said as the demons started toward them.

Max pulled his right foot back a step and took a stance to help his attack. Jr didn't seem to notice the demons or hear what Max had said. He stood there motionless, staring at Claire on the table. His breathing made his shoulders heave up and down in rhythm with Dan's chanting. He flexed his fingers around the handle of his scythe. A blue flame flared up on the tip of the blade and slowly made its way across the entire length of the arch. The flames reached the wooden handle and flared up higher. The flames licked at the air as it started to descend down the handle toward Jr's hand. The flames reached his hand and engulfed it in a huge blue fireball. The demons had advanced in on Max and Jr and were only feet away.

"DJ!" Max shouted.

Jr spun around on his heels, instantly swinging his scythe like an expert swordsman. Blue flames launched off his blade, striking the lead charging demon square in the chest. It exploded into a hissing cloud of smoke. Jr continued to swing his scythe in rotating arch attacks. More flames shot from the blade, causing two more demons to instantly explode into clouds of smoke. Max stood there, looking on in awe. He had never seen Death perform an attack like that with his scythe, and he definitely hadn't taught Jr that move. Max took his axe and swung at another demon charging forward. His massive blade made a quick chore of splitting it in two. The two smoking halves plopped to the ground billowing smoke. Jr swirled his blade and brought it to a quick stop at his side, looking more like Bradford with his katanas than the son of the Reaper with his scythe.

"Stop!" came a shout from behind Jr.

Jr spun around and saw Lucifer standing there with his hand out in a halting motion. A small group of demons who had been charging toward Max and Jr had stopped midstride. Lucifer stood there looking at Jr. His mouth twisted into a small devilish smile. Everything in the room stood motionless except for Lucifer and Jr. Even Max was frozen in place.

"DJ, DJ, DJ," Lucifer started out. "Why are you pursuing this endeavor. We can make an agreement, I'm sure."

"No!" Jr said in a flat, firm tone.

"Look," the Devil said. "I know you weren't interested in my luscious succubi that I offered." He gestured toward the one closest to Jr, and it shimmered as it shifted into a copy of Claire wearing only a see-through scarf. "If you still don't find that enticing enough, maybe I can persuade you with this." Lucifer gestured toward Claire.

Claire's eyes popped open as the tears continued to stream down her face. Her tear-swollen eyes looked at Jr. "DJ, please help me."

Lucifer gestured again, and a piece of duct tape appeared over Claire's mouth. "Let me sweeten the deal a little more." With another hand gesture, the clothes that Claire was wearing shimmered and disappeared. "You can have your way with her. Right here, right now. Just join my side, and you can satisfy your wildest desires with her anytime that you wish."

"Lucifer," Jr said in a methodic tone. "Listen well. I can't wait to send you back to Hell!"

Jr threw his scythe at the Devil with all his might. The blue flames formed a circle as the scythe spun through the air with enormous speed. Lucifer's eyes widened as he barely jumped out of the way. The scythe hit the wall with a thunderous thud as the blade sank halfway up. The scene reverted as the Devil jumped out of the way.

Everything started to move again. Claire's robe reappeared, and the succubi reverted to its original sinful shape.

"Finish the ceremony!" Lucifer shouted to Dan as he resumed his place behind him.

Dan started to chant the incantation again as the entire room of demons focused on Max and Jr. Jr didn't have his scythe; it was stuck in the wall. He balled up his fists. His eyes popped wide with surprise when his fists exploded into balls of blue flame. The demons were beginning to swarm them. Jr started throwing punches at everything that got within striking distance. Max was using his battle-axe with only the precision that the Incarnation of War could do. A bright flash popped into the middle of the sea of demons. Two quick flashes of katana blades appeared followed by wisps of smoke. Jr continued to throw punches as best as he could. Bradford popped in again near Jr's scythe.

He gave it a great heave to pull it from the wall. "DJ!" he shouted as he threw the scythe across the room.

Jr leapt off the ground and caught his scythe. Instantly the blade was on fire again. Jr matched the movements of Bradford's katanas, taking out three demons on his way back to the ground. The sea of the Devil's henchmen seemed unending as the battle continued. The red glow of the room began to pulse and brighten as Dan continued his chant. Jr managed to catch a glimpse of him. Dan had an evil twisted smile forming on his lips. His eyes were black as coal as he held the blade of the Cupio Me Daemonia above Claire's heart.

Jr was snapped back to reality as he felt a hard blow to his head. The force sent him going headlong into the ground. He slid for about ten feet. He jumped back to his feet, scythe still in hand. He spun around and saw four large drooling demons lumbering toward him. He lunged forward using his momentum to enhance his attack. His blade sliced through the first one in the group. The huge cloud of smoke blocked his vision, and he didn't see the next one until it was on top of him. The demon grabbed his wrist, stopping Jr from using his weapon. The demon yanked Jr off the ground and brought him to face height. He seized the opportunity and threw a hard front kick, landing his heel square in the teeth of the demon. It hollered in pain as it released Jr. As Jr dropped, he brought the blade of his scythe down hard on the demon's head. It collapsed instantly. Jr jumped back quickly as he saw the huge blade of Max's axe speeding toward the next one in line. The fourth demon turned to see what was going on and caught a massive fist from Max to the face.

"Thanks, Max," Jr hollered.

Max shoot Jr a look and shouted, "AGAIN!"

That word sparked something in Jr's mind. The training he had gotten from Max came flooding back to his memory. He felt a surge of renewed strength flow into his bones. He stood beside Max as they battled the innumerable amount of Hell's fiends. They made progress toward the ceremonial table where Claire was strapped. Jr surged forward to get to her. The foes seemed unending. For every two they killed, six more filled in the gaps. Jr was beginning to tire as he continued his onslaught. Max seemed to be slowing as well. Jr noticed that he hadn't seen Bradford pop in in a while. How was his dad doing against Sinder?

"Jr look out!" Death's voice rang out through the chamber.

Jr turned around, and his mouth fell open. He saw the huge wall of enemies charging through the pentagram in the hall. He never would have fathomed that Hell could have had that many minions. He braced himself as the wave of demons rushed over him and Max.

Chapter 49

The impact from the sheer number of Hell's minions knocked Jr off his feet. He scrambled to get some traction under his feet. The demons continued to rush into the room. Jr heard the Devil start to laugh a loud, sinister laugh.

"I gave you a chance, DJ." Lucifer laughed. "Now, I will relish in forcing you to watch as I ravish the soul of this girl you so foolishly tried to save. That will be you pain in Hell!" His laughter echoed off the walls.

Rage surged through Jr. He tightened his grip on his scythe as he forced his feet under his body. With all his strength, he shoved his way upward through the wall of demons to get upright. With his feet under him, he quickly scanned his surroundings. He saw a pile of demons on top of Max a few feet away, clawing, scratching, and biting at him.

"Max!" Jr shouted.

Jr swung his scythe in the direction of Max and his attackers. His scythe split a couple demons in half as he pushed his way toward his friend. Max was struggling to get an attacker off his face. Max grabbed at the demon only to have his hand attacked by a number of other demons. Blood was pouring from the bites in his hand. Jr struggled to get to Max. Jr pulled his scythe back to get a swing. His scythe handle came crashing down into his shoulder. A huge clawed hand reached around and clamped down on his face. His head was violently ripped backward. It felt like his neck was going to snap.

"No!" Death shouted.

Jr tried to free his head as he felt hundreds of hands trying to rip his scythe from his grip. He managed to catch a glimpse of his surroundings through the fingers wrapped around his face. He saw his dad's huge black wings being swarmed by a multitude of Lucifer's fiends. Bradford was being pulled in opposite directions by his arms while another demon was clawing at his face. All the succubi in the room began to cackle, sounding like witches instead of the false beauty that they portrayed. Jr felt another pair of large hands grab his arms and wrench them down. He was forced to the ground as his scythe was pulled from his grip. An overwhelming sense of doom and regret for failing to get to Claire swept over him. He closed his eyes.

"Claire, I'm sorry," he whispered. "Please forgive me."

Jr heard a loud crash as the hand around his head released its grip. He looked up and saw a flaming sword come shooting through the roof like a missile. It struck the ground, issuing a blast of flames in every direction, eviscerating a large group of demons closest to the impact. The sword was followed by a figure who shot through the hole in the roof flying like a peregrine falcon. Lucifer looked up, and his eyes went wide with fright. He leapt from behind Dan and headed for the pentagram in the hall.

"Finish the ritual," he shouted to Dan as he ran for the portal.

Hundreds more winged figures came soaring through the roof. The demons scattered in all directions, obviously in chaos. The hands holding Jr down released their grip on him. He jumped up and saw the angels drawing out swords as they landed on the ground. The first one landed next to the flaming sword with a thud as his feet hit the ground. He stood straight and pulled the sword from the ground. Jr's scythe had been kicked across the room from where he was. He looked and saw Dan's grin grow larger as he raised the Cupio Me Daemonia, preparing to plunge it down through Claire's heart.

"No!" Jr shouted.

He took off toward Dan with speed he didn't know that he had. His scythe was in the opposite direction, but that was a problem he would have to deal with. He knew that he had to get there before Dan finished his chants. He raced toward Dan. Like a miracle, every demon who tried to get in his way was immediately hit by a sword-wielding angel, causing violent explosions of smoke. It was different from when Jr would hit one with his scythe. It was instantaneous from the angel's swords. The amount of smoke in the room was increasing quickly. He was only a few feet from Dan when he saw Dan look at him and smirk. Everything seemed to slow in Jr's mind. He saw the muscles in Dan's arm twitch as the blade started to be forced downward.

"DJ!" Jr heard a voice shout.

Jr glanced in the direction of the voice without slowing toward Dan and Claire. The angel with the flaming sword used the tip of his sword to scoop Jr's scythe from the ground and flip it toward Jr. Jr reached out as the scythe came flipping toward him. The handle slapped his palm, his fingers snapped closed around it. It exploded in blue flame, dispersing the few demons next to Jr. He twirled the scythe like a helicopter rotor as he continued toward Dan. He saw the blade of the Cupio Me Daemonia increase in velocity toward Claire's chest. Jr threw his scythe toward the blade. It left his hand and spun through the air. Time seemed to slow to a crawl in Jr's mind. He watched as the scythe flew through the air in agonizing anticipation. Thoughts were racing through his mind. What if he missed? What if he hit Claire instead of Dan? What if Dan's blade found its mark before his scythe got there? Jr's eyes went wide as the scythe spun one last time before reaching its target. The scythe slammed into the blade of the Cupio Me Daemonia right as the tip of its blade was contacting Claire's body. The blade snapped as the scythe passed through it, dislodging the handle from Dan's grasp.

"No!" Dan shouted as he realized that his ritual was ruined. "You insolent little creature," he growled. "The wench will die as my lord Lucifer desires!"

Dan put his hands around Claire's neck and began to squeeze. Jr could hear her gasping for air as Dan tightened his grip. The tears streaming down her face seemed to fuel Jr's speed. He launched into the air tackling Dan, forcing him to release Claire's throat. She gasped in a lungful of air as her throat opened, allowing oxygen to flow into her body. Jr and Dan hit the ground and bounced. They rolled to their feet. Dan grabbed something out of his pocket and swallowed it. His body began to swell in size. His shirt got tight and then ripped in half. Tattered strips of cloth hung loosely around his upper body.

"DJ, look out," Claire shouted as she strained to free herself from her restraints.

Dan ripped the tattered pieces of his shirt off and threw them to the ground. "After I dispense with you, I'm going to have one last go with that little tramp before I send her soul to Lucifer and claim my reward," his words trailed off into laughter.

Dan glared as his laughter subsided and charged at Jr. His shoulder slammed into Jr's torso, picking him off the ground and slamming him down like a linebacker. Jr felt the wind gush out of his lungs, and it felt like his bones were about to crack. The sheer size and strength of Dan after he had taken whatever he had been given was extremely imposing. Dan rolled off Jr and back to his feet. He kicked Jr in the head before he had even started to get back up. The kick sent him sailing through the air. He slid as he hit the ground. He rolled to get his feet back under him as he heard the sound of Dan running at him again. Jr remembered what Max had taught him. He waited until he felt the air start to push toward him from Dan's body before he lunged to the side. He spun and planted a pinwheel kick to the back of Dan's head. Dan stumbled and went to the ground.

Jr glanced around quickly to survey the scene before returning his attention to Dan. The others in his group were still battling the demons with the aid of the angels. The one with the flaming sword was standing back-to-back with Death. Their wings stretched out, forming an impenetrable defense to the side. Their offensive swings were timed perfectly so as not to interfere with the others. The demons were dropping by the handfuls in front of them. Max was holding his own, an expression of sheer anger across his face.

"You bit my hands, I'll break your souls," Max shouted as he swung his battle-axe with precision and power.

Bradford was popping in and out with incredible speed. He had a wild Mad Hatter grin on his face. The angels were fighting with such organization and skill that it made the Spartans look like amateurs. Jr flinched as a bright flash appeared right in front of him.

Bradford stood there with that wild grin on his face as he extended his hand to give Jr his scythe.

"Here," he said. "Now go kick this guy's butt, and go save your girl."

Bradford popped out and instantly popped in right in front of Dan. He slapped Dan across the face and popped back out. His laughter trailed off as he popped away. Dan was furious and spun around, panting like a rabid animal. His shoulders were heaving with anger and rage. He lumbered over to the wall and ripped a stud out of the plaster. He threw it at Jr, aiming straight for his head. Jr swung his scythe to knock it out of the air. Dan took off toward Jr, trying to tackle him again. Jr easily sidestepped him and gave him another kick, this time in the side. Dan roared with anger as he spun around. His face was red; Jr couldn't tell if it was from anger or whatever it was he had taken.

Dan took off again with more speed than Jr was ready for. Dan grabbed him as he ran by and used his momentum to hurl Jr across the room. Jr hit the wall, knocking plaster loose before he fell to the ground. He managed to land on his feet this time. He looked up to see Dan's fist less than an inch from his face. The force put his head through the wall. Before his eyes had enough time to roll back in his head, he felt something grab his feet. He was yanked out of the wall and airborne in an instant. Jr held tight to his scythe as he flew, knowing that if he dropped it, he was done for. He was ready for the impact as he braced to hit another wall. He slammed into the wall and dropped. He rolled as soon as he hit the floor, moving out of the way as Dan kicked at where Jr had been.

Jr sprung up and swung his scythe. He felt multiple hands grab at his body and his scythe. He was jerked backward before he could finish his swing. He was wrestled to the ground by half dozen of demons. Jr pulled his hands up to protect his face from the onslaught that had already started. Two pairs of wings cast a shadow over the minions attacking Jr. Blue-and-white flames blurred through Jr's vision as the blade flashed through. Three demons exploded in smoke as the other three had their bodies sliced in half, the smoke spewing out of the remaining parts.

Death reached down and helped Jr up. He gave his son a nod and flew into the air to the other side of the room. Jr looked around and saw that there was only a few dozen demons left in the room. The pentagram in the hall had disappeared, closing off any chance they had of retreating back to Hell. Lucifer had sentenced them to their demise. Jr turned toward Dan. A bright-red pentagram appeared on the floor in front of Dan. A hand reached out and handed Dan a large red sword. The hand and pentagram disappeared together. Dan grinned as he examined the new blade. He looked at Jr and beckoned him to attack.

The two squared up their weapons as Jr approached. Like a flash of lightning, the two attacked each other. The blades threw sparks as they collided with the other. Their battle continued looking like a medieval duel. Dan kicked Jr in the gut, sending him stepping backward. Dan lurched forward with a swing from his sword. Jr deflected the shot and threw a counterattack. Dan was ready for it and swatted the scythe away. He landed a blow with the butt of his sword on Jr's shoulder. Jr bent down from the impact of the blow. Dan swung an overhead swing aimed at Jr's neck. Jr remembered what Max had taught him. He phased his body out as the red blade passed through his body without harm. The blade hit the ground and stuck from the impact. Dan's eyes went wide from shock at what had just happened. Jr could smell the sulfur on the blade with it so close to his face. Dan roared with anger as he wrenched the blade out of the ground. He swung at Jr with a huge swing. Jr blocked it with his scythe and used the impact to force Dan backward.

Dan came again at Jr. Jr spun around the back side of Dan. He hit Dan in the left kidney with the butt of his scythe. He used his opposite elbow to hit Dan on the ribs on his right side, alternating to the other side. Again he planted a heel in the back of Dan's knee. Jr spun around and threw Dan with a modified hip toss. Dan flew to the side and landed on the ground. Dan got to his feet, his anger and rage evident on his face. He was only a few feet from Claire. He turned and raised his sword as he lunged toward her. Jr shot like a flash to block the swing. Dan knocked off balance and shot to the side. Jr spun around and swung his scythe. Dan turned and threw his sword as the blade of Jr's scythe plunged into his stomach. Dan slumped to the ground when Jr let go of his scythe to grab the sword. Jr reached in horror for the sword as it sailed toward Claire. Jr's fingers grazed the back of the hilt as it passed his reach.

"No!" Jr screamed as he saw the blade sailing for Claire.

Jr watched horrified as he stood there helpless. Bradford flashed in right next to the sword. He swung his katanas, shattering the red sword into a million shards. He gave Jr a wink and popped back out. Jr turned back to Dan as he was slumped bleeding on the floor.

"My lord Lucifer will reward me. You haven't won," Dan said.

Jr ran over to Claire. He reached into his pocket and grabbed his knife. He cut the straps off her hands. She grabbed him and threw her arms around his neck before he could get to her feet. Claire pulled Jr in close and pressed her face into his shoulder and cried. Jr put his arms around her and held her as she cried.

"I love you, DJ," she said as she kissed his ear.

Jr was shocked to hear those words from her. "I love you too," he said.

He turned to cut the straps off her feet. Dan's body was gone as Jr saw a pentagram disappear on the ground. His scythe lay on the floor. Claire got off the table and grabbed Jr again. She shuddered as she squeezed him tightly for a long moment. Death, Max, and the angel with the flaming sword walked up to Jr. The angel looked around and sheathed his sword, dousing the flame as it entered the scabbard.

"Thank you," Claire said as she pulled back.

Jr felt a hand land on his shoulder. "You did well, DJ," the angel said. "Oh, my apologies. I forgot my manners. My name is Michael." He extended his hand for Jr to shake.

Chapter 50

Jr's jaw dropped open as he accepted the handshake. "You mean like Michael the Archangel?"

"In the flesh," Michael responded.

Claire stepped forward. "Um, excuse me," she interjected politely. "Thank you for helping to save me."

"Our pleasure, miss," Michael said. "Father heard your prayers, then Torva here came and talked with Gabriel and said he might need some help."

"Thank you for helping, Michael," Death said as he extended his hand.

Michael laughed at the gesture and grabbed Death in a huge brotherly bear hug. "You know I will always help you, Torva. We are still brothers."

Michael looked around. "Heaven's army, the time to return is upon us." He turned and looked at Jr. "It's good to have finally met you after all these years. Take care of this girl and yourself."

He turned and shot into the sky through the hole in the ceiling. The rest of the angels all waved goodbye and followed Michael out through the roof.

Max spoke up, "Not much for long goodbyes, I guess." He slapped Death on the shoulder. "Torva, I think they want you to visit a little more often." He walked over and picked up Jr's scythe and tossed it to him.

Bradford popped in, "Hey guys, we should head back as well," and popped back out.

"Then let's go," Death said.

Jr grabbed Claire's hand, and with a round of different colored flashes and the entire group was standing in Purgatory. Claire squeezed Jr's hand. Jr looked over and saw the concern on her face. "Where is this?" she asked.

"It's Purgatory," Jr replied. "It's where my parents live."

"Is your dad the Grim Reaper?" she asked timidly.

Death, hearing his name, turned to her. "In the flesh," he said, extending his boney hand. "Well, in the bone anyway. It's a pleasure to finally meet you. Jr and Susan have told me a lot about you."

Claire timidly accepted the hand and gave it a shake. "Thank you," she managed to say.

Jr heard a horse whiny and the sound of galloping hooves. He turned around to get hit by a horse running at him. He grabbed onto the neck. "Morty!" Jr exclaimed. "You're okay!"

"Thanks to your mom and Ivy," Morty answered.

"Um, a talking horse?" Claire asked, bewildered.

Morty gave her a wry look. "Not exactly," he said as he shifted into his car form.

"Okay," Claire said in a shaky voice. "I think I'm in for a lot more surprises."

Morty morphed into his Ducati form. Claire's face turned a little white, and her knees got a little shaky. Morty revved the engine, then turned back into a horse. Claire was standing wide-eyed and in shock about what she had just seen.

"Morty," Jr started, "I'm sorry about what happened. I didn't know what was going on."

"I know, DJ. Mortis filled me in on what happened. On why you didn't hear when I called for help," Morty said. "Lucifer is good at deceiving people and not allowing you to get past his barriers." Morty walked over and put his head on Jr's shoulder. Jr wrapped his arms around his neck and hugged his old friend for a long moment.

Susan and Ivy exited the front door of the house and met the group outside. Susan looked at Claire with the type of concern only a mother could have. "Oh, sweetie, let's get you inside and into some decent clothes," Susan said as she took Claire by the hand. "Ugh, the Devil definitely has zero class when it comes to clothes."

"Okay, thank you, Mrs. Deadwood," Claire said as she followed Susan as she led her toward the door.

"Oh, call me Susan," she said as she gave Claire's hand a squeeze.

Ivy turned to the rest of the group. "If the rest of you will come inside, we have guests in the dining room."

Max laughed as he slapped Bradford in the back. "Now let's feast!"

"What guests?" Jr questioned.

"Let's find out," Death replied.

The group headed toward the door to the house as Morty and Mortis trotted out toward the pasture. The group walked into the dining room. The table was set with a feast that would make Thanksgiving look like a light snack. In the center of the table was a plate with a stack of the most mouthwatering steaks Jr had ever seen before. Jr looked at the rest of the table. There was also a turkey the size of a small cow and a pig that was still steaming from being roasted in a pit. There was an amazing assortment of potato dishes and roasted vegetables, black and red beans with rice, baked beans, and more casseroles than Jr could count quickly. He was shocked to see Josh, Crystal, and Tommy sitting at the table. Before he could say anything, Yvonne walked into the dining room from the kitchen, carrying a tea kettle. A shot of steam came out of the spout as she set it on the table.

"Hey, DJ," Yvonne said as she set the kettle down.

"What are all you guys doing here?" Jr asked.

Yvonne and Jr's voices caught Tommy's attention. "Captain Awesome," he squealed as he noticed Bradford. He took off like a rocket around the table and skidded to a halt as he came face-to-face with Max.

"Hey there, little fella," Max said as he reached down a mammoth hand for Tommy to shake.

Tommy looked back at his parents to see what to do. Josh gave his son a nod of approval. "Hello," he said cautiously as he accepted the handshake.

"Hey Tommy," Bradford said as he walked up next to Max. "This is my friend, Max. He's kind of big, but he's just a giant teddy bear."

"More like a grizzly bear," Max replied as propped himself on his axe. "That food looks delicious."

Crystal walked over to Jr and the rest of his companions. "It isn't polite to stare, sweetie," she said to Tommy. "Glad you're okay, DJ." She gave Jr a hug as Josh was walking over.

"To answer your question though," Josh started, "a guy named Gabriel stopped by and told us that you would be back momentarily. Then a few other guys started bringing in all this food."

"And," Crystal added, "he said to tell your dad not to get hung up on the last conversation that they had. Brothers will be brothers is what he said."

Death stood there with a blank look on his face for a moment, not sure how to respond. Max gave him a look. "I told you they want you to visit more, Torva." Death could only nod.

Susan and Claire walked into the dining room, and Jr's attention was caught. Claire was wearing her normal jeans and T-shirt attire. She looked fairly content based on the events that had just transpired. Jr walked over to where she had entered and took her hand in his.

"Are you going to be okay?" he asked her.

Her eyes started to glisten as a few tears started to make their way to the edge of her eyes. "I think so," she said. "I need to talk to Alfie, though. I'm going to need a new place to stay." Her eyes dropped to the floor. "I can't go back there, to that apartment. I just can't." Her eyes couldn't hold the tears back anymore. She leaned into Jr and buried her face in his shoulder. Feeling helpless, he could only wrap his arms around her in an attempt to comfort her.

Yvonne piped up. "I have a suggestion if Claire is willing," Yvonne said. "I don't want to be alone at the house now that Fred is gone. She could stay at my house for a while. If she wants to."

Claire pulled her head from Jr's shoulder with a few remaining tears etching their way down her cheeks. "Really? You'd do that for me?" Claire asked with a little apprehension.

"Yeah," Yvonne replied. "It would be beneficial to us both."

"Why don't we discuss the details over the meal," Death suggested as he gestured toward the table.

The group gathered around the table and began to take their seats. Death sat next to Susan. Jr and Claire took the next couple of seats, followed by Yvonne and Max. Ivy grabbed Bradford and sat with him, her hands not letting go of his. Josh with his wife and son filled the remaining seats at the table.

"Oh DJ, before I forget," Josh said. "I went by the shop today, and there was a message from Detective St. Claire. He said that he has everything he needs to finish his case and wanted to thank you for the help. He said that he won't need to stop by again."

Jr looked at his friend and gave a slight smile. "So when do we go in tomorrow?"

"You don't," Yvonne said. "All three of us will reopen together in a couple days. You need to get some rest before you go to work."

"I second that," Susan said in her motherly tone. "You are still my son, and I still worry. You need rest."

The meal continued with conversation as the group figured out how to get back to what could be deemed a normal life and realized that it could never be back to the way it was. Jr knew that now that everyone he cared about knew what he was and what his dad was, it could never return. He was glad that he no longer had to hide his identity around them. He was ready to start his relationship with Claire and help his friend get her bike shop back in order. He sat there with a grin forming on his lips as the meal continued.

A while later, Death stood up. "If you all will excuse me, I am way behind in work. But with the help of Bradford, I'm sure we can make short time of the process." Death let out a chuckle.

"Hey," Bradford protested. "I'm supposed to be the funny one, remember?"

Death couldn't help but laugh. "Yes, my timeless friend, but looks aren't everything." He walked out of the room as he grabbed his scythe.

Max let out a thunderous laugh at the jab Death had given to Bradford. Bradford rolled his eyes as he stood up. "Guess I better go help the old guy."

Ivy grabbed his hand. "Hurry back," she said. "I want to spend some time with you."

Bradford smiled at her. "My lady, for you I will make time." He walked out, following Death.

Susan was finishing up as the two exited the room. "Oh, I forgot to give this to you earlier," she said as she handed Jr an envelope.

"What's this?" Jr asked her.

"I don't know. Gabriel said to give it to you."

Jr opened the envelope to find a small piece of paper in it. On the paper was the most immaculate handwriting he had ever seen. The note read, "No one has greater love than this: to lay down his life for his friends. Well done, my young friend." The note was signed Jesus. Jr smiled as he read the note. He knew his future wasn't going to be perfect or easy. He knew that Lucifer wasn't done trying to destroy the world but knew that he could rely on Jesus to get him through it all.

The End

About the Author

Jimmie Hupp was born and raised in the small town of Prineville, Oregon. He has worked as an electrician for twenty-five years to support his family. He is a father of four and has been happily married to his wife, Shellie, for twenty-one years.

Death Jr: The Devil's Rebuke is his first published work written in 2022. Jimmie, however, has been writing short stories since high school. He has been in the creative arts since then, as he was an active member of his Drama Club and in concert/jazz band, playing trumpet, French horn, and percussion.

Printed in the USA
CPSIA information can be obtained
at www.ICGtesting.com
CBHW030443021024
15219CB00027B/304